PRAISE FOR THE
BROTHERHOOD OF WAR SAGA

"Extremely well-done . . . first-rate!"
—*Washington Post*

"Absorbing . . . fascinating descriptions of weapons, tactics, Army life and battle."
—*New York Times*

"A major work . . . magnificent . . . powerful . . . If books about warriors and the women who love them were given medals for authenticity, insight and honesty, BROTHERHOOD OF WAR would be covered with them."
—William Bradford Huie, author of *The Klansman* and *The Execution of Private Slovik*

"BROTHERHOOD OF WAR is a cracking good story. It gets into the hearts and minds of those who by choice or circumstance are called upon to fight our nation's wars."
—William R. Corson, Lt. Col. (Ret.) U.S.M.C., author of *The Betrayal* and *The Armies of Ignorance*

"Griffin has captured the rhythms of army life and speech, its rewards and deprivations . . . a well-written, absorbing account of military life."
—*Publishers Weekly*

By W.E.B. Griffin
From Jove

BROTHERHOOD OF WAR

Book I: The Lieutenants
Book II: The Captains
Book III: The Majors
Book IV: The Colonels
Book V: The Berets
Book VI: The Generals
Book VII: The New Breed
Book VIII: The Aviators

THE CORPS

Book I: Semper Fi
Book II: Call to Arms

THE AVIATORS

Book VIII

BROTHERHOOD OF WAR

BY W.E.B. GRIFFIN

J

JOVE BOOKS, NEW YORK

This Jove book contains the complete
text of the original hardcover edition.
It has been completely reset in a typeface
designed for easy reading, and was printed
from new film.

The typescript of *Brotherhood of War*, Book VIII, *The Aviators*, was prepared on a Sperry PC/IT Computer System, using Perfect Writer Version 2.0 and MicroSoft WORD Version 4.0 Word Processing Software, and printed on a QMS ''Kiss'' Laser Printer.

THE AVIATORS

A Jove Book / published by arrangement with
the author

PRINTING HISTORY
G. P. Putnam's Sons edition published 1988
Published simultaneously in Canada
Jove edition / May 1989

ISBN: 0-515-10053-6

Jove Books are published by The Berkley Publishing Group,
200 Madison Avenue, New York, New York 10016.
The name ''JOVE'' and the ''J'' logo
are trademarks belonging to Jove Publications, Inc.

PRINTED IN THE UNITED STATES OF AMERICA

10 9 8 7 6 5 4 3 2 1

For Uncle Charley and The Bull
RIP October 1979

And for Donn
Who would ever have believed four *stars?*

And for Russ
Who ever would have believed Pee-Wee's Dog-Robber
would grow up to be
a major general, a division commander,
and a university president?

And for Mac
RIP December 1987

I

[ONE]
Pleiku, Republic of South Vietnam
1205 Hours 15 August 1963

When the glistening twin-engine Beechcraft U-8D, painted in the peacetime U.S. Army glossy white, black, and olive color scheme, touched down on the runway at Pleiku, Major Warren H. Hightower, Infantry, USA, the commanding officer of the 170th Assault Helicopter Company, was on the parking ramp waiting for it.

Hightower, a stocky, tanned, and open-faced man of thirty-four, was dressed in a gray tropical-areas flight suit, a brimmed cap, and flight boots. A Model 1911A1 Colt .45 ACP pistol in a leather holster hung from a web belt on his hip. Because he himself had just returned from flying, he'd decided he was not going to change into a more formal uniform just because the battalion commander had gotten on the horn to announce that he and the Battalion S-3 [Plans and

Training] were inbound on their return from Saigon and would the Major please meet the aircraft in the parking ramp.

When the door of the U-8D opened, he regretted his decision. There turned out to be more people on the plane than the two Hightower had expected. Specifically, there were two full bull colonels, one a Green Beret and one in tropical worsted, obviously a member of the palace guard at the Pentagon East, in Saigon. There was also another Green Beret, a captain, a black guy.

Hightower went through the expected routine.

"Sir," he barked, as he raised his hand in a crisp salute, "Major Warren Hightower, commander of the 170th Assault Helicopter Company."

His salute was returned. The battalion commander introduced the colonels and the captain. Hands were shaken.

"Gentlemen, if you'll come with me, we've got coffee, Cokes," Hightower said.

"Where's Lieutenant Oliver?" the Green Beret Colonel asked.

The question surprised Major Hightower.

"Sir, he's on a mission," Hightower said, making a vague gesture toward the Laotian border.

"We wanted to see him," the Colonel from the Pentagon East said. "Weren't you told?"

"No, Sir," Hightower responded. "I wasn't."

"Christ!" the Colonel from the Pentagon East said, impatiently, angrily.

"Something apparently got garbled in transmission," the battalion commander said. "Hightower, how soon can you get him back here?"

Hightower considered that. He had no idea where Oliver was. To get him back now would mean trying to reach him by radio, which might or might not be immediately possible.

"About an hour, Sir. Maybe a little more."

"I don't have that kind of time," the Colonel from the Pentagon East said.

"Is there something I can do, Sir?" Hightower asked.

The Colonel from the Pentagon East looked disapprovingly at Hightower for a moment, then said, "Yes, there is, Major. When you see him, would you please ask him if he will volunteer for a classified mission involving a high degree of personal risk?''

''Yes, Sir,'' Hightower said. He saw in the Green Beret Colonel's eyes scarcely concealed contempt for the Colonel from the Pentagon East.

''If his answer is in the affirmative,'' the Colonel from the Pentagon East said, ''please so inform Colonel Augustus. He will take it from there.''

''I'll be in Dak To,'' Colonel Augustus, the Green Beret, said. ''You're in on their net, I suppose?''

''Yes, Sir,'' Hightower said.

Colonel Augustus nodded. ''I'm Polar Bear Six,'' he said.

''Well,'' the Colonel said, ''since there is nothing more we can do here without Lieutenant Oliver, I suppose the only thing to do is make our piss call and then get the rest of this show back on the road.''

Fifteen minutes after the U-8D touched down, it was airborne again, presumably headed for the Special Forces camp at Dak To.

Once it was gone, Major Hightower had an insubordinate thought: With a little luck, Charlie would throw some mortars at the U-8D at Dak To. And, with a little more luck, the Colonel from the Pentagon East would have to seek cover in a ditch half-filled with the green slime.

Fifteen minutes after that, two Huey HU-1B gunships came fluttering down. One of them, Major Hightower saw, was flown by the twenty-five-year-old first lieutenant of Armor named John S. Oliver, Jr.

Whenever Hightower had occasion to call to mind this young lieutenant (which was more often than he thought of most other lieutenants in his command), his thoughts were almost always positive, even fond. And yet, in addition to whatever the hell was going on with the battalion commander, the Green Berets, and the Colonel from the Pentagon East, Major Hightower had a problem with First Lieutenant John S. Oliver, Jr. Reduced to one word, the problem was tolerance. Major Hightower suspected, correctly, that Lieutenant Oliver simply looked at him with toleration—as opposed to, say, looking at him with respect. In other words, Major Hightower had come to believe that Lieutenant Oliver regarded him—tolerated him—as a well-meaning guy with the best of intentions who just didn't know what he was doing, and that Oliver considered himself far better qualified to command the 170th Assault Helicopter Company than Major Warren H. Hightower.

Oliver's opinion did not come about because he was a lieutenant possessed of an overwhelming ego. Major Hightower, who was in fact a well-meaning guy with the best of intentions, was also honest enough with himself to acknowledge that Oliver was right about him. For one thing, Major Hightower had been In Country about four weeks, and he was perfectly willing to admit that he didn't have one hell of a lot of experience. Lieutenant Oliver, on the other hand, was nearing the end of his twelve-month tour. During that tour he had won the Distinguished Flying Cross, two Bronze Stars, eleven Air Medals, a Purple Heart, and the usual Vietnamese decorations, including the Cross of Gallantry, with Palm.

It could therefore be reasonably argued that Lieutenant Johnny Oliver knew what he was doing. More importantly, Lieutenant Oliver based his unspoken, but sometimes evident belief that he was better prepared than Major Hightower to command the 170th Assault Helicopter Company on the fact that for a month and a half he *had been* its commanding officer.

He had acceded to command after the then commanding officer and the then executive officer had, within three days, been shot down. Though the commanding officer had been seriously wounded, they'd managed to pull him and his crew out of enemy-held territory and shipped them off to the hospital in the Philippines. The exec, who had gone down in Laos, wasn't so lucky. They'd seen him go in, but a diligent search of the jungle canopy later had failed to find his downed aircraft. He was either (probably) dead or (worse) a prisoner of the Viet Cong. Which meant they were carrying him around in the boonies in a wooden cage like a monkey, thus affording the natives the opportunity to spit or throw stones at him, or jab at him with pointed sticks.

Once it was clear that the exec was missing and wasn't going to turn up soon, the decision had been made to give temporary command of the 170th to Lieutenant Oliver, pending the arrival from the States of an officer of the appropriate rank (which would take maybe two or three days, it was then thought). There were no captains currently in the 170th, and while Oliver was not even the senior first lieutenant, he was, in the opinion of the battalion commander, the best man for the job. So, for a couple of days, they would close their eyes to the regulation which decreed that the senior officer present for duty was entitled to the commanding officer's title.

The best-laid plans of the paper pushers nevertheless went agley; and the couple of days became six weeks. First, the Pentagon decided to change the Table of Organization and Equipment of aviation companies like the 170th. The new TO&E provided that the commanding officer be a major, rather than, as previously, a captain. Next, other aviation companies were being formed In Country, and these had to be filled. Since captains were no longer permitted to command aviation companies, the captains who were arriving In Country were farmed out to the newly formed aviation companies.

Thus it was six weeks before Major Warren H. Hightower arrived at the 170th Assault Helicopter Company and signed his name to the General Order stating that, effective this date, he had assumed command of the 170th Assault Helicopter Company, vice 1st Lt J.S. Oliver, Jr., Armor.

Along with Major Hightower came one other major and five captains. Consequently, when Hightower assumed command, Oliver moved from top man on the chain of command to eighth.

He became, in other words, de jure just one of thirty-odd lieutenants. But, in the eyes of most of the lieutenants and all of the noncoms, he remained The de facto Old Man who had been fucked out of his job by some bullshit decision by the REMFs in Saigon. REMF is an acronym for a phrase the first three words of which are Rear, Echelon, and Mother.

Before they'd run him through a quickie Huey course at Fort Rucker, promoted him, and sent him to 'Nam, then Captain Hightower had commanded an aviation company in Germany. He was thus able to judge with a qualified eye how Lieutenant Oliver had commanded the 170th. And his judgment was that the Lieutenant had commanded it well, perhaps even superbly. Morale and motivation were both high. The officers and men liked Lieutenant Oliver, and he had taken good care of their living conditions. As a result, the 170th was a proud, efficient unit. And it manifested what so often is talked about but so rarely realized: cheerful, willing obedience to orders—including those obviously sent up by some REMF in Saigon who had been smoking funny cigarettes.

Major Hightower, who had been around (he was out of Texas A&M and had been in the Army since the Korean War), suspected, of course, that some of the waitresses in the enlisted men's mess/club provided social services beyond opening beer cans and emptying ashtrays, and that the splendid refrigerators in both the officers' and EM clubs may indeed, as rumor had it, have been ''borrowed'' from a PX warehouse in Saigon in a midnight requisition; yet he could find no evidence that the men were either suffering from social disease or ingesting prohibited substances, and he was wise enough not to kick a sleeping dog.

And he found that Lieutenant Oliver had not abused the prerogatives of his command—beyond doing what he would have done himself. The 170th was made up of three helicopter platoons: two ''slick'' platoons, equipped with unarmed Bell HU-1D ''Huey'' helicopters, which were used to transport personnel and equipment; and a ''gun'' platoon, equipped with -B Model Hueys. These carried all sorts of armament, machine guns, 40mm grenade launchers, and 2.75-inch rockets, seven to a pod, with a pod mounted on each side of the ship.

The company commander was provided with a ''slick'' HU-1D equipped with additional radios for command and control. Exercising the prerogatives of command, Lieutenant Oliver had decided that his mission could be best accomplished if he assigned the unarmed Command HU-1D to other duties. Major Hightower heard, but did not investigate, whispers that the Command Slick was thereafter alleged to have made certain unofficial missions which had caused it to be popularly known as the pussy wagon. Lieutenant Oliver had flown instead one of the Gun Platoon's -B Models. This was equipped with a turret-mounted 40mm grenade thrower, two seven-round 2.75 rocket pods, and an M-60 .30 caliber machine gun in each door.

The truth was that Major Hightower would have been happy to serve under Lieutenant Oliver before assuming command himself. And he would have been delighted if Oliver could have become his exec. But that was impossible. Oliver was a lieutenant and he was outranked by five other lieutenants, all the captains, and the other major who had come to the 170th with Major Warren H. Hightower.

Early on, however, Hightower had a quiet word with the captains, in which he suggested that they could all learn from Lieutenant Oliver's broad experience. At the same time he had also made it clear that he himself intended to seek Oliver's advice and counsel whenever he encountered a situation that went beyond his own limited experience. And that, of course, meant just about every situation he expected to encounter. The unspoken point he made was that Oliver, like one of George Orwell's pigs, was "more equal" than other first lieutenants.

It was no surprise to Hightower that Oliver took his reduction of authority gracefully—pretending he was glad to be relieved of the responsibilities that went with command. Though Hightower didn't believe him for a minute, he appreciated the gesture. And he was even touched when word reached him of an overheard conversation between Oliver and a sergeant who had been at the sauce.

It was a fucking shame what those REMFs had done to him, the sergeant had told Oliver, relieving him and putting that asshole in command. But this was Oliver's reply: "Granting all majors are assholes," he said, "our asshole is in the top one percent of all available assholes, and we should be damned glad we got a good one who knows what he is doing."

It was with this background that Major Hightower set out to handle the new situation the Colonel from the Pentagon East and the two Berets had presented him with.

A fuel truck and an ammunition truck drove up to the just landing Huey gunships as Major Hightower walked over to them. The gunships carried a crew of four: pilot, copilot, crew chief, and door gunner. Hightower was not surprised to see Lieutenant Oliver and his copilot, a young warrant officer, manhandling rocket-ammo crates off the truck as the crew chief started to check and refuel the ship, and the door gunner began to examine the weaponry.

It had been Oliver's long-established custom to assist the crew chiefs and door gunners in their labor. Some of the other, newer officers under the Major had not taken readily to that custom. Major Hightower had consequently found it necessary to correct the misimpression held by his executive officer and several of his captains that such assistance was beneath the dignity of officers and gentlemen.

Lieutenant John S. Oliver, a tall, lithe, brown-haired young man, saluted when he saw Major Hightower. The salute was not especially crisp, but neither was it insolent. It was, Hightower thought, sort of a friendly, military wave.

"How did it go, Johnny?" Hightower asked as he returned the salute.

"Two water buffalo and possibly an elephant," Oliver said dryly.

The Huey gunships had just returned from what was officially called an interdiction mission. Technically, they had patrolled the border between Vietnam and Laos. They theoretically stayed inside the Vietnamese border, while searching for supplies passing from North Vietnam down the Ho Chi Minh trails to Viet Cong forces in the south. But they were permitted to engage any targets of opportunity.

Major Hightower was not at all sure whether or not Oliver was pulling his leg with his crack about the two water buffalo and possibly an elephant, but he was damned if he would ask. They had expended their ordnance. They had shot at something. If that indeed had included water buffalo and a suspected elephant, Oliver had his reasons. It was likely, Hightower thought, that they had engaged probable targets: clumps of trees, for example, with truck tracks leading into them.

"Got a minute?" Hightower asked.

"Yes, Sir, of course," Oliver said. "Will it wait until I take a leak?"

"Absolutely."

"Corporal Williamson," Lieutenant Oliver said to the door

gunner, who looked about seventeen, ''I'm sure you will remember my comment about making sure the extra rockets don't go rolling around on the floor?''

''Yes, Sir,'' Corporal Williamson replied, looking chagrined.

Major Hightower and Lieutenant Oliver walked to the latrine behind Base Operations, a wood-and-canvas affair erected above cut-in-half fifty-five-gallon barrels. It was sort of an elevated outhouse.

Both officers wrinkled their noses at the smell of purifying chemicals. Oliver's stream made a ringing sound against the side of one of the cut-off barrels.

''You just had some visitors, Johnny,'' Hightower said after he had finished and was waiting for Oliver to do the same.

''Sir?''

''The battalion commander and two bird colonels. A Green Beret and an officer from Saigon.''

''To see me?'' Oliver asked as he fussed with the stuck zipper on his flight suit. ''What did they want?''

''The Colonel from Saigon asked me to ask you if you would be willing to volunteer for a classified mission involving great personal risk.''

Oliver looked at him incredulously.

''That's what he said, Johnny,'' Hightower said.

''In that case, Sir, with respect, not only no, but *hell* no.''

''Because you're getting short?''

''That too, but those Green Berets are nuts,'' Oliver said, and then asked, ''Is my saying no going to put you on a spot? They wouldn't tell you what they have in mind?''

''I gave you what I have,'' Hightower said. ''And all he said was that I was to ask you. . . . He didn't say anything about encouraging you.''

''Then, hell, no, Sir,'' Oliver said.

Hightower looked at his watch.

''I'm to relay your reply to a Colonel Augustus,'' he said. ''Polar Bear Six. You know who he is?''

''Oh, yeah. He's a real lunatic. The Berets in the camps are crazy enough, but Augustus runs an outfit called Special Operations Group. They make the other Berets seem almost normal by comparison. They go into Laos—and I've heard

North Vietnam, too—for two, three weeks at a time. The Old Man used to say they have a terminal case of death wish.''

''Well, I wish you'd wait around until I see if I can get Polar Bear Six on the horn and tell him what you said. Walk up to the commo bunker with me.''

''Yes, Sir,'' Oliver said.

The commo bunker was a small, sturdily constructed wooden building covered with sandbags. Ten feet away, in a similar but smaller bunker, one of the two available diesel generators gave off a steady roar and sent a thin stream of diesel exhaust into the air.

''There's some Cokes in the fridge, boss,'' the master sergeant who was the NCOIC—Noncommissioned Officer in Charge—said. ''Help yourself.'' In a moment he added, ''You, too, Sir,'' to Major Hightower.

''Thank you,'' Oliver said, asking with a raised eyebrow if Major Hightower wanted something to drink. Hightower nodded, then turned to the sergeant.

''Are you in contact with Dak To?'' he asked. ''If so, will you see if you can raise Polar Bear Six for me?''

''Checked it just a couple of minutes ago,'' the sergeant replied. ''It should be up.''

The link was in, and surprisingly clear.

''You want 'phones, Major? Or should I put it on a speaker?''

''Speaker, please,'' Major Hightower said as he took the microphone the sergeant extended to him.

The voice of Green Beret Colonel Augustus came through the scrambler with unusual clarity. ''This is Polar Bear Six, go ahead.''

''Polar Bear Six, this is Sparrow Six. I have spoken to Oliver. He declines, I say again, he declines to volunteer. Over.''

The response from Polar Bear Six was not what Major Hightower expected.

The unmistakable sound of an amused chuckle came over the air. ''Well, Father said he was smart,'' Polar Bear Six said, not paying much attention at all to proper radio procedure. ''Tell you what, you tell that young man to get in his flying machine and get his ass up here. I want to talk at him. Over.''

''Polar Bear Six, Sparrow Six. You mean now?''

''Yeah, I mean now. Is there some reason he can't?''

''Negative.''

''Polar Bear Six, clear,'' the speaker said.

Major Warren H. Hightower looked at Lieutenant John S. Oliver, Jr.

''Oh, *shit*,'' Lieutenant Oliver said.

''You better take the other ship with you, Johnny,'' Major Hightower said.

[TWO]
Dak To Special Forces Camp
Republic of South Vietnam
1410 Hours 15 August 1963

As the two Huey gunships approached Dak To, a DeHavilland of Canada Caribou roared off the runway. The Caribou, a large twin-engine, high-tailed, short-field-capable transport, was obviously empty now, for it required very little runway to get off the ground; it seemed to leap into the air.

Oliver and his wingman turned on final, flared out, and a foot or so off the ground, moved the gunships into sandbag revetments. Oliver turned the machine off and climbed out.

He reached behind the pilot's seat and picked up what had arrived in Vietnam in a package marked ''Tennis Racquet—Handle With Care.'' The return address on the package was false. The sender, a classmate of Lieutenant Oliver's at Norwich University, had done a Vietnam tour and was aware that the REMFs in Saigon took seriously their prohibition of non-authorized weaponry. They were liable to cause trouble if they detected a shotgun for lethal use near the Laotian border rather than a sports implement for use on one of Saigon's many well-tended tennis courts.

The sender was confident, however, that nine of ten REMFs in Saigon probably thought that everybody in 'Nam got a chance to play tennis and would pass the package without questions. It passed.

Once Lieutenant John S. Oliver had received his tennis racquet, he removed and threw away the magazine plug which limited magazine capacity to a sporting three rounds. The magazine now held five 00-buckshot shotshells, plus one in the chamber. He then neatly sawed off the barrel just above the magazine tube, sawed off the stock immediately behind the cavity for the action spring, and had his houseboy fasten to the barrel and stock a web sling formed from an old U.S. Carbine Caliber .30 sling.

Each of the 00-buckshot shotshells contained twelve pellets. Each pellet was more or less ballistically equal to the bullet fired from a .32 Colt Automatic Pistol [ACP]. It was thus a very efficient people killer, which Lieutenant John S. Oliver had twice so far had occasion to demonstrate.

He now slung the shotgun casually over his shoulder and spoke to Warrant Officer Junior Grade Billy-Joe Daniels, of Salt Spring, Oklahoma, his copilot. Daniels was six feet two, weighed 195 pounds, and was nineteen years old.

"If this base comes under attack while we are here, the SOP"—Standing Operating Procedure—"requires that you get the ship in the air as soon as possible. If you do that, and leave me on the ground, Mr. Daniels, I will find you, no matter where in the wild world you may hide, slice off your balls, and feed them to you."

Daniels chuckled.

"No sweat, boss," he said. "I'll wait for you. What the fuck is going on, anyway?"

"I don't really know," Oliver said, "but I have a sneaking suspicion that I'm not going to like it."

A stocky black man wearing master sergeant's stripes and a green beret walked over to them.

"You Lieutenant Oliver?" he asked. When Oliver nodded, he went on: "Father and the Colonel are in the mess bunker. I'll show you."

"Your name, no doubt, is Judas?" Oliver said, as they walked across the runway toward a large sandbag bunker half buried in the earth. "As in Judas Sheep?"

"No, Sir. Thomas, as in doubting," the sergeant replied with a smile. "I like your shotgun. Does it work?"

"It has so far," Oliver said. "Who the hell is 'Father'?"

"He says he knows you," the sergeant said. "I think that's why you're here."

"Then he's no friend of mine," Oliver said.

Colonel Joseph J. Augustus and a black Green Beret captain were sitting at one of the tables in the mess bunker eating. Steak and eggs, Oliver saw, and concluded that the makings had come in on the Caribou that had taken off as they approached.

Oliver saluted. "Lieutenant Oliver reporting as ordered, Sir," he said.

Colonel Augustus, chewing, laid his knife down, and still chewing, returned the salute. Oliver sensed that Augustus was examining him critically. Finally he finished chewing.

"Sit down, Lieutenant," Colonel Augustus said. "Have something to eat. You know Father, of course." He inclined his head toward the Captain.

Oliver looked more intently at the Captain. "No, Sir, I don't," he said.

"I was at Dak Sut," the Captain said evenly, not smiling. "You took me out of Dak Sut."

Flying an HU-1D into Dak Sut, Oliver had run into a Viet Cong attack. Both he and the slick had been dinged. And for a while it looked as if he wasn't going to make it. This black Beret Captain had apparently been one of the wounded he had hauled out. But he could not remember having seen him before.

"Father tried to get you a Silver Star to go with your DFC for that," Colonel Augustus said. "Predictably, I suppose, some sonofabitch in Saigon downgraded it to the Bronze."

"Sorry, I don't remember you," he said.

The Captain shrugged.

"Father says you have large balls, Lieutenant," Colonel Augustus said.

"The Captain errs, Sir. What I have is a highly developed sense for covering my own ass."

Colonel Augustus laughed. "How do you like your steak?"

"Sir, is there enough to go around? I've got seven other people with me."

"That's what you smell cooking," Augustus said, jerking

his head toward the stoves in the kitchen. "They'll run it out to the revetments."

"In that case, Sir, medium rare," Oliver said, then added, "Quoted the condemned man as he sat down to what he's sure is the standard hearty last meal."

Colonel Augustus laughed. The Captain did not.

"You don't trust me, Lieutenant, do you?" Colonel Augustus asked.

"I'm at sixty-three days and counting, Sir," Oliver said.

"And you've heard about Special Operations, right?" Colonel Augustus went on. "And at sixty-three days and counting, and possessed of a highly developed sense for covering your ass, you want nothing to do with it, or us, right?"

"Yes, Sir, that's about it," Oliver said.

"Well, let me tell you our problem anyway," Augustus said. "And Father's suggestions for solving it. Brainstorm it, in other words. Pick holes in his theory. Nothing dangerous in that, is there?"

A plate with a T-bone steak and two fried eggs was set before Oliver.

"No, Sir, I suppose not," Oliver said, reaching for the salt and pepper.

"Napoleon was right," Colonel Augustus said.

"Sir?" Oliver asked, confused, as he seasoned the eggs.

" 'An army travels on its stomach,' " Augustus said. "Even Ho Chi Minh's army. Interdiction of his lines of supply over here, since they're not going to let us march on Hanoi, is pretty important."

"Yes, Sir," Oliver agreed, wondering if he was going to get a long lecture on the philosophy of warfare before Augustus got to the point.

"We have the means to interdict his supply lines," Augustus went on, "multimillion-dollar airplanes and other weaponry that can, I am told—and believe—drop a round on the speaker's lectern in the Great Hall of the People in Moscow with a 99.9 percent chance of hitting it. But our problem here is that we're not shooting at a target precisely located on a map. We're shooting at moving targets—ranging from a truck convoy to a couple of guys pushing three hundred pounds of rice on a bicycle. You still with me?"

"Yes, Sir," Oliver said.

"The problem is compounded by Charlie's discovery of the tunnel. Spy planes and satellites may be able to read license plates in Havana from sixty-five thousand feet, but nobody has yet come up with a gizmo that can find a target—even an ammo dump with tons of ammunition—that's six or eight feet under the ground. All these Buck Rogers sensing devices, as a matter of fact, have trouble finding a half dozen trucks in the woods—no matter what you might have heard."

"Yes, Sir," Oliver said.

"So when technology fails, you go back to basics. You send in a guy on foot. And he walks around until he finds what he's looking for. Then he sends the coordinates of the target. . . . You get the picture."

"Yes, Sir."

"There is one small problem with this," Augustus said. "You lose a lot of people that way. Too many."

Oliver met Colonel Augustus's eyes, but did not respond.

"The current technique is for a long-range patrol to take a walk in the woods for a week, two weeks, as long as is necessary to get where they are going to see what they can see, and then get out. Father Lunsford has what he thinks is a better idea. I want to hear what you think about it."

"Why do they call you Father?" Oliver asked. "Or is that one of those questions I'm not supposed to ask?"

"My name is George W.—for Washington—Lunsford," Father said, not very pleasantly. "Clear?"

"Yes, Sir," Oliver said.

"We have been losing too many people lately," Father said. "Very highly trained, very valuable people, damned hard to replace. I have decided their getting blown away is a function of exposure. The longer they are running a risk of being detected, the greater the possibility they will get blown away. Reasonable?"

"Yes, Sir."

"Therefore, it follows that the way to reduce losses is to reduce the length of exposure. That seems very logical, wouldn't you say?"

"How are you going to do that?"

Father Lunsford did not respond directly.

"If, say, it is a four-day walk from the border to a suspected tunnel area, where a patrol might linger for say twenty-four hours, and then walk back out, we have a total of nine days' exposure. But let us say that a patrol has to walk through the woods for just one day before reaching the area of interest, spends the same twenty-four hours there, and then has just one more day of walking through the woods to get out. I don't happen to have my slide rule with me, but just off the top of my head it seems that we would be reducing the total exposure by two thirds, and we would thus reduce their risk by the same sixty-six point six six six ad fucking finitum percentum . . . wouldn't you say, Slats?"

"You want to put these people in by chopper?" Oliver asked, but it was actually a statement, an incredulous accusation, more than a question.

"You see, Colonel?" Father Lunsford said brightly. "I *told* you he was considerably brighter than your average run-of-the-mill airplane driver."

Oliver, who'd just registered that he'd been called Slats and didn't like it, and didn't like Captain George Washington Lunsford's tolerant sarcasm either, said nothing.

"Ignoring for the moment your disrespectful attitude toward Army Aviators, of whom my beloved little brother is one, Father," Colonel Augustus said, "I somehow get the idea that Lieutenant Oliver does not share your unrestrained enthusiasm for this notion of yours."

Father Lunsford shrugged.

"Let's try it this way, Lieutenant," Colonel Augustus went on. "Purely for the sake of theoretical argument. We have these givens. We *will* insert and extract a twelve-man, lightly armed team into—purely for the sake of argument—Laos, in an area through which the Ho Chi Minh trails pass. Their mission is to locate suspected dumps of materiel—most of which are believed to be underground—and movements of transport convoys—say, trucks and people pushing overloaded bicycles. Once these targets are identified and reported, our brothers in the Air Force and Navy will make them disappear.

"The teams inserted are quite valuable, so extracting them safely is nearly as important as putting them in undetected. Consequently, for the sake of argument, let us say you have your choice of equipment—anything in the inventory, or anything that can be purchased off-the-shelf in the States and flown over here, cost be damned. Now you tell me how you would insert and extract our teams."

Oliver was chilled. He knew Augustus was dead serious. When he didn't reply immediately, Colonel Augustus went on. "The highest priority is to get them onto the ground undetected. Failing that, we want them in such a place that bad guys looking for them will have difficulty finding them. You understand that their mission is not to engage the enemy, but to locate targets?"

"Yes, Sir," Oliver said, and then without thinking, added, "Jesus H. Christ!"

"What is the first problem you see?" Augustus said.

"Sir, you could put choppers down any number of places, any place four feet wider than the rotor cone," Oliver said. "But Charlie knows that, too. And taking out long-range patrols is one of his high priorities. So you start with the risk of trying to sit down on a spot where there's a machine gun trained. The way around that would be to use suppressive fire on the landing zone, but that would sure tell him where you were landing. Even if that LZ wasn't already defended, scratch that helicopter."

"So you would say that you couldn't fire on the LZ before landing?" Augustus said.

Oliver realized that his mind was racing. He felt a little lightheaded.

"Sir," he said, and the words came out in a rush, "you could probably do it this way: four choppers, two slicks, and two gunships. Before you go out, you pick six, eight, ten LZs, all small ones. The gunships fly, say, a half mile off the route of the slicks, and high. One slick makes an approach to an LZ. If there's nobody there, he off-loads his half of the team, and the other slick comes in with the other half. If somebody *is* there, he tries to get away. If he succeeds, fine. In any event, if he lands in a hot LZ, the gunships come in and take it under fire. Then, if necessary, pick up survivors. I could pick up, say, three people by dumping most of my ammo load . . . half of the people on a slick . . ."

"*You* could, could *you*?" Colonel Augustus asked softly.

Oliver met his eyes. "And the other gunship, theoretically speaking, could pick up the other three people."

Colonel Augustus grunted. "And how would you get them out under normal conditions?"

"That would be easier. A team in would know which LZs Charlie is covering. It would be best if they could find one that isn't being covered. But, failing that, they'd have to duck while we suppressed it—" He started to say something else and then stopped.

"Come on," Colonel Augustus said softly, gesturing with his hands.

"On the insertion, at the increased risk of hitting a hot LZ," Oliver said, "you could make touch-and-goes at two, three LZs without putting the teams off. Charlie wouldn't know if you had put them off or not. So he would have to put a lot of people to work running around in the woods, looking."

Augustus grunted again.

"It's perfectly clear to me why Father thinks you're considerably brighter than your average run-of-the-mill airplane driver," Colonel Augustus said. "The true test of somebody else's intelligence is the degree to which he agrees with you. Would you be crushed to learn, Lieutenant Oliver, that Father Lunsford came up with a plan that is, give or take a minor detail, almost identical to yours?"

Oliver didn't reply.

"I want to restate that," Augustus said. "I hope, Captain Lunsford, that you are appropriately crushed, having seen Lieutenant Oliver—in what, ninety seconds—come up with a plan very much like the plan that took you two weeks to dream up."

"Great men tend to think alike," Father Lunsford said solemnly.

Colonel Augustus laughed.

"How soon could you get set up to do it?" he asked Oliver. "Forty-eight hours give you enough time?"

"I didn't hear the word 'volunteer,' Sir," Oliver said.

"Oh, come on," Augustus said. "Forty-eight hours give you enough time?"

"Yes, Sir."

II

[ONE]
Dak To Special Forces Camp
Republic of South Vietnam
1615 Hours 11 September 1963

It is incumbent upon a commander, First Lieutenant John S. Oliver, Jr., reminded himself, feeling like a horse's ass, *to inspire confidence in his men by example. If a commander exudes an aura of calm, of confidence, it is contagious. A good commander never lets his doubts become known to his men.*

At the moment he felt neither calm nor confident. In just about forty-five minutes he was going to insert a Special Operations Group (radio call sign *Bulldog*) long-range patrol twenty miles over the other side of the Laotian border.

The team consisted of twelve people. On the Number One slick would be its commander, Captain George Washington Lunsford; its radio operator, Master Sergeant William

Thomas; and four Nung tribesmen, mercenaries, who were used as technical advisers. The Nungs were paid a monthly retainer plus sixty dollars each time they crossed the Laotian border. The Number Two slick would carry a new guy, a mean-looking little Italian lieutenant named Fangola, and five more Nungs.

The plan called for three diversionary touch-and-goes before the drop. And the patrol would actually get off at the fourth LZ. Following that there would be two more diversionary touch-and-goes before the slicks flew back across the border and returned to Dak To.

The planning and timing of the mission had to be based on two considerations. There had to be time for the patrol to get away—say a thousand meters, maybe fifteen hundred—from their LZ before darkness fell. And then there had to be additional time before it became dark for the slicks to make the two diversionary touchdowns. The determination of timing had consequently been based on the official hour for sunset.

Oliver didn't think that was going to work. The monsoon season was already beginning, the skies were overcast, and the weather was sure to grow worse before it grew better. So he suspected that it was going to be dark as hell long before there was official permission for darkness to fall from the United States Air Force Meteorological Service, Southeast Asia. He was also worried that the weather might close in after the team was inserted, and then they might not be able to bring them out for days.

Though technically Father Lunsford was in charge, the responsibility for making all this work was not Lunsford's but his.

Battalion had put the four choppers, their crews, and some maintenance personnel on TDY—Temporary Duty—to Special Operation Group, and Father was in command of that; but short of his calling the whole thing off, Father would indulge him in anything aeronautic he wanted. And this meant that Oliver had to live with the choices he'd made: If, on the theory that it would get dark earlier, he had chosen to go in early, the sun would have doubtless broken through the cloud cover and given Charlie another thirty minutes or more to look for Father and his men. But since he had actually decided to go with Official Sunset, it *would* surely get dark earlier, and so Father would not have much time to take a long walk through the woods before it was too dark to see his hand in front of his face. Or there would not be time to make the follow-on diversionary landings.

To make matters worse, the weather was going to be shitty for the next couple of days at least. But when he told Lunsford that, Lunsford said the patrol still had to go. They just couldn't put it off.

They had two targets this time: a newly reported, suspected fuel and ammunition dump, in caves, and a convoy of Russian-built trucks coming down from North Vietnam to that dump. With a little bit of luck, Father said, they would find not only the dump but the trucks unloading there.

The intelligence about all this was supposed to be pretty good.

Oliver doubted that, too.

But what really bothered him was a gut feeling. Something was going to go wrong.

"Take not counsel of your fears"—General George S. Patton, Oliver quoted to himself. It didn't help much.

Father Lunsford walked up to where Oliver was sitting on the floor of the cabin of his gunship.

Lunsford was wearing fatigues, with no insignia of any kind. There was a black band around his forehead—a net. Oliver supposed that Lunsford could pull it down over his face, the way stickup men pulled a woman's stocking down over their faces before they stuck up a liquor store. But in his own experience, Oliver had never seen one of those nets used as anything but a headband.

"Here you are, Tiger Lead," Father said, and tossed something to him. "Don't say I never gave you anything."

Tiger Lead was Oliver's radio call sign for the mission.

It was a pistol, a 9mm Parabellum Browning automatic.

"What's this?"

"A small token of my admiration," Father said. "If you can come up with some clever way to smuggle them out of the country into the States, we can get rich."

"What the hell are you talking about?"

"You will notice there is no serial number," Father said.

"Gangsters, I am told, like that. I figure I can lose one or two per patrol—on the field of battle—without causing questions to be raised. And I hear that you can get four hundred bucks for one of those, even more—but say four hundred. Four hundred times say twenty-pistols is—eight thousand bucks. You figure some clever way to get those into the States, we can rent some very interesting female companionship."

He didn't know if Lunsford was pulling his leg or not.

"I am a Norwich graduate," Oliver said. "We do not, as I have previously informed you, have to rent female companionship. But on the other hand, neither do we accept postcoital gratuities. A simple round of applause is sufficient reward."

Lunsford laughed and then grew serious. "You look worried, Slats. Something wrong?"

"I don't like the weather," Oliver said.

"I don't want to abort this unless we have to."

"I'm at thirty-seven days and counting," Oliver said. "Caution increases as days remaining In Country decline."

"People who get too cautious get killed."

"You believe that?"

"I don't know," Father Lunsford said. "It *sounds* good. We going or not?"

"*Mis-ter* Daniels!" Oliver called loudly, à la Charles Laughton calling for Mr. Christian in *Mutiny on the Bounty.*

"Sir!" WOJG Daniels responded in a shout from the left, copilot's, seat of the Huey gunship.

"Sound 'Boots and Saddles,' " Oliver called. "The Cavalry rides again!"

Oliver could hear the whine of the gyros starting up as Billy-Joe Daniels threw the master switch.

"I really get to keep this?" Oliver said, holding the Browning up.

"Try not to shoot it," Lunsford said. "My information is they're worth more in NRA New condition."

"Thank you," Oliver said, then pushed himself upright. He and Father Lunsford looked at each other a moment, and then, as Lunsford walked to one of the slicks, Oliver got in the right seat and started strapping himself in.

[TWO]
Landing Zone Mike
1725 Hours 11 September 1963

There was excitement in the voice of one of the slick pilots. The excitement came clearly over the FM between-aircraft radio:

"Tiger Lead, this sonofabitch is hot! Jesus Christ, he's down!"

"Here we go, hot and heavy," Oliver said over the intercom to his crew. He was flying. And Billy-Joe Daniels's responsibility as copilot was controlling the maneuverable 40mm grenade launcher in the nose. Oliver pressed the switch on the stick to the next, radio-transmit, detent. "On the way," he said, and a moment later, "What's going on? For Christ's sake, report!"

"Bikini One is down, crashed on landing."

"Survivors?"

"I think so," Tiger Two said.

"On the way," Oliver repeated, aware that it was unnecessary to repeat it.

The two Huey gunships had been flying just over a half mile to the right rear, and above, the slicks. It took them no more than thirty seconds to reach Landing Zone Mike.

Twice during that thirty seconds Oliver tried unsuccessfully to communicate with Bulldog Six, but as he picked out the shape of the downed Huey against the jungle background, the AN/ARC-44 FM radio came to life.

"Tiger Lead, Tiger Lead, Bulldog Six, we're down, we're down!"

Lunsford had at least survived the crash.

"I have the LZ in sight," Oliver replied. "Where the hell are you?"

"In the trees to the north of the LZ," Lunsford's voice came back. "There's a light machine-gun and maybe half a dozen AKs across the LZ."

Oliver couldn't see a thing.

"Tiger One, we've got to take out those weapons. Give me some smoke in the middle of your position. I'll hit everything but the smoke," Oliver called, even as he pointed the nose of the gunship toward the LZ.

There was a stream of 2.75-inch rockets from the rocket pods, and a steady thumping sound as the 40mm grenade launcher, fired by Billy-Joe, brought the enemy positions under fire. After that died and he overflew the target, the sharper sound of the .30 caliber M-60 machine gun started up. It was being fired by Corporal Williamson from the right-side door.

"Bulldog Six, how many survivors?" Oliver asked.

"The pilot and copilot didn't make it," Lunsford replied.

Oliver made up his mind what had to be done as he banked the gunship steeply.

"Tiger One," he called to the other gunship, "we're going to make one more gun run. We'll expend as much as possible and then touch down on the next go-around. It's a big LZ and I think we can each take out four of the people. You cover me as best you can. After I'm out, I'll cover you while you pick up the remaining four."

"Got you," Tiger One replied.

Oliver moved the mike button to "radio transmit" again.

"Father, I'm coming in. When we touch down, run like hell," Oliver ordered. "Four people only. Tiger One will then come in for the rest."

There was no reply.

Oliver completed his turn, then made another run at the LZ. Billy-Joe fired the 40mm grenades that were left, and there was another stream of 2.75-inch rockets from the pods. Oliver heard the chattering of the M-60 machine gun as he pulled out. He touched the intercom button.

"Throw out the extra rockets," he said. "And whatever else is loose back there."

"Guns, too, boss?" Corporal Williamson's voice came in his earphones.

"Yeah, everything," Oliver said. With four people coming aboard, he was going to have a hard time getting the gunship back in the air.

He completed the turn and made another approach, hoping that Charlie would think he was about to make another firing run.

And then he flared it quickly and put it on the ground.

Master Sergeant "Doubting" Thomas, moving with surprising speed for his bulk, came running toward the helicopter, with three Nungs on his heels.

The last wasn't fully in the cabin when Oliver tried to get back in the air.

Goddammit, it's heavy!

The gunship shuddered and finally lifted off. The moment it was a foot off the ground, Oliver spun it, dropped the nose, and started to move away, picking up airspeed.

There was a dull pinging sound, and a moment later the *beep beep beep* of the systems-failure alarm. But because he was too intent on getting the bird over the trees, Oliver didn't even look at the control panel. He cleared the trees by inches.

"We have trouble," Billy-Joe said calmly.

Oliver looked at his control panel.

The master systems-failure light in front of him was flashing red, and so was the hydraulic-systems warning light on the console between the pilot's and copilot's seats.

He didn't need the lights. He could tell from the brute force needed to move the controls that he had lost all hydraulic power.

"Get on the controls with me," he ordered Billy-Joe. "We've lost hydraulics."

And then he felt the ship shudder as other things started coming apart.

"Shit!" he said. Then he depressed the mike button. "Tiger One, we've been hit. I've got no hydraulics and the warning-light panel looks like a Christmas tree. I'm going to have to sit this thing down quick. Where are you?"

"I've just cleared the trees," Tiger One responded. "I have Bulldog Six plus three."

"What are we going to do?" Billy-Joe asked matter of factly.

They were at only five hundred feet—and less than a mile from the LZ.

Oliver didn't reply. There was really no choice. With a little bit of luck, the ship would stay together long enough to make a landing.

If the tail rotor will stay together just a couple more seconds!

"There, to the right," he said to Billy-Joe. "Stay on the controls with me!"

With both of them working the controls with all their might, they managed to steer the gunship toward a small opening in the jungle not much wider than the rotor cone.

And then he saw that the clearing was *not* as wide as the rotor cone.

Billy-Joe made the same judgment.

"Oh, *shit*!" he said.

Oliver flared the gunship out high, just above the treetops. He was in effect landing there—except that the ground was twenty feet below him instead of a couple of inches.

The gunship stopped flying and fell straight down.

The tail rotor struck the trees; the tail-rotor shaft severed.

A moment later the gunship hit the ground in a slightly nose-down attitude. The skids instantly collapsed, absorbing some of the shock. And then the fuselage touched the ground with a bone-jarring crash.

The tail boom ripped off.

The main rotor head and the transmission tore loose and shifted forward.

The rotor blades, still moving, sliced the nose of the gunship off neatly, with a horrifying screech of torn metal, just forward of the instrument panel.

Almost as if it was happening to someone else, Oliver waited for the next blade to slice through his door, and then him.

Instead, it struck the ground and stopped.

"Jesus H. Christ!" Billy-Joe said.

Oliver looked at him a moment, and then they both unfastened their seat and shoulder harnesses. They stood up and just walked forward, where the nose and instrument panel had been.

Then, as if waking up, Oliver became aware that the engine was running out of control. He knew what caused that: When the transmission and main rotor head had shifted forward on impact, the short shaft between the engine and the transmission had either broken or torn loose. Because there was no load on the engine any longer, it was about to tear itself apart.

When that happened, it would scatter parts as lethally as a hand grenade, except that the parts would be bigger.

When he looked into the cabin, he saw that Staff Sergeant Paul Thornton, the crew chief, had not only survived the crash but was already on his feet, working on the quick-disconnect on the fuel line. Seconds later the insane howl of the engine suddenly died.

"Tiger Lead, Bikini Two. Tiger One just went in. Crashed. He hit hard. Shit, it blew up."

Oliver looked at the walk-around, emergency FM transceiver in his hand. He didn't remember grabbing it before leaving the gunship. He put it to his mouth.

"Bikini Two," Oliver replied, "why did Tiger One go down? Are there any survivors?"

"I think he got hit after he cleared the LZ. Looks like some people came out of it."

"Bikini Two, we're on the ground," Oliver said. "Even if we had another ship to pick us up, it couldn't land where we are without hitting the trees. I'm going to torch the bird and dee-dee out of here. We'll call you on the emergency radio later."

He walked quickly to the side of the crashed ship and looked inside.

"Everybody all right back here?"

"The black guy took a slug in the leg," Corporal Williamson said matter of factly. "Where the fuck are we?"

"Sergeant Thomas to you, asshole," Thomas said. "He told me he didn't think it got an artery, and he can still move."

"We're going to torch the ship," Oliver said, "and then dee-dee into the jungle."

"If you torch it they'll know where we are," Thomas said.

"They know where we are anyway," Oliver replied, thinking simultaneously, *I don't have to explain myself to this guy.* "Maybe if they think we crashed, they won't be so anxious to look for us."

"And maybe they will," Sergeant Thomas said.

"You find the thermite grenades, Billy-Joe?"

"Williamson threw them out," WOJG Daniels replied.

"Shit!"

"I know how to set it on fire," Staff Sergeant Paul Thornton, the crew chief, said.

"Do it, Paul," Oliver ordered.

Master Sergeant Thomas took a small, hand-held radio from his pocket and spoke into it.

"Bulldog Six, Three. We're down."

"Three, Six, we'll find you. Eight," Father Lunsford replied.

"What does that mean? Eight?" Oliver asked.

"It means whenever the little hand points to eight, I'll key this thing for fifteen seconds," Sergeant Thomas said. "He'll home in on us."

"And they'll send somebody to pick us up, right?" Corporal Williamson asked.

"Not today," Oliver replied. "Not in this soup. And it's dark already. Probably first thing tomorrow."

He felt Sergeant Thomas's eyes on him, met them, and saw in them that Thomas thought that he was either a fool or a liar.

"Let's get into the jungle," Oliver said, and pointed toward the east.

"I think we ought to go west," Sergeant Thomas said.

"Do what I tell you, Sergeant, will you, please?" Oliver said, coldly furious.

Master Sergeant Thomas shrugged his shoulders and moved to the east.

Oliver looked at the helicopter. Sergeant Thornton had somehow—Oliver had heard no noise—ruptured a fuel cell. JP-4 was spilling out, forming a puddle. Thornton took a Zippo from his pocket, opened it, and worked the lighter-fluid-soaked cotton wadding out of the bottom. Then, using the lighter, he ignited the wadding and tossed it into the puddle of JP-4. It burst into flame, and a moment later there was a small but growing cloud of dark smoke. The JP-4 fuel was really beginning to burn.

"That ought to do it, boss," Thornton said. "I'll stay and make sure."

Oliver and Thornton waited fifty feet from the downed gunship until the JP-4 was burning furiously, then they followed Master Sergeant Thomas and the others into the jungle.

When two hours later the first Nung mercenary appeared, silently stepping out of the forest in the near absolute darkness, he so frightened Oliver that he really thought for a moment he was going to faint or be sick to his stomach, or both.

He leaned on a tree, weak and dizzy, while the mercenary conducted a whispered conversation with Master Sergeant Thomas, of which Oliver understood not a word. In what Oliver, with growing annoyance, decided was in Thomas's own sweet time, Thomas came to him.

"Father took a couple of hits," Thomas explained laconically.

"Where is he?"

"They're bringing him," Thomas said impatiently. "As I was saying, the pain must be pretty bad, 'cause Father gave his radio to this guy and took a needle. One of the Nungs took some hits, too, so that's three people who can't walk out of here."

"We're going to have to walk out of here, Thomas," Oliver said. "There's no other way. The rain is not going to stop."

"I say we wait until it clears," Thomas said. "They know we're here; they'll send something—maybe an Air Force Jolly Green Giant—after us."

"You don't listen good, do you, Sergeant?" Oliver flared. "I said the weather is not going to lift. And Charlie is going to comb this area looking for us. We have to move; and given that, I think we should walk toward Vietnam, not away from it."

"You don't think Charlie will think we'll head toward 'Nam?" Thomas asked. "And look for us there?"

"I think I've had enough of this discussion, Sergeant," Oliver said. "If Father Lunsford is out of it, I'm in charge."

"Yes, *Sir*!" Thomas said with exquisite sarcasm.

Father Lunsford was truly out of it. When he appeared, ten minutes later, supported on one side by a Nung mercenary and on the other by Technical Sergeant Peter Alonzo, the crew chief of the other shot-down gunship, he was deep—literally—in the arms of Morpheus.

Sergeant Alonzo told him that the pilot, copilot, and door gunner of the gunship had been killed in the crash when they went in; he had been thrown free and was bruised and sore but otherwise all right.

Captain George Washington Lunsford's reaction to their predicament was a cheerful smile and certain philosophical observations.

"For yea, though I walk through the valley of death," he pronounced, smiling happily, "I will fear no evil for I am—or maybe Doubting Thomas is—one or the other—the meanest sonofabitch in the valley!"

"How are you, Father?" Oliver asked.

"It smarted," Lunsford said, his face serious, frowning. "Oh, my, how it smarted! You may have noticed that I have availed myself of the proper medication?"

"I've noticed."

"I place this brave little band of brigands and all-around feather merchants in your capable hands, Brother Oliver," Father said. "There being nobody else around to hand it over to. Doubting Thomas is all balls, and one hell of a radio operator, but he can't find his ass in the dark with both hands."

Then he smiled even more brightly. A moment later, he went limp, and his eyeballs rolled white.

[THREE]
United States Air Force Hospital
Clark Air Force Base
Republic of the Philippines
3 October 1963

"Attention to orders," the portly little light bird with the Adjutant General's Corps insignia on his lapels said more than a little pompously. "Headquarters, U.S. Military Assistance Command, Vietnam, 30 September 1963. . . ."

"Excuse me, Sir," Captain George Washington Lunsford said very politely, "I can't quite hear you." He gestured toward his right ear, implying that he was a little hard of hearing.

Lunsford, wearing a purple bathrobe, was sitting on the bed; and the light bird had just pinned on him the Purple Heart medal (fourth oak leaf cluster) which had been given to the Colonel by an AGC captain, who had accompanied him.

The AGC light bird then turned to Oliver, cleared his voice, and boomed, "Award of the Silver Star Medal. For valor in action against an armed enemy, the Silver Star Medal is herewith awarded to First Lieutenant John S. Oliver, Jr., Armor. United States Army. Citation: Shot down while attempting to recover by helicopter a long-range Special Forces patrol operating in enemy-controlled territory in the vicinity of Dak Pek, Republic of Vietnam. . . ."

"So *that's* where we were. I *wondered* where we were," Captain George Washington Lunsford said, wonderingly, innocently.

The AGC light bird glared at him and then continued. "Lieutenant Oliver, then assigned to the 170th Assault Helicopter Company, after managing a safe landing of a severely damaged HU-1B helicopter, established contact with the Special Forces patrol, three of whose members, including the commanding officer, were wounded. He then assumed command of the entire force of thirteen men and successfully, over a period of nine days, led it through enemy-controlled territory to friendly lines. During this period there were three encounters with enemy forces. For the last five days of the withdrawal operation, Lieutenant Oliver was suffering from shrapnel and small-arms wounds to his right arm and chest, and refused available pain-deadening medication in order to maintain his full mental faculties.

"Lieutenant Oliver's extraordinary courage, superb leadership, coolness in combat, and outstanding professional skill reflect great credit upon himself and the United States Army. Entered the military service from Vermont."

The AGC light bird handed the orders to a Medical Service Corps captain and reached for the Silver Star box. Captain George Washington Lunsford put his fingers in his mouth and whistled. Then he applauded.

The AGC light bird spun around and glared at him again.

"Sorry, Sir," Lunsford said. "I guess I got a little carried away. I mean, the Lieutenant saving my life, and all."

With visible effort the AGC light bird restrained himself from saying what was in his mind and turned back to Oliver.

He pinned the Silver Star on his bathrobe, then offered his hand.

"Congratulations, Lieutenant."

"Thank you, Sir," Oliver said.

The AGC light bird turned and marched out of the room, trailed by the Captain.

"You're out of your fucking mind, Father, you know that?" Oliver said.

"I always get carried away on emotional occasions like that," Father replied with no evident sign of remorse.

The AGC Captain came back in the room. He tossed Oliver another blue medal box.

"Purple Heart," he said. Then he looked at Lunsford. "Hey, wiseass, you were almost a little too smartass for your own good. I just had to talk the Colonel out of jerking you off the evac flight in the morning."

"He was going home?" Oliver asked.

"You both are," the Captain said. "He almost didn't. I guess the Colonel figured he'd rather have somebody else go through the paperwork of court-martialing you."

"For what? Applauding this splendid young officer's superb achievements on the battlefield in defense of Mother, and apple pie, and who knows what else?"

"Keep it up, Lunsford, you'll dig your own grave," the Captain said and walked out of the room.

"You're insane," Oliver said to Lunsford. "Don't you want to go home?"

Lunsford looked at him a moment, shrugged, then opened the drawer of his bedside table. He took out an envelope, opened it, and held up a sheet of paper.

"Attention to orders," he said.

"You're not nearly as funny as you think you are," Oliver said.

"You just stand there at attention like a good little lieutenant," Lunsford said and resumed reading. "Headquarters, U.S. Army Special Forces Group, Vietnam, 25 September 1963. Special Orders Number 203. Paragraph eleven. Award of the Combat Infantryman's Badge. The Combat Infantryman's Badge is awarded to First Lieutenant John S. Oliver, Armor, 170th Assault Helicopter Company, for service in ground combat while serving as acting commanding officer, Special Forces Team C-16, near the Laotian border during the period 11 to 21 September 1963.''

''Jesus, is that for real?''

''Yeah, it's for real,'' Lunsford said. He tossed a Combat Infantry Badge to Oliver, who dropped it and had to pick it up. When he was erect again, Lunsford handed him a small sheet of green paper, officially termed a distribution form, but universally called a buck sheet.

Oliver read it. On it, in pencil, was written, ''For a skinny honky, you ain't all that bad a Green Grunt. Take care of yourself. M/Sgt D. J. Thomas.''

Oliver looked at Lunsford.

''Well, Slats,'' Father said, ''you ever had carnal congress with a lady of the Philippines?''

''Not yet.''

''Well, since we're not gonna be able to do anything about that tonight, you're gonna still just have to hold your breath.''

[FOUR]
The Army Aviation Center & Fort Rucker, Alabama
25 October 1963

The MP on the gate leaned down and put his hands on the door of the Desert Sand 1963 Pontiac convertible. He glanced quickly inside, and then at the driver. The driver was in civilian clothes; but to judge by the luggage in the back seat, he was almost certainly in the service.

''Help you, Sir?''

''Reporting in,'' Lieutenant John S. Oliver said. ''PCS.''

Permanent Change of Station.

''First stop is the MP station, Sir,'' the MP said. ''Just—''

''I know where it is,'' Oliver interrupted.

''They'll give you a temporary car-pass until you can get your vehicle inspected and registered. Then you go to the AG office.'' The Adjutant General. ''That's over by the post office—you know where it is?''

Oliver nodded.

''They'll take care of you from there,'' the MP said, and then added, ''I never saw a pink car before. New, huh?''

"Yes, it is," Lieutenant Oliver said. "And it's *Desert Sand*, not pink."

The MP didn't argue, but his face said that he knew pink when he saw pink.

Since it was his home state, the car had Vermont plates, but Oliver had actually bought it in San Francisco the day after he had returned to the United States. He had always wanted to drive across the country, and this seemed to be a good opportunity to do so. Especially since he was in no rush whatever to go home.

Oliver had left Father Lunsford in the other bedroom of their suite in the Mark Hopkins. When he left, Lunsford was snoring loudly in the arms of a very tall, very thin, Afro-American/Spanish/Tahitian stewardess who had been on the Northwest Orient Airlines Honolulu–San Francisco leg of their journey. Once Oliver was on the street in front of the hotel, he got in a cab and had himself delivered to the nearest Pontiac dealer.

Two hours later, the deed done and almost all of his travelers checks gone, he was back in the hotel working himself up to defend to Lunsford his notion of driving across the country. Lunsford was certain to declare him mad.

He was wrong again about Lunsford.

"Sometimes, my boy, you are not as dumb as someone looking at you might surmise," Lunsford said. "I forget how many miles a day it is the Army considers a reasonable day's drive, but four hundred pops into my mind. That will give us at least a week, not chargeable as leave. We will drive, drink, wench, arising fresh the next morning to drive, drink, wench . . ."

"You sound as if you're going with me."

"I will even help a little, not much, but a little, with the gas," Father said.

"I thought you would want to get home."

"I'm going to have to psych myself up for that," Lunsford said. "I gather *you* are not terribly impatient to rush into the arms of your family, either?"

"My parents are dead," Oliver said. "My family is my sister, her husband, and their house apes."

Father looked at him for a moment, then replied, "Mine

are alive. Unfortunately, before they got it right, they had three other children, to whom I am something of an embarrassment."

"How?"

" 'Soldiers and Dogs Keep Off the Grass'?" Father Lunsford said. "My two brothers are doctors, medical doctors, like the old man. My sister is a PhD, married to an MD. High-class folk like that don't really want to mess with a lowlife sol-juh, Johnny."

"You're kidding."

"Not a bit. And what makes it worse is that Big Brother Number One, and Dear Old Sis, and of course her husband, are what is known as 'progressive.' Which means, in other words, that they're knee-jerk liberals who regard Uncle Ho as sort of a Southeast Asian George Washington, and who regard me—carrying this analogy along merrily—as sort of a black Hessian peasant stupidly standing in the way of freedom, a brave new world—et cetera et cetera. It gets a bit stiff sometimes, at dinner. I once livened things up by throwing my brother-in-law off the porch into a snowbank. They were delighted."

"Delighted?"

" 'He who uses violence confesses he has lost the argument,' " Father quoted. "That's their Holy Writ. You'll see what I mean when you meet them."

Oliver's first impression of Father Lunsford's family was that they were all very bright, very charming people. But by the end of the second day, however, he'd come to divide them as Father had, into two groups: Father's father, mother, and Big Brother Number Two, who were great people, and all the rest, who obviously believed that anyone who did not agree with their pronouncements vis-à-vis geopolitics had been shortchanged in the brains department.

Oliver's own time at home turned out to be just about what he expected. His sister's twelve-year-old boy, his nephew, had moved into Johnny's room; and Johnny's stuff had been moved to the basement. He should have kept his mouth shut, but he had a couple too many drinks and pointed out that since the house was half his, he didn't think it unreasonable that a room in the ten-room place should be set aside for him, even if he wasn't home.

His sister had thereupon thrown one of her screaming fits—tears alternating with outrage. How could he be *so* ungrateful for all she and her husband had done for him!

The next morning Johnny left.

After thinking about it all the way down from Vermont, he called Father's home when he was passing through Philadelphia. But Father had already left. His mother told Johnny that Lunsford had been recalled to duty and was at Fort Bragg—which Oliver didn't believe for an instant. The Army would not recall people from convalescent leave until Russian T-72 tanks started rolling down Pennsylvania Avenue.

When he reached Fort Bragg, he found that his guess was correct. Father confessed he just couldn't take it anymore at home. So he had rented a garden apartment in Fayetteville and was going to booze and wench with his peers until his leave was up. Oliver spent the next two and a half weeks with him, then drove the Desert Tan (and *not* by God *pink)* Pontiac to Fort Rucker.

After Lieutenant Oliver left the MP at the Rucker gate, he found his way to the AG's office. When he got there, he discovered that he was on the shit list. The AG had attempted to make contact with him at his leave address of record and had been unable to do so. Parties at the LAOR had reported they had no idea where he was. Army regulations required that personnel on leave keep the appropriate authorities notified of their location.

"What did you want?"

"You were supposed to go to Fort Devens, Massachusetts, for a physical en route here," the AGC Captain said.

"Would you like me to go back, Sir?"

"Don't be a wiseass, Lieutenant."

"Sorry. What would you like me to do?"

"I suggest you go over to the station hospital and take the physical. Report back to me when you have."

He spent the afternoon taking the physical. And because he did not want to fool around with the billeting office about getting a BOQ, he drove into Dothan and spent the night in a motel.

When he returned to the AGC Captain's office the next morning, he learned that the Army had sent him another communication:

Lieutenant John S. Oliver, Jr., Armor, was promoted Captain, with Date of Rank 1 October 1963.

III

[ONE]
Office of the Commanding General
The Army Aviation Center & Fort Rucker, Alabama
12 December 1963

Major General Robert F. Bellmon sat in his high-backed leather chair in his office on the second floor of the Post Headquarters Building. He had pulled out the lower-right-hand drawer of his desk and was using it as a footstool. Bellmon was forty-five years old, just over six feet tall, and weighed 180 pounds. He wore his brown hair closely cut, but just long enough to part. He was wearing a Class A uniform, an Army Green blouse and trousers.

On the breast of the blouse he wore his Combat Infantry Badge and aviators' and parachutists' wings, but no ribbons. There was a wide ("General's") black band around the cuffs of the blouse, and another black band down the trouser seams. And two silver, five-pointed stars were pinned to each epaulet. But with those exceptions, there were few visible differences between his uniform and those worn by captains, or for that matter, by PFCs.

His feet were clad in old and soft from wear, but highly polished tanker's boots. This footgear was not prescribed by uniform regulations, and might indeed be proscribed, but Bellmon had worn tanker's boots as a young tanker, and he had always found them comfortable. . . . And of course no one at Fort Rucker was going to tell him they were unauthorized.

On General Bellmon's desk was an eight-inch-high stack of officers' service records: ten of them, each holding the official story of the military career, so far, of seven lieutenants and three captains. Each man had been proposed to General Bellmon as a replacement for his present aide-de-camp.

When Bellmon was on the fifth of the ten, that of Captain John S. Oliver, Jr., Armor, he realized that he had probably come across the young man he was looking for.

Captain John S. Oliver, Jr., was twenty-five years old. He was a bachelor, regular army, Armor, Presbyterian, an aviator, and a Norwich University graduate, class of 1959. Norwich, the Military College of Vermont, is the oldest of the private military colleges in the United States, and it has sent its graduates off to be regular officers, predominantly Cavalry (later, Armor), since the early 1800s.

Oliver, according to his records, was just back from Vietnam. And this interested General Bellmon. But it interested the General more that Oliver was a captain. Since he had not been in the service long enough to win that promotion routinely, ergo, he had made it on the "five-percent list."

What that meant, Bellmon knew, was that the Captains' Selection Board had been authorized (but not required) to select for promotion a number of lieutenants, not exceeding five percent of the total selected, from "below the zone of consideration." In effect, that meant the Board could pick lieutenants of outstanding ability and demonstrated performance who did not have the required time in the Army (or else the time as lieutenants) normally required for promotion.

Those on the five-percent list were selected by reviewing their service records and efficiency reports. One of the factors certainly considered in the case of Lieutenant Oliver was that his rating officer had recommended him "without qualification, to command a company in combat," and described him as having "an unusual grasp of the principles of leadership and warfare uncommon in someone of his youth and service."

It probably hadn't hurt Lieutenant Oliver's chances very much, either, that when the Board examined the portion of his service record devoted to awards and decorations they learned that he had come home from Vietnam with two Purple Hearts for wounds received in action against the enemy. Reading further, Bellmon saw that one of the Purple Hearts was connected with Oliver's receipt of the Distinguished Flying Cross.

> *. . . Seriously wounded while flying an aerial supply mission in the vicinity of Soc le Dug, Republic of Vietnam, Lieutenant Oliver managed not only to complete the delivery of desperately needed supplies, but, ignoring grievous and painful wounds to his leg and neck, remained on the ground, constantly under heavy enemy mortar and machine-gun fire, while wounded were loaded aboard his aircraft. He then took off, under fire, and flew the severely damaged aircraft more than sixty nautical miles. He managed a successful landing of the aircraft moments before losing consciousness.*

Reading further, Bellmon saw that the second Purple Heart was connected with Oliver's Silver Star, the service's third-highest award for gallantry.

> *Shot down while attempting to recover by helicopter a long-range Special Forces patrol operating in enemy-controlled territory in the vicinity of Dak To, Republic of Vietnam, Lieutenant Oliver, then assigned to the 170th Aviation Company, after managing a safe landing of a severely damaged HU-1B helicopter, established contact with the Special Forces patrol, three of whose members, including the commanding officer, were wounded. He then assumed command of the entire force of thirteen*

men and successfully, over a period of nine days, led it through enemy-controlled territory to friendly lines. During this period, there were three encounters with enemy forces. For the last five days of the withdrawal operation, Lieutenant Oliver was suffering from shrapnel and small-arms wounds to his right arm and chest, and refused available pain-deadening medication in order to maintain his full mental faculties.

Captain Oliver met all the criteria Bellmon had established in his mind for his new aide-de-camp; in fact, Oliver was more than he had hoped for. But he laid his record on the desk and picked up the next one, and read that.

General Bellmon was by nature and training methodical. Although, when the occasion demanded it, he could be imaginative, he was a great believer in precedent. He had found that it was often valuable to profit from the experience of others.

The precedent he was about to follow had been the practice followed both by his father, the late Lieutenant General Thomas Wood Bellmon, Jr., and by his father-in-law, the late Major General Porterman K. Waterford: both men replaced their aides-de-camp on an annual basis.

The office of aide-de-camp originated back in a time when communications were primitive. And aides functioned then as the chief messengers for generals. General officers would point to an aide and give him a message, either written or oral, and the aide would climb aboard his horse and gallop off to deliver it to another senior officer.

That function of aides-de-camp had begun to grow obsolete, however, with the introduction of the heliograph—the technique of sending messages by flashing mirrored sun's rays. But by then general officers had found it handy to have bright young officers around them to perform errands. And such became the custom. As a consequence, in the modern Army, promotion to general officer brings with it the assignment of an aide-de-camp.

Some maintain that the modern-day function of aides-de-camp is to be general officers' social secretaries. And there is more than a grain of truth in this. But aides do much more than that: essentially, insofar as it is humanly possible, an aide makes sure that the machinery of his general's professional life (and often his private life, too) runs smoothly. In practice this means that aides-de-camp end up becoming what their peers, the platoon leaders and company commanders, commonly call them: *dog-robbers*—guys who would rob a dog if that's what it took to better serve their generals. If that meant running errands, the aide ran errands. If that meant getting an inebriated Mrs. General home safely from the Officers' Club, he drove her home. If it meant pushing canapes, he pushed canapes.

Major General Bellmon believed such a perception of the role and function of aides to be unfortunate and limited (though partially true). As far as he was concerned, an aide-de-camp had two responsibilities: one to his general and one to himself. His responsibility to his general was to relieve him of minor, time-consuming, administrative details. And to himself: a bright young officer standing quietly in the background could learn more about how the Army was really run in six months as an aide than he could in the year-long course at the Command and General Staff College.

Like a chief of staff—perhaps even more so—the value of an aide-de-camp was based on his ability to read his general's mind, so that he could do, or have done, what the general wanted done, even before the general so much as expressed his desire. That, in practice, meant that the general had to *like* his aide. And since for the period of his assignment he became sort of a member of the general's family—an obedient, wanting-to-please son, so to speak—the aide had to like and be liked by the general's family as well. An aide who had trouble concealing his opinion that the general's wife was an old bitch, for example, would be unsuitable. And so would an aide the general's wife believed to be an unpleasant young man or an unsatisfactory role model for her son.

And a year on the job was enough. By then a young officer had learned about all he was going to learn from proximity to his general (by being privy, for instance, to meetings either officially or socially confidential), and it was time to give some other deserving, and suitable, young officer a chance.

The experience wasn't all that made service as a general's

aide useful to a young officer's career. There was also the general's efficiency report of his performance. A good efficiency report on an aide's record could make a tremendous difference even years later in his career. If Colonel Jones, say, now being considered for brigadier general, had served his general well when he was a lieutenant, that meant he had been constantly examined by a senior officer presumed to be a better judge of military potential than, for example, a captain.

When he had finished all of the records, Bellmon had seen that he had, without thinking about it, separated the ten folders into two stacks. There were three records in one stack and seven in the other.

He pushed a button on his intercom and summoned the incumbent aide-de-camp.

"Jerry, arrange for those three to come in for a chat. Am I busy tomorrow afternoon?"

"Yes, Sir, you're full," Captain Thomas replied.

"Then first thing Monday morning," General Bellmon ordered. "Schedule Captain Oliver last."

"Yes, Sir."

[TWO]
Near the Village of Grosse Rollen
Kreis Hersfeld, Hesse,
Federal Republic of Germany
1455 Hours 12 December 1963

Colonel George F. Rand, who was forty-four years old, exactly six feet tall, and weighed 165 pounds (ten more than he had weighed when he had graduated with the class of 1940 from the United States Military Academy at West Point), was sitting in a jeep on a small, snow-covered knoll near Hersfeld, in Hesse, overlooking the border between the Federal Republic of Germany and the German Democratic Republic.

He was dressed in a borrowed parka and what he thought of as a Royal Canadian Mounties hat, which was furry and had built-in earmuffs. At the moment he had the earmuffs down. Because he had not pinned colonel's eagles to either the hat or the shoulders of the parka, he was virtually indistinguishable from the PFC who sat beside him at the wheel of the jeep.

He had borrowed the jeep and driver from the motor pool of the 14th Armored Cavalry Regiment, giving as explanation to the motor officer, a captain, that he wanted to run into town. That was not true, and the lie made him a little uncomfortable. But he rationalized the guilt away by looking at what he was doing as "thinking Jesuit": the ends justify the means—sometimes.

If he had told the truth about why he wanted the jeep—that he wanted to have a look at a patrol actually on patrol—his arrival at the border would have been preceded by a flock of radio messages warning anybody of the 14th Cav near the border that one of those asshole brass hats from Seventh Army was running around loose up there, so cover your ass. Or words to that effect.

At the very moment Rand was doing his own checking out, the 14th Armored Cavalry Regiment was being officially inspected by a team under the personal direction of the Inspector General of the Seventh United States Army. That luminary, also a full colonel, was not especially pleased to have Colonel Rand around while he and his people were doing their thing, but there was nothing he could do about it.

Colonel George F. Rand was Chief, Combat Readiness Branch, Office of the Assistant Chief of Staff, G-3, Headquarters Seventh United States Army. It was his responsibility to know the state of combat readiness of each of the tactical units in Seventh Army. And if it was not what it should be, it was his business to see that training was implemented to bring everything up to snuff.

The Inspector General had argued, however, that it was his job to go onto the scene and check out what was there. He was supposed to do the inspecting and report his findings through proper channels. This procedure would ensure that, in due time, the proper information would be made available to the Chief, Combat Readiness Branch, Office of the Assistant Chief of Staff, G-3, Headquarters Seventh United States Army, for whatever purpose he wished.

Colonel George F. Rand was perfectly willing to have the IG and his platoon-sized entourage of experts count and inspect the rations in the combat stocks, and see that the ammunition in the bunkers would go off if necessary, and have a look at the other indicators (disciplinary actions, the AWOL and reenlistment rates, and so forth) of a unit's morale and efficiency. And he would not only believe what the IG told him, he'd be grateful for the information.

But Rand was not satisfied with that. He was convinced that his own responsibilities did not begin when the IG's reports landed on his desk, and that they went beyond whatever actions the IG's reports might suggest. His conviction in this case was based on long personal experience in the Army, in and out of combat, as well as on his own reading of the strategic and tactical situation the 14th Cav actually faced.

The conventional wisdom, which actually had its start with the Allied and Soviet troop disposals at the end of World War II, was that if the Russians decided to attack Western Europe, they would move from East Germany into Hesse, in the American Zone. The Soviets and their surrogates, the East Germans and the Poles and the rest of what had become the Warsaw Pact nations, would attack with a massive employment of armor and strike toward the Rhine, the English Channel, and into France. All these forces would go through Seventh Army like a hot knife through butter. Or at least so the theory held.

The geography of the area will permit a massive flow of tracked vehicles and their supporting equipment through only one relatively flat area, near Fulda. This area is known as the Fulda Gap.

If the Russians did decide to come through the Fulda Gap and make for the Rhine, the training responsibilities of G-3 would be put on the shelf, and the plan's (which was another way of saying, operational) responsibilities would be of paramount importance.

Colonel Rand did not personally think the Russians would ever try to come through the Fulda Gap. In his professional judgment, for one thing, they seemed to be getting pretty much what they wanted without waging a major war. Why fight the United States when you don't have to? For another, he was unable to believe that they would be able to secretly marshal the tanks, artillery, and troops, much less the incredible amounts of food, fuel, and ammunition they would need without getting caught at it.

In Colonel Rand's scenario, the moment intelligence (which is to say anything from a guy on a bicycle to the most esoteric electronic detection by satellite) picked up a Warsaw Pact buildup of the magnitude necessary to come through the Fulda Gap, other forces, political and military, would come into play.

Colonel Rand had no doubt whatsoever that the Russians would continue to try to satisfy their historic hunger for territorial expansion. That hunger went way back before the 1917 Revolution, before there were communists to give it new meaning and ideological force. And he believed it would continue long after communism ended up on the rubbish pile of history. But he didn't believe that expansion would begin here at Hersfeld—despite the conventional wisdom. In other words, he did not seriously believe that the 14th Armored Cavalry would be on the receiving end of the first blow.

Even so, he operated on the premise that it would. And consequently, he devoted a great deal of his effort and thought preparing and planning for an event he didn't think would happen.

He did this partly because he was a soldier who believed, quietly but firmly, that a soldier is honor bound to carry out his orders to the very best of his ability—even if he has profound doubts as to their wisdom. And some of it was because he knew that he was entirely capable of evaluating a politico-military situation and coming up with the absolutely wrong answer. He had demonstrated this once before, early in 1942, when he was a young officer still wet behind the ears. It was then his professional judgment that to permit the Philippine Commonwealth to fall to the Japanese would be more than just a stupid geopolitical blunder, it would be simply unthinkable.

Or at least so it appeared to him from his own personal vantage point. Rand was stationed on the Philippines when the Japanese attacked Pearl Harbor.

It was absolutely clear to him at the start of 1942 that the logical way to fight the Second World War was to permit the Germans and the Russians to bleed themselves dry of materiel and personnel, while at the same time diverting the bulk of American military assets then available to reenforcing the Philippines and fighting the Japanese to a standstill. Eventually, what was described accurately at the time as the sleeping colossus of American industrial might would get its act in gear, and war production not needed to contain the Japanese could be diverted to Europe. By that time the Russians would have worn down the German war machine.

Colonel George Rand had had plenty of time to consider how wrong his assessment was. "The aid" that he and everybody else in the Philippines expected tomorrow, or the next day for sure, had not come. Meanwhile the Japanese were forcing American troops down the Bataan Peninsula. And still no aid. And yet they still expected it even after they'd lost the Bataan Peninsula and were being shelled round the clock on the fortress island of Corregidor.

The aid hadn't come on the Death March either. Nor had it come when Lieutenant George F. Rand, in absolute violation of the Rules of Land Warfare prescribing the treatment of captured commissioned officers, had been loading powder into land mines in a Korean factory, while existing on a baseball-sized ball of rice a day plus an occasional dried fish.

But something can be learned, if not salvaged, from any experience, and Colonel George F. Rand believed that he had the rare professional experience of service with troops who were asked to provide more than should have been asked of them—troops facing impossible odds while simultaneously running out of food, ammunition, rations, and hope.

So if his estimate of the Soviets was wrong, and they did decide to come through the Fulda Gap, the troops of the 14th Armored Cavalry would be to World War III what the 26th Cavalry had been in the Philippines. They would fight until they ran out of people and ammunition and hope, and then they would be rolled over.

Thus Rand considered it his responsibility to know, as well as he could, exactly how long the symbol on his map that stood for the unit would represent an asset in place—rather than a gravestone marking where a unit had been.

Part of the information he needed to make that judgment would come from the IG, and part of it from the action and casualty reports that would flow when hostilities began. But an important factor in making that judgment would be an actual assessment of the troops: Would they do what could reasonably be expected of them, or fold quickly? Or would they earn themselves a place in military history as the 26th Cavalry had? Could they too be a unit that would go on fighting long after they really had nothing to fight with, and in the knowledge that "the aid" wasn't coming, and that a rational human being would conclude that further resistance was pointless?

And Rand had decided—not only with the 14th Armored Cav, but with all Seventh United States Army tactical units that would be in trouble if the balloon went up—that the only way to make that judgment was to go take a personal look.

After War II, Rand had commanded a company, and later a battalion, and in Korea a regiment. He knew what happened when a unit was about to be honored by the visit of an inspector general and his platoon of nit-pickers. A company, battalion, or regimental commander put his best equipment and his best people on display for inspection. And he sent the worn-out equipment and the misfits, commissioned and enlisted, someplace where they would be out of sight.

Such as on patrol now, when the rest of the regiment, all shined up, was on display for the IG in the *Kaserne*.

Rand believed that you don't judge a unit's efficiency by looking at its best men and at its newest and best-maintained equipment. You do it by finding out where the junk and misfits are being hidden, and by looking at the equipment you find, and, more importantly, by talking to the officers and men.

A patrol appeared, two hundred yards away and a hundred feet below where Rand's jeep sat. Three jeeps, and two M-48A5 tanks, moving at fifteen or twenty miles per hour down an icy, snow-covered dirt road, twenty yards from the first (of three) fences separating West Germany from East Germany.

Rand watched them for a moment, and he was sure that the parka-clad figure in the front seat of the lead jeep had seen him as well.

"OK, son," Rand said to the PFC at the wheel. "Let's go talk to those guys."

The jeep moved slowly and cautiously down the knoll until it reached the road, and then turned left, in the direction of the patrol.

"Stay on the road," Rand ordered.

The two jeeps stopped, nose to nose. The parka-clad figure in the lead patrol jeep jumped out. He was wearing a Royal Canadian Mounties hat, too, but he did not have the ear flaps over his ears. There was a second lieutenant's gold bar pinned to the front of the cap, and when Rand looked a little closer, he saw bars pinned on the parka.

I know why they hid this guy, Colonel Rand thought. *He looks as if he'll be fifteen next week.*

The Lieutenant looked at Rand, searched for and found no insignia of rank, saw the somewhat battered face, and logically concluded that he was dealing with a sergeant.

"Is there some reason you're blocking my way?" he asked.

Firm, but not arrogant, Rand decided. Second lieutenants, especially young ones who know they look young, tend to be arrogant.

"Unless you're headed for something that won't wait, I wanted to have a word with you, Lieutenant," Rand said.

"I'm on patrol," the Lieutenant said. Rand knew that the Lieutenant was beginning to question his first snap decision that he was dealing with a sergeant. Rand decided to take him off the hook.

"My name is Rand, Lieutenant," Rand said. "I'm a colonel on the Seventh Army staff. I wanted to look at a patrol."

The Lieutenant saluted. Crisply.

"Sir, Lieutenant Shaugnessy, Commanding Patrol B, Region Three. Sir, I did not see any insignia of rank."

"I borrowed the parka," Rand explained. "I'd like to talk to your men and have a look inside the tanks. But before we do that, I expect you'd better tell them why you've been stopped and by who, and why."

"Yes, Sir," Lieutenant Shaugnessy replied.

There was radio equipment and a radio operator in the back of the jeep. The radio operator had heard the conversation.

"Blue Fox, Blue Fox, This is Blue Fox Bravo," he said.

"Go ahead, Blue Fox Bravo."

The radio operator extended his arm and handed the microphone to Lieutenant Shaugnessy.

"This is Blue Fox Bravo Six," Shaugnessy said into the microphone. "We have halted near Position Barbeque Three Six, and are conversing with Colonel Rand of Seventh Army."

"Say again, Bravo Six?" Shaugnessy repeated the message.

"Blue Fox Bravo Six, advise when resuming movement."

"Affirmative, Blue Fox. Blue Fox Bravo Six out."

Rand was pleased with what he had seen. Not only were the radios working, which was not, in his experience, always the case, but the operator and the Lieutenant had followed the approved radio procedure.

More important, from Rand's viewpoint, was the way the radio operator had behaved. He was alert and he had tried to be helpful. If he hadn't liked his boy-faced lieutenant, for instance, he would not have started to call their headquarters until he was told to. And then, after he was told, he would manage not to make contact, so the Lieutenant would stand there before the brass hat from Seventh Army with egg on his face.

Rand walked to the jeep. The radio operator looked as if he were two weeks older than the Lieutenant. He had the drawstring of his parka hood drawn tightly around his face. He had been wearing goggles; they were now pushed up on his forehead.

"They maintain your radios all right, son?" he asked.

"Yes, Sir," the radio operator said.

"Do I detect a slight hesitation?" Rand asked, smiling.

"You really want the truth?"

"Yes, I would like the straight poop."

"I generally fix my own radios," the radio operator said.

"Because Third Echelon Maintenance can't, or won't?"

"What happens, Sir, is when you swap boxes, the way you have to, you're liable to turn in a radio with a little malfunction, like a diode blown or something. And what you get back is a radio looks like it got run over by an M-48."

"And doesn't work?" Rand asked sympathetically.

"Oh, they work all right, the guys in the shop know what they're doing, but they don't give a rat's ass what it looks like . . ." He paused, obviously remembering that he was talking to a senior officer and had gone too far, too profanely. ". . . Sir."

Rand was pleased. He was not much of a spit-and-polish soldier, and he thought there was entirely too much time wasted within the Army making things glisten that would work as well lubricated and painted olive drab. But it was also true that a soldier who cared about how his equipment looked was likely to take better care of it than one who didn't.

"How do you like this job?" Rand asked.

"Better'n sitting around in a maintenance van, Sir," the radio operator said.

"Blue Fox Bravo, this is Blue Fox. Blue Fox Bravo, this is Blue Fox."

The radio operator shrugged apologetically and spoke to the microphone.

"Go, Blue Fox."

"Is there a Colonel Rand with you? I spell, Roger, Able, Nan, Dog."

"Affirmative, Blue Fox," the radio operator said.

"Blue Fox Bravo, can you get Colonel Rand to the mike?"

The radio operator handed Rand the microphone.

What this is going to be is the troop commander, or maybe some major, or light colonel, who was just told I am here, is afraid I'm going to see or hear something he would rather I didn't see or hear, and wants me to know that at least he knows what's going on.

"Rand," Rand said.

"George, this is Donn. Where the hell have you been? Seventh Army's about to have kittens."

Donn was the commanding officer of the 14th Armored Cavalry, a just-promoted very young full colonel officer who was, as they say, going to go places. There were stars in his future.

Colonel Rand was aware that he was the opposite. He was getting more than a little long in the tooth as a colonel (he'd made colonel in Korea, nine years before) and it was growing more painfully evident each day that he had gone as far as he was going to go.

"Did they say why?"

"No. But there's a U-8 on its way to Fulda to pick you up. And as soon as I get off the horn, I'm going to send an H-13 to pick you up and carry you to Fulda." The H-13 was a Bell two-place, bubble-canopy helicopter. "What the hell are you doing out there, anyway?"

"Looking at the troops you're hiding from the IG."

"What makes you think I'm hiding anything or anybody, George?"

"I like what I found, Donn. These people not only look like soldiers, but they know what they're doing. You ought to be proud of them."

Out of the corner of his eye, Rand saw the radio operator's eyes light up, and was pleased. His comment would spread through the troop very quickly.

"I am, goddammit," the Colonel of the 14th Armored Cavalry Regiment said. "It's you that are making me look like a horse's ass. 'I'm sorry, General, I just don't seem to be able to lay my hands on Colonel Rand at this moment. But I'm looking. Have patience.' "

"I'm sorry if I've embarrassed you, Donn," Rand said.

"You damned well should be," Donn said cheerfully. "Hold one. The chopper is on the way. ETA four minutes. Don't disappear again."

"What do I do with the parka and the eskimo hat?"

"Give it to the chopper driver. You leave anything here at the *Kaserne?*"

"No. Thank you, Donn."

"My pleasure. Come again. Blue Stallion Out."

It is nice, Colonel Rand thought, *to be a very young full bull colonel, with your own regiment, Old Blue Stallion himself, looking forward to a first star, and then maybe an epauletful. It is infinitely nicer than being a senior colonel pushing paper around a headquarters and wondering what kind of a job you can get on civvy street when you finally face facts and put in for retirement.*

As he handed the microphone back to the radio operator,

he heard the first faint *flucketa-flucketa* sounds of a helicopter coming toward them.

[THREE]
Office of the Commanding General
Headquarters, Seventh United States Army
Stuttgart/Vaihingen, Federal Republic of Germany
1830 Hours 12 December 1963

It was after-duty hours, and the desks in the General's outer office normally occupied by his secretary, aide-de-camp, and sergeant major were vacant. Off the outer office, in a small room occupied during duty hours by the sergeant major's clerk and another clerk typist, the FOD—Field Grade Officer of the Day—and the CQ—Charge of Quarters—had set up shop to answer the phones and otherwise hold things down overnight.

The FOD was a lieutenant colonel wearing the insignia of the Quartermaster Corps. Though Colonel George F. Rand could not remember having seen him before, he knew who Rand was.

"Sir," he said, standing up behind one of the desks when he saw Rand walk in, "the General expects you. Go right in."

The General's door was ajar but not open. Rand rapped his class ring against the doorjamb.

"Who is it?"

"Rand, Sir."

"Come in, Colonel."

Rand stepped inside, closed the door behind him, and saluted.

"For a while, Colonel," the General said, "no one seemed to know where you were."

"I went out and looked at a patrol, Sir."

"And how is Blue Stallion and his merry lads?"

"That's a pretty good outfit, Sir. Morale's high. They know what they're doing. And they seem to think very highly of Young Blue Stallion himself."

"They alone or you too?"

"He's as bright as they come. And a nice guy. Unflappable. He's going to wear stars, I'll bet on it."

"You should never bet on who will get to wear stars and who won't," the General said. "You've been around the Army long enough to know that, George."

Colonel Rand looked at the General curiously, wondering if Blue Stallion had somehow turned up on the General's bad-guy list.

"Yes, Sir," Rand said.

"The reason I had you brought back from Hersfeld, George, is that I'm having a few people in for drinks tonight and I wanted you there. Pamela's called Susan, so I suspect when you get home she'll be dressed and waiting for you."

"May I ask what the occasion is, Sir?" Rand asked. He was more than a little surprised at what the General had told him.

"A little combination farewell party and celebration among old friends, George. We got a DA TWX. There's a PCS" —Permanent Change of Station—"to Benning, and a name sent the Senate for confirmation as a BG. You ever hear of the 11th Air Assault Division, George? Eleventh Air Assault Division [Test]?"

"No, Sir, I haven't."

"You have no idea what it is?"

"No, Sir. It probably has something to do with The Howze Board. They're experimenting with aerial battlefield mobility. I heard they might run a troop test at Benning, but I can't imagine a division-sized test."

"Neither can I," the General said. He, like every other senior officer in the Army, knew that Defense Secretary McNamara had appointed a board under Lieutenant General Hamilton R. Howze, a pillar of the Armor Establishment (and thus, inevitably, "The Howze Board") to see how Army battlefield mobility could be enhanced with Army-owned aircraft. The Air Force, of course, was enraged at what it considered an invasion of its prerogatives. "What do you think of the whole idea, George?"

"I don't really know enough about what they're doing to judge, Sir," Rand said. "It seems to me that the moment they start forming aviation units larger than a battalion, the Air Force is going to go right through the roof."

"I thought you were pretty good pals with Bill Roberts,"

the General said. "He's got McNamara's ear and he's been pushing Army Aviation for years."

Brigadier General William R. Roberts was an artilleryman who had spent his career around small, light Army aircraft. But he was more famous as the officer who had first said out loud what a lot of Army people knew in their hearts but were too prudent to say: "Since the Air Force obviously has little or no interest in anything but jet fighters, bombers, and Intercontinental Ballistic Missiles, if the Army needs aircraft on the battlefield, we're going to have to get them ourselves." It was also generally believed that Roberts had sown this heretical seed in Defense Secretary McNamara's ear while Roberts was assigned to Research and Development in the Pentagon. It was generally believed, in other words, that he was in large measure responsible for McNamara's establishment of The Howze Board.

"We're classmates," Rand said. "I see him every once in a while. But no, Sir, not pals."

"I find that very surprising," the General said.

"Sir?"

"You're to report to the 11th Air Assault Division [Test] not later than 31 December," the General said.

"Jesus!" Rand said, genuinely surprised. "I wonder why."

"The TWX didn't say. Just that you will be there before 31 December."

"Well, if they are conducting a division-size test, that implies at least one regiment. Maybe they're going to give me a regiment."

"No, I know it's not that," the General said, and when Rand looked at him in surprise added, "They don't give regiments to brigadier generals, George."

He came from behind the desk, holding a silver, five-pointed star in his hand. He handed it to Rand.

"I. D. White gave this to me when I made brigadier," the General said. "You can't put it on yet, George, you're still BG Designate. But when the orders come down, I would be sort of pleased if this was the first star you did pin on. I can't think of anyone who deserves it more."

• • •

The General's prediction was correct. When Brigadier General [Designate] George F. Rand walked through the front door of his quarters thirty-five minutes later, Susan Rand was indeed suitably dressed and coiffured to take cocktails and dinner with the Commanding General of the Seventh United States Army.

She looks good, George Rand thought. *Three kids and twenty-three years of marriage and she still turns me on.*

She was also, George Rand saw, annoyed.

"You could have called, damn you," she said. "I didn't know until this moment, when you walked through the door, whether you were going to show up for this whateveritis or not."

"I wasn't close to a phone," he said. "Sorry."

"Baloney."

" 'Hello, dear,' " he mocked. " 'Welcome home. How was your day?' "

"I don't give much of a damn, frankly, about your day. But vis-à-vis mine, at three o'clock this afternoon, the General's wife called, and in that regal manner of hers commanded our presence for cocktails and dinner. What's going on, George?"

"What would you like first? The good news or the bad?"

"The bad, I think. It will fit in nicely with my mood."

"Pack," George Rand said.

There was a moment's hesitation before Susan Rand replied.

"Where are we going?"

"Benning."

"When?"

"I have to be there no later than 31 December."

"Damn it, they did it again!" Susan Rand said. "Why is it everybody else in the U.S. Army gets anywhere from sixty days' to six months' notice of a PCS, and you get—what—three weeks?"

"You don't have to be there by 31 December—I do."

"Oh, no, George. Whither thou goest, et cetera. But, damn it, I just finished putting up the Christmas tree!"

"I'm going to the 11th Air Assault Division," Rand said. "Correction, the 11th Air Assault Division [Test]."

"What's that? I never heard of it."

"Neither did I until about a half an hour ago," he said. "Rather obviously it has something to do with The Howze Board and Bill Roberts and the Army's Air Force. I had heard they were doing, or going to do, a troop test at Benning. But a division-size troop test surprises me. I haven't had a chance to find out more."

She looked at him thoughtfully.

"What are you going to do? Chief of Staff?"

"No."

"Then what else can you do as a colonel? Go back to being a Division G-3? Back to commanding a regiment? Can you get out of it? Didn't they even ask you?"

"No, they didn't ask me, and no, I don't think I can get out of it. I don't want to get out of it."

"Oh, to hell with them, George! Tell them you don't want the assignment. Put in your retirement papers. If the Army isn't smart enough to give you a star, to hell with them."

"That's the good news," George Rand said.

IV

[ONE]
Quarters #1
Fort Rucker, Alabama
1915 Hours 12 December 1963

Major General Robert F. Bellmon answered his home telephone a little testily. He did not like taking unscreened calls. But his wife, who considered screening his calls to be one of her wifely duties, was not at home. And his daughter, Marjorie, who was, had the apparent intention of setting a *Guinness Book of Records* mark for Longest Hours Spent By One Twenty-One-Year-Old Female Under a Shower Head.

''Bellmon!'' he snapped, snatching the telephone from its wall cradle in the kitchen.

''Oh, hell,'' his caller said. ''I hoped Barbara would pick up.''

It took Bellmon a moment to identify the voice of Brigadier

General Paul T. Hanrahan, Commandant of the Special Forces School and the titular head Green Beret.

"She's not here at the moment, Red," Bellmon said. "Is there anything I can do for you?"

"There is, but I would rather have had the chance to ask her if you were in a good mood before I asked."

"I'm one of the world's most gracious men," Bellmon said. "I thought you knew that, Red."

"Then who was it that answered the phone? A visiting ogre?"

"Was it that bad?" Bellmon said, now smiling.

"Would you like to swap stories about who had the lousiest day?" Hanrahan asked.

"I don't know about you, General," Bellmon said, "but *my* day, as usual, was nothing but sweetness and light. And it ended with the entirely satisfying feeling that things had indeed got better and better in every way."

Hanrahan laughed.

"What can I do for you, Red?"

"I'd like one of your officers," Hanrahan said.

"Just one? I've got about two dozen I'd be delighted to send over there in the morning. One colonel in particular."

"Just one, Bob. One particular one."

"That's what I was afraid of."

"One little captain," Hanrahan said. "You probably won't even know he's gone."

"Why do I suspect I am being charmed out of my socks?"

"Perish the thought."

"Have your G-1 tell my G-1 you can have him," Bellmon said. "There, doesn't that prove what a nice guy I am?"

Hanrahan's voice grew serious.

"Robert, your G-1 has told my G-1 I can't have him. That's why I'm calling you."

What the hell is going on here? If my G-1 has told Hanrahan's G-1 he can't have somebody, that should be it. We must need him here. And Hanrahan is fully aware that he's asking me to pull the rug out from under my G-1 by overturning one of his decisions.

"Who is this captain?" Bellmon asked. "More importantly, why do you need him?"

''To instruct in the training of long-range patrolling for Vietnam,'' Hanrahan said.

''He's a snake eater?''

''No, he's an airplane driver,'' Hanrahan said. ''But he has 'Nam experience—''

''And his name is John S. Oliver, Junior, right?'' Bellmon interrupted.

''Yeah. You know him?''

''I'm about to make him my aide, Red,'' Bellmon said.

''Your G-1 apparently didn't tell my G-1 that,'' Hanrahan said. ''If he had, I wouldn't have bothered you.''

''If you need him bad, you can have him,'' Bellmon said.

Bellmon could hear Hanrahan inhale.

''Let me start this from scratch,'' he said. ''What happened is that Joe Augustus came back from 'Nam last week. I guess you know he runs that Special Operations Group?''

''His brother's here, running SCATSA. He told me.'' SCATSA stands for Signal Aviation Test and Support Activity.

''Well, Joe and one of my guys, Father Lunsford—''

''I don't recall the name, should I?''

''Captain. Black guy. Mean sonofabitch. He was running the long-range patrols for Joe Augustus. Anyway, they came up with an insert-extract technique using two slicks and two gunships. It cut their losses, which were pretty bad, down pretty low. Joe Augustus wants to train our people before we send them over there.''

''Why?''

''There's a chopper shortage over there, you haven't heard?''

''There's a chopper shortage everywhere. The 11th Air Assault tests have drawn down everybody,'' Bellmon said.

''Well, that's part of it. Joe is having trouble getting choppers to practice with over there, that's part of it. The other part is sort of psychological. Your Captain Oliver's apparently been in on it from the beginning. As has Father Lunsford. People pay attention to people who know what they're talking about. So when Father told me your man Oliver wasn't doing anything really important over there—that was before I heard you had made him your aide—I figured he would be more valuable here. So I told my G-1 to call up and ask, et cetera, et cetera. Otherwise, Bob, I would have taken no for an answer.''

''Red, I repeat,'' Bellmon said, ''if you think you really need him, you can have him.''

''No,'' Hanrahan said. ''Thanks, but no thanks. He's a regular, Norwich, I think, and a tour as your aide is more important to him, and the Army, down the pike, if he's as good an officer as Joe and Father say he is. So, quickly changing the subject, how's the family? Bobby graduates this year, doesn't he?''

''He's captain of the fencing team,'' Bellmon said. ''Everybody else is fine. How's Patty?''

''Everybody's fine. You're not sore I called, Robert, are you?''

''Don't be silly. Come see us, Red.''

''You're the one with all the airplanes, you come see us,'' Hanrahan said.

''I will, I really will,'' Bellmon said. ''It was good to hear your voice, Red.''

I wonder why I told him I had already picked Oliver to take Jerry Thomas's place. I guess maybe I already had and was just going through the motions.

[TWO]
Office of the Commanding General
The Army Aviation Center & Fort Rucker, Alabama
1545 Hours 15 December 1963

Starting at quarter to three in the afternoon, the three semi-finalists came in to see Bellmon. Aware of it—and wondering why—Bellmon was in a foul mood from the moment they began arriving.

He finally realized it was because he was wasting time: his own time and the time of two of the nominees. Unless Captain John S. Oliver, Jr., came in drunk, or there was an unpleasant chemical reaction between them, Oliver had the job.

The first two bright young officers did not please him any more than he had expected they would. Courtesy and respect differ from servility, and Bellmon was well aware of that difference. He didn't want a manservant; he wanted a nice young man who could simultaneously be helpful and acquire professional knowledge.

And, just as Bellmon had expected, Captain John S. Oliver made a favorable first impression when he entered, saluted, and announced, "Captain Oliver, John S., reporting to the commanding general as ordered, Sir."

Oliver, Bellmon noticed, was not wearing any of the ribbons to which he was entitled, neither those representing awards, nor the I-Was-There ribbons. All he had on his blouse breast were his aviators' wings and the Combat Infantry Badge, the latter worn above the former, which General Bellmon thought reflected the priority which should be accorded to the two qualification badges.

Or, Bellmon wondered sourly, *has he taken the trouble to find out that I don't wear ribbons, either, most of the time, just the badges? Imitation is the most sincere form of flattery.*

But after he considered that briefly, he began to wonder where Oliver had gotten the CIB; Oliver had been assigned to an aviation company, and aviation companies do not award the Combat Infantry Badge.

"Where did you get the CIB?" Bellmon asked.

"I did a short, involuntary tour with the Berets, Sir," Oliver said.

"When you got shot down and had to walk out, is that what you mean?"

"Yes, Sir."

"And they cut the orders?"

"Yes, Sir."

Bellmon made a grunting noise. That had just turned Oliver's Silver Star citation into the real thing, and not just the prose of an imaginative citation writer in an aviation company. If the Berets had given Oliver the CIB, that meant they thought he had earned it.

I should have guessed that; Red Hanrahan would not have gone to all the trouble to try getting him reassigned over there if he thought he was just one more airplane driver. They think this young man is one of their own. Will that be a problem?

General Bellmon went on to reflect that while he admired

the Green Berets—some of his best friends were Green Berets—he would not want his daughter to marry one.

Does that maybe apply to an aide who's an unofficial Green Beret, too? An aide is close to being a member of the family.

Don't be ridiculous. This young man is obviously a clean-cut young fellow. Just because the Green Berets want him, that should not make him guilty by association.

"In ten words or less, Captain," Bellmon said, smiling at Johnny Oliver, "tell me why you would like to be my aide-de-camp."

"Sir, with respect, I don't want to be your aide."

"Then what are you doing here?"

"I was ordered to report to the General, Sir."

"And you weren't told why?" Bellmon asked, confused.

"Sir, I supposed that it was something to do with my making a nuisance of myself."

What the hell is this?

"What kind of a nuisance?"

"Sir, I don't want to be a Chinook IP," Oliver said—an *I*nstructor *P*ilot.

"Is that what they have planned for you?"

"Yes, Sir. I'm just about finished with the transition course."

"And what makes you think they're going to make you an IP?"

"I heard they were, Sir. And when I asked Colonel Matthews, he admitted it."

"What's wrong with being a Chinook IP?" Bellmon asked. "As I understand it, that would be a feather in your cap. We have far more applicants for Chinook training than we have spaces."

"Yes, Sir," Oliver said. "That's what I told Colonel Matthews, Sir. I told them he should give it to somebody who wanted it."

"And you, obviously," Bellmon said sarcastically, realizing that he was more than a little annoyed with this young pup, "can think of other assignments where your talents would be of greater benefit to the Army?"

The intercom at that moment came to life.

"General, Mrs. Bellmon is here," his secretary announced.

"Ask her to come in, please."

Barbara Waterford Bellmon came into the office. She was a lanky, tanned, and freckled woman who looked considerably younger than her husband, although barely a year separated them.

Bellmon wondered if she had come to examine the prospective aides-de-camp. That was unlikely, although she had every right to do so; she would be spending as much time with the aide as he would.

"Bobby has been stabbed," Barbara Bellmon announced. "Run through by a plebe d'Artagnan."

"What?" General Bellmon asked. He thought that either he hadn't heard her right or she wasn't taking the situation seriously.

"The tip of the other kid's épée came off just as he lunged at Bobby," Barbara said. "The Point just called. Lew's aide. He said Bobby's in no danger but is experiencing some discomfort. No wonder."

The Point was of course West Point. Bobby was Robert F. Bellmon, Jr., who the following June would graduate from the United States Military Academy and march off in the Long Gray Line . . . in the footsteps of his father, his grandfathers on both sides, and two of his four great-grandfathers. Lew was Brigadier General Lewis M. Waterford, who was running the Corps of Cadets and was Barbara's baby brother.

"Where was he hurt?" General Bellmon had asked.

"It took some doing to get that out of Lew's aide. And now that I have it, I have no intention of repeating it in mixed company. I don't even know this young man."

"Excuse me," General Bellmon said, "Barbara, this is Captain John Oliver. Captain, my wife."

"Hello," Barbara said, smiling and giving him her hand. "I don't think I've seen you around, have I?"

"No, Ma'am, I don't believe so."

"Captain Oliver was sent here to be interviewed to replace Jerry," General Bellmon told her. "We had just reached the point where he said he would rather not be my aide, thank you, when you walked in."

Barbara looked at John Oliver with interest. "I don't blame you, of course. I wouldn't want to work for the old grouch either. But I'm part of the deal, and I'm much more pleasant than he is."

"Captain Oliver was just about to tell me where he *does* think he should be assigned," Bellmon said. "Go on, Captain."

Barbara Bellmon heard the sarcasm in his voice and gave him a dirty look. Bellmon saw that his wife liked young Captain Oliver, and he knew that she was damned seldom wrong about her snap judgments of young men. Or old ones, either.

"Sir, if I'm going to be teaching something, I think I should be teaching from my 'Nam experience, probably in the 11th Air Assault."

"What about teaching insertion-extraction techniques to the Green Berets at Fort Bragg?" Bellmon asked evenly.

Oliver considered that for a moment before replying.

"Yes, Sir. I hadn't thought about that, but I could do that."

"You're too junior to be given command of a company," Bellmon told him. "You just made captain. And the question of you being assigned to Fort Bragg has come up and been decided against."

"I didn't know that I was being considered for an assignment at Bragg, Sir," Oliver said, and Bellmon saw that he was obviously telling the truth. "I've already run a company, Sir. I commanded the 170th Aviation Company for seven weeks," Oliver argued politely. "Which leads me to think I might do that again successfully."

"How did that happen?"

"The company commander went in, Sir," Oliver said, matter-of-factly, which Bellmon translated to mean he had either been shot down or for some other reason crashed to his death. "The exec was flying in the left seat. I was senior."

Bellmon saw in Barbara's eyes a new interest in Captain Oliver.

"Captain Oliver came home from 'Nam with a Silver Star and a DFC," Bellmon said.

"Did he?" Barbara said.

"Anyway, the TO and E now calls for a major to command

aviation companies,'' Bellmon went on. ''The most you could hope for would be a platoon. More than likely, if they offered to make you a Chinook IP, it was intended as a reward for your service in Southeast Asia. And in that circumstance, I can understand why they're annoyed with you for throwing it back in their faces.''

''Davis,'' Barbara said. ''Interesting parallel. And he even looks like him.''

It took General Bellmon a moment to take his wife's meaning. When he did, he smiled and grunted.

''Captain Davis, Captain Oliver, was a young Armor officer much like yourself at this stage of his career. A West Pointer. He'd gotten into Korea early and done some rather spectacular things.''

''Silver Star, too,'' Barbara Bellmon interjected.

''So when I. D. White, who was then commanding Knox—I suppose you know who General White is?''

''Yes, Sir,'' Oliver said, smiling. ''Class of '20. 'Norwich Forever.' ''

''Oh,'' Barbara Bellmon said, brightening. ''Are you Norwich, Captain?''

''Yes, Ma'am.''

''We have a *very dear* friend who just graduated from Norwich, don't we, dear?'' Barbara Bellmon said very sweetly.

''Oh, Jesus, Barbara!'' General Bellmon said disgustedly, confirming Oliver's suspicion that Barbara Bellmon was zinging her husband.

''He was in the class of '63 and a half,'' she went on innocently.

''Ma'am?'' Oliver said, confused.

''She's talking about a—friend—of ours who got caught up in this OPERATION BOOTSTRAP nonsense,'' Bellmon said, ''and was *ordered* to Norwich.''

OPERATION BOOTSTRAP was an Army Personnel program designed to ensure that all regular service commissioned officers had a baccalaureate degree; those who could acquire a degree in twelve months or less were sent to college on duty and at government expense.

''Yes, Sir,'' Oliver said uneasily.

''I have nothing against education, and certainly not against

Norwich,'' Bellmon decided he had to explain, ''but in this case, the officer who got hung up in OPERATION BOOTSTRAP was a lieutenant colonel—''

''And my husband felt sorry for him, and went up to see him, and when Bob found him, he was on the campus ski slopes, surrounded by twenty-year-old beauties from the University of Vermont,'' Barbara Bellmon said, laughing.

''Wearing a hat with a goddamned tassel!'' Bellmon added, and then he shook his head and laughed, too. Then he went on. ''But we were talking about a *distinguished* Norwich graduate, not Craig Lowell.''

''Craig graduated with honors in German and Russian,'' Barbara argued.

''He spoke German before they sent him up there,'' General Bellmon said.

''Anyway, Captain, Colonel Lowell is now the Army Aviation Officer on the staff of STRIKE COMMAND at McDill,'' Barbara Bellmon said.

''If we can get back to this,'' Bellmon said impatiently. ''I suppose you know, Oliver, that General White's now Commander in Chief, Pacific,'' Bellmon said.

''Yes, Sir.''

''Well, as I was saying, when I. D. White was commanding Knox during the Korean War, he needed an aide, and he offered Davis the job because he felt it should go to some officer who'd already been to that war, and because he was sure that he—General White, I mean—wasn't going to get to go to Korea. There were no plans then to send an armored division to Korea, and based on his long experience with Army politics, General White was convinced they weren't going to give command of a corps, with no armored divisions in it, to an Armor general.''

''So General White was apparently nicer to Captain Davis than my husband has been to you,'' Barbara said, ''and Davis took the job—''

''And was on it I guess three weeks,'' Bellmon interrupted his wife, ''when there was a telephone call from the Chief of Staff. The President had just sent General White's name to the Senate for his third star, and how soon could he leave for Korea to take command of X Corps?''

"Davis went with him, of course, Davis is now on the lieutenant colonels' list—" Barbara Bellmon said.

"He made it," Bellmon interrupted. "I saw it in *Armor*."

"Are we getting through to you, Captain Oliver?" Barbara asked.

Captain Oliver looked at her, nodded his head, then looked at General Bellmon, and then back at her.

"Yes, Ma'am," he said. "You are very persuasive indeed."

"Speaking of promotions," Barbara said to her husband, "did you hear that George Rand was selected for brigadier?"

"No," he said, and turned to Oliver to explain. "A classmate." And then turned back to Barbara. "Where did you get that?"

"From Susan," Barbara said. "She called from Germany."

"Well, I'm glad to hear it," Bellmon said. "George Rand is a good man. But I'd hate to have their telephone bill if she called everybody in the Army to tell them he finally got his star."

"She called me to see what I could tell her about the 11th Air Assault," Barbara Bellmon replied. "George has to report there not later than the end of the month."

"Now *that's* interesting," Bellmon said. "I wonder what the hell that's all about? So far as I know he's never thought much of aviation."

"Maybe O. K. Wendall asked for him," Barbara said.

"More likely Bill Roberts. They've always been pretty close."

"They have *not,*" Barbara said. "My God, in 1945, Bill was a lieutenant colonel at twenty-four, and George was a captain."

"What did you tell Susan about the 11th?" Bellmon asked.

"Well, the truth, of course," she said, smiling innocently. "That it's the most important innovation in modern warfare since the internal combustion engine, and that instead of giving it to you and Bill Roberts, two fully qualified aviation types, they turned it over to a couple of parachutists with political influence—"

"God, you didn't?" Bellmon exclaimed, only then realizing she was pulling his leg. ''Wait a minute,'' he said, and looked at Captain John S. Oliver, Jr. ''Captain, if you are going to be privy to throne room gossip like this, you're going to have to be officially a member of the palace guard. I'd like to have you as my aide, but only if you want the job. A simple yes or no will suffice.''

Barbara Bellmon winked at Captain John S. Oliver, and nodded, and smiled encouragingly.

''Yes, Sir,'' Oliver said. ''I would like to be your aide.''

Bellmon grunted, then leaned forward and pushed his intercom button and summoned his aide-de-camp.

''Jerry, do you know Captain Oliver?''

''Yes, Sir.''

''Why aren't I surprised?'' Barbara asked.

''I always told you, Jerry, to either shape up or ship out,'' General Bellmon said. ''Meet your replacement. See how much you can teach him before you go on Christmas leave.''

''Yes, Sir. Welcome aboard, Johnny.''

''I think that's *my* line, Jerry,'' General Bellmon said as he offered his hand to Captain John S. Oliver.

[THREE]
Room Seven, Building T-124
Fort Rucker, Alabama
17 December 1963

Building T-124 was one of a dozen identical two-story, frame BOQ—Bachelor Officers' Quarters—buildings scattered around Fort Rucker. Room seven, which was on the right side of the second floor, at the end of the corridor, and which offered windows on two sides of the building, was one of the better accommodations available in T-124. So situated, room seven afforded its occupant cross-ventilation while removing him as far as possible from the noises a number of young men living in the same building are capable of making, drunk and sober.

Room seven was actually a suite. By the entrance door, there was a small, narrow room, which was furnished with a GI desk, chair, and bookcase, and which was somewhat grandly identified as the ''study.'' The bedroom had a single bed, an upholstered armchair, a straightback chair, a bedside table, and a chest of drawers. There was also a closet with a curtain hanging over it.

Room seven shared a water closet and a tin-walled shower stall with room six.

Before he had become aide-de-camp to General Robert F. Bellmon, room seven had been assigned to Captain John S. Oliver as a perquisite of rank. When he had first arrived on the base, however, he had initially declined the chance to have his quarters there, since somebody was already occupying the room, even though it was his right to evict the current occupant by virtue of Rank Hath Its Privileges. Then the other shoe, Rank Hath Its Obligations, had been dropped. Because most captains, for that matter, most lieutenants and warrant officers, were already married and so were living in family quarters, it turned out that he was the Senior Officer Occupant. And when he was informed that, as such, he would be responsible for maintaining order and discipline in Building T-124, he had reconsidered.

The only changes made to Captain Oliver's quartering situation since his appointment as aide-de-camp to General Bellmon were that he had been relieved of his Senior Officer Occupant duties, and that two telephones had been installed in room seven, leaving him with a total of three.

The installation of the first telephone had been accomplished after what he considered a noble victory over Army discrimination. There had been only two telephones in Building T-124 when he moved in—a handset connected to the post switchboard sitting on a small table in the upstairs corridor, and a pay phone mounted on the wall in the downstairs foyer, at the main—side—entrance to the building.

Private-line telephones, he had been told, were "not available" for bachelor officers living in BOQs. If bachelor officers had to call off the post, they could feed coins to the downstairs pay phone. And if they wanted to make or receive on-post calls, they could use the handset upstairs.

Captain Oliver had already been annoyed at the special treatment, by policy, given to married company-grade officers. Now that there was nearly adequate family housing on the post (there was never fully adequate housing; that, like perfection, was an objective never reached), a second lieutenant coming to Fort Rucker who had paused at the Cadet Chapel on graduation day long enough to get married was assigned a two-bedroom home—with living room, two full-tiled bathrooms, a study, a fully equipped kitchen, a washer and dryer, and even a two-space carport to keep the car out of the sun and rain.

As a captain, returning from 'Nam a certified hero and wounded veteran, Johnny Oliver had been ordered into quarters about the size of the second john's family-housing living room. He was forced to park his car in an unpaved parking lot, and he had to share his shower and the crapper with a complete stranger. He had been willing to swallow that, but he found himself unable to accept being told that he couldn't have a lousy goddamned telephone of his own.

And so Oliver went to see the Assistant Post Signal Officer about his problem. But he got nothing for his trouble but a brushoff. "It's policy," the Assistant Post Signal Officer told him. "Why don't you just live with it?" he went on. Then he jocularly suggested that Oliver find a wife and get the whole ball of wax. Johnny Oliver was sorely tempted to tell the Assistant Post Signal Officer, a jolly, balding, mustachioed major, to go fuck himself. But that would have constituted conduct both prejudicial to good order and discipline and unbecoming an officer and a gentleman.

The IG—Inspector General, a senior officer charged, among other things, with investigating and correcting injustices—wasn't much help either. He offered the friendly suggestion that submitting an official complaint over something "as frivolous as this" was going to earn Oliver a reputation as a troublemaker.

Oliver had then submitted a *suggestion.* He tucked four neatly typed pages into one of the Third Army Commander's suggestion program boxes placed at various locations around the post. He suggested— actually argued eloquently, with lots of polysyllabic words—that since it was clearly Army Policy, with which he of course had no argument, to provide second lieutenants who happened to be married with far nicer quarters, including private telephones, than the Army could furnish bachelor captains, and since this tended to cause morale problems among said captains, that an orientation program be prepared and delivered to all bachelor captains, explaining to them how Army efficiency and morale was improved by treating married officers better than bachelor ones.

Three days after he submitted the suggestion, two sergeants and a corporal from Post Signal appeared to ask him where he wanted his telephone. He never heard any more about his suggestion.

It was a victory, but he had wondered more than once if it wouldn't turn out to be Pyrrhic and that he had become known as a wiseass. That worry had been added to his determination not to spend the next two years teaching people how to fly the Chinook. And both worries had been added to his fear that he was now a Certified Troublemaker. All of which was in his mind when two days ago he had been ordered to report to the Commanding General. He had thought then that in deference to his hero badges, he was about to get a word to the wise from the Head Man himself. It had never entered his mind that he would be asked to be the Head Man's aide.

But that had happened. And with his appointment came two more telephones for his room, both personally paid for by General Bellmon: one was listed as the residence number of the aide-de-camp and the other not listed at all. That was the number, Jerry Thomas had told him, that General Bellmon would use when he called Johnny Oliver in the BOQ. The General did not want to find it busy.

Captain Jerry Thomas had also pointed out to him that while it was true that there were some general officers in the Army who had not served as aides-de-camp, there were far more general officers who *had been* dog-robbers in their youth. It was, Thomas argued, one of the wider rungs on the military career ladder. If Oliver did well as Bellmon's aide, it probably would help him get on the five-percent list for promotion to major. But if he screwed up, got relieved for cause, he could count on never having to buy a silver eagle for his epaulets, much less a general's star.

Now that the job, to his genuine surprise, was his, Oliver intended to perform it to the best of his ability. And he realized he was as nervous putting the dog-robber's golden rope through his epaulets as he had been the day he had assumed command of the company in 'Nam after the Old Man and the exec had gone in.

There had been serious question in his mind then about his ability to deliver what the Army expected of him. And there was serious question, for different reasons, that he could deliver now.

When Jerry Thomas had explained the basic, both specific and general, items that would be expected of him, he'd started with Oliver's wardrobe. An aide-de-camp cannot get by with a faint old gravy stain on his uniform, much less frayed collars or cuffs. But since Oliver was able to wear—simply by having the trousers hemmed—uniforms right off the Quartermaster Sales Store racks, he was able to get by with three new sets of greens, and two of blues, that didn't cost him as much as they would have cost someone who required extensive alterations, or even tailor-mades. But the QM didn't sell mess dress, and he winced when he wrote the check for that elaborate, and in the performance of his new duties, essential, uniform.

And Jerry also subtly let him know that the Great Stalk, as Oliver thought of it, would have to be put on ice for a year. An aide-de-camp did not have the time to pursue a casual dalliance, much less a courtship. And he also understood that the weekends at Panama City Beach, and the all-night poker games, and the happy hour at the club or Annex #1, would all have to be sacrificed on the altar of being a good aide to General Bellmon.

As for specific responsibilities, Johnny's days would begin with his driving to Post Headquarters to pick up the interesting overnight TWXs—Teletype Messages—and to read the FOD's—Field Grade Officer of the Day—Log to see what had come to Bellmon's official attention during the night. This ranged from enlisted men (and sometimes officers) confined in the hands of civil authorities, to airplane crashes, to dependent wives having at their husbands with whatever lethal weapon was conveniently at hand.

Bellmon wanted to read these reports over breakfast, Jerry explained, so he wouldn't be surprised when he went to his office.

On the other hand, this particular duty carried with it one

of the unofficial perks. Johnny would usually be eating breakfast with General Bellmon, Jerry told him. In fact, he'd be eating a good many of his meals with Bellmon. And most of the time that would be at Quarters #1.

And Jerry went on to explain all the other daily, and weekly, and irregular responsibilities Johnny would be expected to perform. And then, finally, Jerry gave him a discreet and respectful but thorough briefing about the General himself—down even to the General's private wealth.

Bellmon had told Thomas early on that he was fortunate in not having to live on his military pay, and that meant walking a narrow line between taking advantage of the creature comforts he could afford and not rubbing his affluence in anybody's face.

As a general officer Bellmon was entitled by law to an aide, an orderly, and a driver. Out of his own pocket, Thomas told Oliver, Bellmon augmented this staff with a cook and a maid, husband and wife. These were black civilians from Ozark who arrived at Quarters #1 before Oliver did and left at four-thirty—unless there was a dinner or a cocktail party, or something else that required their services.

Off-duty GIs took care of the yard and household chores, cutting the grass, sweeping the drive, washing the cars, and serving as bartenders and waiters. But Oliver was expected to keep track of who did what and for how long, and to prepare the checks for Mrs. Bellmon's signature. The Bellmons paid promptly and well, Thomas said, and their staff were both fiercely loyal to them and proud of their jobs.

The first task Oliver performed on his own, without Captain Jerry Thomas looking over his shoulder, was setting up the General's Christmas party. At the time, Jerry was about to move on to his next assignment; he would take a delay en route Christmas leave to visit his family, before reporting to the 11th Air Assault Division [Test] at Fort Benning. Before leaving, Jerry had a few last words for Oliver.

Among these: "It's the General's custom to say a few kind words about his departing aide at the Christmas Dinner," he said with a little grin. "At which time he gives him—me—a small present.

"Since I am required to profess absolute surprise," Jerry

continued, "I can't be involved in the logistics. Marjorie will help you."

Marjorie was Miss Marjorie Bellmon, the Bellmons' daughter. She was not quite a year younger than Bobby, but already through college and working at the bank in Ozark. Oliver found her delightful, but he was baffled by his physical reaction to her. She was tall, and lithe, and splendidly bosomed, and ordinarily he would have fallen in love with her in about thirty seconds flat.

But somehow that hadn't happened. There had been simply no physical spark, as if Mother Nature had turned off the lust switch. Their relationship had immediately become like brother and sister. A brother and sister who were *very* fond of each other, which was not, in Oliver's own experience, the way that usually worked.

As far as he could recall, he had never liked his own flesh-and-blood sister, even as a kid, before their parents had been killed in an automobile crash when he was six. His sister had then been nineteen, and married. After the crash, he had been reared by her and her husband. And that was possibly the reason she didn't like him either. No young bride wants the responsibility for raising a kid.

He had never particularly liked his sister's husband, Charley, either; and though Charley's treatment of him had been decent, Oliver had figured out at fourteen that he was going to have to leave "home" sooner rather than later.

He and his sister had inherited, equally, the family business, a medium-sized truck stop. There would not be room for him as a partner in the business, not so much for the money—there was enough of that to divide—but because there was room for only one boss. And his sister's husband occupied that spot.

Consequently, Charley had been glad to see Johnny Oliver go off to Norwich. And he'd been barely able to conceal his relief when Johnny told him he had decided to accept a regular commission when he graduated.

She and Charley had given him a Mustang as a graduation present, a gift tempered by his knowledge that not only had the Mustang been bought with his money, but that it had been given to him in order to delay the accounting he was entitled to by the terms of his parents' will.

When he turned twenty-one, halfway through his last year at Norwich, he had stopped being their ward. Under the law, as well as the terms of the will, he was entitled to an accounting of his inheritance, together with a share of the profits from the truck stop.

There had been neither. Instead, there was some talk, never put into a specific proposal, that his sister and Charley would buy him out. But whenever he tried to raise the subject (as he had on graduation day, and again when he'd come home from 'Nam), it always seemed to be a bad time to discuss it.

He knew he was eventually going to have to do something about all that, to force the issue, and take care of his rights—not to mention his money. He was sure, however, that doing it, bringing it all into the open, would probably mean a screaming scene and a visit to a lawyer. And the idea of taking his sister into court over money was unpleasant. She had, after all, raised him.

But not now, he thought (he was at the moment dressing in the bedroom of room seven). *Not yet. Sufficient to the day is the bullshit thereof. And besides, screw it, it'll wait. And they'll wait.*

And it was always easier to think about more pleasant subjects—such as Marjorie Bellmon. *Why isn't she my sister,* he thought, *instead of that bitch?*

But then, what the hell. Marjorie doesn't have to be my sister for us to like one another. I don't have to want to love her, or make love to her, just because I'm a man and she's a girl. There is nothing wrong having a friend who happens to be of the other gender.

And he knew for certain that Marjorie was going to be a friend, just as her mother was becoming. It had taken Oliver about three days to figure out that Marjorie was just like what her mother must have been like at that age. He remembered, in this regard, some sage advice from a crusty old retired master sergeant at Norwich: "Before you rush to the altar with some dame, take a long hard look at her mother; that's what yours will look and act like in twenty years." Oliver was sure he'd never be rushing up to the altar with Marjorie

Bellmon. But she was a terrific girl just the same. And he was glad they were friends.

As he let all these thoughts spin around his head, Captain John S. Oliver, for the first time wearing all the regalia of an aide-de-camp to a major general, examined his appearance in the cheap, distorting mirror on the wall of room seven.

The cavalry sabers superimposed on a silhouette of a tank, the insignia of Armor, which he'd worn on his lapels even as a cadet at Norwich, had been replaced with a Federal Shield, at the top of which were two stars, representing the rank of the general officer he was now expected to rob dogs for.

A golden rope, called an aiguillette, hung from his blouse epaulet—apparently intended, he thought just a bit cynically, to tell those who didn't know what an aide's lapel insignia was that he was something special.

Just now, Oliver was about to fly to Fort Devens, Massachusetts, where General Bellmon was being forced to attend a post commanders' conference. Captain Jerry Thomas was going partway with them during that trip. On their way back they would drop him off in North Carolina, near his home. From the moment Thomas got out of the airplane, Johnny would assume responsibility as General Bellmon's aide.

His self-examination in the distorting mirror was interrupted by a knock at his door. It was the General's driver, picking him up before they went to fetch the General at his quarters.

He took one last look and walked out of the room.

[FOUR]
The United States Military Academy
West Point, New York
18 December 1963

Captain John S. Oliver, newly appointed aide-de-camp to Major General Robert F. Bellmon, inquired of the nurse on duty the location of Cadet Captain Robert F. Bellmon, and was directed to the third door from the end of the corridor on the right.

Oliver walked down the highly polished linoleum and pushed the door open without knocking. He fixed the good-looking young man in the bed with what he hoped was a suitably West Point stern glower. Then, absolutely solemnly, he made the sign of the Cross, four times, once in each direction, and looked at Bobby.

Cadet Captain Bellmon was dumbfounded. Oliver was wearing the Army Aviation Center insignia on his shoulder and the insignia of an aide-de-camp to a major general on his lapels. That should have made him his father's aide, but Bobby knew that his father's aide was Captain Jerry Thomas.

''No questions, Mister?'' the mysterious aide snapped.

''No questions, Sir,'' Bobby replied.

''You should ask questions. You can learn all kinds of interesting crap that way. For your general fund of military knowledge, Mister, that was an act of exorcism,'' Captain Oliver said.

''Sir?''

''I'm Norwich,'' Oliver said, waving a hand with a school ring. ''We always do that when we are surrounded by the demons of the Long Gray Line.''

Bobby had no idea what was going on.

''Where did you get stuck, Mister?'' Oliver demanded.

Bobby was so surprised at the question that he blurted the truth: ''Sir, in the balls.''

Oliver's eyebrows rose in surprise.

''No wonder your mother was delicate about the subject,'' Oliver replied, and then, taut-voiced again: ''At God only knows what cost to the taxpayers, Mister, the U.S. Government is trying to turn you into an officer and a gentleman. An officer and a gentleman, Mister, would say, 'In the scrotum, Sir.' Or, 'In the groin, Sir.' Not 'In the balls.' Try to remember that.''

''Yes, Sir,'' Bobby replied. ''Sir, may I ask who you are?''

''Look at all this stuff,'' Oliver replied, pointing to the Aviation Center patch on his sleeve, and the golden aide-de-camp's rope, and finally to the aide's insignia. ''Don't they teach you clowns anything up here? Think, Mister! Apply yourself!''

''Are you my father's aide, Sir?''

''Correct. A little late, but correct. You win the all-expense-paid trip to downtown Brooklyn.''

"Sir, is my father here?"

"I just left him at a post commanders' conference at Fort Devens," Oliver said. "I didn't have the foggiest idea what was going on, so he took Jerry Thomas in with him. Jerry sends his best regards, by the way. I'm the *new* aide."

"But my father sent you, Sir?"

"Oh, no," Oliver had said. "And I think it would be best if we kept this little chat a secret between you, me, and your mother."

"My mother sent you?" Bobby asked, surprised.

"No," Oliver said. "But she was worried when she heard they weren't going to let you come home for Christmas. Your uncle has not been what you could call a fountain of factual information about you, and since I was in the neighborhood, I thought I would drop by on the way home."

"Sir, I don't understand."

"Well, in my solemn professional Army Aviator's judgment, our aircraft could not be trusted to cart such an august personage as your father around before I took it on a test flight. I was thus engaged, test-flying it, you see, when I happened to look out the window, and, *lo and behold!* there it was, the West Point School for Boys, right there below me. So I figured, what the hell, why not? If I didn't stay long, I probably wouldn't catch anything penicillin can't handle, and then I could go home and whisper in your mother's ear that there is absolutely nothing to those nasty rumors about you carousing with nurses instead of coming home. So here I am."

"My father doesn't know you're here?"

"Of course not. If he did, he would almost certainly ask why I didn't test-fly the bird in circles over Fort Devens."

"You're not going to get in trouble?"

"Not unless you spill the beans," Oliver replied, then asked, "They hurt?"

"Sir?"

"Your gonads, Mister. The family jewels. I see the ice bag. I asked if they hurt."

"Yes, Sir, some. And that's not an icebag, Sir."

Oliver's eyebrows rose.

"Really?" he said in what could have been either awe or delight.

"They're swollen, Sir."

"That I have to see," Johnny Oliver had said.

"Sir?"

"Show me what you have hidden under the sheet, Mister," he said.

Very carefully, and furiously aware that his face was flushing, Bobby pulled the sheet off.

"Fantastic!" Johnny Oliver said. "If I didn't see it with my own eyes, I wouldn't believe it. Purple grapefruits! How did that happen?"

"Sir, apparently a vein leaked."

"Would you like a souvenir?" Oliver said, and dipped in his pocket and came out with a Minox camera. He held it up questioningly.

"Sir, I don't know . . ." Bobby protested.

"I can think of many times in your military career, Mister, where a color photograph of those outsize balls would be a great thing to have. What they call a conversation starter. Those balls should really be chronicled for posterity."

Bobby was so off-balanced by this genial madman that he spoke aloud the next thing that popped into his mind: "Sir, is that the Distinguished Flying Cross?"

"You sound surprised," Oliver replied. "You didn't think they'd let some shit-for-brains six weeks out of flight school ferry your old man around, did you? What about the picture? Trust me. Ten years from now you'll be glad to have it."

"OK," Bobby said, throwing military courtesy out the window. "Why the hell not?"

Oliver took half a dozen snapshots and then dropped the camera back in his pocket.

"They look like they'd really hurt," he said.

"They don't except when I try to walk," Bobby replied.

"Then don't walk," Oliver said. "You need anything? Cigarettes, booze, anything?"

"No, Sir. Thank you."

"You're sure? You tell me what you want and I'll smuggle it in."

"Nothing, Sir. Thank you."

"I'd offer to leave the film," Oliver said. "But I think they'd shit a brick if you had the PX process them. They're really obscene. I'll have them souped and printed by a pal of mine at Rucker and send you the prints and negatives."

"Thanks."

"And you call your mother on Christmas Eve. That's not an order, of course, just a friendly suggestion. If you don't, I will see that photographs of your medical affliction are circulated among the Corps of Cadets."

"Yes, Sir, I'll call her."

"They give you a hint how long they'll be that way?" Oliver asked.

"The doctors say they'll go down in a couple of days."

"I will never again say that West Pointers have no balls. I have seen absolutely spectacular proof to the contrary."

Captain John S. Oliver winked at Cadet Captain Robert F. Bellmon, Jr., tossed him a mockery of a salute, and walked out of the room.

V

[ONE]
Room Seven, Building T-124
Fort Rucker, Alabama
1915 Hours 22 December 1963

When his telephone rang—it was the one listed in the book for the Aide-de-Camp to the Commanding General—Captain John S. Oliver had settled in for the evening—or possibly for the next two days—in his quarters.

At noon, after he had tied up all the loose ends of the General's Christmas Party, he had been relieved from duty and told he would not be expected to make himself available until December 26. So all that remained on his schedule was a vague notion that he might go to church somewhere, on either Christmas Eve or Christmas Day.

Annex #1 of the Officers' Open Mess, a one-floor building, T-125, next to Building T-124, was the place where he normally passed a large part of his off-duty hours drinking beer and playing the pinball machine. But that, he had decided, was no place to spend the joyous Yuletide season. On such occasions, the patrons, mostly young lieutenants and warrants who for some reason had not been able to get Christmas leave, were prone to partake freely of intoxicants, and this sometimes resulted in chairs (or lieutenants) being thrown through windows.

When summoned to suppress blithe spirits in Annex #1, the first question the MP OD—Military Police Officer of the Day—asked was almost invariably, "Who's the senior officer in here?"

Captain Oliver did not wish to respond affirmatively to that question, so he decided he would do his Christmastide drinking right here in the room.

Therefore he had stopped by the PX and taken One Each of everything that looked reasonably interesting (or erotic) from the paperback book rack, and then from the magazine rack. After that, as sort of an emergency ration in case he didn't feel up to going to the club for breakfast, he had laid in from the canned goods counter twenty dollars' worth of goodies, ranging from smoked oysters through pickled shrimp to two cans of spaghetti and meatballs. And then he had acquired from the Class VI Store two half-gallon bottles of Johnnie Walker. The Army classified intoxicating beverages as Class VI supplies. One of these was Red Label (for display and thus for visitors); the other was Black (for his personal consumption, and thus concealed in the closet).

Then he had showered and dressed, more or less, in civilian clothing—a sweater and a pair of blue jeans. He had settled himself comfortably in his one armchair, having moved it so that he could both rest his feet on his bed and watch (if by some miracle there should be something worth watching) the small television sitting on top of the chest of drawers.

"Captain Oliver, Sir," he said to the telephone.

"Major Picarelli, Captain, I'm the AOD." The Aerodrome Officer of the Day.

"Yes, Sir?"

"The tower just got a call from a civilian Cessna 310H," Major Picarelli said. The Cessna 310 is a twin-engine, four-place aircraft. "And he wants to land here. Said it's been cleared with the General. The FOD doesn't know anything about it, and when I called Quarters One, the maid said the General's not there."

"The General said he was going to the PX, Sir," Oliver said, which was the tactful way of saying that the General had been dragged there, kicking and screaming, by Mrs. Bellmon to do last-minute shopping.

"Well, what should I do with the Cessna?"

"Sir, I suggest you give him permission to land. I'll come out there and see what it's all about."

"He's about ten minutes out."

"I'll leave right away, Sir."

The phone went dead in Oliver's ear.

Oliver dressed quickly, replacing his blue jeans with uniform trousers. After he put his shoes back on, he slipped his arms into his overcoat, the neck of which he buttoned. If he didn't take the overcoat off, no one would ever know that he was wearing a sweater with a picture of a stag on it under the uniform overcoat.

As he reached Base Operations, the Cessna taxied up to the transient parking area. It glistened and looked brand new.

"Are you Captain Oliver?" a voice said at his ear. Oliver turned and found himself looking at a swarthy major wearing the AOD brassard.

"Yes, Sir."

"What the hell is this all about?" Major Picarelli asked. "The tower just got another call. An Air Force Special Missions jet is five minutes out. They're supposed to pick up a Colonel Felter. Post locator says there's no Felter, colonel or otherwise, on the post."

"I really don't know, Sir," Oliver said.

He pushed open the glass door from Base Ops to the tarmac and walked toward the Cessna as its engines died.

As he reached the aircraft, the door opened and a small man in civilian clothes got out. He stood on the wing root and struggled into an overcoat, then reached inside the airplane and came out with a briefcase.

Oliver walked to him.

"Sir, I'm Captain Oliver, General Bellmon's aide. May I help you?"

"What happened to Captain Thomas?" the small man asked, pleasantly enough, smiling, putting out his hand. "I'm Colonel Felter."

"Sir, I've taken Captain Thomas's place," Oliver said as another man emerged from the airplane and jumped to the ground from the wing root. He was tall, mustachioed, and very handsome. And he was wearing a tweed jacket, a tattersall shirt and a foulard, and a Tyrolean hat with a large brush in the band.

"Sir," Major Picarelli said, "an Air Force plane is about to land, to pick up a Colonel Felter. Is that you?"

"Uh huh," the small man said. "Craig, this is Bob's new aide."

"How are you, Captain?" the handsome man said, offering his hand first to Oliver and then to Major Picarelli. "I'm Colonel Lowell. You want to give me a hand tying this thing down?"

"Yes, Sir."

This is the guy the Bellmons talked about, the one who did a BOOTSTRAP *at Norwich. I wonder who the little colonel is. And whose airplane is this?*

As Oliver was shoving wheel chocks in place, a Learjet in Air Force markings whooshed in from the sky and landed. There was the sound of the thrust reversing, and then it turned off the runway and taxied rapidly toward Base Operations.

"Sir," Oliver said to Colonel Lowell, "I don't believe General Bellmon expects you."

"No," Lowell said. "The original idea was that I would take Colonel Felter to Atlanta and have the Air Force meet him there. But then I decided to hell with that, let them come here and get him."

Colonel Felter then took a step forward. He didn't look, Oliver decided, like your typical John Wayne movie-type colonel: he was slight, short, and balding, and he wore a suit that looked as if it came from a rack in a Sears, Roebuck bargain basement. But he certainly acted like a colonel. "Captain," he said, "is there a phone around here? I want to talk to General Bellmon." Before Oliver could reply, Felter added, to Lowell, "With that damned airplane here, I can't take the time to go into the post."

''Yes, Sir, there's a phone just inside Base Operations,'' Oliver said.

The Learjet stopped right in front of Base Operations, ignoring the signals of a ground handler, who wanted it to park somewhere else. The door unfolded from the fuselage, and an Air Force master sergeant got out, looked for and found Felter, and marched over to him and saluted.

''Anytime you're ready, Colonel Felter,'' he said.

''I've got to make a quick phone call,'' Felter said. ''I'll be right with you.''

''We have a telephone aboard, Sir,'' the master sergeant said.

''I want to use one here,'' Felter said, and walked toward Base Operations.

Major Picarelli, Oliver noticed, had apparently decided not to make AOD-type noises about whether the civilian airplane had permission to land at Cairns Army Airfield. Oliver ran after Colonel Felter, got there in time to push the door open for him, then told the sergeant behind the counter to hand him the post phone book.

''General Bellmon is in the PX, Sir,'' Oliver explained to Felter. ''I'll get him on the line for you.''

''This is General Bellmon,'' Bellmon's voice, all business, came on the line a minute or two later.

''Hold on for Colonel Felter, please, Sir,'' Oliver said, and handed Felter the telephone.

''I'm out at your airfield, Bob,'' Colonel Felter said, which Oliver found fascinating, as colonels do not customarily refer to general officers by their first names. ''Craig flew me up from McDill.''

Oliver couldn't make much of the one side of the conversation he could hear, and then the conversation was over. Colonel Felter handed him the telephone.

''Johnny, I'm glad you were available,'' General Bellmon said. ''Could I impose on you further and ask you to take care of Colonel Lowell? Bring him to the house, or wherever he wants to go?''

''Yes, Sir, of course,'' Oliver said.

''I've been meaning to warn you about those two,'' Bellmon said. ''I just never found the time.''

Warn me about them? What the hell does that mean?

"I can handle it, Sir."

"Call me and let me know what happens, please, Johnny."

"Yes, Sir."

The line went dead.

Felter put out his hand.

"Thank you very much, Captain," he said. "Merry Christmas."

"My pleasure, Sir," Oliver said. "Merry Christmas to you, too."

Felter nodded at Major Picarelli, then walked back out of Base Operations. He walked directly to the Learjet and climbed the stairs. The Air Force master sergeant followed him aboard, and the door closed. The engine starter whined, and a moment later the Learjet started taxiing away.

"Can I mooch a ride from you, Captain?" Colonel Lowell asked.

"I'm at your service, Sir," Oliver said. "Where would you like to go?"

"Into Ozark, if that's not too much of an imposition," Colonel Lowell said.

"Not at all, Sir," Oliver said.

"Thank you very much for your courtesy, Major," Lowell said to Major Picarelli, and shook his hand.

"My pleasure, Sir," Major Picarelli said.

"My car is right outside, Colonel," Oliver said.

"Thank you very much," Lowell replied.

They stepped into Oliver's Pontiac convertible and drove off Cairns Airfield, and then through Daleville.

"Colonel, I'm brand new at this aide business, so this may be the kind of a question a good aide shouldn't ask, but what's going on?"

"What do you mean?"

"That fancy civilian airplane, the Air Force jet, Colonel Felter . . . ?"

"The airplane is mine," Colonel Lowell said.

Jesus Christ! Oliver thought, *that's a third-of-a-million-dollar airplane. Does he really mean it's his, or what?*

"Colonel Felter is one of General Bellmon's oldest friends," Lowell went on. "You mean he hasn't mentioned him?"

"No, Sir," Oliver said.

"He's one hell of a soldier," Lowell said, "who at the moment works in the White House. He carries the title, and the clout, which is more important, of Counselor to the President. The jet came here because the President wanted to see him, and if you're the President, you can dispatch Learjets like taxicabs."

Oliver digested that for a moment.

"Where are we going in Ozark, Sir?" Oliver asked several minutes later as he turned onto the road through Fort Rucker that led to Ozark.

"One twenty-seven Melody Lane," Lowell replied. "Know where it is?"

"No, Sir."

"I'll give you directions. My nephew, more or less, lives there. Lieutenant Geoff Craig. You know him?"

"No, Sir."

"He's in flight school," Lowell offered. "Just back from a tour as a Beret in 'Nam. I thought maybe you knew him there."

"Sir?" Oliver asked, confused. *How did this guy know I was in 'Nam?*

"Oh, Barbara's told me all about you, Oliver. I know how you got your CIB. And, of course, that we are fellow graduates of Norwich."

Oliver looked at him in surprise.

"So tell me, Oliver," Lowell said. "What's the status of Bobby's balls?"

"They were rather swollen the last time I saw them, Sir."

"Was there a prognosis? How long will he be immobile?"

"He told me, that was what—four days ago?—that the medics told him they would go down in a couple, three, days."

"Mrs. Bellmon told me she was very touched by that visit of yours to see Bobby," Lowell said.

"I hope it doesn't get back to the General," Oliver said.

"She is also heartsick that Bobby won't be home for Christmas," Lowell said. "She didn't say anything, but I know her that well. She's thinking it is, in effect, his last Christmas as her baby boy. He graduates in June. No telling where he'll be next year this time."

" 'Nam, very possibly," Oliver agreed.

"Have you got hot and heavy plans for tomorrow, Oliver?" Lowell asked.

"No, Sir."

"Well, at two tomorrow afternoon, I have to pick up my cousin Porter and his wife—Geoff's parents—in Atlanta. And bring them here. If I left here early tomorrow, I could pick up Bobby at West Point first. I think if I did that, that would be a very nice present for his mother."

"How are you going to get him out of the hospital?" Oliver asked.

Lowell waved his hand, signifying that was a minor problem that could easily be solved.

"I was going to ask Geoff to come along and work the radios," Lowell said. "The problem with that being I'm not sure he can work the radios . . ."

"Sir, if you're asking me to ride along, I'd be happy to."

"OK," Lowell said. "Then the first thing I'll do when I get to the house is call Barbara's brother. . . . You meet him when you were up there?"

"No, Sir. I know about him, though."

"Well, I'll call him and ask him what he thinks. And if we can go get Bobby, we will."

One hundred twenty-seven Melody Lane was the largest house on its street in the subdivision. It was a long and rambling frame house behind a wide lawn. There was a three-car carport. And, as Oliver pulled into the driveway, he saw in one of the spaces Marjorie Bellmon's MGB convertible.

Marjorie yelped with pleasure when she saw Lieutenant Colonel Craig W. Lowell, and then she kissed him and hugged him.

Then she saw Oliver.

"Oh, poor Johnny!" she said. "And you were supposed to be off duty."

"No problem," Oliver said.

"Well, I wanted you to meet the Craigs anyway," she said. "So it won't be entirely a waste. Geoff, this is my father's new aide, John Oliver."

Geoff Craig bore a strong familial resemblance to Craig W. Lowell.

"How do you do, Sir," he said, "I'm sorry you got hung up with this. I would have gone to the airfield . . ."

"No problem," Oliver said.

"Well, at least let me offer you a drink. That's Ursula," he said, pointing at a wholesome-looking blonde. She smiled shyly. "How do you do?" she said, and Oliver detected a German accent. "Thank you for bringing Colonel Lowell."

"What'll it be?" Geoff Craig pursued. "We have everything."

"Nothing, thank you," John Oliver replied. "I'm just waiting for the answer to a phone call Colonel Lowell is making."

"Well, at least take off your coat," Geoff Craig said.

"I'm fine, thank you," Oliver said.

"Uncle Craig, order him," Marjorie said.

"Take off your coat, sit down, and let Geoff fix you a drink," Lowell said as he reached for the telephone. "Operator, I want to speak to Brigadier General Lewis Waterford at the U.S. Military Academy at West Point."

"What's that all about?" Marjorie asked.

"We're going to see if we can't go get Bobby tomorrow," Oliver said.

"Can you?" she asked. "Mother would be ecstatic."

"We're about to find out."

"Take off the goddamn coat," Lowell said. "And relax. You're among friends."

Oliver unbuttoned the coat, revealing the sweater.

"Marjorie said I'd like you, Captain," Geoff Craig said. He took Oliver's arm and led him to a well-stocked bar. "Choose!" he said.

"Thank you," Oliver said.

Obviously this is much nicer than sitting alone in that room, reading Playboy *and drinking by myself. Then why am I uncomfortable?*

Because these people are a family, and behaving like one, and that is a societal arrangement with which I have virtually no experience.

[TWO]
Lawson Army Airfield
Fort Benning, Georgia
1235 Hours 4 January 1964

The Cessna 0-1E "Birddog" making its approach to Lawson was a high-winged, single-engine, two-passenger, fixed-landing-gear aircraft primarily intended to direct artillery fire, but it was often used, as it was being used now, as an aerial jeep, carrying a single passenger from here to there more quickly than he could be taken in a wheeled vehicle.

The pilot of the 0-1E touched the mike button.

"Lawson, Army Four Oh Four understands I am number two to land after the Caribou on final." Lawson, at the edge of Fort Benning, served as Benning's airfield.

The tower came right back, with more than a hint of impatience in his voice.

"Four Oh Four, you are number two. Number two. Watch out for turbulence behind the 'Bou."

"Four Oh Four, Roger," the Cessna 0-1E pilot said.

Compared to the 0-1E, the DeHavilland CV-2 Caribou was enormous. The Caribou was a transport aircraft, which was not, in fact, by other standards, all that big, being only a bit larger and more powerful than the Douglas C-47, the standard Army Air Corps transport in World War II. Large flaps and two Pratt and Whitney R-2000 1450hp engines permitted the 'Bou to almost leap into the air from very short landing strips. In the rear of the 'Bou's fuselage there was a door that converted to a ramp large enough for the two jeeps which could be carried aboard.

Landing on short fields was accomplished by rapidly reversing the pitch of the propellers, so that instead of pulling the aircraft through the air, they exerted exactly as much force—2900 horsepower—in the other direction. That much force stopped the 'Bou as if an invisible hand had grabbed it.

That much force also caused turbulence on the runway behind the 'Bou. And since it was fairly standard practice for 'Bou pilots to reverse their propellers the instant their wheels touched down—even when landing on wide, long, concrete runways—the Lawson tower considered it prudent to warn Army 404 about possible turbulence.

The warning was unnecessary. The pilot of 404 had once seen an aircraft identical to the one he was flying land too close behind a Caribou. The same invisible hand that brought the Caribou to a short stop had grabbed the little 0-1E, thrown it fifty feet in the air, turned it over, and then slammed it down onto the runway on its back.

The pilot of 404 made a very slow final approach to the active runway, making sure that the turbulence had dissipated before he touched down. And then he braked harder than he liked, to get off the runway as quickly as possible and make it available to the long line of aircraft that was behind him in the landing stack.

In January 1964, Lawson Army Airfield was the second-busiest airfield in the United States. In terms of landings and takeoffs, it was second only to O'Hare Field in Chicago, and ahead of even Atlanta, LaGuardia, and LA. The airplanes at Lawson were smaller, of course, than the transports sitting down at O'Hare; but O'Hare had more runways, and at O'Hare several hundred rotary-wing aircraft were not sharing the facility with their fixed-wing brothers.

Lawson had been designed and built in War II primarily for the C-47 aircraft used in the training of parachutists. For military parachuting—the theory and practice of vertical envelopment—had had its birth and first tests at Benning.

And now another theory of war was being tested here.

Depending on who was talking, it was either the inevitable evolution of the theory and practice of vertical envelopment, the Airborne State of the Art. Or else it was an entirely new concept of battlefield maneuverability that did *not* trace its beginnings to parachuting, and which would, more importantly, make parachuting (at least insofar as it was a means to invest a battlefield) as obsolete as catapults.

The 11th Air Assault Division [Test] was now stationed at Fort Benning, where it was testing the evolutionary/revolutionary theory that Army divisions of the future would be airmobile. Meaning that the next war (which most knowledgeable observers believed was already in progress in far-off Vietnam, just waiting to burst into flame) would be fought by soldiers who would arrive at the battlefield in helicopters and not in trucks or by parachute. These soldiers, further, would be resupplied by air, either by fixed- or rotary-wing aircraft, while they leapfrogged around the zone of conflict unhindered by rivers and mountains and swamps and other inhospitable, unpleasant terrain.

Ninety-five percent of the aircraft that crowded Lawson Army Airfield now belonged to the 11th Air Assault Division. The other five percent belonged to visitors to Fort Benning, such as the pilot of Army 404, who had flown up from Fort Rucker, a hundred miles to the south.

''Lawson, Four Oh Four, I just turned off the active. Request permission to taxi to the transient area,'' 404's pilot called.

''Four Oh Four, there's no room in the transient area. Turn right on the taxiway and park where you see the other Birddogs.''

Right on the taxiway was away from Base Operations. The windshield of the Birddog was now covered with raindrops. If he turned right and parked where he had been told to park, he would have perhaps a three-quarter-mile walk through a cold drizzle to Base Ops.

''Shit,'' the pilot of 404 said, then nudged his throttle and turned right on the taxiway.

After he'd found a space to park and got out, he saw that there were neither tiedown ropes conveniently waiting for him, nor even chocks for the wheels. Thus, he had to dig them out of the Birddog's fuselage and drive stakes in the ground before he could hook up the tiedowns.

Finally he had the chocks in place. After that he reached in the back of the Birddog, took out a battered GI briefcase, and closed the window. He looked up and down the taxiway, hoping to see a truck or a jeep that would spare him the long walk through the drizzle. But he was not surprised when he saw none. He swore again and started to walk toward Base Ops. He was so far down the field that the taxiway here was grass, not macadam. His shoes were quickly wet and mud splattered.

A hundred yards from the Birddog, a DeHavilland Beaver came taxiing down the dirt taxiway. The pilot of 404 walked deeper into the ankle-high dead grass to get out of the way of its prop blast.

The copilot of the Beaver, in the right seat, turned to the pilot.

"You see what I saw?" he asked.

"I'll be goddamned," the pilot replied.

The copilot reached for his microphone.

"Lawson, I thought maybe you'd like to know there's a major general marching through the mud and rain down here at the end of zero seven. I can't imagine why, but he looks a little pissed."

"Aircraft calling Lawson tower, identify yourself and say again your last transmission."

"I said the General looks pissed," the copilot said, and then put the hand-held microphone back in its holder.

Two vehicles left the vicinity of Base Operations within the next ninety seconds. One was a jeep. It was painted in a yellow and black checkerboard pattern and flying a white and black checkerboard flag from a pole welded to its right-rear bumper. The second was a glistening Chevrolet four-door sedan with an array of antennae and a similar white and black checkerboard flag.

The Chevrolet overtook the jeep before it reached the pilot of Army 404. It stopped, and the driver and an officer wearing the golden rope of an aide-de-camp jumped out of the front seat. The driver went to the front of the car and snatched a vinyl cover off a plate the size of a license plate, exposing two silver stars. The aide, a good-looking young captain wearing glistening parachutist's boots, saluted crisply.

"General, I'm terribly sorry about this."

Major General Robert F. Bellmon returned the salute and handed him the briefcase.

"Don't worry about it," he said, as he fished a handkerchief from his pocket and wiped his glasses with it.

The jeep pulled up, and a very natty lieutenant colonel in stiffly starched, form-fitting fatigues jumped out. He saluted.

"Sir, Colonel Sawyer. I'm the AOD. General, the tower swears they did *not* get a Code Eight." When an aircraft communicating with an airfield tower announces "Code Eight," it means that a major general is aboard.

"I didn't give one," General Bellmon said, offering his hand to the AOD. "I figured you looked busy enough without my adding to your burden. How do you do, Colonel?"

"Sir, it wouldn't have been a problem."

"I decided it would," Bellmon said.

"Sir, I'll have your aircraft moved to Base Ops," the AOD said.

"You're not listening, Colonel. I don't want to add to your burden. Just have it fueled, please. I can find it where I left it."

"Yes, Sir," the AOD said as Bellmon entered the Chevrolet.

"How are you, Sergeant?" Bellmon said to the driver.

"Just fine, thank you, Sir. Sorry you had to walk. We was waiting for you."

"This is the Infantry Center, isn't it?" Bellmon said with a smile. "The walking branch? You ever hear, Sergeant, 'When in Rome . . .'?"

The aide got in the front seat and turned to face General Bellmon.

"General Campbell's compliments, Sir. He hopes that his scheduling lunch at Riverside will be all right with you, Sir."

"Fine with me. I always like to see how the other half lives," General Bellmon said.

The quarters of the Commanding General of the U.S. Army Infantry Center & Fort Benning, Georgia, like the quarters of commanding generals throughout the Army, were officially known as Quarters #1. But universally throughout the Army—indeed, throughout the armed forces—those of the Benning commander were known as "Riverside."

Bellmon's Quarters #1 at Fort Rucker, Alabama, had no corresponding unofficial title, although General Bellmon, *en famille,* had variously described them as *this doghouse; this goddamned dump;* and once, waxing eloquent, as *a splendid example of the contempt in which general officers of the Army are held by those horses' asses on Capitol Hill.*

Quarters #1 at Fort Rucker had been built, six years before, in ninety days, as part of a multimillion-dollar family-housing project for the married officers and noncommissioned officers of Fort Rucker. Most of the houses were duplexes, sharing a common wall. But single quarters had been provided for senior officers. Quarters #1 was slightly larger—just slightly—than any of the other one-family houses. But it was built to the same general pattern. That is to say, it was one-story, frame, with half brick and half shingled walls, eight-foot ceilings, and narrow corridors. Bellmon had also, fairly, said it *looked like a housing development for the underprivileged.*

Riverside, on the other hand, could fairly be described as a stately mansion—with high ceilings and wide corridors and other amenities suitable to persons of exalted rank. Built long before World War II, it sits behind a wide lawn, surrounded by massive trees. And it is steeped in history. George Catlett Marshall and Douglas MacArthur and Dwight David Eisenhower and Vinegar Joe Stilwell and George S. Patton and Maxwell Davenport Taylor and James Van Fleet and Matthew B. Ridgway and a thousand other soldiers with stars on their epaulets had all sat at one time or another at the highly polished antique table in the downstairs dining room.

When Major General Robert F. Bellmon entered Riverside, he smiled, shook Major General William C. Campbell's hand, and rendered the just as *de rigueur* kiss to the cheek of his host's wife. After that he considered again the difference between these quarters and his. And then he thought, *I wouldn't swap jobs to move in here.*

"The others are already seated, Bob," General Campbell said. "You want a drink?"

"I'm flying, Bill, I'd better not."

"Yourself?" Eleanor asked. "I mean, you flew up here by yourself?"

"What you really meant was that you didn't know they let old men like me fly by themselves," Bellmon said.

"No, I did not," she protested.

He smiled at her.

Beginning to wonder, Eleanor? Whether we're going to get away with this, and that if we do, whether Bill will be on the sidelines?

He walked beside General Campbell down a wide, carpeted corridor to the downstairs dining room.

Places had been set at that same table for four general officers.

[THREE]

Three of the five officers at the meeting described in the General's diary as *Private luncheon, in quarters* were major generals (two stars). One of these was the host, William C. Campbell, who was Commanding General, U.S. Army Infantry Center & Fort Benning. The remaining two were brigadier generals (one star). One of these was William R. Roberts. Roberts was also the youngest officer at table, and the most recent (1940) graduate of the United States Military Academy at West Point. Major General Campbell was '38, and Major Generals Harrison O. K. Wendall and Robert F. Bellmon were '39. They had all known each other at West Point and they'd frequently been in touch since. They were, in varying degrees, friends.

The fifth officer at table, who rose as Bellmon walked into the dining room, was also a member of the Class of '39.

He smiled when General Campbell said, "Bob, I believe you know *General* Rand?"

"Well, I'll be damned," Bellmon said, then walked quickly to him, put out his hand, and grabbed his shoulder. "That star looks good on your shoulder, George."

"I'm not quite used to the weight," Rand said. "It's only been up there a couple of hours."

"Well, brace yourself," Bellmon said. "It will get heavier."

"As, I think, I am about to find out," Rand said, gesturing around at the others.

"Well, I'll tell you this," Bellmon said. "It's not what you think it will be."

"Particularly if you're operating from a position of massive ignorance, as I am," Rand said.

"Well, you're in good company," General Wendall said. "We all have that problem."

Major General Harrison O. K. "Hok" Wendall was Commanding General of the 11th Air Assault Division [Test]. The 11th Air Assault was immediately subordinate to, in theory, Continental Army Command [CONARC] at Fortress Monroe, Virginia. CONARC was charged by statute and custom with the development of tactics and equipment.

In practice, however, the 11th Air Assault Division [Test]

belonged to the U.S. Army Deputy Chief of Staff for Operations. Though there were several reasons for this, the chief reason was that Secretary of Defense Robert Strange McNamara was in the Pentagon, and so was DCSOPS. McNamara was fascinated with the notion of battlefield aerial mobility, and thus with the 11th Air Assault Division [Test]; and he obviously had plans for it.

When McNamara had a question to ask or some suggestion to make about the 11th Air Assault, he didn't want to have to get on the telephone or summon someone to the Pentagon from someplace like Norfolk. He wanted action *then.*

He got it from DCSOPS.

It was also true that McNamara knew that DCSOPS not only believed in the 11th Air Assault Division [Test] but also in the concept of air mobility that was behind it. And this was something of a minority opinion within the upper echelons of the Army. Since McNamara wanted his orders obeyed, not circumvented, and his suggestions listened to, not politely tolerated, he got all this from DCSOPS.

The problem wasn't that the Army establishment was *opposed* to the idea of an Army Aviation Division, but rather that most senior officers were convinced that the whole concept was moving too fast. It hadn't been thought through—much less anywhere near adequately tested. They believed, further, that Ham Howze and the other "aviator types" were getting carried away on the wings of their own enthusiasm. And it was also perfectly clear to them that the priority given to the 11th Air Assault Division—indeed, to the whole damned idea—was diverting assets (money, property, and personnel) that were needed elsewhere. And *that* situation, they believed, was going to get even worse.

When the five general officers lunched at the highly polished table in "Riverside," their meal consisted of pork chops, mashed potatoes, applesauce, green beans, and apple cobbler; and their conversation was mostly small talk—gossip of wives and children, and classmates and friends.

It was only when a white-jacketed steward cleared the table, set out a large silver coffee service, and left the room that they got down to business.

"We're about to be sandbagged by our friends in blue," General Hok Wendall said.

"Is that a general philosophical observation, Hok, or is there something specific in your mind?" Bellmon asked.

"Both." Wendall chuckled. "Specifically, BLUE BLAZES II."

BLUE BLAZES II was a maneuver. Its stated purpose was to move what amounted to a regimental combat team—that is, a regiment of troops, augmented by artillery and other forces—from Fort Benning to Fort Stewart, near Savannah, Georgia. The force would maneuver against an "enemy" force for ninety-six hours and then be withdrawn to Fort Benning.

Its more general purpose was to test whether a force that large could in fact be effectively and efficiently transported by Army aircraft to a battle zone, supplied and reinforced solely by Army aircraft for four days, and then returned to Benning.

"What's the problem?" Bellmon asked.

"Chinooks, lack of," Hok Wendall said.

"Nobody has enough Chinooks," Bellmon said.

"The original idea, as you know," Wendall went on, "was to simulate Chinooks. Use whatever transport we have, primarily CH-34s, but some Caribous and Otters too, to move the materiel from here to there. And then, when the test is evaluated, to use tonnage and time data to compute how many Chinooks could have done the same thing."

"The first time I maneuvered with tanks," Bellmon said, "they were 1936 Ford ton-and-a-half trucks. They had 'tank' written on the doors and windshields."

If General Wendall was interested in this bit of historical lore, he gave no sign.

"And then George had an idea," Wendall went on, nodding toward General Rand.

"Oh?"

"The Air Force," Rand said, "is going to say—and you know it, Bob, no matter how squeaky clean honest we are about it—that our simulation figures are slanted in our favor."

"Sure, they will. That's a given. Just be damned sure of your figures," Bellmon said.

"Particularly in the area of maintenance man-hours per flight hour, fuel consumption, and availability," Rand went on.

"What George came up with, Bob," Hok Wendall said, "is a way out. Something that would collapse their bag of hot air before it was filled."

"George is very clever," Bellmon said, meaning it. "I suspect that's why you asked for him. I'm all ears, George."

"We form two provisional Chinook companies," Rand said. "Actually use thirty-six Chinooks. The Air Force wouldn't be able to refute the data we actually developed."

Bellmon nodded his agreement. "Where are you going to get the Chinooks?" he asked, and as the words came out of his mouth, he understood Rand's idea and what they wanted from him.

"There are twenty-three Chinooks at Rucker," Hok Wendall said.

"No," Bellmon said. "Not possible."

"I'd only need them for ninety-six hours, Bob," Rand said.

"Five are assigned to the Board," Bellmon said, referring to The U.S. Army Aviation Board, the organization charged with testing aircraft and associated materiel. "So you couldn't have them, period. The eighteen in the school fleet are about half what I need. Eight are in use for enlisted training. And ten are all I have to train pilots."

"I'd only need them for ninety-six hours, Bob," Rand repeated, reasonably.

"I don't know why I'm arguing about this," Bellmon said. "But no, you would need them for at least one hundred forty-four hours, six days. Twenty-four hours to get them here ready to work, ninety-six hours—which will, and you know it, probably be extended—for BLUE BLAZES II, and then another twenty-four, almost certainly more, to get them back to work at the school."

"Bill says," Hok Wendall said, nodding at Major General William C. Campbell, the Fort Benning commanding general, "that he'll pay for fuel and TDY pay for the air crews, and he'll work something out with you about contract maintenance."

"No," Bellmon said. "Thank you, Bill, for the thought. But I cannot, I will not, shut down my Chinook operation for six days. Do you realize how many people that would leave sitting around on their hands? How much that would delay training? You're already screaming at me for pilots. How I am going to turn out pilots or mechanics if I don't have any aircraft to train them on?"

"I keep saying this, Bob," George Rand said. "We only need them for ninety-six hours."

"And I keep saying it's just impossible."

"I've been thinking of making the proposal officially to General Howze," Hok Wendall said.

"If you do, and he approves—which seems damned unlikely to me—I'll take it to DCSOPS," Bellmon said. "My God, don't make me the heavy in this. The 11th Air Assault is not the only unit in the Army that needs Chinooks. They're programmed for Germany. Christ, I've even got to send three, and crews for them, to the Arctic Test Board. And what the hell is going to happen to the training program if you cowboys dump a couple of them?"

"Cowboys?" Hok Wendall asked just a little coldly.

"I know all about the relaxed safety standards," Bellmon said. "And to repeat, don't make me the heavy in this. I'm as much interested in getting the 11th off the ground as you are. But not at the expense of the seed corn."

There was no reply from Generals Wendall or Rand. Bellmon looked at Brigadier General William R. Roberts.

"Bill?" Bellmon asked. "You think I'm wrong?"

"No, of course not," Roberts replied.

"Why doesn't that surprise me?" Wendall asked.

"That was a low blow, Hok," Bellmon said coldly.

General Wendall met his eyes for a moment and shrugged.

"Yes, it was," he said. "I didn't mean it the way it sounded. No offense, Bill?"

"No, Sir, none taken," Roberts said.

Bullshit on both counts, Bellmon thought.

"Well, George," Hok Wendall said, smiling, "it looks as if you came up with a splendid idea whose time has just not yet come."

"It would appear that way, Sir."

"And I'm sure, Hok, that if you did decide to go to Ham Howze, you would tell me, wouldn't you?"

"That's your low blow for the day," Wendall said, his smile forced. "That makes us even."

A white-jacketed orderly appeared with yet another silver pot of coffee.

"Not for me, thank you, Sergeant," General Bellmon said, waving the pot away.

"I heard, Bill," General Wendall said to General Roberts, "that your mentor has formed an unholy alliance with the Chief of Staff and is already making noises that when it's up to strength, the 11th should be redesignated as the First Cav."

The First Cavalry Division, organized and equipped as a regular infantry division, was at the time stationed in Korea.

"Mentor meaning who?" General Roberts asked somewhat sharply.

"Ol' sabers-on-the-tank I. D. White," Wendall said.

When the old insignia of Armor, a silhouette of a World War I tank, had been redesigned as a front-on view of a World War II tank, then-Major General I. D. White had insisted, with all of the enormous persuasion of which he was capable, that Cavalry sabers be superimposed on it.

"Seems like a splendid idea," Roberts said. "Or are you just pulling my chain?"

"I heard that, too," General Campbell said.

"No kidding?" Bellmon asked.

"And you flyboys are going to be issued riding breeches and sabers," General Campbell continued, "and Smokey the Bear campaign hats."

"Screw you, Bill," General Bellmon said, tempering it just slightly with a smile. "Is there anything else?"

"George has a favor to ask you," O. K. Wendall said. "I told him what I knew you would say, but he wants to ask anyway."

"Shoot, George," Bellmon said.

"General Wendall tells me that as the man who writes the regulations for pilot training, you also have the authority to waive them," George Rand said.

"Go ahead and ask, George, but if the question is what I think it's going to be, the answer will be sorry, no."

"I just got here. I've got a lot to learn. I just don't have the time to take six weeks or two months to go to Rucker and learn how to fly, and I think everybody agrees that I have to get myself rated. There are qualified people here, former Rucker IPs, who could teach me how when I could find a few loose hours."

"Sorry, no," Bellmon said. "I warned you."

"For what it's worth, George," Bill Roberts said, "I agree with Bob. When you're learning how to fly, you don't need anything else on your mind."

Rand glowered at Roberts. On Roberts's breast were the wreathed and starred wings of a Master Army Aviator. Roberts had been the first aviator so designated. He was, de facto and de jure, the Army's most experienced aviator. He could hardly be told to mind his own business, although that thought ran through George Rand's mind.

"Bob," General Wendall said quickly, as if he sensed the possibility of a blow-up, "why don't you call Barbara and tell her you're weathered in? We can run the wives off and get drunk. I for one think not only that are we entitled, but that we have a duty to celebrate George's star."

"Plenty of room here, Bob," General Campbell said.

"Rub it in, you bastard," Bellmon said. "Hell, I'd really like to. But I can't." He looked at his watch. "Christ! I've got to get the hell out of here." He looked at Brigadier General George Rand. "George, whenever you feel you can take the time from here, you call me. I promise you, I will run you through a flight program, taught by the best people I have, and as quickly as you can get through it. But they need you here alive, and I'm not going to be responsible for you killing yourself."

"I understand, Bob," Brigadier General Rand said, although he did not.

VI

[ONE]
Quarters #1
Fort Rucker, Alabama
1810 Hours 11 January 1964

Miss Marjorie Bellmon, only daughter of Major General Robert F. Bellmon, telephoned Captain John S. Oliver, aide-de-camp to Major General Robert F. Bellmon, catching him just as he was leaving the office. Bellmon had left a half hour before.

"Guess what?" she said.

Captain John S. Oliver did not have to guess. He instantly understood that for the fourth time since he had become aide-de-camp to Major General Robert F. Bellmon he was about to rescue Miss Marjorie Bellmon from automotive breakdown and deliver her to her home.

Her MGB had carburetion problems. No mechanic in the area had any idea what caused them, but the symptoms were well known. Whenever it was raining and she was driving home from the bank, the MGB burped, coughed, and died. Usually, she would have the car towed to the Ford dealer where she had bought it, and then she would have either Geoff or Ursula Craig drive her home. When neither of them were available, she would call Johnny Oliver. He didn't mind. It wasn't the General's Daughter leaning on the General's Aide, but a friend asking a friend for a favor.

"Where are you?" Captain Oliver asked.

"By the auxiliary field, about three miles from the Ozark gate."

"You want me to call the Ford place?"

"To hell with them. Johnny, would you pull it home for me?"

"Be right there," he said. "What are you going to do with the car?"

"I'm going to take Daddy's forty-five and put a merciful round in the radiator," she said. "But there's no sense taking it back to the Ford place."

"We'll be there in ten minutes," Oliver said.

"*We'll* be there? Is he *still* following you around, happily wagging his tail?"

"That's true," Oliver said.

"He" was Cadet Captain Robert F. Bellmon, Jr., who was at the moment sitting on a leather couch, reading a copy of *Armor* magazine.

Since Johnny and Lieutenant Colonel Craig W. Lowell had brought Bobby home for Christmas leave, General Bellmon had encouraged Bobby to tag along after him and his aide during the duty day. Oliver wasn't sure if that was because the General wanted to show Bobby off—in his complete-to-cape Cadet Gray uniform—or whether he considered it part of Bobby's education.

And then, when Bellmon finally turned him loose at the end of a day, Bobby had taken to tagging along after Oliver alone. This turned out to be at once flattering and annoying, but Oliver didn't have the heart to run him off. And, in any event, it was about to be over. Bobby was catching the 8:05 Southern Airways flight to Atlanta, and thence to New York, tonight.

"We'll be right there," Oliver said. "Don't put it out of its misery yet. Somebody has to know how to fix it."

"If that's Marjorie, and her car is broken down again," Bobby said, raising his eyes from *Armor,* "it's her own fault."

"How do you figure that, Mr. Bellmon?" Oliver asked.

"I told her the fuel line is fouled," he said. "All she has to do is blow it out."

"Well, I'm glad you're going with me to get it, then, Mr. Bellmon," Oliver said. "As full of hot air as you are, you should certainly be able to blow it out better than that air compressor at the Ford place has already done it, three times."

"I didn't know it had been blown out," Bobby said.

"Engage your ears, and your brain, Mr. Bellmon, before you operate your mouth," Oliver said. "Come on, let's go."

They found Marjorie and her MGB without trouble, and Johnny went through the motions of trying to start the car himself, correctly predicting it wouldn't do a damn bit of good. Then he fastened a nylon rope to the bumpers of both cars and towed the MGB to Quarters One.

The three of them were shoving it backward into the carport when Barbara Bellmon came out.

"Oh, not again!" she said.

"If it doesn't heal itself over the weekend," Johnny said, "Marjorie has promised to put it out of its misery."

"I'd like to put the salesman who sold it to her out of his misery," Barbara Bellmon said. Then she turned to her son. "I hope you're all packed. If you're on the 8:05 plane, I want to leave here at seven."

"Johnny can take me to the airport, Mom, you don't have to bother," Bobby replied.

"*Captain* Oliver is *not* the family chauffeur, Bobby," Mrs. Bellmon said angrily. "You really have a hell of a lot of nerve, Bobby! I'll take you, or Marjorie will."

"I'll run him in, Mrs. B," Johnny said. "I'm going to Dothan anyway."

"Don't let him push you around, Johnny," Mrs. B said. "He's just like his father, pushing people around."

Johnny Oliver remembered the old soldier's advice to look at the mother if you wanted to see what the daughter was going to be like twenty years later, and decided it was equally applicable to men. General Bellmon in his youth had probably looked like Bobby did now, and was probably as stuffy, self-righteous, and naive. And in twenty-five years, Bobby would probably be just as good a general officer as his father was, and even, conceivably, as wise.

"No problem," Johnny said. "The airport's on my way."

Oliver really had no intention of going to Dothan on his own. But taking Bobby to the airport would spare Mrs. B having to drive him in, and it would take only an hour, back and forth.

"Well, at least let me give you something to eat, Johnny," Mrs. Bellmon said. "I insist."

"I accept," Oliver said. "Thank you."

"If you think he's bad now, Mother, wait till they pin that gold bar on him. Then he will be really insufferable."

Bobby Bellmon gave his sister the finger. Their mother pretended not to see it.

When they were on U.S. 231, headed for Dothan in Oliver's Pontiac convertible, Cadet Captain Robert F. Bellmon, Jr., rested his back against the door and asked, "Johnny, what do you think of my sister?"

"She's my boss's daughter," Oliver replied. "I don't think about her."

"You know what I mean."

"Oh, you mean, what do I think of her as a *female*, a representative of the allegedly gentle sex?"

"Yeah."

"Mr. Bellmon, that falls into the category known as none of your fucking business."

"I'll tell you what the Old Man said. He and Mom were talking, and the Old Man said, 'She could do a lot worse.' She being Marjorie, of course, and you being who she could do a lot worse than."

"Isn't there something in the Sacred Honor Code of Hudson High making it a high crime and misdemeanor to refer to a major general, who just happens to be your father, as the Old Man, much less eavesdropping on his conversations and then reporting what you overheard?"

"Hey, I'm on your side. I think you and Marjorie would make a good pair."

"Don't hold your breath, Mr. Bellmon," Oliver said. "Nothing like that is going to happen."

"You never can tell."

"Bobby, shut up."

[TWO]
Building T-124
Fort Rucker, Alabama
2045 Hours 11 January 1964

When he pulled into the parking lot behind the BOQ, for a moment Johnny Oliver thought that Marjorie had somehow miraculously brought her MGB back to life, and for some reason had come to the BOQ. Then he saw that the MGB had a Fort Rucker Temporary registration card—an oblong piece of cardboard taped to the rear window, and that it had Texas license plates.

He scooped his laundry and dry cleaning out of the back seat of the Pontiac and started toward the building. Then he stopped and went back to take another look at the MGB. Something had caught his eye, and now he saw what it was. It was, he decided, the legendary MGB of Many Colors, like Joseph's robe in the Good Book.

One fender was blue and the other was dark maroon. And between them was a flaming-yellow hood. The body was British Racing Green, and so was one of the doors. The other door matched the hood.

Oliver shook his head and walked into the building and up the stairs and down the corridor to room seven. And with some effort, while balancing the laundry and dry cleaning with one hand, he pulled the key out of his pocket with the other and got the door open. There was an envelope on the floor. He dumped the laundry and dry cleaning on the bed and went back for the envelope.

It held a neatly typed note from the sergeant in the billeting office:

1330 10 Jan
Capt. Oliver:
We ran out of space. I had to put a 2nd Lt in Six. Just as soon as there is room for him in a Student BOQ, I'll move him.
Sincerely Yours,
SFC Wilters

Oliver had learned that having room six (the other side of the bathroom) empty was another perquisite of being the General's aide. He wondered why that was, but didn't question the custom. And then his mood turned darker. To wit: The enforced camaraderie he now faced with a new roommate reminded him of the prejudice he was forced to suffer as a bachelor. And this was one more proof of that prejudice: they hadn't moved this second lieutenant into some second lieutenant's family quarters when they ran out of space in the Student BOQs.

Oliver crumpled up the note and the envelope and scored two baskets in the tin wastebasket by the desk in the "study."

Then he walked down the corridor and got a waxed-paper bucket full of ice from the ice-maker. He carried it back to his room, took the good bottle of Johnnie Walker from the closet, and made himself a drink. After that, he took off his blouse and tie and started putting his laundry and dry cleaning away.

There came a knock on the door to the latrine.

"Come," Oliver said.

A very short officer put his head through the doorway.

"Captain Oliver? I'm Lieutenant Newell. They moved me in next door. There's no room in the Student BOQ."

"Welcome to the Rucker Hilton," Oliver said. "Come on in. Pour yourself a drink."

"No, thank you, Sir. I just wanted to introduce myself."

"Oh, have a drink. Drinking and screwing aren't any fun by yourself."

"I'm married, Sir," Newell said.

"Well, good for you, but so what?"

"The billeting sergeant made it pretty clear that I was not to have females in the room."

"Why?" Oliver asked. "I've been in whorehouses with fewer broads than are usually here on weekend nights."

"I think his point was that I wasn't to disturb you, Sir."

"Oh, Jesus!" Oliver said, and then had a fresh thought. "If you're married, where is she? If she was here, you'd have a whole damned house to yourself."

"Home, Sir. El Paso. I'm National Guard, and we're not authorized dependents."

That explains why, Oliver thought, *this guy doesn't look, or act, like your typical bushy-tailed second john fresh from an officer basic school.*

"When did they stop drinking in Texas?" Oliver asked.

"Well, if you're sure, I'd like a drink. It's been a bitch today."

"Then we have something in common," Oliver said. And then he thought of something else. "Is that MGB of Many Colors outside yours?"

"Yes, Sir."

"No one is watching," Oliver said, handing him the bottle of Johnnie Walker. "You can call me by first name—John—within the walls of our little home."

"My name is Joseph," Newell said.

"I knew it would be. As in 'Joseph's Coat of Many Colors.' Is there some story behind that technicolor MGB?"

Newell smiled.

"I rebuilt it," he said. "Or I made one that runs out of three that didn't."

He didn't mix the scotch with ice. Raising the glass of straight whiskey to Oliver, he said, "Thank you," and then took a sip. "That's good booze."

"May I infer, Joseph? Do people really call you Joseph?—What does your wife call you?"

"Butch."

"Dutch?"

"Butch," Newell said. "From the haircut." He rubbed his hand over his crew cut. "I always wore it like this." He looked at Oliver a moment. "My father calls me Joe and my mother calls me Jose. I'm a Mex-Tex, or a Tex-Mex."

"And do you carry a chip on your shoulder because of that?"

"Why do you ask?"

"Because I think I'm going to call you Jose and I wouldn't want you running to the minority affairs officer and raising a bitch about it."

Newell smiled. "Jose's fine," he said.

"As I was saying, Jose. Would it be reasonable to presume you know something about MGBs?"

"Yeah. Why?"

"Why would an MGB—one which has had its fuel line blown out three times—cough, sputter, and suffer complete engine malfunction every time it's driven in the rain?"

"Sounds like a cracked distributor head," Newell said after a just perceptible hesitation.

"I looked for that."

"Where it cracks most often is in the center lead—the wire from the coil?—and it's damned near impossible to see. And then when you run it in the rain, a sort of mist gets through the radiator, or up from under the engine, condenses in the molding, and shorts it out. You've got an MGB?"

"A friend of mine does. I have just decided, Jose, that our enforced association is going to be fortuitous."

Newell smiled at him.

"I'll look at it, if you'd like," he said. "I've got a new distributor cap in my trunk. They're always cracking. I think they make them out of papier-mâché."

[THREE]
0830 Hours 12 January 1964

Johnny Oliver and Jose Newell started work on Marjorie Bellmon's MG early the following morning. By that time Johnny had learned quite a lot about Second Lieutenant Joseph M. Newell, Signal Corps, Texas Army National Guard, the new occupant of room six.

For one thing, he now knew that Jose Newell was just half an inch taller than the minimum prescribed height for commissioned officers, and five pounds heavier than the minimum prescribed weight. Over their fourth drink, for which they had adjourned to the bar of Annex #1 of the Officers' Open Mess next door to the BOQ, Jose told him that that made him five and half inches shorter and twenty pounds lighter than his wife. He produced a picture of the lady, a statuesque blonde in a cowboy hat, hanging tightly on to Jose's arm and looking down at him with an expression that was visibly near ecstasy.

Twenty-three years before, Joseph M. Newell, Sr., then twenty and working for the railroad in El Paso on a tie-tamping machine, had enraged his family and Anglo-Texan sensitivities generally by taking to wife one Estrellita Gómez. Miss Gómez, eighteen at the time, had similarly enraged her family and Tex-Mex sensitivities generally by running off to Las Vegas with a Protestant gringo.

Joseph M. Newell, Jr., had been born the day after his parents' first wedding anniversary. He had always been a runt, he told Johnny Oliver, which both sides blamed on the weak blood of the other. And he'd always been so dark he looked Spanish.

In time, though, a sort of armed truce had been reached between the families, largely through the good offices of Monsignor Antonio Delamar, rector of El Paso's Our Lady of Guadalupe Roman Catholic Church. Monsignor Delamar managed to convince Lita Gómez Newell's mother that the marriage was valid in the eyes of God, that Lita and Joe were not living in sin, and that Little Jose was not illegitimate. All this followed, the Monsignor told her, because the Holy Father himself had pronounced that many Episcopal priests had valid holy orders, and that the wedding had been performed by such a cleric.

Similarly, the Reverend Bobby-Joe Fenster of El Paso's Second Church of the Nazarene, Full Gospel, had managed to convince Mrs. Archie Newell that since it was true that God did indeed move in mysterious ways, perhaps there was a purpose in what had happened between Joe and that sweet little Mex girl. There was no disputing the fact that she'd gotten him away from the bottle, Praise God, something she had to admit *they* had been unable to do. And the Mex girl wasn't trying to get Joe to convert—not that he would, of course, but some of them did. . . . And he'd hate to tell her what he'd heard about how some Roman Catholic women did that.

And later, when the time came for Little Joseph/Jose to

begin school, the Reverend Fenster told Mrs. Newell he personally found nothing wrong in Little Joe going to the parochial school, especially since Joe's wife felt so strongly about it. He had Monsignor Delamar's word on it—and, giving the Devil his due, Delamar was an honorable man—that the nuns wouldn't try to convert the boy. And Mrs. Newell knew full well it was a shame what they were teaching in the public schools. Little Joe wasn't going to hear in the Saint Agnes Parochial School that human beings are nothing more than super developed orangutans.

When Jose Newell was a junior in high school, he joined the Texas National Guard. The first summer they sent him to basic training. And the summer after he graduated, the National Guard sent him to radio school at Fort Monmouth, New Jersey. He learned enough there to get taken on at Lone Star Aviation at the El Paso airport, where he repaired aviation radios. During that time his boss took him for his first airplane ride, in a Cessna 172. And from that moment, Jose Newell knew that all he wanted to be in life was an aviator.

He soloed in a Piper Cub. Subsequently he picked up what to Oliver seemed a nearly incredible thousand hours by swapping his electronic expertise for time, and by flying as an unpaid copilot on business aviation airplanes. He had a commercial multiengine land ticket with an instrument rating.

And while he was doing this, he went to Officer Candidate School in the Texas National Guard and at Fort Benning, giving up two weekends a month and taking six weeks' unpaid vacation two summers in a row to do it. He had by then met and wooed Lucy, and decided that there was no real future for them in his being an airfield bum. He had seen, he said, too many guys in leather jackets and wire-rimmed sunglasses hanging around airfields competing with two hundred similarly qualified pilots for whatever rare flying jobs were available.

The airlines, Jose Newell continued, wanted six-foot, preferably blond, Anglo-Saxon pilots who had several thousand hours of Air Force or Navy/Marine jet time. (He said this without rancor, accepting it as the way things were.) And the Air Force and Navy/Marines were accepting for flight training only college graduates, so that was out, too. Air charter companies, or corporations hiring pilots, were even worse.

But when Jose Newell had graduated from OCS they commissioned him a second lieutenant in the Signal Corps, and he thought that might open a door that would let him fly without becoming an airfield bum.

There had been a Texas Army National Guard Aviation Company at the airfield that flew Sikorsky CH-34s. As a civilian, the commanding officer (who was a friend of Jose Newell's) flew a Beech King Air for an El Paso real estate operator. The deal struck was that because the helicopter company desperately needed someone to maintain its avionics, Lieutenant Newell would transfer into it from the Field Artillery unit he belonged to . . . providing the helicopter company sent him to flight school.

Six months after Jose Newell transferred to the National Guard helicopter company, he was ordered to active duty for the purpose of attending the prescribed course of instruction leading to designation as a rotary-wing aviator.

"What I figure," Jose Newell, somewhat thickly, told Johnny Newell just before they called it a night, "is that if the Army is as hard up for avionic maintenance officers as the National Guard, maybe I can wangle extended—maybe even indefinite—active duty, college degree or no college degree."

"I don't really know what I'm talking about," Oliver told him, "but I thought there was a board here that would rate you on your civilian experience. It seems pretty silly to send you through the whole course when someone with your experience should be able to transition to choppers in a couple of weeks."

"Catch-22," Newell replied. "They will rate regular or reserve officers on indefinite active duty, but not National Guard. And without a goddamned degree, I can't come on active duty, much less get a regular commission. But there's always an exception to every rule, and I intend to be it."

When they drove into the driveway of Quarters #1 in Jose Newell's MGB of Many Colors, Captain John S. Oliver saw no sign of life within the house. So they went right to work on Marjorie Bellmon's MGB.

It turned out that Jose Newell's shot-in-the-dark diagnosis had been right on the money. He pulled the cap from the distributor, wedged a screwdriver into the coil wire hole, held it up to the light, and showed Oliver a tiny crack.

Two minutes later, with a new cap in place, the engine coughed into life.

"It sounds like a thrashing machine," Jose said. "Who tuned this thing, anyway?"

As Jose Newell, with all the delicacy of a surgeon, was adjusting the MGB's timing, Miss Marjorie Bellmon, sleepy-eyed, in a bathrobe, came into the carport from the kitchen.

"Does this mean I won't have to shoot it?" she asked. "Or is that too much to hope for?"

"I am the compleat aide," Johnny said. "All problems solved, the difficult immediately, the impossible a few minutes later. Marjorie, say hello to Jose Newell, Master MG Mechanic, who I imported all the way from Texas to get your ridiculous little machine running. Miss Bellmon, Ma'am, Lieutenant Newell of the Texas National Guard. My new roommate."

"Hi," Marjorie said. "And welcome, welcome, welcome! But don't let me disturb you. I'll put some coffee on, and get some clothes on. And you just keep doing what you're doing. *Please*!"

"Very nice," Jose Newell said, softly, after Marjorie had gone back in the house.

"She's a pal of mine, Jose, that's all," Oliver said.

Newell's eyebrows rose in question.

"You've heard about love at first sight? Well, with Marjorie and me, it was pals at first sight. Once I got used to the idea, I found I like it that way."

"That's interesting," Jose said, and returned his attention to the engine.

Fifteen minutes later, as Captain Oliver and Lieutenant Newell were being served poached eggs atop English muffins by Miss Bellmon in the kitchen, the phone rang and Oliver rose to answer it.

"Stay there," Marjorie ordered. "Dad's up. I heard him. And it's your day off."

A minute after that, Major General Robert F. Bellmon walked into his kitchen. He was wearing a uniform shirt and trousers, but no tie, and he was unshaven.

Oliver and Newell rose to their feet.

"Good morning, General," Oliver said.

"I thought I heard your voice out here," Bellmon said distractedly.

He's upset as hell about something, Oliver thought.

"Sir, this is Lieutenant Newell," Oliver said.

"Who just brought my car back from the dead," Marjorie added.

Absently, General Bellmon nodded at Newell.

"One of the Board's Chinooks just went in," Bellmon said. "Badly. The other side of Enterprise. The crew's apparently dead."

"Oh, God!" Marjorie said softly.

"I'm going to the crash," Bellmon said. "You want to come along with me, Johnny?"

When Bellmon looked at him, Oliver gestured at his civilian clothing. He was wearing a red nylon ski jacket and blue jeans.

"So what?" Bellmon replied. "Call Hanchey and lay on a bird for us."

Oliver went to the note pad fixed to the wall beside the telephone and scribbled on it. Then he tore the sheet of paper off.

"Call this number, Jose," he said. "Tell them to have a Huey warmed up by the time the General and I get there."

"Yes, Sir," Jose Newell said.

"Give that piece of paper to Marjorie," General Bellmon ordered. "Lieutenant . . . what's your name?"

"Newell, Sir."

"Lieutenant Newell can come with us. We may need another pair of hands."

[FOUR]
Hanchey Army Airfield
Fort Rucker, Alabama
0905 Hours 12 January 1964

Though it was Lieutenant Joseph M. Newell's first ride in a Bell HU-1-Series helicopter, it was not his first ride in a helicopter. So he knew more or less what was going on in it.

He found a headset and plugged it in, and listened as Bellmon and Oliver went through the takeoff checklist. He found that interesting, not just in itself, nor because the pilot went through the list very carefully, but because General Bellmon himself had chosen to sit in the right, pilot's, seat.

Oliver's voice came over the earphones.

''Hanchey . . . where the hell is the radio plate? Hanchey, this is Army HU-1B Helicopter, radio call unknown, Code Eight, in front of Operations.''

''Go ahead, Code Eight.''

''Six One Seven,'' General Bellmon's voice came metallically over the intercom. ''The call-sign plate fell off. The glue came off. This is Army Six One Seven.''

''Six One Seven for liftoff from present position,'' Oliver said. ''VFR, Local.'' That referred to the Visual Flight Rules.

''Hanchey clears six one seven for takeoff. The time is ten past the hour. There is no traffic in the area. The winds are five from the north, gusting to fifteen. The altimeter is two nine eight niner.''

''Six One Seven, light on the skids,'' Oliver said.

''Hanchey, have you got a location on the Chinook crash?'' General Bellmon's voice came over the intercom.

The Huey was by then four or five feet off the ground, moving away from the Hanchey hangers and parking ramps, north, into the wind, accelerating rapidly.

''All I have, Sir, is north of Enterprise,'' the Hanchey tower replied.

''OK,'' Bellmon's voice said, and then, ''Johnny, call Cairns and see what they have.''

There was a popping in the earphones as Oliver changed radio frequencies.

''Cairns, Army Six One Seven.''

''One Seven, Cairns.''

''Can you give me a position for the Chinook crash?'' Oliver asked. At the same moment, General Bellmon decided he had sufficient horizontal velocity and needed next a little altitude.

Jose Newell had to grab the aluminum pole through which the nylon straps of his seat were woven as Bellmon put the Huey in a steep climbing turn to the west.

He really can fly this thing, Newell thought, and then wondered why that surprised him.

"Army Six One Seven, Cairns. A crash emergency has been declared. No aircraft will fly into or over the ten-square-mile area north of U.S. Highway 84 and west of Alabama Highway 27. Those are the roads leading west and north from Enterprise. Six One Seven, acknowledge."

"This is General Bellmon," Newell heard Johnny Oliver say. "Where's the crash?"

"Sir, are you aboard Six One Seven?" Cairns asked.

"Yes, I am," Oliver said.

"Sir, the Chinook went in about five miles north-northwest of Enterprise."

"Are you in contact with Colonel McNair?" Bellmon's voice came over the earphones.

"Colonel McNair is at the crash site, Sir."

"OK," Bellmon said. "Six One Seven is going to the crash site. ETA five minutes."

"Yes, Sir," Cairns said.

Three minutes later, Second Lieutenant Joseph M. Newell heard Major General Bellmon said, "Oh, shit, there it is. *God*damn!"

Newell stuck his head out the door of the Huey. Eight hundred feet ahead of and below them, in a stand of very young pine trees, was the oblong, squarish fuselage of the crashed Chinook.

The U.S. Army CH-47-Series helicopters were manufactured by Boeing-Vertol, successor company to Piasecki Helicopters, which had designed and manufactured the CH-21 "Flying Banana." Like the CH-21, the Chinook used two equal-sized rotary wings, rather than, as in Sikorsky and Bell helicopters, one large rotary-wing and a smaller antitorque tail rotor. Powered by two 2650-shaft horsepower turbine engines, either of which could power both sixty-foot-diameter rotors in an emergency, the Chinook had a maximum gross takeoff weight of about fourteen tons, with a payload of about seven tons. The engines were mounted outside on each side of the rear rotor pylon, so that the fuselage, wide enough for a jeep or light artillery piece, was unobstructed. There was a ramp at the rear to facilitate loading.

The triple-bladed front rotor of the crashed Chinook was collapsed over the cockpit; the rear rotor was nowhere in sight. The left engine had been ripped from the rear pylon by the force of the crash. And the right engine had also been ripped loose, but was still connected by wire and cables to the pylon.

The stand of pine trees, all the same size, looked to Jose Newell to be about a quarter of a section of land. It was a tree farm. There was no sign of trees having been torn down or uprooted, except in the immediate vicinity of the crashed Chinook. That meant that the Chinook had fallen to the ground like a rock, Newell thought (and found the thought very uncomfortable). It had come down with little or no horizontal motion.

The crash itself was almost in the center of the tree farm. At the far side was an open field where four helicopters were sitting: three Hueys, two of them with Red Cross Aerial Ambulance markings, and a Hughes OH-6, a small, high-performance helicopter Newell had seen before only in pictures.

The field was half a mile from a dirt road, and Newell could see cars, trucks, police cars, and fire engines waiting there. They were apparently unable to get through a fence to cross the field.

Bellmon dropped the Huey close to the ground and flew over the Chinook low enough for Jose Newell to notice something he had missed when he had first caught sight of the downed helicopter: the fuselage was no longer straight; its forward and aft sections had been bent downward by the force of impact. The plexiglass windows on the roof of the cockpit were broken, and he saw people in the pilot's and copilot's seats inside. For an instant he wondered why they hadn't gotten out. And then he understood why: they were dead.

Without thinking about it, he crossed himself.

They reached the end of the stand of pines, and Bellmon prepared to land the Huey. A man wearing an International Distress Orange flight jacket came running out and tried to wave them off. Bellmon ignored him. With a just perceptible bump, the Huey sat down.

[FIVE]
5.3 Miles NNW of Enterprise, Alabama
0920 Hours 12 January 1964

The man in the International Distress Orange flight jacket who tried unsuccessfully to wave off General Bellmon's helicopter turned out to be an Army Aviation Board major.

He ran angrily to the Huey as it settled onto the field, but then recognized Bellmon.

When Bellmon climbed out, the Major saluted.

"I'm Major Crane, Sir," he said. "I didn't know it was you, General."

"No way you could. What happened?"

"The pilot declared an emergency, Sir," Major Crane reported. "He said he was experiencing severe vibration. Then he said he'd lost the rear rotor. Then he said he was going in."

"You heard him?" Bellmon asked.

"Yes, Sir. Colonel McNair and I were in the area, in the Hughes. We had spoken with them a minute or two before."

"Where is Colonel McNair?"

"At the Chinook, Sir. We were the first ones to get here. Cairns had them on radar and gave us a vector here. He sent me back here, Sir, to wait for the photographers."

Bellmon nodded and then walked briskly toward the treeline, with Oliver and Newell trailing behind him.

When he saw Bellmon and the others coming through the trees, Colonel John W. McNair, the President of the U.S. Army Aviation Board, also wearing an International Distress Orange flight jacket, was leaning against one of the young pines, fifty feet from the downed Chinook.

The Aviation Board, which was stationed on Fort Rucker, but was not subordinate to the Army Aviation Center, was charged with testing aircraft and associated equipment to reveal design discrepancies and to determine the levels of maintenance and spare parts which would be required to operate the aircraft, and its support equipment, in tactical use.

He straightened up and waited for them. He touched his hand to his forehead in a casual salute.

"Hello, Mac," Bellmon said, returning the salute. "Bad business, this."

"I'm surprised to see you here, General," McNair said.

"Why does that surprise you, Mac?" Bellmon replied icily.

"I meant so soon, Sir," McNair replied uncomfortably. "Hell, the medics just got here."

"Any idea what happened?"

"The tail rotor came off," McNair said, gesturing vaguely in the direction of the Chinook's rear pylon. "They came down like a stone. They were at twenty-five-hundred feet."

"Jesus!" Bellmon said.

He walked to the Chinook. Oliver followed him, and when he got closer took his Minox from his trousers pocket and started shooting pictures.

Colonel McNair saw him and trotted after him.

"What are you doing?" McNair demanded.

Bellmon stopped and turned.

"He's taking pictures, Mac," Bellmon said. "Since I don't see any official photographers around, that strikes me as a pretty good idea."

"The photographers are on the way," McNair said, and then, "CONARC will have to clear those pictures before they're released, Sir."

"What the hell is the matter with you, Mac?" Bellmon flared. "You didn't really suppose that Oliver was going to pass those pictures out to the press, did you?"

"No, Sir, of course not," McNair said. "I'm a little shaken, General."

Bellmon snorted and walked close to the Chinook.

At first glance, the copilot appeared to be bent over the control panel as though searching for something. But what that meant, Bellmon knew, was that he himself wasn't looking closely enough. He steeled himself, took a good long look, forced the nausea and the feeling of faintness down, and backed away. He turned around.

"You can knock off the picture taking, Johnny," he said. "Here come the photographers."

Oliver took the Minox from his eye and looked where Bellmon was pointing. Three soldiers and an officer, all laden down with cameras and photographic equipment, were trotting—panting with the exertion—through the young pines.

"I think you had better give that film to Colonel McNair's

people, Johnny,'' Bellmon said. ''After you've had them make me a set of prints.''

''Yes, Sir,'' Oliver said.

One of the photographers set his camera case on the ground, then started to trot toward the crashed fuselage.

''Hold it right there, son,'' Bellmon called, and then turned to Colonel McNair. ''Mac, how do we know this thing isn't going to blow up?''

''The fuel tanks didn't rupture, Sir,'' McNair said. ''And we've put three extinguisher loads into the engines and the panels.''

''OK, son,'' Bellmon said, gesturing to the photographer. ''Be thorough, but make it quick. Get the cockpit first.''

He turned again and walked around the Chinook. When he got to the back, he saw that the force of impact had caused the rear ramp door to open. When he looked inside, he saw that the pylon supports had buckled, apparently when the engines had torn loose. Then he saw the crew chief. He was lying on the fuselage floor, facedown, arms and legs spread, in a darkening, half-inch-deep puddle of blood.

He stared a moment and then completed his trip around the fuselage. Behind him he heard the sound of retching. He wondered if it was Oliver, or Oliver's second-lieutenant friend. But it would not have been right to turn around and look. He forced himself, instead, to set up in his mind the actions that would be required of him next, and the best way to accomplish them.

He went to Colonel McNair.

''The tanks didn't rupture,'' Bellmon said. ''That's something, I suppose.''

Colonel John W. McNair had of course informed General Bellmon not three minutes before that the tanks had not ruptured. Nevertheless, if he took offense at Bellmon checking this out for himself, the only sign was a tightening of his lips.

''Yes, Sir, it is. As hard as they must have hit, you would have thought the tanks would have ruptured.''

''Aside from the loss of the crew, the Air Force is going to love this,'' Bellmon said. '' 'If the Air Force, which has the necessary experience, and expertise, were conducting the testing, this tragedy could have been avoided,' '' Bellmon quoted. ''If I can hear my brother-in-law saying that, you can imagine what the other bastards are going to say.''

''Yes, Sir, I'm afraid that's just what's going to be said.''

''And O. K. Wendall tells me—and I believe—that without the Chinook, the 11th Air Assault can't hack it.''

''I agree with General Wendall, Sir,'' Colonel McNair said.

''And if the 11th Air Assault can't hack it, there goes the whole ball game,'' Bellmon said. ''The Army will be back where it was before, begging the Air Force for close-in air support.''

''I wouldn't go quite that far, Sir,'' Colonel McNair said. ''I believe that Army Aviation is an idea whose time has come.''

Bellmon grunted but didn't reply.

''What has to be done, Mac,'' he said, closing the subject, ''is to find out what went wrong here and fix it right now. And if that sounds like I'm telling you what to do, I'm sorry.''

''I agree completely, Sir.''

''How do you plan to handle the next of kin?'' Bellmon asked.

''Sir, I don't understand the question.''

''This is a suggestion, Mac, just that. But if it would help you to get things moving . . .''

''Oh,'' Colonel McNair said, and paused thoughtfully. ''Yes, Sir, that would help. If you would tell them that I'm here, trying to find out what happened, and that I'll come just as soon as I can . . . that would be a big help, Sir. I appreciate it.''

''OK,'' Bellmon said. ''You need anything else from the post, Mac, just speak up.''

''Yes, Sir, thank you, Sir.''

''Let's go, Johnny, we've done all we can do here,'' Bellmon said.

VII

[ONE]
Quarters #36
The U.S. Army Infantry Center
Fort Benning, Georgia
1015 Hours 12 January 1964

Susan Rand, barefoot, came down the stairs two at a time, ran into the living room, and grabbed the telephone. She was wearing a cotton blouse, mostly unbuttoned, and a pair of faded slacks. And nothing else. She had been in the shower.

The quarters assigned to General Rand were identical to, and four doors down from, the quarters he had been assigned during his last tour at Fort Benning. These were commonly referred to as Colonels' Quarters—two-story brick structures that had been constructed in the late 1930s to house captains.

Downstairs were the living room, the dining room, the study, the kitchen, and a toilet. There was a sun porch to the right and a small, screened-in porch at the back. Upstairs were three bedrooms, a smaller room known as the sewing room, and the bathroom. And above that was an attic. Some attics, though not the one in Quarters #36, had been finished, providing a little additional space under the eaves.

The last time a captain had occupied one of the houses on "Colonels' Row" had been in the very early days of War II. Rank hath its privileges, and captains and majors and lieutenant colonels had been moved elsewhere to accommodate colonels and generals. The post-War II Army had not shrunk to pre-war levels, so the quarters had continued to house colonels. Then Korea had come along, and now Vietnam was heating up. There were not sufficient quarters to house all the general officers assigned to Benning in generals' quarters, so Rand's promotion had not brought with it larger quarters than the ones he'd lived in the last time he was there.

That didn't bother either Rand or his wife. Colonels' quarters were plenty large, and they were comfortable. And compared to the quarters—half of a converted frame barracks—the Rands had occupied at Benning when newly promoted Captain Rand had reported for duty following his thirty-day Released POW Rehabilitation Leave, they were positively luxurious.

"Colonel Rand's quarters," Susan Rand said, answering the phone.

"Don't you mean 'General,' Susan?" Major General Robert F. Bellmon inquired teasingly.

"Oh, God," she said. "Bob, I was in the shower. I don't know where the hell he is."

"Could you find him? It's important."

"Maybe the garage," she said. "Hang on, Bob. If he was going someplace, he would have told me."

"Thank you."

Brigadier General George F. Rand came into the living room two minutes later. He was wearing oil- and grease-stained khakis, and his face and hands were grease-stained.

"Bob?" he said to the telephone.

"Yeah. Good morning, George."

"I was in the garage, trying to get the station wagon started. We stored it in Columbus while we were in Germany, and now that we finally had it hauled out here, it doesn't want to run. What's up?''

''I couldn't get through to Hok,'' Bellmon said.

''He's flying. Over near Fort Gordon.''

''We lost a Chinook this morning,'' Bellmon said. ''One of the Board's. Bad. The tail rotor came off, and it went in from twenty-five hundred feet.''

''Jesus Christ! The crew?''

''A captain, a lieutenant, and a staff sergeant. They all bought it,'' Bellmon said. ''Just as soon as I get off the phone, Barbara and I are going to call on the families.''

''Is there anything we can do?''

''What I want you to do is round up the Vertol tech reps and get them down here right away. Can you do that without O.K.'s permission?'' Technical Representatives of the various manufacturers—that is airframe, engine, and avionics engineering and maintenance employees—were assigned to Forts Rucker and Benning, and elsewhere, to provide technical support.

General Rand thought that over very briefly. In the absence of Major General Harrison O. K. Wendall, he was the division commander.

''I'll get right on it,'' he said. ''And call you and tell you when they've left.''

''It might be a good idea to send a Lycoming tech rep, or reps, if you can lay your hands on one,'' Bellmon said. ''I want to be able to tell the Air Force what caused this accident, and how we're fixing it, by the time they get their act in gear.''

''I understand,'' Rand said. ''Is there anything else we can send you?''

''I can't think of a thing at the moment.''

''I'll get back to you, General, as soon as I have anything to report,'' Rand said.

Bellmon hung up without saying anything else.

Rand broke the connection with his finger.

''What was that all about?'' Susan asked.

''Under other circumstances, seeing you standing there in your wet T-shirt . . .''

''It's not a T-shirt, it's a blouse,'' Susan Rand said, her face flushing when she looked down and saw how the wet cloth was clinging to her chest. ''In other words you're not going to tell me?''

''A Chinook crashed,'' he said. ''Killing the crew. Bob wants our tech reps sent down there right away.''

''Oh, my!'' Susan Rand said, then: ''You go in the kitchen and get that grease off of you; there's some Lava soap under the sink. I'll lay out a uniform for you.''

He nodded absently and then dialed the number of the field-grade OD.

[TWO]
Office of the Commanding General
The Army Aviation Center & Fort Rucker, Alabama
1020 Hours 12 January 1964

Bellmon put the handset in the cradle and looked up at the door. Captain John S. Oliver was standing there, now in uniform.

''That was quick, Johnny,'' he said. In a remarkably short time, Oliver had dropped the General off behind Quarters #1 (technically violating Bellmon's own rules about aircraft activity in the housing area), returned the Huey to Hanchey Army Airfield, gone to his own quarters, changed into a uniform, and then come to the General's office.

''It's amazing, Sir,'' Oliver said. ''MP radar breaks down whenever a car with a Number 1 Post decal on it gets near.''

Bellmon flashed him a quick, disapproving look. *He's telling the truth; he must have gone like hell to get here this quickly. Still, he wasn't speeding because of my de facto immunity, but because he knew he was really needed here as quickly as he could get here.*

And then General Bellmon saw who was standing behind Captain Oliver.

''Good morning, Sergeant Major.''

''Good morning, Sir,'' the sergeant major said. He was a stocky man in his late thirties, sharp-featured, his hair cut so close the skin of his scalp was visible.

''Oliver send for you?'' Bellmon asked.

''The AOD called me, General,'' the sergeant major said. ''I went right out to the Board.''

He walked into the room and laid three service records on Bellmon's desk.

"The sergeant and the Captain lived in quarters, General," the sergeant major said. "The Lieutenant lived in Ozark. The notification teams are on their way. You want me to put in calls to DCSOPS and CONARC, Sir?"

"Send a priority TWX to DCSOPS, info to CONARC," Bellmon ordered. "Very brief. There has been a fatal crash. We are investigating. I don't want to give them a chance to say something on the telephone I don't want to hear."

"Yes, Sir," the sergeant major said.

"Get the TWXes out, and then, if you will, come with us to see the sergeant's family. Then you come back here and hold the place down while Oliver and Mrs. Bellmon and I go see the others."

The sergeant major nodded his acceptance of the orders, then asked, "What about the press, Sir? There have been calls. The PIO's out here."

"Tell him to say the same thing we're telling DCSOPS," Bellmon said. "And that he is not, *not,* to permit the press anywhere near the crash site until the accident-investigation people are through out there."

"Sir, I took the liberty of notifying the Chief of Staff. He's on his way in."

"Good man," Bellmon said. He exhaled audibly and moved his fingers around the papers on his desk. "The car here, Johnny?"

"Yes, Sir."

"I just talked to General Rand at Benning, Sergeant Major," Bellmon said. "He will telephone reporting when the Vertol tech reps, and Lycoming, if he can lay his hands on one, will leave Benning. When he does, notify Colonel McNair and the Accident Investigation Board that they're on the way. You better make arrangements to billet them, and lay on a car—two cars, as many as they'll need—for them."

"Yes, Sir," the sergeant major said.

One of the telephones on Bellmon's desk rang. Oliver grabbed it.

"Commanding General's Office, Captain Oliver, Sir."

"Johnny, this is Geoff Craig. Have you got names for the

people that went in on the Chinook? Was Lieutenant Jack Dant one of them?''

''Who told you a Chinook went in?'' Oliver replied, aware that Bellmon was looking at him with what was certainly curiosity, and more likely grave annoyance.

''It was on the radio,'' Geoff Craig said. ''Dant lives behind us. He's been flying a Chinook for the Board. His wife heard that one went in. She called the Board and they wouldn't tell her zip. So she came here. She's hysterical. Ursula just took her back to their house. I'm not asking to be told who it was, but, Jesus Christ, why can't we tell her if it's *not* Jack? She's pregnant, Johnny.''

Oliver had trouble finding his voice.

''Geoff, the notification team is on the way. But for Christ's sake, you keep your mouth shut until they get there.''

''Oh, *shit*!'' Geoff Craig said, and the line went dead.

''I presume, Oliver,'' Bellmon said icily, ''that you carefully considered the effect of what you just said before you said it.''

''Sir, that was Lieutenant Geoff Craig. Lieutenant Dant lives—lived—behind him in Ozark. Dant's wife, who's pregnant, heard about the crash on the radio and is hysterical. Denying that it was Dant would be despicable, and 'no comment' under the circumstances would have been the same thing as telling him. So I told him.''

Bellmon thought that over for a full ten seconds.

''You were right,'' he said finally. ''OK. Let's go.''

[THREE]
1105 Hours 12 January 1964

''Johnny,'' Major General Robert F. Bellmon said, ''I've been thinking.''

Oliver, who was sitting beside the driver in the front seat of the Chevrolet staff car, turned on the seat to face Bellmon, who was in the rear with Mrs. Bellmon.

''Yes, Sir?''

''There ought to be a better way than the way we did it earlier to communicate between a chopper—or my chopper, a command chopper, anyway—and a telephone.''

"Yes, Sir," Oliver said.

On the flight back from the crash site, Bellmon had wanted to ask questions and issue orders to people on the post. The only way this could be done was for the tower operator to call whomever Bellmon wanted to deal with on the telephone and then relay what Bellmon had to say.

"Not only was it inconvenient, but it tied up the tower operator," Bellmon said.

"Yes, Sir."

"See what can be done," Bellmon ordered. "Put it up close to the top of the list."

"Yes, Sir," Oliver said. He took a small wire-bound notebook from his shirt pocket and wrote *chopper phone* in it.

He had worked for Bellmon long enough to understand what that was all about. Bellmon had the habit, which Oliver found admirable and intended to emulate, of keeping himself from dwelling on a problem he had no immediate control over by forcing himself to think of something else. At the moment that something else had been access to the phone lines from a chopper.

What he was not allowing himself to dwell on was what they had just gone through twice, and were en route to go through again: dealing with the family of a soldier who would not be coming home that day because he was dead.

They had arrived at the sergeant's quarters while the notification team was still there. Notification teams consisted of a commissioned officer, who was of equal or superior rank to the deceased, but was in no case lower in rank than a captain; a chaplain, preferably of the same faith as the deceased; a physician; and an officer of the Adjutant General's Corps, who would explain to the surviving spouse what benefits were immediately available to her and her family and assist in making funeral arrangements.

The AGC officer at the sergeant's quarters had been a self-important paper pusher, a first john. But that didn't matter, because they had had the sergeant major with them, and whatever paper had to be pushed in behalf of the sergeant's family, he would push himself.

It had occurred to Oliver then that the last time he had encountered death in a family situation was when his parents had been killed. He'd seen some death since, but in 'Nam. Here it was worse. The dead are out of their misery; for the survivors, the misery is just starting.

The notification team sent to the Captain's quarters was leaving as the Commanding General, his wife, and his aide-de-camp arrived. The widow had been a carbon-steel-tough lady who had maintained her composure behind her shocked eyes, and had even insisted on making coffee.

"Sir," the driver said softly to Oliver, "aside from Ozark, I don't know where we're going."

"You know where Melody Lane is?"

"No, Sir."

"Well, where we're going is the next street from Melody Lane, and I know how to find that."

On the outskirts of Ozark, Johnny saw a staff car, loaded with officers, heading in the other direction back toward the post.

"I think that was the notification team, General," Oliver said.

Bellmon grunted but didn't reply.

They found Brookwood Lane without difficulty; it was the street before Melody Lane. And they found 123 Brookwood just as easily. There were cars parked all over the street in front of a modest, relatively new "ranch house." Oliver saw it had the number he was after.

When they were out of the car and walking up the driveway, Oliver could see the back of Geoff Craig's house through the carport.

He walked to the door and pushed the doorbell button. He could hear the chimes inside playing, "There's No Place Like Home." A moment later the door opened.

A striking redhead appeared. She was fashionably dressed, blue-eyed, with lips a sensual red lipstick slash against her pale skin. Her hair was cut short in what Oliver thought of as Roaring Twenties Flapper Style. The redhead looked at him with what, for a moment, he thought was recognition. But that look, even before she spoke, was replaced by a look of anger. Or contempt.

"What do you want, Johnny?" she snapped.

How does she know my name? Oliver thought. *I would remember her; she's gorgeous. . . . But where?*

He hesitated just long enough for Bellmon to step in.

''Good morning,'' he said. ''I'm General Bellmon and this is Mrs. Bellmon. We've come to offer our condolences.''

''Oh, Jesus Christ!'' the redhead said disgustedly.

''I beg your pardon?'' Bellmon asked.

''The widow is unavailable, General.''

''Ma'am?'' Bellmon asked, confused by the hostility.

''She's been sedated. She was hysterical, thanks to you. And the last thing in the world she needs to see right now is another goddamned uniform.''

The door slammed shut.

''My God!'' Barbara Bellmon said softly. ''What was that all about?''

''I haven't the faintest idea,'' Bellmon said.

''Let me try,'' Barbara said. ''There has to be some misunderstanding—''

''No,'' Bellmon said, not loudly, but in an unmistakable I-will-be-obeyed tone of voice. He looked at Oliver, fixed him with a cold stare, and said, ''The first thing that pops into my mind, Oliver, is that whatever is going on here is connected with that telephone conversation you had with Lieutenant Craig. I hope I'm wrong, but whatever it is, you will stay here until you find out what it is. Then—without opening your mouth beforehand—you will tell me what you found out. Clear?''

''Yes, Sir.''

''Come on, Barbara,'' Bellmon said, and took his wife's arm.

''What telephone call with Geoff?'' Barbara asked.

Bellmon did not respond, and his wife did not press him. They got into the staff car, the driver closed the door, got behind the wheel, and the car drove off.

Now what the hell do I do? Oliver wondered.

The question was answered for him about a minute—which seemed much longer than that—later. The front door of the ranch house opened and Geoff Craig came out.

''This is a real bitch, isn't it?'' Geoff said. Then, without waiting for Oliver to reply, he gestured toward his own house and went on: ''Come on, I need a little liquid courage. And you look like you could use one too.''

Oliver started to decline, to tell him "Sorry, I'm on duty." But then he changed his mind. *To hell with it,* he decided. *I'll drink vodka.*

As they walked through the Dant carport, Johnny asked, "Who's the Dragon Lady? What the hell was that all about?"

"I don't know her name," Geoff said. "She's a friend of Joan Dant's. She was there when that fucking chancre mechanic showed his ass. Maybe she shouldn't have run the Bellmons off, but I don't blame her for being pissed. I'm pretty fucking pissed myself."

"I don't have any idea what you're talking about," Oliver said.

By then they had crossed the adjoining backyards, separated by a low line of hedges, and were at the Craigs' back door. Geoff opened it, and Oliver followed him inside.

Geoff went to the bar, gestured toward a bottle of Ambassador Twelve-Year-Old scotch, and raised his eyebrows in question.

"I better not," Oliver said. "You have any vodka? I go from here to report to the General."

Geoff found a bottle of vodka and a glass and handed them to Oliver. Then he poured an inch of scotch in another glass, drank it down, grimaced, and poured another inch.

"He was a good guy," he said. "What the hell happened? You know?"

"We were out there," Oliver said. "A few miles north of Enterprise. They lost the rear rotor and went in like a stone, straight down from twenty-five hundred."

"Christ!" Geoff said, exhaled audibly, and then took a sip of the scotch. "He wasn't back from 'Nam a year . . . eight months," he added thoughtfully, "something like that. Maybe less. His wife is seven months gone."

"Tell me about the chancre mechanic," Oliver said. "In fact, start from the beginning."

Geoff shrugged. And then, obviously collecting the facts in his mind, he walked into the living room and opened a cigar box on a table beside a Charles Eames chair. He held up two until Oliver shook his head no, then put one back in the box. After that he went to a drawer in the kitchen cabinets and took out a box of wooden matches. And after that he went through what to Oliver was an unnecessarily slow ritual of lighting the long, fairly thick, nearly black cigar. He finally got it going, took a puff, looked at the glowing end, and turned to face Johnny Oliver.

"Dant was over here about six," Geoff said. "He saw my lights on. I was cracking the goddamned books. He made me a deal. If he could borrow my car, he would go by the Commissary and the Class VI store and pick up steaks and beer and booze. Then Joan wouldn't have to drive him to work. What the hell, it saved me a trip out there to get the booze, so I let him have it."

"You were pretty good friends?"

Geoff hesitated a moment before answering.

"No, not really. He was really a hotshot. Big deal. A Board Test Pilot, dealing with a student schmuck like me. But Ursula and Joan are pretty close, so what the hell? Anyway, when he left, I went back to the books. Joan came over—she usually does—about half past eight. So I retreated to the office. About quarter to nine, the two of them come in the office, and they tell me that they heard on the radio that a large chopper went in, and they're afraid maybe it's Dant. So, wiseass that I am, I tell them that if the radio station knows, the Board knew, and if it was Jack, they would have called and told her. Or something. They come back in thirty minutes and tell me Joan's called the Board, and they won't tell her zilch. I told her to come home and sit by the phone, and I'll see what I can find out. So I called the pilots' lounge at the Board, and there's no answer. So I called the Board OD—another chickenshit sonofabitch—and he tells me to mind my own goddamned business. So that's when I called you."

"I'm on Bellmon's shit list for telling you what I did," Oliver said. "He was there when you called. We were just back from the wreck."

"How did Dant buy it?"

"For however long it takes to drop from twenty-five hundred feet. They must have known they were in the deep shit. But they kept their cool. They made radio reports, and they cut the switches. There was no fire. It came down straight and level. They were still in their seats when we got there."

"How the hell can a rotor come off?" Geoff asked.

Oliver shrugged helplessly.

"Tell me about the chancre mechanic," he said.

"Well, after you gave me the word, I went over there. I didn't say a word, not to Joan, and not to Ursula. That was tough, 'cause Ursula kept telling her everything was just ginger-peachy. I was there about five minutes when the notification team arrived. Jesus Christ, that was a bitch. Joan looked at me, and I know she knows I knew."

"You did the right thing," Johnny Oliver said.

"Tell me about it," Geoff said. "Well, they were all right. Some major from the Board, a guy from the AG, a chaplain, and a doctor."

"What about him?" Oliver asked.

"Oh, he was all right," Geoff said. "Joan knew him. He's a baby doctor, I think. Anyway, he gave her some pills and told her not to take them unless she thought she really needed them—"

"Then what chancre mechanic are you talking about?" Oliver interrupted.

"Chancre mechanics, plural—two of them," Geoff said. "They came as the notification team was leaving. By then the house was getting full of people."

"Including the Dragon Lady?"

"She got there right after the notification team did. I don't know I told you who she is. Some friend of Joan Dant's. But she was helpful. And then, as I said, these two chancre mechanics show up, and they ask to speak to Joan alone, so they go into the bedroom. The redhead goes with them. The next thing I hear is Joan wailing, I mean, really wailing, howling, like a run-over dog. And then the redhead throws them out. She can throw a real mad. And has a very *colorful* vocabulary. She told the tall sonofabitch—I don't remember the words, but you could tell he didn't expect to hear them from a woman—"

"I don't understand," Johnny said.

"The clowns weren't doctors . . . I mean, they aren't assigned to the hospital treating people. They're pathologists, the redhead told me they said. Anyway, what they're doing is studying the effects of a crash on the body. What they wanted was Joan to sign some paper authorizing them to cut up Dant to see what the damage was. Not the cause of death, if you follow me, but the other damage. How many bones were broken, what happened to the organs. . . . You get the picture? Not an ordinary autopsy. They wanted to cut him up in little pieces . . . and *'retain specimens.'* In other words, put his brain and his liver and whatever in jars.''

''Oh, shit! And they told the wife what they wanted?''

''After she told them no, they told her how important it was, and how she was selfishly standing in the way of science. That's when the redhead threw them out. Five minutes later you showed up. The redhead had calmed Joan down to the point where she wasn't moaning, and she'd just told me what happened, when you rang the doorbell.''

Oliver exhaled audibly and shrugged.

''Put a uniform on, Geoff,'' Oliver said.

''What the hell for?''

''Because we're going out to see Bellmon and you're going to tell him what you told me.''

''I don't think I want to do that,'' Geoff Craig said.

''I'm not asking you, Geoff,'' Oliver said.

Geoff Craig's eyes and lips tightened. He met Oliver's eyes and locked with them for a long moment.

''What the hell,'' he said. ''I'll have to go out there anyway to get my car back, won't I?''

''The damage is done here,'' Oliver said. ''The thing to do is see that it doesn't happen again.''

''You don't really think Bellmon will do anything about it, do you? Those clowns will say they were just doing their duty.''

''I don't know if he will or not, but I think we have to find out.''

''You get me their names, Johnny, and I'll make sure they don't do it again,'' Geoff said, almost conversationally, and with a smile.

Johnny Oliver suddenly remembered that before he had gone to flight school, Geoff Craig had been a Green Beret. And Johnny Oliver had seen that look, and that smile, on the faces of Green Berets before.

''And get yourself court-martialed,'' Oliver said.

''No way. They would have to ask me why I did it. They

wouldn't like the answer. And they really wouldn't like to see it reported in the newspapers: 'Decorated Vietnam Veteran Charged with Assault on Army Doctors.' "

"Don't be a damned fool," Johnny Oliver said.

"Did it ever occur to you, Captain," Geoff Craig said, "that the trouble with you Regular Army career types is that you worry more about your sacred careers than about right and wrong?"

"Get dressed," Oliver said flatly.

"Yes, Sir, Captain," Geoff said, and gave a mocking salute.

[FOUR]
Office of the Commanding General
The Army Aviation Center & Fort Rucker, Alabama
1145 Hours 12 January 1964

There were several hundred first lieutenants currently undergoing flight training at the Army Aviation Center. Major General Robert F. Bellmon knew little about any of them except that they almost invariably exceeded the criteria established (in the most part by him) for the selection of officers for flight training. That is, they met stiff physical standards, they had exceeded a specific score on what was the Army variation of an IQ test, and, over all, they had been judged to be worth the expenditure of an awesome amount of the Army's money—the money being devoted to the effort to teach them how to fly.

Moreover, since there were three times as many applications for flight training as there were spaces, it had been possible for the selection boards to select the cream of the applicants. In a very real sense, Bellmon thought, the first lieutenants in flight training were the crème de la crème. And under any other circumstances he would have been very favorably impressed with First Lieutenant Geoffrey Craig, who at the moment sat in a leather chair at the other side of Bellmon's desk.

He was tall and well set up, and he looked like an officer. You could deny it all you wanted to, but looks did count, and young Craig looked like a recruiting poster. His uniform was impeccably tailored. And, beyond all that, there was obviously some substance to Lieutenant Craig: on his chest, in addition to his parachutists' wings, were ribbons representing the Silver Star; two Bronze Stars; four Purple Hearts; service within the Republic of South Vietnam; and an array of foreign decorations, including the two awards of the South Vietnamese Cross of Gallantry, with Palm.

But, unlike most of the other student pilots at Rucker, young Craig had already considerable acquaintance with General Bellmon. In fact, the General happened to know a good deal about Craig. And that was the trouble. For there was much that he didn't like about Craig, the General thought, acknowledging his own prejudices.

But the main thing he didn't like was that Geoff Craig was a Green Beret.

Like many senior officers, Bellmon was philosophically opposed to the idea of "elite" military organizations. In his experience, the contributions made in the past by the parachute divisions, Ranger battalions, and especially by Special Forces, did not justify their extra cost in terms of materiel, training time, and the transfer of the brightest people from ordinary units to the special ones. Furthermore—although he knew it wasn't their fault; they were encouraged to do so—parachutists, Rangers, and especially again Green Berets, thought of themselves as better soldiers than ordinary troops, and they acted accordingly.

At the moment Geoff Craig was filling in flight school one of the spaces allocated to Special Forces, and not a space filled from out of the Armywide selection process. And that rankled Bellmon—though he acknowledged in fact that if Craig had competed against his peers, Armywide, he probably would have been selected anyhow. But the point was that he *hadn't* competed. He had been sent to flight school by Brigadier General Paul T. Hanrahan, Commandant of the U.S. Army Center for Special Warfare, at Fort Bragg, as a sort of consolation prize: Craig had gotten his commission in Vietnam, literally on the battlefield. Though he hadn't wanted to take it, he had agreed to do it—after being assured that as soon as he was sent home, he could resign.

Between the time of his commissioning and his return

home, resignation privileges of ''critically needed'' commissioned officers (which included everybody in Special Forces) had been suspended. Under normal conditions, that would have meant that Craig would have been assigned to Bragg training would-be Green Berets.

But Craig had friends in high places—most particularly his father's cousin, Lieutenant Colonel Craig W. Lowell.

Lowell had served as a teen-aged second lieutenant in Greece with Red Hanrahan when Hanrahan had been a lieutenant colonel. They had been Green Berets, in other words, before there were Green Berets.

And so Bellmon could now see Red Hanrahan and Craig Lowell (two members of the elite taking care of another, younger, fledgling) smiling smugly while they worked out what had to be done with Geoff Craig. Since Geoff had to spend a little more time in uniform, they would send him to flight school—with absolutely no concern that the space could be better used by some young officer who would either fly for the 11th Air Assault or elsewhere in the ''ordinary'' Army.

Bellmon recalled now, angrily, how Red Hanrahan had tried to have Johnny Oliver transferred to Bragg.

The only reason he backed off then was because I wanted Oliver for my aide. Otherwise he would have been indignant if I had refused the transfer. The implication being that what Oliver could do for the Berets was vastly more important than anything he could do here.

And Geoff himself already showed all the signs of Green Beret behavior: which is to say, he already felt free to ignore regulations that applied to lesser mortals. Specifically, Bellmon had learned (unofficially; if he had heard officially, he would have had to do something about it) that Geoff had a twin-engine Beech at the Ozark airport. While the Army was teaching him to fly helicopters, he was being taught to fly the Beech by an IP he had hired—in blatant violation of a prohibition against offpost flying, period.

Still, despite all the negatives he felt about young Craig, Bellmon was aware that he had to think carefully before taking any action concerning him. For he knew he was emotionally involved in what was going on.

''Geoff,'' he said, ''the story you've brought me about those pathologists who went out to see Mrs. Dant is what the lawyers call hearsay. You did not actually hear—''

''No, Sir. The redhead—''

''Whose name we don't know,'' Bellmon interrupted.

''I believe the redhead,'' Geoff said, and remembered to add, ''Sir.''

''But it's hearsay,'' Bellmon insisted.

''General,'' Geoff said, ''respectfully. I didn't want to bring this to you. Captain Oliver made it an order.''

''What's your point, Geoff?''

''Sir, why don't you just forget I came in here?''

''And you'll deal with it?'' Bellmon asked softly.

Geoff smiled and shrugged. And Bellmon looked at him icily; he was quite aware of what Craig intended to do to the pathologists.

''Lieutenant,'' he said, ''I don't know if you know this or not, but my wife and I were having cocktails in Washington with your—with Colonel Lowell—the day your father telephoned and said that you were in the Fort Jackson stockade about to face a general court-martial for breaking your drill sergeant's jaw. I know how you came to be a Green Beret. I would have hoped you had learned something in the time that has passed.''

Lieutenant Geoffrey Craig's face went white.

''Now you listen to me,'' Bellmon said. ''You will let this matter drop right where it is. Right where it is. If one of those doctors who allegedly said something he probably should not have said so much as cuts himself shaving, you had better have an absolutely airtight alibi. You may be a Green Beret, but you are first and foremost, to the exclusion of anything else, a commissioned officer. And you will behave like one. Do you understand me?''

''Yes, Sir.''

''You will discuss this—what may or may not have happened at the Dant home—with no one else. Is that clear?''

''Yes, Sir.''

''That will be all, Lieutenant,'' Bellmon said. ''Thank you for coming in to see me.''

Geoff stood up, came to attention, and saluted. Bellmon returned the salute. Geoff did an about-face and marched to the door.

"See that he gets home somehow," Bellmon said to Johnny Oliver when the door had closed behind Geoff. "You and I are going out to Cairns. They're bringing the Chinook back with a Flying Crane."

"Yes, Sir," Oliver said, and started for the door. Before he reached it, the sergeant major opened it and walked in.

"I thought you would want to see this, Sir," he said, and handed Bellmon a TWX.

OPERATIONAL IMMEDIATE

HQ CONARC FT MONROE VA 1620Z 11JAN64
COMMANDING GENERALS, ALL SUBCOMMANDS

1. FOLLOWING FROM HQ DA FURNISHED FOR COMPLIANCE.

2. RECEIPT WILL BE ACKNOWLEDGED BY TELEPHONE AND REPEAT AND URGENT TWX.
CARTER, GEN, CG CONARC

OPERATIONAL IMMEDIATE

HQ DEPT OF THE ARMY WASH DC 1600Z 11JAN64
COMMANDER-IN-CHIEF, US ARMY PACIFIC
COMMANDER-IN-CHIEF, US ARMY EUROPE
COMMANDING GENERAL, US ARMY ALASKA
COMMANDING GENERAL, US ARMY SOUTHERN COMMAND
COMMANDING GENERAL, US ARMY CONTINENTAL ARMY COMMAND

1. EFFECTIVE IMMEDIATELY ALL REPEAT ALL CH47(SERIES) CHINOOK AIRCRAFT ARE GROUNDED, WHEREVER LOCATED. CH47-SERIES AIRCRAFT IN FLIGHT WILL BE CONTACTED AND REDIRECTED TO LAND AT THE NEAREST MILITARY OR CIVILIAN AIRFIELD.

2. RECEIPT OF THIS ORDER WILL BE ACKNOWLEDGED BY URGENT TWX. NO REPEAT NO REQUESTS FOR EXCEPTIONS ARE DESIRED.

3. A TEAM OF USAF ACCIDENT INVESTIGATION EXPERTS ARE BEING SENT FROM WRIGHT-PATTERSON AF BASE OHIO TO FT RUCKER ALA TO ASSIST IN DETERMINING CAUSE OF FATAL CH47 ACCIDENT WHICH OCCURRED AT FT RUCKER THIS MORNING. THE POSSIBILITY EXISTS THAT ACCIDENT WAS CAUSED BY A DESIGN DEFICIENCY COMMON TO ALL CH47-SERIES AIRCRAFT.

FOR THE CHIEF OF STAFF:

WINDSOR, LT GEN, DCSOPS

Bellmon handed the TWX to Oliver.

"That's the message I didn't want General Windsor to give me over the phone," he said.

"Yes, Sir," the sergeant major said.

"Well, get the FOD to call them and acknowledge it," Bellmon said. "And then send them a TWX. I presume you've called Cairns?"

"Yes, Sir."

"And then call the hospital and tell them I want to see the commanding officer. And I also want to see here immediately the officers who went to see Mrs. Dant requesting permission to perform an autopsy on Lieutenant Dant's remains."

"Yes, Sir."

"Sir, I thought you were going out to Cairns."

"I am."

"When will you be back, Sir?"

"I don't know, Sergeant Major. Have them wait for me."

VIII

[ONE]
Cairns Army Airfield
Fort Rucker, Alabama
1220 Hours 12 January 1964

Major General Bellmon and Captain Oliver, who were standing in front of Base Operations, with the AOD hovering nervously around, could hear the CH-54 coming a long time before they could see it. It was the largest, most powerful helicopter in the world. Designed and built by Sikorsky, it was universally called the Flying Crane, despite all efforts of the Army to label it Tarhe, after some obscure Indian tribe.

Bellmon wondered now, for the hundredth time, what idiot was responsible for the Indian-name nonsense, and how much time and money had been wasted on the whole aircraft-naming business. Each aircraft had an official designation: a letter defining the type of machine, and a number. The H-13 was, in other words, Helicopter, type 13. The O-1 was a liaison airplane, type O-1. And the CH-47 ''Chinook'' was Cargo Helicopter, type 47.

For some reason ''Chinook'' had stuck. But few of the other Indian names had. The H-13 and the O-1 had also been assigned Indian names, but everybody called the H-13 the H-13, and the O-1 the O-1. Somehow the Indian name of the O-1A, the twin turboprop observation plane, the ''Mohawk,'' had also stuck. But the HU-1s were universally called Hueys. And more often than not you got a blank look when you referred to almost any other aircraft in the Army's inventory by its Indian name.

The troops called aircraft what they wanted to—Huey and Flying Crane or whatever. Whenever the name they gave an aircraft was the same as the one the Army officially dubbed it, that was coincidence and nothing more.

In industry, Bellmon thought, *if some middle-level manager came up with a stupid idea like that, wasting time and money on something that wasn't important in the first place, you could find out who he was and fire his ass. In the Army, you were stuck with the dumb sonofabitch.*

''There it is, Sir,'' Johnny Oliver said, and pointed to the east.

The Flying Crane, with the fuselage of the crashed Chinook dangling beneath it, was approaching Cairns low and slow. It was not alone in the sky. There were three Hueys and a Hughes OH-6, which had another infernal Indian name, but which, like the two other Light Observation Helicopters, was universally called the Loach. These others served to illustrate how enormous the Flying Crane was. *They look like porpoises around a whale,* he thought, *or maybe starlings around an eagle.*

As Bellmon watched, the OH-6 suddenly lowered its nose and picked up speed and then headed across the field as the Flying Crane continued its approach to the runway.

Mac McNair's in the Loach, Bellmon thought. *Supervising. Jesus* Christ! *Does he really think he knows more about the Crane than the people he's assigned to fly it? Now he's going to land, get out of the Loach, and get in the way of the people who have to put it on the ground.*

And then he had another thought: *I am in Disposition Condition Four. I will have to watch myself.*

''Let's walk over there, Johnny,'' Bellmon said evenly. He turned to the AOD. ''Major, there may be a call—''

''I'll have someone standing by to fetch you, General,'' the AOD said.

As they approached Hangar 104, they saw that the aircraft normally parked there had been moved. What stood instead on the concrete parking pad between Hangars 103 and 104 was a tank transporter Lowboy, a multiwheeled open trailer which sat very low (hence the name) to the ground. The intention, obviously, was to lower the crashed Chinook onto the Lowboy and then move it inside Hangar 104. Normally Hangar 104 was crowded with aircraft having their avionics worked on by SCATSA, but he saw that it was now just about empty.

There were over a hundred people scattered around the area. Some of them with reason to be there, but the great majority were just spectators who had somehow heard that the crashed Chinook was being brought home.

What McNair should be doing is getting these people out of the way.

As if on cue, Colonel Mac McNair's Loach landed. McNair stepped quickly out of it, trotted to the nearest officer he could see, and spoke to him. Then the officer started shooing people off the parking area. McNair walked to the Lowboy, where half a dozen officers and noncoms were standing, and then started looking around for the Flying Crane.

With a little bit of luck, the little bastard will get blown away by the downblast; he doesn't weigh a hundred and twenty pounds. Serve him right.

''Good afternoon, General,'' a voice said, and Bellmon turned to see Lieutenant Colonel Charles M. Augustus, the bald, barrel-chested SCATSA Commanding Officer. He was saluting.

''Hello, Charley,'' Bellmon said, returning the salute. ''Bad business, this. Have you met Johnny Oliver?''

''No, Sir,'' Augustus said. ''But I heard about him. How are you, Captain?''

''How do you do, Sir?'' Oliver said.

"The word is," Augustus said, "that they've grounded them, worldwide, 'pending determination of airworthiness.' "

"It just came down. That hurt you?"

"Yes, Sir. Bad. I have all kinds of radiation-pattern problems, especially with the FM antennas. I need another hundred hours' flight time."

"Can't be helped, Charley," Bellmon said.

"General, how would you feel if I went to the Chief Signal Officer and explained my problem?" Augustus asked.

The question momentarily surprised Bellmon. Signal Corps Lieutenant Colonels do not normally communicate directly with the Chief Signal Officer of the Army, who is not only a major general, but a member of the palace guard in the five-sided Palace on the Potomac.

But then Bellmon remembered that Lieutenant Colonel Augustus was not a typical commanding officer. For one thing, he had recently been selected for full colonel. For another, when he had come to Rucker, Bellmon had checked him out. He'd wondered why the Signal Corps had insisted on getting Augustus a space in the Blue Courses (the quickie flight-training program for senior officers), even though there were a number of Signal Corps full colonels who were not only already wearing wings, but who seemed better qualified to command SCATSA than Augustus.

What he'd learned about Augustus was that he was one of that small group of Signal Corps officers he thought of as warriors rather than technicians. For instance, Augustus had gone ashore on D-Day in Normandy as a nineteen-year-old second lieutenant in the Rangers, and he'd been a captain two days later. In Korea, he had served with Task Force Able, a hush-hush operation that operated behind the Chinese and North Korean lines. And between Korea and his assignment to Rucker, he had the reputation of being the Chief Signal Officer's hatchet man, sent from one Signal Corps unit to another around the world looking for deadwood to trim.

Although it was physically on Fort Rucker, SCATSA was directly subordinate to the Chief Signal Officer and not to Mac McNair at the Army Aviation Board. McNair, who understandably thought that SCATSA should be there to fix the

Board's avionics, and nothing more, period, was often unhappy with Augustus. For Augustus considered that his mission was to provide Army Aviation generally with the best available avionics—his choice, not McNair's. McNair had tried a half dozen times to have Augustus transferred and had failed. The Chief Signal Officer was pleased with what Augustus was doing, and how he was doing it, Q.E.D., or Augustus would not be Colonel (Designate) Charles M. Augustus.

As Bellmon considered this, he noticed that the insignia of rank on Augustus's flight jacket was still the silver leaf of a lieutenant colonel. Most officers made a beeline for the PX to obtain the insignia of their new rank as soon as it was announced they had been selected for promotion. Augustus, to his credit, obviously thought he had better things to do.

In balance, Bellmon concluded, the only thing wrong with Augustus that he could call to mind was that he was too chummy with the Green Berets, not just with his own brother, which was understandable, but in particular with Colonel Dick Fullbright, who Bellmon thought was a real pain in the ass.

"You think going to the Chief Signal Officer would do any good, Charley?" Bellmon asked.

"There's no sense in sending Chinooks to Vietnam, General, if they can't communicate with combat arms units on the ground," Augustus said.

"The larger question would seem to be the one about whether we're going to be able to put Chinooks in the field, period," Bellmon replied. When Augustus didn't answer, he went on: "If your question is, 'Would I be annoyed?,' the answer is 'No, I wouldn't.' I don't think it will do any good—the TWX came from DCSOPS himself—but good luck. If you get permission to fly one, maybe we can too."

"I think we're going to find something stupid happened here," Augustus said, gesturing toward the Chinook as it was maneuvered toward the Lowboy.

"Pilot error?" Bellmon asked a little coldly.

"No, I mean something like a nut that didn't get tightened. A wrench that got into the transmission. *Something really stupid.*"

Bellmon shrugged and turned his attention to the Chinook.

The Flying Crane hovered over the Lowboy and then, just perceptibly, moved closer to the ground. The Flying Crane had a second set of pilot's controls, in a sort of second cockpit, which face to the rear. It was being flown from that position now. The rear-cockpit pilot could see what he was doing; the pilot up front could not.

When the Chinook fuselage touched the Lowboy there was a faint thump and then a creaking sound.

Ground handlers jumped onto the Lowboy and disconnected the cables. When they were through, one at a time, they raised their arms over their heads in a signal. When all of them had their arms in the air, there was a change in the sound of the engines, and the Flying Crane rose straight up for fifty feet, turned so the nose was pointing toward the runways. And then, dropping its nose to gain speed, it flew away.

Bellmon started to walk toward the Lowboy and then turned to say something to Colonel Augustus. Augustus wasn't there. He looked around for him and saw him entering Hangar 104.

''He's headed for a telephone,'' Bellmon said to Oliver. ''I wouldn't be really surprised if he got away with it. Having the Chief Signal Officer lean on DCSOPS, I mean. He's an interesting—capable—fellow.''

''Yes, Sir,'' Oliver said. He thought: *And I'll just bet he would know how to rig a radio so that Bellmon can talk on the phone from a chopper. I'm damned sure going to ask him.*

Bellmon walked up to Colonel John W. McNair, who saluted.

''Two things, Mac,'' Bellmon said. ''First, I called George Rand at Benning and told him to send his Vertol tech reps—and the Lycoming ones if he can lay his hands on them—down here right away. It's important that we learn what caused this as soon as we can.''

''Thank you, Sir.''

''Second, there was an unfortunate situation at Mrs. Dant's home involving two pathologists from the hospital.''

''I don't quite understand, Sir.''

''Don't spread it around, Mac. This is just for you. But they asked the widow for permission to retain 'specimens,' and then told her which specimens they would like to have.''

"Goddamn!"

"I'll deal with it," Bellmon said. "But when you go over there . . . I thought you should know the situation."

"Yes, Sir. Thank you. Are we grounded?"

"Worldwide. And the Air Force, in what I am sure is a gesture of interservice camaraderie, is sending an accident-investigation team from Wright-Patt." The U.S. Air Force maintains a large aviation-engineering facility at Wright-Patterson Air Force Base, Ohio.

"The bastards were probably sitting around on their packed suitcases," McNair said, "waiting for something like this to happen. I don't need the sonsofbitches."

"They are to be shown every courtesy, Mac," Bellmon said.

"Yes, of course, Sir," McNair replied. "But in point of fact, we know as much about these choppers as anybody; more than they do."

"As soon as you find out anything, I want to know. No matter what time it is."

"Yes, Sir. We'll keep at it until we find out what happened."

Bellmon offered McNair his hand, and what could have been a smile, and then started back toward Base Operations.

In the staff car, as they drove past Hangar 104, where the Chinook was being slowly pulled into the hangar, Bellmon said, "What did we forget to do, Johnny?"

"I'm speaking from a position of ignorance, Sir; I don't know what we're supposed to do."

"We've dealt with the families. We're doing everything possible . . ." He paused and thought that over. "We're doing everything possible to determine the cause of the accident. The press. . . . Goddamn, we've forgotten the press!"

"I'll check with the PIO," Oliver said.

"You check with the PIO," Bellmon parroted. "He generally prepares a statement for me. I do not—*not*—want to talk to them. Make sure that what he has me say is the right thing and then tell him to release it."

"I could call and read it over the phone, Sir."

"No. If you don't have enough sense to know what should,

and should not, be said, you shouldn't be working for me. Just call and tell me that the PIO is handled."

"Yes, Sir."

"Your car is at the office?"

"Yes, Sir."

"Well, then. Go see the PIO and then you can take off."

"I'm available, Sir, for anything else you need me for."

"There is a hoary old Army saying, Captain Oliver," Bellmon said, "that you should never *counsel* an officer, or for that matter, a corporal, in the hearing of his peers or juniors, when you perceive that he has done something he should not have done and when you wish to make sure he does not make the same error in the future."

"Yes, Sir?" Oliver said, not sure where Bellmon was leading.

"That applies to what is next on my agenda. I am about to have a piece of the surgeon and those two medical clowns who went to see Mrs. Dant, and I don't think it would be a good idea if you were there when I tear it off."

[TWO]
1440 Hours 12 January 1964

The public information officer, a lieutenant colonel, seemed a little discomfited when Captain Oliver deleted several words, changed several others, and added a few more to the statement the PIO had prepared for the General to issue. And he was a little more discomfited when the Captain told him he could release it that way.

"You don't think the General would want to initial it?"

"No, Sir, that's just fine the way you wrote it."

"I would hate to put something out that he didn't like," the PIO said.

"So would I, but he told me to do it," Oliver said. "May I use your phone, Sir?"

"Help yourself."

"Office of the Commanding General, sergeant major speaking, Sir."

"Oliver, Sergeant Major. Is he available?"

"No, Sir, he is not."

"What's going on?"

"He's eating three assholes new assholes, Sir, and may I offer the comment that he's doing so with great skill and artistry?"

"Well, they deserve it."

"Yeah, they do," the sergeant major said. "Something I can do for you, Captain?"

"Tell him when he's finished that everything's OK at the PIO."

"Yes, Sir."

"Anything for me to do there, Sergeant Major?"

"Can't think of a thing, Sir."

"Then I guess I'm through," Oliver said. "I won't be leaving the post, if I'm needed, Sergeant. Try Annex #1 if I'm not in my room."

"All work and no play, Captain," the sergeant major said.

"That applies to sergeants major, too, Sergeant Major."

The sergeant major chuckled and hung up.

"Thank you, Colonel," Oliver said, and left the PIO office, a small frame ex-orderly room building. He got in the Pontiac and then remembered the film in the Minox. He was supposed to turn it over to the Aviation Board, but only after he'd had a set of prints made for the General.

When he drove to the Post Signal Photo Lab, he found that it was closed. Then he told himself he should have known better, it was Saturday. But the Aviation Board had its own photo lab, a mile or so away, and it was open. Although they were busy, when he told the DA civilian-in-charge what he had, he souped the film immediately. And then, in what Oliver thought was a remarkably short time, he produced a stack of wet 8½ × 11 prints.

"If you were to feed them to the drier, Captain—"

The drier was an enormous stainless steel drum. Prints were laid glossy side down on the drum, which was heated and slowly rotated. In one revolution of the drum, the prints were dried. Because it was such a slow process, Oliver was almost forced to study what the photographs showed. They had been expertly cropped during enlargement, producing up-close views of the pilots dead in the cockpit, the crew chief dead in the fuselage, and the torn-off engines and broken fuselage.

And the photolab had obligingly made two copies of each, which forced Oliver to examine them twice so he could separate them into two sets.

"One of these stacks for the Board?" he called to the DA civilian.

"No. I'm going to make eleven-by-fourteens for them," the DA civilian said. "You're pretty good with that Minox, Captain."

"Thank you."

When all the prints were dried, and in two envelopes, Oliver drove by Post Headquarters. Neither the staff car nor any of Bellmon's cars were in the parking lot, but the sergeant major's glistening four-year-old Cadillac was there, with its red (for enlisted) post decal, No. 1, so he went in.

"All work and no play, Sergeant Major," Oliver said.

"He said you'd be by with the pictures," the sergeant major said.

Interesting. I guess he expected me to have them printed before I quit. What if I'd forgotten?

"Here they are, two sets," Oliver said.

"I'll take one," the sergeant major said. "He won't want two. You hang on to the others. I'll have the FOD's driver take them to Quarters #1."

The sergeant major took the pictures out, examined them carefully, then put them back in the envelope. "Hell of a way to buy the farm," he said. "They must have known for a long time they were going to get it."

"Yeah. Why don't I put this set in the safe?"

"Because I just gave the keys and the log to the FOD and we'd have to go through all that when-was-it-opened-and-why-and-by-who bullshit if you did," the sergeant major said.

"OK. Tell me, Sergeant Major, what is the classification status of material that *will* be classified *before* it's actually officially classified?"

"I thought you were a nice guy, Captain," the sergeant major said, "but nice guys don't ask questions like that of a tired old sergeant."

Oliver laughed; and, taking the envelope with the pictures in it, he walked out of the office and drove to the BOQ.

Jose Newell's MGB of Many Colors was nowhere in sight, and Oliver was disappointed. He didn't want to go to Annex #1. The word that the Chinook had gone in would by now be common knowledge all over the post, and the guys in the annex would regard the General's dog-robber as a prime source for the straight poop on what had happened. And when the General's dog-robber declined to go into details, it would confirm the general consensus that dog-robbers as a class were uppity pricks who thought they were better than other people.

It would have been nice if Jose had been around to share a drink, but since he wasn't, Oliver decided to have one anyway. He hung his blouse in the closet, pulled down his tie, and made himself a stiff drink of the good scotch, reminding himself as he sat down to be careful. If he spilled booze on his trousers, it would be necessary to have the whole damned uniform dry-cleaned. Otherwise the blouse and trousers would be of a different hue, and that was not permitted for a dog-robber.

After he finished the first drink, he decided, (a) to change out of the trousers, which were still pressed sharply enough for another day's wear; and (b) to have another drink—of the ordinary scotch. But just then the telephone rang.

It was his telephone, the one, in other words, listed in his own name.

"Captain Oliver."

"Johnny, this is Liza Wood."

Who? . . .

"Hello, Liza Wood."

"I just wanted to apologize for climbing all over you."

Nice voice. Who the hell is Liza Wood? . . . Apologize?

"What?"

"I said, I just wanted to apologize—" Liza Wood said, and interrupted herself. "You don't have any idea who I am, do you?"

"Sure, I do."

"No, you don't," she said, and laughed, and he liked the sound of her laugh, too. "The Dragon Lady," she added. "I heard what you said to Geoff Craig in the carport."

"Oh."

Liza Wood is the Dragon Lady; that makes her that spectacular redhead in the Roaring Twenties hairdo who slammed the door in our face at the Dants'. Of course. She said "carport."

"If you heard that, Miss . . . Mrs.? . . . Wood, then I owe you an apology."

"You really don't remember me, do you?" she replied, as sadly, he thought, as surprised. "It's Mrs. Wood. I'm Allan Wood's wife. *Widow.*"

The image of Allan Wood—First Lieutenant Allan M. Wood—Artillery, Texas Aggie, classmate in Fixed Wing Class OFW 61-17, blond-headed, barrel-chested, thick-necked, Rebel—appeared instantly in Oliver's mind's eye. And then, as clearly, he saw Mrs. Wood. Not the high-fashion, tough-as-nails Dragon Lady, but a sweet and lovely madonna named Elizabeth, swollen with child, makeup-less pale face surrounded by a halo of soft red hair, holding shyly, lovingly, on to Allan's hand.

What did she say? Widow?

"What did you say?"

"I said, I'm Mrs. Wood. Allan's widow."

"I didn't know about that," Johnny Oliver said softly. "Jesus *Christ*!"

"It's almost eighteen months," Liza Wood said. "About the time you went to 'Nam."

How did she know when I went to 'Nam? That I went?

"Oh, God, I'm sorry, Elizabeth," Oliver said. "I didn't know. How did it happen?"

"He 'lost consciousness as a result of wounds caused by enemy small-arms fire and consequently lost control of his aircraft, which crashed,' " Liza Wood said softly but bitterly, and obviously quoting words she had read so many times she had memorized them. "Allan was flying a Beaver, trying to land it on some Green Beret mountaintop."

"I hadn't heard," Oliver said softly.

"I didn't think you had. I thought I would have heard from you if you had."

"Yeah, of course."

"I hate to hide behind my widow's weeds, Johnny, but

maybe if you told the General and his wife that I went through what Joan Dant went through today, they would understand why I acted the way I did."

"Geoff told me what happened," Oliver said. "And I took him to see General Bellmon, and I have it on impeccable authority that those two chancre mechanics. . . . Well, I don't have all the details, but they won't do anything like that again. But Geoff didn't know who you were . . . or about Allan."

She didn't answer for a long moment, then she said, "Well, I called to apologize, and now I have."

"Wait!" he said. "Don't hang up!"

Another long pause, then: "Why not?"

"I'd like to see you, Elizabeth, to talk to you," Oliver said.

"I call myself Liza now," she said after a moment. " 'Elizabeth' has too many memories connected with Allan. And for the same reason I don't think I want to see you. Not today, anyway. We'd wind up talking about Allan, and after what happened to Joan Dant today . . ."

Jack Dant got killed, not his wife. But I know what she means.

"Then we won't talk about Allan," Oliver blurted, and hearing what he had said, winced.

There was a long silence.

"That was a strange comment, Johnny," Liza said finally.

"I didn't mean it the way it sounded."

"How did you mean it?"

"I really wasn't thinking about making a pass at you," Oliver said. "You can believe that or not, it's the truth."

"Is that supposed to reassure me?" Liza asked. When there was no reply, she added, "I can handle passes, Johnny. I have had passes made at me by every sonofabitch in pants in Ozark, and by a surprising number of women, starting the day after Allan's funeral. Most of which began with offers to help me through my grief."

"The truth of the matter," Oliver said, somewhat coldly, resenting the implication that he was trying to get into her pants, "is that I am sitting here in my little cell, feeling sorry for myself, for . . . for a number of reasons. The only thing I have to look forward to tonight is getting drunk alone. Compared to that, having a couple of drinks with a pretty woman, even if that meant having to talk about her dead husband and my dead friend, seemed, at the moment, to be a desirable alternative.''

After the longest pause yet, Liza said, ''It no longer does?''

''Yes, of course it does. Could you come out to the club. . . . No, of course not. I forgot about the kid.''

''The *kid*, whose name is Allan, is with his grandparents. I took him over there when I heard about Jack Dant. But I don't want to come out there.''

''OK. Sorry.''

''I'd ask you here for a drink,'' Liza said. ''But there's nothing in the house.''

Is that a gentle putdown? Or am I supposed to offer to bring my own bottle?

''They sell all kinds of booze at the Class Six,'' Johnny said.

''You bring a bottle and I'll go to the A & P and get something for supper. What would you like? Stupid question. I'll get steaks. It's the fifth house from the Dants'.''

''What would you like from Class Six?''

There was another, the last, hesitation, and then the phone went dead in his ear.

She hung up. Because she didn't want to tell me what to get at the booze store? Or because she was on the edge of withdrawing the invitation?

[THREE]
123 Brookwood Lane
Ozark, Alabama
1705 Hours 12 January 1964

Johnny Oliver found without trouble a mailbox with WOOD painted on it, pulled the Pontiac to the curb, got out, took out the bags from the back seat, and walked up the driveway.

Liza Wood's house was larger than he expected it to be, almost as large, and thus almost as expensive, as Geoff Craig's house. And a colonel had been the original occupant of Geoff's house, not a first john. There was a Buick station wagon and a Chevrolet Corvair convertible in the carport.

He saw the glow of lights in the kitchen, and went to the

kitchen door. As he was looking for a doorbell button, the door opened.

"I don't know why they put front doors on these houses," Liza said. "They never get used."

Johnny saw that Liza had changed clothing since he had seen her at the Dants' (only a few hours before, but it seemed like days). But the blouse or shirt or whatever it was called, and the slacks, if that name applied to stretch trousers that hooked under the feet like ski pants, were as high-fashion as the dress she had been wearing earlier.

"Hello," he said.

"Hello, Johnny. Come on in."

He went inside and set the paper bags on a butcher block in the center of the kitchen.

"Is that your strategy, Johnny? Ply the widow with booze? What have you got in there, anyway?"

He felt his face flush with anger.

He tore both bags down their sides so the bottles were exposed.

"That's a bottle of scotch, a bottle of bourbon, a bottle of gin, and one of vermouth. Plus some wine. You hung up on me when I asked what you wanted from Class Six. So, trying to be a nice guy, I got some of each. And I already told you, trying to jump your bones is not on my agenda."

He turned to look at her.

She had moved back against one of the kitchen counters and had raised a leg so that her foot rested against the counter—a posture that served to draw the silk blouse tight against her chest. While he was sure it was entirely unintentional, the result was that he was made acutely aware of the curves of her body. "Sorry," she said, and then raised her eyes to his and said it again: "Sorry. I mean it. You always were a nice guy. I should have remembered."

After a moment he nodded his head curtly.

She pushed herself away from the kitchen counter and walked to the butcher block.

"Gin," she said, as she picked up the bottle. "It's been a long time since I had a martini. Thank you."

"I didn't know what you wanted."

Jesus Christ, she smells good. That's either a very expensive perfume, or I am in the terminal stages of lackanookie.

"Would you mind if we ate soon, right away? I didn't have any lunch."

"Neither did I," he said.

"You know how to light charcoal?" she asked.

"Yes, but my culinary skills end there."

Liza laughed. "No problem. I'm the compleat housewife. You start the fire—the grill is in the fireplace in the living room—and I'll make us a drink. Would you like a martini? Is that what you drink?"

"Martinis and me don't agree. They make me think I'm irresistible."

"They won't make me think that," Liza said. "One won't hurt you. I hate to get all the paraphernalia out to make just one martini, and one is all I'm going to have."

"OK. Why not?"

"Take off your blouse and I'll get you an apron," she said. "That's a new uniform, isn't it?"

"Thank you," he said. "Just about."

He unbuttoned the blouse.

"Captain," she said. "When did that happen?"

"When I came home from 'Nam," he said, handing the blouse to her.

"You must have made it on the five-percent list," she said as she walked out of the room carrying the blouse. When she didn't return immediately, he twisted the top loose on the gin bottle and started opening drawers looking for an opener for the vermouth.

She returned with a glass martini pitcher, two glasses, and an apron with HEAD COOK printed on it.

"Allan's," she said as she handed it to him.

He nodded.

"The charcoal and a can of lighter fluid are in the utility room," she said, pointing.

He got the fire going, then returned to the kitchen. There was a large pot on the stove now, and Liza was peeling potatoes. When she saw him, she put the knife down.

"You're not the barbeque type," she said. "You look distinctly out of place and uncomfortable in that apron."

"I'm your standard bachelor type."

"Yes," she said. "I often wondered about that."

"What about that?"

Instead of answering him, she wiped her hands on a towel and then went to the martini pitcher, which was filled with ice. She spilled the ice into the sink, then added fresh ice from the refrigerator.

"Allan always said that the key to a good martini was making sure that the *pitcher* was ice cold before you added the ice and the gin."

"Oh."

She carefully poured gin into a measuring cup, then poured that into the pitcher, added a few drops of vermouth, and began to stir it vigorously.

"Does it make you uncomfortable when I keep talking about Allan?" she asked.

"I don't see how it can be avoided."

She stopped stirring the mixture, went to the refrigerator, and took martini glasses from the freezer section. She poured the martinis with all the care of a chemist, then handed one of the glasses to Oliver.

"I won't mention Allan again," she said, "nor what happened down the street."

"It's all right, Elizabeth," he said, then corrected himself, *"Liza."*

"Mud in your eye, *Captain* Oliver," she said. "That gives us something to talk about. Did you make it on the five-percent list?"

He nodded, then sipped the martini. It was good, but he resolved to have no more than the one in his hand.

"And how did you get to be the General's dog-robber?" Liza asked. "Or is that rude, the dog-robber business?"

"I would rob somebody else's dog for him. He's quite a guy. But not my own dog."

She laughed, making him aware of her perfect teeth and the contrast of her lipstick against her skin.

"How'd you get the job?"

"I was sent over to see him. I didn't even know I was being considered. As a matter of fact, I thought I was in trouble.

I'd been making a pain in the ass of myself; they wanted to make me a Chinook IP.''

''Something wrong with that? Talking to Jack Dant gave me the idea that flying a Chinook was good duty.''

''I had a company for a while, a little while, in 'Nam. And I wanted—still want—another one. And I didn't want to spend two years teaching people how to fly. That gets dull in a hurry, and it's a dead end. You do a good job and you wind up a career IP. Not for me.''

''So how did you get to be Bellmon's aide?''

''The Department Commander sent me over. Now that I've had a chance to think about it, I think he was sympathetic. He couldn't let me go—I had all the brownie points to be an IP: total time, 'Nam time, that sort of thing—but if I was picked as the aide, that would get me out of it. He didn't tell me that, and when I walked in Bellmon's office, I thought I was going to get one of those words to the wise: 'For your own good, Captain, shut up and do what you're told.' I didn't know he needed an aide until he asked me why I wanted the job. At first I told him I didn't, but then I changed my mind.''

''Sorry?''

''No. He's a nice guy. I like his family.''

''Especially Marjorie?''

''You know her?''

''She's a friend of Geoff's wife. I've met her. Nice girl.''

''Her, too,'' Oliver said. ''I even like Cadet Captain Bobby, of the Long Gray Line.''

''Marrying the General's daughter is supposed to be a passport to good assignments,'' Liza said. ''Maybe you ought to go for her, Johnny.''

That's a hell of an odd thing for her to say.

''That's just not in the cards. We're pals. She looks at me as sort of a brother.''

''Huh,'' Liza grunted. ''So there's nobody special, Johnny?''

What the hell is she doing? Looking for a husband?

''No,'' he said.

She looked at him and saw what he was thinking.

''I know what you're thinking,'' she said. ''You're wrong. I'm not looking for a husband. Generally, I'm doing very well, thank you, in the real estate business. And specifically, I'm not about to marry another soldier. Once down that path is more than enough. You can relax.''

''How did you know what I was thinking?''

She didn't respond directly to his question.

''What that was was simple female curiosity. I used to wonder why you never had a girl.''

''Miss Right just hasn't come along,'' he said, lightly sarcastic. ''I'm still looking for the Aviator's Dream Girl.''

She laughed. ''The rich nymphomaniac who owns a liquor store?''

''Why not?''

''Allan used to say you were really afraid of women. That someone had hurt you and you weren't going to let that happen again.''

''You two talked about me?'' he asked, surprised and annoyed.

''You really don't know, do you?'' she said. ''We used to find nice girls for you. You would take them out, they could confess to me they really liked you, and then you would never call them again. No more than twice, anyway. What was that all about? Was Allan right about you? Are you afraid of women? Did somebody really disappoint you?''

''I don't know what you're talking about,'' he said, angry and uncomfortable.

She looked at her glass. ''I better not have any more of these. I'm feeling this one already.''

''There's more in the pitcher.''

She looked.

''So there is,'' she said. ''You want to live dangerously? And kill it? Then I'll put the pitcher away and remove the temptation.''

''Why not?'' Oliver said and drained his glass.

''You're not supposed to do that,'' Liza said with a chuckle. ''You're supposed to sip them.''

''I'll sip the seconds.''

''Oh, what the hell,'' Liza said, and drained hers. Then she refilled his glass, emptying the pitcher. There was considerably less martini in the pitcher than had appeared. His glass was only slightly over half full.

And he poured half of that into her glass.

She looked at it.

"I don't think chugalugging the first was such a good idea," she said. "I feel flushed."

"Then throw the rest away. I don't want any more." He went to the sink and emptied the glass. She handed him her glass. Their fingers touched. He started to empty her glass in the sink and saw it had been emptied.

"Now what?" she asked.

"Why don't we open the wine? And keep the booze for another time?"

"All right," she said. "Good idea."

She went to the wine, picked it up, and said, gaily, "Just think, four years ago some barefoot peasant in France squashed these grapes just for us."

The gaiety is forced. What the hell did I do wrong now?

She handed him the bottle, then found and handed him a corkscrew. While he was opening the wine, she went and found glasses.

"They're dusty," she said. "They haven't been used since . . . in a long time."

She held the glasses out to him, and he poured wine.

"Mud in your eye, Liz," Oliver said, raising his glass to her.

"Nastrovya," she replied and touched glasses and smiled at him and took a sip.

"Nice," he said, about the wine.

"Yes, it's very nice. I better finish peeling the potatoes. We're having french fries and a salad. Will that be enough?"

"Plenty."

"There's peas and lima beans in the freezer. They wouldn't take long."

"Steak and fries and salad will be enough."

"How long will the steaks take?"

"I have no idea," Oliver said, "but I suspect that first you have to wait until the black lumps in the grill turn gray."

She looked at him, not understanding. Then she did. *"Charcoal."* She laughed, met his eyes for a moment, then looked away. "I forgot. You're not the domestic type, are you?"

"No, Ma'am, I'm not."

"Well, go see if the little black lumps are turning gray," she said. "That will give us a starting point, anyway."

"Sure."

He went back to the charcoal grill and looked at the coals. They seemed to be starting to acquire a layer of ash.

What I need is something to stir them, to push them around.

He went to the kitchen door to ask Liza for a tool of some sort. She was standing by the sink, her head tilted back, taking a pull from the neck of the gin bottle. He was so surprised that he didn't move until she set the bottle down and started to look guiltily over her shoulder.

He walked quickly back to the charcoal grill, sensing that she had seen him. Confirmation of that came immediately.

"You weren't supposed to see me do that, damn you, Johnny," she called to him. He was very uncomfortable. He swore softly, then marched to the kitchen door and back inside. She was facing the sink again.

"You say something?"

There was no reply. And then he saw her back shaking, and knew she was crying. He walked close to the sink.

"Liza?" he asked softly. "Have I said something I shouldn't have?"

She shook herself from side to side, no.

"What's the matter?" he asked.

"Oh, Jesus!" she sobbed.

He touched her shoulder.

"Hey, whatever it is, it'll be all right. I'll fix it."

Now she snorted, and laughed.

"*That's* what I'm afraid of," she said, and turned around and looked into his eyes.

That's why there was no booze in the house! Why she wanted martinis. She's been hitting the bottle!

"You been drinking a little too much?" he asked gently.

"Oh, God," she said in exasperation, then chuckled a little bitterly. "That's not what's wrong with me."

"Then what is?"

Her hand came up and touched his cheek.

"I think you're going to be the thing that's wrong with me. Damn, I knew I shouldn't have called you!"

The hand on his cheek went around to the back of his neck and pulled his face to her.

And then they were kissing. Very chastely, but the warmth of her lips seemed to have an astonishing effect on him. He felt his heart thumping.

"Now do you know what's wrong with me?" Liza asked. "And you thought I was a lush!"

He bent his head to hers, and this time the kiss was not chaste. Her body pressed against his. There was no question what was going on.

Finally they broke apart.

She looked into his eyes. Her face was flushed, and her hair, for the first time, was out of place.

"Don't say anything," Liza said. "Just lock the door. I don't think my mother-in-law will come over here, but there's no sense taking any chances."

When he had locked the kitchen door, she took his hand and led him through the house into the bedroom.

IX

[ONE]
123 Brookwood Lane
Ozark, Alabama
1725 Hours 12 January 1964

"I'd love to know what you're thinking right now," Elizabeth Wood said to Johnny Oliver, "except maybe I really don't want to know."

He was lying on his back, and he'd been staring at the ceiling. He turned his head to look at her. She had pulled a sheet modestly over her; and she too was staring at the ceiling.

What I'm thinking, God forgive me, is that on a scale of one to ten, that piece of ass was a low four, maybe even a three. Her fault or mine? A little guilt trip, maybe? "Allan, ol' buddy, you didn't come back, so I'm jumping your wife"? But not to worry: she didn't like it much. Except toward the end, she lay there like a piece of cold liver. Without any life at all in her eyes. They were blank; she didn't see me.

"I feel very lucky," he said.

"You scored, you mean?" she said quickly.

"Hey, that's not what I meant."

He rolled over on his side and supported himself on his elbow.

It probably is my fault. Christ, she's absolutely gorgeous!

He touched her face, and felt her stiffen.

"How about privileged?" he asked, softly.

She turned her face and looked at him.

"I'm trying very hard to feel ashamed of myself."

"What for?"

"Come on, Johnny. *'What for?'* "

"I say again, 'What for?' "

"This is Allan's bed."

"Not anymore, it isn't," Johnny Oliver said. "It's *your* bed now. You, single, not you the couple."

Her face grew tight at that, and her lips pressed together.

Thinking that she might want him to comfort her, he put his hand on her shoulder and tried to pull her to him. But her whole body stiffened then, and he pulled harder. And finally she gave in and came to him, and he lay back and put his arm around her shoulder. He thrashed around until he was under the sheet with her. Then he kissed her hair.

"It's unfair," she said. "A man gets randy, and he goes looking for a little, and he's one of the boys. A sex-starved woman who gives into an impulse is a slut."

"I don't think you're a slut."

"Thank you," she said, and playfully kissed his chest. "Even if you don't mean it, and wouldn't have dared to agree with me."

He laughed, and when his chest moved, he was aware of her breasts on his abdomen.

"What if I'm pregnant?" she asked.

Jesus, what if she is? That's all I need, a problem like that.

"If you are, we'll deal with it," Johnny said, hoping he sounded more sincere than he felt.

"If I am, just to clear the air, it's my problem, not yours."

"Is this what they call postcoital depression?"

She chuckled. "Probably."

"Well, I'm not depressed," he said. "I feel better than I've felt in months."

You're pretty good at this lying bullshit, Oliver. When they throw your ass out of the Army, you can probably make a good living as a gigolo.

"Has it been that long for you, Johnny, months?"

"Yeah," he said. "It has."

That is, if we don't count that nurse at Fort Devens who just loved aviators.

"It's been two years for me," she said. "Allan went to 'Nam two years ago next week."

After a moment Johnny said, "I was one of those they sent to chopper school after fixed wing. They sent six of us from that class. The rest went right to 'Nam."

"How many from your fixed-wing class, all of you that went to 'Nam, are dead?"

"I don't know," he said. He thought it over. "Five, six, I suppose."

"You sound pretty callous."

"I don't mean to. It's a war. People get killed in wars. Always the other guy."

"You didn't get hurt?"

"I got shot, if that's what you mean."

"Where?"

"If you move your hand about four inches lower, you will feel a zipper," he said.

She moved her fingers and found the scar and traced it with the balls of her fingers. And then she suddenly sat up to get a look at it.

"My God, that's awful!"

"It wasn't as bad as it looks."

He gave in to the temptation to touch her breast, and then to cup it in his hand.

Now I'm getting horny again. What's going on? It is time, Oliver, to fold your tent and silently steal away, grateful that you didn't hang yourself up with a widow woman.

She looked down at him but didn't speak.

He felt himself growing erect.

And this time he wanted her to look at *him*, to be aware of *him*.

"Put your hand on it," he said.

"On what?"

"What do you think?"

"Johnny!"

He took her hand and directed it toward his groin. She closed her eyes, but she touched him. And then she rolled onto her back.

He guided himself into her. She pulled her knees back, but she turned her face to one side and kept her eyes tightly shut.

For a moment he stiffened. And then he stopped thrusting into her. There was no response. *Have I embarrassed her?*

Then he said, quietly, "Do you think this is sordid? Is that why you won't look at me?"

She shook her head but didn't respond.

And then he understood what she was doing, and he felt anger nearly overcome him.

It's not me after all! It's him!

That's pretty fucking perverse. Really sick. Am I just imagining it?

Goddamn it, goddamn her, *that's* just what she's doing!

"Look at me," he ordered.

She shook her head from side to side, no.

"Look at me, goddammit!"

She turned her face to him, opened her eyes, and glowered at him. He started to thrust at her again. Her eyes closed.

"Open your goddamned eyes!" he said.

They opened. He wasn't sure if she was angry or frightened. Maybe both.

"Don't you pretend I'm Allan!" he said, coldly furious.

There was pure hate in her eyes.

"That's obscene," she said disgustedly.

"You're goddamn right it is," he said and stopped moving in her. "And that's what you were doing. That's what happened before!"

"Let me up," she said, coldly. "Get off of me."

"No fucking way," he said. "You said you wanted some after two years and now you're going to get it. But it's going to cost you. You're going to know it's me and not him.'' Then he started thrusting into her again.

''You sonofabitch,'' she hissed angrily, looking at him now, tears running down her cheeks. ''You miserable sonofabitch! I hate you!''

He could feel her loins were responding to his.

Oh, God, don't let me come, not yet! Not until she realizes that I'm alive and in her, and Allan is really dead.

''Say my name,'' he said hoarsely, barely able to speak.

''Goddamn you!''

''Say it!''

''John. Johnny.''

''Say, 'I want you, Johnny.' ''

''I don't *want* to!'' she said, an entreaty.

''Say it!''

She sucked in her breath audibly.

''Oh, God!'' she moaned.

''Look in my eyes, and say, 'I want you, Johnny.' ''

''No!''

''You're fucking *me*, not a ghost!''

''Oh, *goddamn* you!''

''Say it!''

''I want you, Johnny! Oh, God, I want you, Johnny!''

He felt her begin to convulse as his orgasm overwhelmed him.

When he came to his senses, he was lying on her and she was crying. He rolled off her and pulled her onto him and held her tightly, until her convulsions stopped, until her breathing became normal again.

''Are you all right?'' he asked.

''I don't know,'' she said, icily, matter-of-factly. ''I've never been raped before.''

''You crazy bitch!'' he said, furiously, pushing her off him, sitting up in the bed, swinging his feet to the floor. ''Raped? Are you fucking kidding? I didn't drag *you* into this goddamned bedroom. I didn't pretend you were a goddamned woman who was two years dead.''

He started to get up. She moved quickly across the bed, and, hanging on to him, one arm around his neck, the other on his shoulder, prevented him from getting up.

"I'm sorry," she said.

He sat without moving. His body was tense and his muscles were like stone.

When she's let me go, I will get up. To hell with this!

She started to cry.

Bullshit! I'm not going to fall for that!

He could feel her warm breath on his back, and the pressure of her breasts.

He shook himself, violently, free of her, and turned to look at her, and all of a sudden he had his arms around her again. He held her against his chest, rubbing her back tenderly, and her hair, and after a while, she stopped crying.

And then she rolled away from him.

"I think you'd better go, Johnny," she said, softly, evenly.

He turned his head to look at her. Her face was turned away from him.

He rose from the bed and found his clothes, then got dressed and left.

[TWO]
The Officers' Open Mess
Fort Rucker, Alabama
0815 Hours 13 January 1964

First Lieutenant Charles J. Stevens, a long, lanky Arkansan, put his tray, which held ham and eggs, biscuits, two half-pint containers of milk, coffee, and the *Dothan Eagle*, on the table and unloaded it item by item, wordlessly. The table was already occupied by Second Lieutenant Joseph A. Newell and Captain John S. Oliver, who were in uniform. Stevens was dressed in a baseball cap, scuffed cowboy boots, blue jeans, a faded corduroy shirt, and a red ski parka.

" 'May I sit down?' " Oliver said, mockingly. "Why, *certainly* you can. I'm always grateful for your company."

"Fuck you, Oliver," Stevens said matter-of-factly. He put the empty tray on an adjacent table, took off his parka, put that on the table, and then sat down.

"What we have here, Jose," Oliver said, "is absolute proof of the theory that you can take the shitkicker out of the boonies, but you can't get the boonies out of the shitkicker."

"What are you, Jose?" Stevens said, "the aide-de-camp to the aide-de-camp?"

"Its name is Stevens," Oliver said. "I had to spend four years with the sonofabitch in college."

"What is that you're eating?" Stevens said, jabbing at Oliver's plate with his fork. "A breakfast steak? Are you putting on the dog or did you really do something energetic last night requiring a high-protein intake . . . such as getting laid?"

"I don't know what he did, but when I looked in his room last night at half past eight, he was sound asleep, looking satisfied," Newell said.

"Didn't anyone ever tell you, little man, that second lieutenants are to be seen and not heard?" Stevens said to Newell.

"Hey! Lay off. He's a pal of mine," Oliver said.

"No offense," Stevens said cheerily. "The reason I'm slumming, Johnny, sitting here in public with you and this talkative second lieutenant is that I figured you'd have the poop on what happened to Jack Dant."

"You knew him?" Oliver asked in reply.

Stevens nodded. "And so did you, at least sort of."

"What does that mean?"

"When you were doing your first John Wayne walkathon, he did most of the looking for you," Stevens said.

"What's a John Wayne walkathon?" Jose Newell asked.

Stevens turned his face to Newell, held his index finger before his lips, and said, "Sssssh!"

"I didn't know that," Oliver said.

"He had the only Special Instrument Ticket around. They wouldn't let anybody else fly in that shit."

A Special Instrument Flight Certificate was the highest of the several grades of certification of competency to fly aircraft on instruments (only). It authorized the holder to take off completely on his own discretion—that is, without regard to visibility and other flight-safety standards established for less-qualified pilots.

"How did he hear about it? He wasn't in the 170th."

"It was the 123rd," Stevens said. "I told him. He really laid his balls on the chopping block for you, Johnny."

"Charley," Oliver said, visibly disturbed, "I never heard this until just now."

Stevens looked at him sharply a moment, saw that he was telling the truth, and then, smiling, turned to Newell.

"John Wayne here ran out of gas in an Otter and had to sit down in the boonies, in Charlie's backyard," he said. In the military phonetic alphabet, the abbreviation for Viet Cong (VC) was spoken "Victor Charlie." "We thought maybe he'd walked away from it—God is supposed to take care of fools and drunks, and Johnny is thus dual qualified—but we couldn't go look for him, because of the weather. Our battalion commander was very interested in his safety record—"

"That's not fair, Charley," Oliver protested.

Stevens put his finger in front of his lips and went "Sssshh!" again.

"We were just about to divvy up his personal gear between us, when Jack Dant comes out of the soup in his Mohawk with all that lovely terrain avoidance radar in it and says that since Oliver can't find his way out of a men's room by himself, maybe we should go looking for him—"

"You said 'we,' " Oliver interrupted him. "You said, 'We should go looking for him.' You were with him, weren't you, Charley?"

"You ever hear the phrase, Jose?" Stevens asked, ignoring him, " 'like something the dog dragged in'? When the Air Force went in with a Jolly Green Giant to fetch him, John Wayne here looked like something no self-respecting dog would drag anywhere."

"Answer the goddamned question," Oliver said.

"Yeah, I went along and worked the radios," Stevens said. "What the hell, you owed me fifty bucks and pair of sunglasses."

"Thank you, Charley," Oliver said.

"The point of all these war stories is that I know for a fact that Jack Dant was one hell of a pilot. So what happened to him?"

"The tail rotor came off," Oliver said. "They went straight down from twenty-five hundred feet."

" 'The tail rotor came off'?" Stevens parroted incredulously.

"The entire rotor head was gone," Newell said. "It was nowhere near the fuselage."

"You were there?" Stevens asked. "What are you, some kind of engineer? Expert?"

"He was with me," Oliver said. "Jose's Texas National Guard. He's got a civilian ticket and a lot of hours. Now he's going through flight school."

Stevens considered that a moment, grunted, then asked, "They just sat there and waited for it?"

"They got on the radio, called a Mayday, reported what had happened."

"And then boom, so long?"

Oliver nodded.

"I went by his house last night," Stevens said. "I heard a very unpleasant story about two flight surgeons—"

"Out of school, Charley, it's true."

"Goddamn! Have you seen her?"

"I went there with the Bellmons, but we didn't get to see her. Allan Wood's widow—"

"The Ice Princess," Stevens interrupted.

"Is that what you call her?"

"I wrote her a letter when Allan went in," Stevens said. "No reply. So when I came home, I went to see her. Allan and I were pretty close, and I was . . . Anyway, I figured maybe she didn't get the letter and went to see her. And she made it plain in about two minutes that she was not interested in auld lang syne or anything connected with the Army, or, in particular, with Army Aviators. Thank you for calling, and don't let the doorknob hit you in the ass on your way out. What about her?"

"She wouldn't let us in. Slammed the door in our faces."

"Bellmon must have liked that," Stevens said.

"He told me to find out what was going on, and left."

"And the Ice Princess told you?" Stevens asked.

"A guy named Geoff Craig—he lives behind the Dants—told me."

"That's right. You know him, don't you?"

"I do, but how do you know that?"

"Green Grunt? In flight school? Supposed to be rich as hell? Same guy?"

"Yeah."

"You remember when Foo Two damned near got overrun?"

"I heard about it," Oliver said. "I was in the hospital."

"Oh, yeah. That's right."

"Foo Two?" Newell asked.

"Green Grunt base on top of a mountain," Stevens explained. "An A-Team and a couple of hundred slopeheads. They fuck up Charlie's supply routes—"

"Why Foo Two? I thought those bases had—what do I say?—Army names," Newell pursued.

"It probably had one, but the Green Grunts called it Dien Bien Phu Two because they were surrounded and up to their ass in VC," Stevens explained. "That got shortened to Foo Two."

"Was Geoff Craig at Foo Two?" Oliver asked.

"He was the only American who came through it," Stevens said. "Everybody else got blown away except one master sergeant who Charlie carried away. When we got there the next morning, there was VC all over the place. And you know they usually haul their dead off. Craig was pretty glassy-eyed. He was as deaf as a post from firing mortars and machine guns all night in that rock fortress . . . you remember that, Johnny?"

"In the center of the camp, what they used as the ammo dump and the backup CP?"—Command Post.

"Yeah. Well, anyway, Craig went there when the attack started, him and a dozen of our Vietnamese. While Charlie was wiping the rest of the place out, they couldn't get to the fortress because of the machine guns and the mortars. And they couldn't take out the fortress with their mortars because it was all solid rock—except for the roof, which was railroad ties and dirt maybe six, seven feet thick. So he spent the night firing mortars and machine guns, and he couldn't have heard an atom bomb go off when we got there."

"He didn't get wounded?"

"Some little shrapnel dings, and rock splinters. Shit like that. He took a zing on the face, and he burned his hands changing machine-gun barrels. But they didn't *hit* him. He was deaf and glassy-eyed, but that's all. So instead of med evacing the poor bastard, Green Grunts being what they are, they hung a gold bar on his collar, left him in command of a new A-Team, less officers. We took the A-Team in when we took out the bodies."

"I heard he got a commission in 'Nam," Johnny Oliver said. "I didn't hear how."

"How'd you meet him?" Stevens asked.

"He's related to a friend of Bellmon's, a light colonel named Lowell. I drove Lowell out to his house one time, and he invited me in for a drink. And Craig's wife and Bellmon's daughter are pals. I didn't know you were friends."

"We're not. I saw him only that one time, at Foo Two. And I spoke to him here one time, and mentioned that, and he made it plain he didn't want to talk about it," Stevens said.

"Well, anyway, Craig told me what had happened with those goddamned doctors, so I dragged him out here and made him repeat it to the General."

"Is Bellmon going to do anything about it?"

"He already has," Oliver said. "They won't do that again. Even after they grow new assholes."

Stevens grunted.

"So how did the Ice Princess treat you?"

"All right," Oliver said carefully.

"Well, don't get your hopes up. She isn't about to let you into her pants."

"Apparently you're speaking from experience?"

"Not really," Stevens said. "She didn't even give me a shot at it. But on the same subject, tell me about Bellmon's daughter."

"No," Oliver said. "I will not."

"Ah ha—so you do have ambitions along that line. You are determined to be a general, aren't you?"

"You're on dangerous ground, Charley," Oliver said.

"She's not giving you any, huh?"

"I would be very surprised to learn she's giving anybody any," Oliver said. "She's a very nice girl."

"In that case how about introducing me?"

"Fuck you!" Oliver said, laughing incredulously.

"I'm serious, Johnny. Why not?"

"Because I really like her, she's a pal of mine, and I don't want to have to kill you for what I'm sure you have in mind."

"What I have in mind is meeting a nice girl," Stevens said. "I have fucked my way through all of the local talent, and what I am looking for now is a nice girl."

"Bullshit. A stiff prick has no conscience."

"Hey," Stevens said. "I'm serious. I know she's a nice girl. I can tell by just looking."

"She is a very nice girl," Jose said.

"You know her?" Stevens asked, and then when Newell nodded, said, "OK, then *you* introduce me."

"I'll introduce you, Charley," Oliver said. "That doesn't mean she'll go out with you. But I'll introduce you. And if you get a half-inch out of line with her I'll—"

"I just said, goddamn it, I want to meet a *nice* girl. I don't need your help to get laid, thank you very much, *Captain* Oliver."

"I'll bring her to the Norwich Dinner," Oliver said. "That's two weeks away."

"OK," Stevens said. "Thanks, Johnny."

"I'll be damned if I don't think you mean it," Oliver said.

The enormous black woman who presided over the cafeteria on Sunday mornings waddled across the floor to their table.

"The Gen-rul's on the phone for you, Captain Oliver," she said. "He didn't give his name, but I knows his voice."

"Thank you," Oliver said.

"Man's work is sun-to-sun," Charley Stevens pronounced solemnly, "but a dog-robber's work is never done."

Captain John S. Oliver gave Lieutenant Charles J. Stevens a gesture known as the finger and then went to the telephone behind the serving counter. Oliver ducked under the serving rail and picked it up.

"Captain Oliver, Sir."

"Johnny, they just called me and said they have found the cause, or think they have, of the Chinook crash. I'm about to go out there. I thought perhaps you'd like to go."

"Yes, Sir, I would. Shall I get the car and pick you up?"

"I'll pick you up. Is that friend of yours with you by any chance?"

"Lieutenant Newell? Yes, Sir."

"There is a good deal of what I think is legitimate curiosity on the post about what happened yesterday," Bellmon said. "Sometimes, Johnny, when you want to get the straight word out, you can do that better by word of mouth than with an official statement. Do you take my meaning?"

"Yes, Sir. I'll bring Jose Newell with us. But you're going to have to tell him it's all right to talk about it, Sir."

"OK," Bellmon said. "I'll leave right away. Unless you've just started your breakfast?"

"No, Sir, we're finished. Sir, there's someone else with us. Lieutenant Stevens. He's a classmate of mine, and he flew with Lieutenant Dant in 'Nam."

Bellmon hesitated only momentarily.

"Bring him too, Johnny," he said and hung up.

[THREE]

"I'd like to apologize for my appearance, Sir," First Lieutenant Stevens said to Major General Bellmon as Bellmon's Oldsmobile drove through the Officers' Open Mess parking lot.

"Not necessary," Bellmon said automatically, then added: "Anytime I see a Norwich man with his zipper closed and wearing shoes, I know he's doing his best."

There was absolute silence in the car. It was an astonishingly gauche thing for a general officer to say to two lieutenants and a captain.

They stopped at the end of the parking lot, by Chapel #1, a frame building painted white. Oliver saw what was set up in movable letters on the church bulletin board:

Monday
1500 Hours
Memorial Service For
1st Lt John Marshall Dant

"I think the last time I said that," Bellmon said, "was twenty-three, no, twenty-four years ago. At Fort Knox. I was a lieutenant, right out of the academy . . . I meant no offense, Lieutenant.''

''None taken, Sir.''

''When Johnny came to work for me,'' Bellmon said, ''my wife read the riot act to me. I was not to make any Norwich jokes. And I haven't. I suppose when Johnny told me you were classmates, I subconsciously decided the prohibition didn't apply to you. But I shouldn't have said it and I'm sorry.''

''We Norwich men understand what is considered humor at West Point, Sir,'' Oliver said.

''Now we're even, Captain Oliver,'' Bellmon said, mockingly stern. ''Any further witticism on your part will be considered impertinence.''

''Yes, Sir.''

''What's in that envelope, Johnny?'' Bellmon asked.

''It's a second set of the pictures I took at the crash site, Sir. I thought they might be useful out at Cairns. Newell and I were going out there—before you called, I mean.''

''I thought that's what they might be. Show them to Lieutenant Stevens.''

Stevens examined the pictures. He exhaled audibly, and, very softly, said, ''Shit.''

They were now at the main gate. The MP on duty had been leaning against the wall of the guard shack, casually waving cars past him. But suddenly, on recognizing General Bellmon's car, and then Bellmon, he snapped to attention and saluted crisply.

''I had what may sound like a callous thought looking at those,'' Bellmon said, as he returned the salute. ''The Chinook fuselage is stronger than I would have believed.''

''Maybe the pine trees cushioned the impact,'' Stevens said. ''Maybe . . .''

''I'm not sure what the physics are,'' Bellmon said. ''What happens, specifically, when you lose one of your rotors? With the countertorque dynamics gone, what happens?''

''Nobody saw it go in?'' Stevens asked, adding, ''Sir.''

''No.''

''What happened when you were shot down, Johnny? Did you lose a rotor?'' Bellmon asked.

"No, Sir," Oliver said. "I lost hydraulics. And I was flying a B-Model Huey anyway, so it wouldn't be the same thing."

"I saw a Twenty-one lose its *front* rotor," Stevens said. "It just . . . went down. No wild gyrations, nothing like that. The nose just dropped and it went down."

"I understand you flew with Lieutenant Dant in Vietnam," Bellmon said.

"Yes, Sir."

"Have you seen Mrs. Dant since this happened?"

"Yes, Sir."

"Are you aware of the visit Mrs. Dant was paid by two medical officers?"

"Yes, Sir."

"I'd like your opinion, Lieutenant," Bellmon said. "Think it over before replying. Would it help or exacerbate things if those two doctors, and the hospital commander, apologized to Mrs. Dant?"

"Sir," Stevens said, after a moment. "I don't think Mrs. Dant wants to see either of those two assholes ever again."

"OK," Bellmon said.

When they reached Cairns Airfield and drove up to Hangar 104, there was a staff car with a covered general officer's plate parked in a space reserved for general officers. The driver, who had been leaning on the front fender, straightened as he recognized Bellmon.

"Who the hell is that?" Bellmon asked rhetorically as he pulled in beside it.

The staff car driver saluted.

"Good morning, Sergeant," Bellmon said as he returned it. "Who are you driving around?"

"General Rand, Sir."

"I didn't know he was on the post," Bellmon said, smiling at the sergeant and then turning his attention, eyebrows raised, to Oliver.

"Sir, neither did I," Oliver said.

"Well, I'm glad that someone has apparently taken care of him," Bellmon said, and then entered a two-story concrete-block building that had been built along the hangar wall.

How the hell was I supposed to know he was on the post?

Oliver thought angrily, and then came up with the answer: *Because I am the aide-de-camp, and aides-de-camp are supposed to know when there are visiting general officers on the post, and they are supposed to tell the General about them. Generals don't like other generals running around loose on their post.*

When this one showed up, the FOD knew about it. Otherwise General Rand would not have been assigned a car and driver. And the SOP says the FOD will notify the aide. And the SOP also says the aide will keep either the General, or the sergeant major, or the FOD, aware of where he is. When the FOD tried to call me, and I wasn't in my quarters—when I was off, Jesus Christ, with Liza—he notified the sergeant major. And I told him that I would either be in my room or Annex #1. Where I wasn't. So he covered for me, and did what had to be done.

I have just had my ass eaten for dereliction of duty. And he neither raised his voice nor made a specific accusation. Oh, shit!

[FOUR]

Pipe-and-sheet-steel work platforms had been set up around the rear pylon of the crashed Chinook. There were half a dozen people up there, about all the platforms would hold, and one of them was Brigadier General George F. Rand.

Dangling from a crane above the rear pylon was the rotor hub assembly, which had not been anywhere in sight at the crash site. It was only the assembly center; the blades were gone.

"Good morning," General Bellmon called, raising his voice enough to be heard.

Rand saw him and immediately started coming down the steps of the ladder. Another man came with him, a civilian in a leather World War II Air Corps flying jacket. Johnny Oliver did not recognize who he was.

"Good morning, General," Rand said, saluting.

"I didn't know you were on the post, George," Bellmon said. "My people been taking care of you all right?"

"Just fine," Rand said. "When I came in last night, your

sergeant major said you'd had a bad day and asked if there was anything he could do for me. I said all I wanted to do was pay my respects, and that could wait until morning."

"Hell, I'll have to tell him we're old friends," Bellmon said. "You should have stayed with us, George."

"I'm in your VIP quarters. And since I invited myself, I'm grateful for that."

"Don't be silly," Bellmon said. "You never need an invitation here."

"When General Wendall came back from Fort Gordon, he sent me down here, first to see if we could find out what caused the crash, and then to ask you for any ideas you have about getting the grounding lifted."

"Well, we're glad to have you," Bellmon said.

"Do you know Harry Schultz, General?" Rand said.

"Sure. Harry used to be here before he went to Benning."

Who the hell is Harry Schultz? Oliver wondered.

"Nice to see you again, General," Schultz said, offering Bellmon his hand. "Bad circumstances."

"Are you the one who found out what caused it, Harry?" Bellmon asked.

"Tom Everly did," Schultz replied. "I'll bet he's right. I was just showing General Rand what Tom found."

"Why don't you show me?" Bellmon said, and started up the ladder. Schultz followed him.

General Rand looked at Oliver.

"Sir, I'm General Bellmon's aide, John Oliver," Oliver said. "I'm afraid I owe you an apology."

"What for?" Rand said, offering Oliver his hand.

"Well, for not being around when you arrived, Sir."

"Your sergeant major took good care of me—no problem."

"Well, I should have been available, Sir."

"I said, no problem."

"Sir, I have some photographs I took yesterday at the crash site. Would you like to see them?"

"Very much," Rand said. Oliver handed them over.

"Lieutenant Stevens, you want to come up here?" Bellmon's voice came from the work platform. "You, too, Newell."

Oliver looked around for them. They were making themselves as inconspicuous as possible against the hangar wall. He saw Rand's eyes examining Steven's cowboy hat and boots.

"Lieutenant Stevens flew in 'Nam with Lieutenant Dant, who was flying the right seat in this, Sir," Oliver explained. "Lieutenant Newell was with us at the crash site yesterday."

"I see," Rand said. "Did you serve in Vietnam, Captain?"

"Yes, Sir."

"Have you flown one of these?" Rand asked, nodding toward the Chinook.

"Yes, Sir," Oliver said. "Before I became General Bellmon's aide, they were going to make me an IP. I took the transition course."

"There are two schools of thought about this aircraft," Rand said. "One is that it's a fine machine and the other that it's a flying coffin. Which way do you feel?"

"I think it's a fine machine, Sir," Oliver said.

Rand grunted.

Bellmon came down the work-platform steps.

"Have a look, Oliver," he said. "If you like."

"Thank you, Sir," Oliver said, and went quickly up the stairs to the work platform.

Newell and Stevens came down as he went up. Both of them shook their heads.

Schultz had seen him coming, and waited for him. The panels over the rotor head and transmission had been removed. Schultz pointed at something inside.

What the hell am I being shown?

"Look at that, will you?" Schultz said.

And then comprehension came; he knew what he was looking at.

Each Chinook pylon had three rotor blades, each of which was almost exactly twenty feet long. These fitted into hub assemblies, which contained the mechanism to control their pitch, and which in turn were connected to the transmission.

The rear rotor-head assembly had torn loose from the transmission, flailed around, and then flown off. The cause for this was obvious. It had lost one of its three blades. The moment that happened, the assembly, grossly out of balance, had begun to tear itself loose.

On the rotor-head assembly itself, Oliver saw the now empty bolt holes where the rotor blades had been fastened to the assembly, four bolts for each blade. The bolt holes for two of the three blades were perfectly round. Where the third rotor blade had been mounted, two bolt holes were battered, twisted, elongated, and torn. The other two were round. What had happened, obviously, was that two bolts had lost their nuts and then vibrated out of their holes. And that allowed that blade to wobble, and the strain had been too great for the assembly; the remaining bolts had torn free.

It had all happened in probably no more than a couple of seconds. By the time the pilots had sensed that something was wrong, the tail rotor assembly had thrown a blade; and then it started tearing itself to pieces.

What had caused the accident was a lousy nut. It had either failed from metal fatigue, or, even less pleasant to consider, it had not been safety-wired in place.

Oliver refused to consider the one other possibility, sabotage, although that was just about as likely as a criminally negligent mechanic, who would now never be caught, or a pair of nuts failing one right after the other.

"Ain't that something?" Schultz said bitterly.

Oliver didn't trust himself to respond beyond saying, "Thank you, Mr. Schultz."

He went down the work-platform steps.

Bellmon met his eyes.

Is he pissed at me because of General Rand? Or at the world generally because of what we've just seen?

"Oliver," General Bellmon said, "I have just volunteered your services to take General Rand back to Benning. Any reason you can't do that?"

"No, Sir. I'll be happy to."

"I hate to ruin your day off," General Rand said.

"Don't worry about it," General Bellmon said. "Captain Oliver gets plenty of time off, don't you, Oliver?"

"Yes, Sir," Oliver said.

X

[ONE]
Base Operations
Cairns Army Airfield
Fort Rucker, Alabama
1005 Hours 13 January 1964

Brigadier General George F. Rand, ignoring the FLIGHT PERSONNEL ONLY signs on the doors, followed Captain John S. Oliver into the Weather Briefing Room, and then into the Flight Planning Room. No one said anything, of course. The only people in the Army who dare ask general officers what they are doing are other general officers.

Rand listened intently as an Air Force master sergeant delivered his assessment of the weather to be encountered between Cairns and Lawson, and he even glanced over Oliver's shoulders as Oliver took notes.

"We're above minimums, Sir," Oliver explained. "But I think we'll file an instrument flight plan anyway."

"Why?" Rand asked simply.

"Well, Sir, if the rubber bands break, that way Lawson will know when we don't show up when we're supposed to and can come looking for us."

Rand stared at him without comprehension for a moment, long enough for Oliver to consider that his mouth had just run away with him again. Then Rand's lips curved in a faint smile, and he mimed, twirling his finger, a small boy winding up his balsawood airplane. Then he grunted.

"For someone in my job, Deputy Commanding General of the 11th Air Assault Division," Rand said, "I know damned little about flying."

That's so. I wonder why they assigned you to the 11th.

"Sir, General Bellmon said you're going to go through a Blue Course," Oliver said. "I think you'll find it isn't really as mysterious as it might seem."

"You ever hear, Captain, what they say about teaching old dogs new tricks?" Rand said. "I've been feeling pretty ignorant at Benning, but in the last twenty-four hours you experts—unintentionally, of course, it's not a criticism—have really made me aware of my awesome ignorance."

"Sir, I remember the first time I got close to an M-48, at the Armor School. I was awed. Six weeks later I could change tracks on it."

"Well, I hope you're right," Rand said.

In Flight Planning, Oliver explained each step as he prepared his flight plan. Rand seemed fascinated, but didn't ask any questions, and Oliver wondered if he was a quick learner or whether he was afraid of asking what might be a dumb question.

Ten minutes later, after Oliver had the U-8F trimmed up to climb to the altitude Atlanta Area Control had assigned Army 917, he turned to General Rand and said, "Sir, it is absolutely forbidden to permit nonrated personnel to touch the controls of an aircraft in flight. Having said that, would you like to try?"

Rand smiled at him.

"I wouldn't know what I'm doing," he said.

Oliver pointed to the radio compass and then to the altimeter.

"That's our course," he said. "You keep those two needles crossed. And what we're doing—we're at fifty-two hundred feet—is climbing to ten thousand. The little airplane on the artificial horizon shows our attitude with relation to the earth. It shows we're going up. And the rate-of-climb indicator"—he pointed to it—"shows we're climbing at about five hundred feet a minute. The phrase would be, 'Keep what you've got.' "

When Rand put his feet on the rubber pedals and his hands on the wheel, Oliver disengaged the auto pilot.

"You've got it," Oliver said.

He restrained the smile that wanted to come to his lips. Rand was excited.

He didn't do badly. The altimeter crept slowly up to ten thousand feet.

"Now see if you can level it off," Oliver commanded.

The plane leveled off, then nosed down. And then Rand overcorrected and the nose went up again.

"Atlanta Area Control, Army Nine One Seven at ten thousand," Oliver said to the radio. He started to take the wheel. Then he changed his mind.

"There's nobody up here but us," he said. "Just be a little more gentle."

"Army Nine One Seven, maintain flight level ten thousand on present course."

"Roger, Atlanta."

"Army Nine One Seven, you may switch to one twenty-one point three at this time."

"Roger, Army Nine One Seven switching to one twenty-one decimal three," Oliver said.

The undulations diminished. General Rand finally got it in straight and level flight about 9,800 feet. Oliver figured that was close enough. He adjusted the trim and retarded the throttles.

"Lawson, Army Nine One Seven," Oliver said into the microphone.

"Nine One Seven, Lawson."

"Nine One Seven is sixty miles south of your station, IFR at ten."

"Roger, we have you on IFF."

"Nine One Seven for approach and landing. We have a Code Seven aboard."

"Nine One Seven, Lawson. Maintain your present heading. You may commence descent to three thousand at your option. Report when passing through five thousand. Would you care to identify the Code Seven?"

"Nine One Seven leaving ten thousand. Rand. I spell Roger Able Nan Dog. We will require ground transportation."

"Nine One Seven, Lawson, roger on wheels for General Rand."

"Now we start to go down," Oliver said to General Rand. "The problem with going down is that you pick up airspeed. When the needle on the airspeed indicator goes past the red mark, the wings come off. So what you do is take your foot off the gas."

Rand looked at him and smiled.

"I'll do that," Oliver said as he reached to retard the throttles. "You just push the nose down a little and try to go down as fast as we came up—five hundred feet a minute."

"There's a lot to remember, isn't there?" Rand said as he ever so carefully pushed forward on the wheel.

"After a while, Sir, it becomes automatic."

Rand's reply surprised him.

"Have you got heavy plans for the rest of the day, Oliver?"

"No, Sir. I'm at your disposal."

"What about the airplane? Do you have to get it back to Rucker right away?"

Oh, Christ! I'm going to spend the afternoon giving bootleg instruction.

"No, Sir. I don't think General Bellmon is going anywhere. I'll have to call and say I'm delayed."

"The reason I wanted to come back here is to brief General Wendall, and probably General Roberts, on what happened to the Chinook. It just occurred to me that you are far better qualified to do that than I am. And we left the tech reps at Rucker."

"I'm at your disposal, General."

"And I think maybe you should take over flying this thing again."

"Yes, Sir," Oliver said, wondering if there was some kind of a reprimand in that decision. Rand had seemed as happy as a ten-year-old playing with his Christmas electric trains.

Oliver put his hands and feet on the controls and said, "I've got it."

He trimmed it up for a five-hundred-feet-a-minute descent, turned on the autopilot, and turned around in his seat to dig into his Jeppesen case, on the seat behind him, for the Lawson Approach Chart.

"I was about to ask you what the hell you were doing," General Rand said. "It would have been a dumb question. You obviously turned on the autopilot. So maybe I am learning a little."

"Sir, when you go to the Blue Course, I don't think you'll have any trouble."

"That brings us back to the old dog/new tricks business," Rand said. "But thank you, Captain, for letting me fly . . . if it could fairly be called that."

"What I was doing just then, General, was dumb. I was getting the Lawson Approach Chart"—he waved it in his hand—"which I should have taken out before I took off. I've been here before, of course, and I know the field. But the whole idea of the Jeppesen system is to have the latest information—not what you think it is—in front of you. It's little dumb mistakes that ordinarily wouldn't matter—like that—that kill people."

Rand grunted again. He thought. *An interesting man. Most junior officers wouldn't make a confession the way he just did to themselves, much less to a senior officer who would never have known the difference.*

[TWO]
Headquarters, 11th Air Assault Division [Test]
Harmony Church
Fort Benning, Georgia
1330 Hours 13 January 1964

"Thank you very much, Captain," Major General Harrison O. K. Wendall said. Oliver had just shown the photographs of the crashed Chinook to Wendall and half a dozen other senior officers, including Brigadier General William R. Roberts. At the same time he had explained what the experts at Rucker thought had caused the crash.

"The thing to do is check everything here and see if any other blades are about to come off in flight," Brigadier General Roberts said.

Wendall glared at him. That Roberts was right did not, in his judgment, give him any right to tell the 11th Air Assault Division [Test] Commander what to do.

Roberts seemed immune to the cold look.

"I find it hard to accept that the safety wiring would fail," Roberts said. "What I think we're going to find is that some mechanic screwed up. But we have to look."

"Dave," General Wendall said to a man who was in golf clothing. Oliver came to understand he was a colonel. "Get the maintenance officers on it right away. I want every Chinook pylon inspected right now."

"Yes, Sir."

"I think that's all we'll need you for, Captain," General Wendall said. "Thank you again."

"Sir, if it would be all right, I'd like to hang around until that's done. I know General Bellmon would like to know what you find."

"Help yourself," Wendall said. "We'll get you a ride back to the airfield."

"I'll take him," General Rand said. "After I take him home and feed him some lunch."

Susan Rand did not seem at all surprised or annoyed when her husband showed up with a strange captain to feed. But, she said, since she hadn't known when her husband would be back, she and the kids had just finished eating. She could come up with something edible, though, in half an hour. "In the meantime," she said to Oliver, "there's beer or anything harder you might like."

"I'm flying," Oliver said. "But thank you anyway."

"I'll make some coffee," General Rand said. "I shouldn't be drinking anyway."

Oliver had expected the "something edible" to be either cold cuts or maybe a hamburger, but it turned out to be stuffed pork chops, spinach, rice, fresh biscuits, and apple pie à la mode.

Mrs. Rand sat down with them while they ate, but when she served the coffee and the apple pie, she left them alone.

Oliver immediately sensed that Rand wanted to pick his

brain, not so much about the Chinook crash, but about Vietnam, and combat flying versus flying anywhere else. It was a debriefing, Oliver realized, skillfully administered, and designed to fill what Rand obviously considered blank spaces in his fund of knowledge.

It was flattering that Rand would want his opinion of so much, but it was also disconcerting, for Oliver was afraid he would paint an inaccurate picture. Thus he found himself carefully thinking over his answers before he gave them. The process forced him to think for the first time about many things he had learned in Vietnam . . . and temporarily put out of his mind.

The discussion lasted more than an hour, though Oliver didn't notice the time passing. But he did realize how tired he was when Rand finally said, "Unless you want some more coffee, Johnny, maybe we had better go down to Lawson and see how the inspection is coming." He wondered how long Rand had been calling him by his first name.

As if on cue, Mrs. Rand reappeared and told Johnny that it had been nice to meet him, that he should give her very best to the Bellmons when he got "home," and that she hoped she would see him soon again.

When she was done, Oliver had the somewhat cynical thought that this was not the first time the Rands had managed a debriefing like this—with his wife first putting you at ease, and then Rand himself skillfully picking your brain.

These two are bright as hell, like the Bellmons. Why am I surprised?

When they got to Lawson Field, the Colonel who had been in golf clothes was now in uniform. He walked up and announced that every pylon had been examined. No belts were loose; every nut and bolt in the pylons that was supposed to be safety wired had been safety wired.

And then he said, "I really hate to do this to you, Captain, but I have as many Chinook maintenance people as we could round up, plus a flock of Chinook pilots and crew chiefs, in the hangar next door. Do you suppose you could give them the briefing you gave the General?"

Oh, shit!

"Yes, Sir," he said. "I'd be happy to."

It was a quarter after six when he finally got in the air again, and a little after seven when he parked the U-8F on the ramp at Cairns. He went in Base Ops and turned in the paperwork, then he called the General.

"General Rand called me and said he was finally letting you go," Bellmon said. "And he said you did a first-rate job of briefing the senior people and then the flight crews and maintenance people. Good job, Johnny."

"Thank you, Sir."

Well, I guess I'm off the shit list.

"Did General Rand mention they inspected their Chinooks, and there was safety wire all over?"

"Yes," Bellmon said. "And we inspected the fleet here and found three unwired bolts. I've got the maintenance contractor coming in for a chat at eight o'clock."

Well, God help that poor bastard.

"Yes, Sir."

"See you in the morning, Johnny," General Bellmon said and hung up.

The telephone he'd used to speak with Bellmon was a B-line; that is, it was not connected to the civilian trunk to Ozark. There was a pay phone in the lobby of Base Operations, but there was a TEMPORARILY OUT OF SERVICE sign hanging from its mouthpiece. There was an A-line in the Operations Officer's office, and he called Liza Wood from there, under the disapproving eye of the AOD.

"Hello," he said.

"Who's this?"

"John Oliver."

"Oh. I didn't recognize your voice."

"I just got in," he said. "Otherwise I would have called earlier."

"Why?"

"I thought we could have a drink or something."

"I don't think that would be possible. Sunday is the only full day I have with Allan."

"Sorry, I didn't think about that. How about tomorrow?"

"I don't see how we could. I'm going to Jack Dant's memorial service, and then Ursula Craig and I are going to help her with the people who call afterward."

You are being shot down, Oliver. What you hear in those bullshit excuses is the polite way a lady says piss off. What did you expect?

In his mind's ear he heard her say, "I've never been raped before," and "I think you had better go, Johnny." He closed his eyes.

"I understand," he said. "Well, I'll call again sometime."

"Why don't you?" she said. "Good night, John."

He put the telephone in its cradle.

Why the hell am I so disappointed? Why the hell did I call in the first place?

"Captain," the AOD said, "I don't want to be a prick about it, but that phone is not for personal calls."

Oliver looked at him.

Good little aides-de-camp do not tell AODs who are majors to go fuck themselves.

"Yes, Sir," Oliver said. "Sorry, Sir."

When he got to the BOQ, Jose Newell's MG of Many Colors was in the parking lot, but he was not in his room.

Oliver found him and Charley Stevens in Annex #1, telling Fort Monmouth stories. Fort Monmouth, New Jersey, is the home of the Signal Corps. He remembered that Stevens was another flag-waver. Charley was drunk.

"I'm celebrating my transfer," Stevens said. "You can buy me a drink."

"Transfer where?" Oliver asked as he waved the bartender over.

"SCATSA," Stevens said. "They need a replacement for Jack Dant. Guess who is the only Signal Corps first john checked out in Chinooks on the post?"

"I thought Jack Dant was assigned to Aviation Board?"

"He was," Stevens replied. "But SCATSA pools their pilots with the Board, and they just happen to be one first john short of their TO and E."

"When are you going over there?" Oliver asked, aware that something was bothering him about what Stevens was telling him.

"TDY effective tomorrow, the orders will catch up with me later."

"Are you happy about it?"

''I'm fucking ecstatic, doesn't it show?''

Oliver suddenly understood.

''You sonofabitch, you volunteered, didn't you?'' Oliver challenged. ''You called Colonel Augustus and volunteered!''

Stevens didn't reply.

''What the hell is the matter with you? We only *think* it's missing safety wire on those bolts. It could be metal fatigue or something else.''

''Somebody has to fly the sonsofbitches,'' Stevens said. ''Why *not* me?''

''Because you stuck your neck out often enough in 'Nam,'' Oliver said. ''Let somebody else have a turn.''

''Yeah, but I didn't get on the five-percent list like some people I know,'' Stevens said thickly. ''Now maybe I can.''

Oliver shook his head.

''You're crazy, Charley.''

''Up yours, Johnny. And, fuck you—I'll buy my own drink.''

''Give this asshole whatever he wants,'' Oliver said to the bartender.

Charley Stevens wrapped an arm around Oliver's shoulder and kissed him wetly on the forehead. ''For a dog-robber, you ain't so bad yourself, asshole.''

[THREE]

With less effort than he thought it would take, and with an assist from Second Lieutenant Jose Newell, Captain John S. Oliver managed to convince First Lieutenant Charles J. Stevens that the path of wisdom was to get something to eat, and then go to bed, so that when he reported for his first day of duty with SCATSA, he would be bright-eyed and bushy-tailed rather than bloody-eyed and reeking of booze.

They went to a fast-food joint in Daleville, just outside the main gate. And they ate greasy hamburgers and french fries under the disapproving eyes of a dozen or more enlisted men who without saying anything managed to convey that they thought the three officers had invaded their turf.

Oliver's unlisted phone was ringing when he walked into his room.

"Captain Oliver," he said, answering it.

"Sergeant James, Sir. How nice to find the Captain at home," the sergeant major said cheerfully. "And on *my* very first try."

"You're in a very good mood for an old man this time of night, Sergeant Major," Oliver said. "May I thus infer that I'm in trouble?"

"Not now you're not," James said. "Now that I've found you. Would you care to guess who couldn't find you and who assigned me the job?"

"I was having a hamburger."

"I'm disappointed," Sergeant Major James said solemnly. "The General and I had visions of you surrounded by half-naked women, drinking from the neck of a bottle of hard liquor."

Oliver chuckled. "Why was he looking for me?"

"You bring his plane back in one piece from Benning?"

"Yes."

"You think they serviced it?"

"They always do, but I'll check. Am I, are we, going somewhere?"

"The General will meet you at Cairns at 0400 tomorrow morning. You will by then have filed a flight plan Cairns-Lawson-Eustis." The Army Airfield at the U.S. Army Engineer Center, Fort Eustis, Virginia, near Washington, D.C., served as the de facto Pentagon air terminal. Army aircraft were, for all practical purposes, denied use of Washington's National Airport.

"How long are we going to be gone?"

"Up and back in time for Lieutenant Dant's memorial services," Sergeant James said. "You'll be cutting it close."

"You know what's going on?"

"You ever meet the DCSOPS, Captain?"

"No."

"Prepare yourself," Sergeant James said. "And a *very* good night, with many *pleasant* dreams, to you, Sir." Then he hung up.

When Oliver called the AOD at Cairns, the prick who had jumped on him about using the telephone identified himself. Oliver asked him if 917 had been serviced.

"I really don't know," the AOD said.

"Sir, could you find out?"

"Is it important?"

"Yes, Sir, I think so."

"You dog-robbers think a lot of things are important that aren't," the AOD informed him.

"General Bellmon expects to take off in that airplane at 0400 tomorrow," Oliver said. 'He won't be able to do that unless it gets serviced between now and then." After a moment he added, "Will he, Sir?"

"I'll take care of it, Captain," the AOD said.

"Thank you very much, Sir."

As he wound his alarm clock, Oliver considered that the AOD was a particular type: *Prick, Officer, Bald-headed, Field Grade, Mark Three. That being true, it's entirely possible that if he discovers that Nine One Seven hadn't been serviced, he'll "forget" that I called him rather than take the time and trouble to find someone to top off the tanks and replenish the oil and wipe the windshield.*

And that being the case, Oliver decided it would be prudent to set his alarm for 0230 rather than 0300. Bellmon wanted the plane ready to go; he would not be interested in how Oliver arranged that; and he would not be sympathetic to an excuse that the AOD had promised to do it.

When he got to the field a few minutes after three, his face festooned with tiny squares of toilet paper from a disastrous session with a dull razor blade, he discovered that 917 had not been serviced. The NCO in Base Ops told him the AOD had gone to meet with the FOD. He could, the sergeant said, get him on the radio if it was important.

"Scare up a fuel truck, Sergeant, please," Oliver said, "and have them top off Nine One Seven."

"Sir, I don't think one is available this time of morning."

"Why the hell not?"

"Well," the sergeant said, somewhere between reasonably and righteously, "if a plane comes in at this time of the morning, they rarely go anywhere before five, or six. And if one came in last night, it should have been serviced when it landed."

"Well, Sergeant, Nine One Seven came in about seven last night, and it has not been serviced. The General wants to take off in Nine One Seven at 0400. Now what do you think we should be doing about that?''

''I guess I better go get a fuel truck,'' the sergeant said. ''But I'll need somebody to man the extinguisher. That's SOP.''

''You get the truck and I'll handle the extinguisher.''

''What about the phone? Who'll answer the phone?''

''If the phone rings while we're gassing the airplane, we will just let the sonofabitch ring, OK?'' Oliver said sarcastically.

''Yes, Sir,'' the sergeant said with more than a hint of contempt in his voice.

Congratulations, Oliver. You handled that beautifully. You are a real leader of men, who has just made another significant gesture to buttress the opinion held by most senior NCOs that officers generally, and dog-robbers in particular, are pompous assholes.

When they had finished topping off the tanks, he went to Weather Briefing. An Air Corps staff sergeant there, who looked no older than seventeen, painted, between yawns, a detailed picture of the dismal weather he could expect to encounter between Rucker and Washington. To make matters more interesting, it would worsen as the day passed and they were on their way back.

He would be in the soup all day. It was even possible that if they got into the Army Airfield at Fort Eustis, they wouldn't be able to get out. He remembered then that he had not brought a change of linen. If they weathered in, he wouldn't be able to change his socks or his underwear. He hated that.

General Bellmon and Harry Schultz, the Boeing-Vertol tech rep from Benning, were in the lobby of Base Operations when Oliver came out of Flight Planning. Schultz was unshaven and wearing the same World War II leather pilot's jacket Oliver had seen him wearing the day before. General Bellmon was in his overcoat, buttoned around his neck. He carried a blouse and shirt on a hanger. He was also unshaven.

That mysterious behavior was explained as they got into 917. Bellmon took off the overcoat and Oliver saw that he was wearing an old athletic jacket under it.

''Would you like to fly, Sir?'' Oliver asked.

"I'm going to catnap in the back," Bellmon said. "If we run into any weather or something wake me."

"Yes, Sir."

Forty minutes later, at Fort Benning's Lawson Army Airfield, a man walked up to the U-8F as Oliver was shutting down the engines. He was attired in a zipper jacket worn over a gray cotton sweatsuit, and he was carrying two plastic-bagged hangers of uniforms and a small pillow under his arm. Oliver recognized him only after Schultz had opened the door and gotten out onto the wing to reach down for the luggage and pillow.

"You stay right where you are, Harry," Brigadier General William R. Roberts said, quickly declining Schultz's offer of the seat in front. "I'm going to crap out with General Bellmon in the back."

Three minutes after that, as Johnny Oliver pushed the throttles of the U-8F to takeoff power and told Lawson he was rolling, he thought wryly, *Oh, what a grand and glorious aviator you must be, Johnny Oliver, to be at the controls of a flying machine with both the Army's most experienced airplane driver and the headman of the flying school trying to go to sleep in the back seat, placing full trust in you as you soar off into the wild blue yonder.*

A moment later he thought that it really wasn't the blue yonder; he wasn't going to break out of the soup at all. Weather had told him it topped out at fifteen thousand or so, and he wasn't going over ten thousand, and would thus be in the gray soup all the way. But aside from that . . .

[FOUR]
262 Winding Glen Road
Silver Spring, Maryland
0720 Hours 14 January 1964

As soon as they landed at Eustis, Harry Schultz disappeared in the direction of Base Ops. Generals Bellmon and Roberts helped him tie down the airplane.

How many lowly captains, Oliver thought, *have had the Army's most experienced aviator and the Commandant of the*

Aviation School help them *tie down an airplane in a freezing drizzle?*

When the three of them approached Base Ops, they found Harry Schultz waiting with a huge man in a Navy officer's uniform. Oliver was not at all surprised when Schultz introduced him as Commander Bull Jenkins, but he wondered who the hell he was. No explanation was offered, and Oliver believed that good little aides should not ask questions.

Bull Jenkins drove them in a Buick station wagon to Silver Spring. Once there, Bellmon gave directions, and they ended up in front of a two-story brick house. Everybody got out.

"Thanks, Bull," Harry Schultz said.

"My pleasure, Admiral," Commander Jenkins said. "Anytime."

Admiral?

Commander Bull Jenkins saluted, got back in his Buick, and drove off.

Harry Schultz said, to Oliver, "Bull was my aide when I had Guantánamo."

"Sir, I had no idea you were an admiral," Oliver said, feeling like a fool.

"The operative word, Johnny," Schultz said, "is *'was.'* What I am now is the Vertol tech rep, and you don't say 'Sir' to tech reps."

"Yes, Sir . . . ooops," Oliver said.

Schultz chuckled and patted Oliver's arm, directing him up the walk to the front of the two-story house. Bellmon and Roberts were already there. There were lights visible in the rear of the house, and as Oliver watched, lights came on in what was probably the living room, and then over the door.

A middle-aged man in a bathrobe, holding a cup of coffee in his hand, opened the door, but he made no move to open the glass storm door. He was Lieutenant General Richard J. Cronin, Deputy Chief of Staff, Operations, United States Air Force. He was also Major General Robert F. Bellmon's brother-in-law.

"What I think I'm going to do is to go back in the kitchen and pretend I didn't hear the chimes," General Cronin said. "I don't want to see you guys. Good God!"

"Open the damned door," General Bellmon said. "It's cold out here."

"Dick, for God's sake," General Roberts said.

"Who is it?" a female voice demanded impatiently, and then appeared, also in a bathrobe. "Bob!" she said, pushing past the man in the bathrobe, unlatching the storm door and opening it. "What's the matter with you, Dick, why didn't you open the door?"

"I was hoping they'd go away," he said perfectly seriously. "I know why they're here."

"What?" she asked as she held the door open and hurried them through. "What is all this, Bob? What *are* you doing here at this time of the morning?"

"Don't ask, Helen," the man in the bathrobe said.

"Why didn't you call or something?" the woman said, kissing Bellmon's cheek and then Roberts's. "You, too, Bill? What's going on?"

"How are you, Helen?" Roberts asked.

"Do you know Harry Schultz, Dick?" Bellmon added.

"No, I don't think so," Dick Cronin said. "Wait a minute, sure I do. You were at the War College, weren't you? Well, it's good to see you, at least, Admiral."

"I'm on their side, Dick," Schultz said.

"With respect, Sir, I'm sorry to hear that."

"And this is my aide, Captain John Oliver," Bellmon said. "Johnny, this is General and Mrs. Cronin. United States Air Force."

General Cronin, and then his wife, offered Oliver their hands.

"Well, whatever this is all about, it will wait until I can get some coffee into you. And breakfast," Mrs. Cronin said. "You haven't eaten, have you?"

"No, we haven't," Bellmon said. "Thank you, Sis. And we'll need, Bill and I, your bathroom to shave and change."

"Well, you know where it is," she said. "Take Bill with you and I'll get started in the kitchen."

"Where are the kids?" Bellmon asked.

"Nobody's home," she said. "So there's room for everybody if you're staying. Unless you're going out to the Farm?"

"We're not staying, but thank you," Bellmon said. Then

he added, ''As soon as we finish at the Pentagon, we have to get back for a memorial service for a pilot we lost.''

''Apropos of nothing whatever, of course,'' General Cronin said.

Bellmon glared at him but didn't reply directly. He handed Oliver an attaché case. ''While General Roberts and I are changing, Johnny, why don't you show General Cronin the photographs of the Chinook accident? There's some new ones in there, too. Harry can show him what happened.''

''Jesus Christ, Bob!'' Cronin protested angrily.

Bellmon touched Roberts's arm and guided him toward the stairs.

Cronin looked coldly at Johnny Oliver.

''Aides are supposed to learn how things are run, Captain,'' he said. ''I hope you don't come to the conclusion that this is the way things are supposed to be done.''

''Dick!'' Mrs. Cronin protested. ''Whatever this is all about, it's certainly not the Captain's fault.''

''No,'' General Cronin said, ''it isn't. I know whose fault it is. I'm sorry, Captain. Come on in the study.''

Johnny and Schultz followed Cronin through his living room to a small room equipped with a desk and a wall lined with bookshelves. There was no window.

There was a silver-framed photograph on the desk. A wedding picture, taken outside the chapel at West Point. Oliver saw a second lieutenant, wearing U.S. Army Corps insignia, and the woman who had just defended him, and a lieutenant colonel, and brigadier general, and their wives. And a cadet wearing corporal's chevrons. The cadet corporal was now Major General Robert F. Bellmon. The Brigadier General was almost certainly, Oliver decided, former Lieutenant General Robert F. Bellmon, Jr.

General Cronin took the two envelopes of photographs from Oliver and sat down at the desk.

''Please sit down, gentlemen,'' Cronin said and began to study the photographs.

Mrs. Cronin came in with coffee just as he said, ''Good God!''

''May I see those?'' Mrs. Cronin asked.

"No," General Cronin said immediately, sharply. Then, "Oh, what the hell. Have a look if you'd like."

"Are they classified, or what?"

"Probably," General Cronin said. "They should be. But there's never any telling with your brother."

"Oh, my God!" Mrs. Cronin said as she looked down over her husband's shoulder. She looked at Oliver, then at Schultz, and walked out of the room.

"OK," Cronin said, looking at Oliver. "What have I seen?"

"The tragic results of inadequately supervised maintenance," Harry Schultz answered for him. "What happens when you don't put safety wire where there is supposed to be safety wire. And what happens when an inspector signs off a job without going to the trouble of actually checking to see that it's been done properly."

"That's a *theory*," Cronin replied. "There is also a metal-fatigue theory, and several other theories having to do with basic design inadequacies."

"There is another theory," Bellmon said, walking into the room, tying his tie as he walked, "that there was great jubilation in the Air Force when this aircraft went in."

"Goddammit, Bob!" Cronin exploded. "No one likes fatal accidents! Jesus Christ, how can you say something like that?"

"Because it's true," Bellmon said. "Because that goddamned accident-investigation team of yours was off the ground at Wright-Patterson three minutes after they got the TWX."

"They should have been at Rucker all along," Cronin replied. "And I have pretty reliable information about who kept them from being there."

"And I still don't," Bellmon said. "I have no intention of feeding a Trojan horse."

"You're paranoid," Cronin said. "We're not the enemy."

"The hell you're not," Bellmon said. "You bastards wouldn't give us the support we told you we needed, and you thought it was hilarious when we said, 'OK, we'll do it ourselves,' and now that it looks like we *can* do it ourselves, you're doing everything in your power to screw us."

"Stop it!" Mrs. Cronin said angrily, rushing into the room. "You're not going to start in on that argument again, not at this time of the morning. I mean it."

"Sorry," Bellmon said.

"You remember what happened the last time!" she said, still angry.

There was silence in the small room.

"Breakfast is ready," she said. "Come and eat it. Where's Bill?"

"Bill has learned to be very careful around sharp instruments like a razor," Bellmon said. "He's a little slow, but he'll be along in a minute."

"Well, you two knock it off and come out and eat."

"In just a minute, honey," Cronin said.

"Don't start it up again, Dick," Helen Cronin said. "I mean it. You either, Bob."

Both of them raised their hands in a gesture of surrender.

When she had gone, Cronin looked at Schultz.

"If you were to tell me, Admiral, that it is your best professional judgment that this accident is, as you say, attributable to gross, damned near incredible, sloppy maintenance, I'd take your word."

"I'm not an admiral anymore, Dick," Schultz said. "I'm the Vertol tech rep."

"I'm asking you as an admiral."

Schultz's lips twisted in thought momentarily.

"General," he said finally, formally, "it is my judgment that there is nothing wrong with the rotor assemblies on Ch-47-Series helicopters. I would bet my life that this accident was caused by a mechanic's error; that a safety wire, or wires, that should have been installed was not, or were not, installed."

Cronin looked at him intently for a moment.

"The trouble, Harry," he said sadly, "is that at our age and position we're betting other people's lives, not our own." He looked at Oliver. "Can you fly this machine, son?"

"Yes, Sir."

"Would you feel safe in taking one of them for a ride, right now, without further investigation of the cause of this accident? Were you at the crash site, by the way?"

"He took those pictures at the crash site," Bellmon said.

"Let him answer, Bob," Cronin said softly but sharply.

"I would pull the inspection panel and look at the rotor head myself," Oliver said. "But, yes, Sir, I would fly it. Confidently."

"I would have been surprised if you said anything else," Cronin said, resignedly. "Isn't that why you brought him along, Bob, because you knew I would ask that question and you were sure of what his answer would be?"

"I suppose it looks that way," Bellmon said, "but no. He's here because he's my aide and I needed someone to drive the airplane. And I didn't know until just now what his answer would be. Now that I think of it, if I were Johnny Oliver I would be more than a little insulted at your implication that he would lie for me or for anybody else."

"No offense was intended, Captain," General Cronin said.

"None taken, Sir," Oliver said.

Bellmon was not through. "He doesn't have to kiss my ass, Dick, for a good efficiency report," he said angrily. "He came home from Vietnam with a Silver Star and a DFC."

"I said I meant no offense," Cronin said.

Bellmon was still not through.

"And he's Norwich, a regular."

Cronin ignored the outburst. He waited a moment to give Bellmon a chance to calm down, then he asked, "Spell it out, Bob. What do you want from me?"

Bellmon took a moment to frame his thoughts.

"Yesterday the Chief Signal Officer went to our DCSOPS and pleaded the necessity of having the Chinook grounding lifted—"

" *'Yesterday'?* " General Cronin parroted.

"Yesterday. Sunday," Bellmon said. "He didn't get anywhere. DCSOPS said he couldn't do a thing without Air Force acquiesence, the pressure was on. Bill Roberts and I are going to be in his office first thing this morning, and we're going to hit him again. We just don't have the time to wait for a full-blown accident-investigation report. Anyway, he's going to give us the same speech: he can't do anything without Air Force acquiescence. Whereupon I will say, 'Call Dick Cronin. The Air Force DCSOPS is willing to go along.' "

"And what am I supposed to say to my Chief of Staff," Cronin demanded, "when he hears about this and calls me in?"

"Tell him the truth. Tell him that we absolutely have to have the Chinook experience, both at Rucker and with the 11th Air Assault, before the 11th goes to Vietnam, and that the risk is justified."

"The problem with that, Bob, is that the Chief of Staff devoutly believes that as soon as Lyndon Johnson finds out what McNamara has been letting you guys get away with, he'll tell him to cut Army Aviation back to where it belongs." Johnson had become President less than two months earlier.

"Back to Key West, you mean, Dick?" The roles and missions of the Army, Navy, Marine Corps, and Air Force, including what aircraft the Army were permitted to have, had been spelled out in an agreement signed at Key West in 1948.

"Exactly," General Cronin said. "And when that happens, Army Aviation, of the size you're trying to make it—an Air Assault *Division* with its own large, complicated, and thus properly belonging to the Air Force, airplanes, and the supporting logistics—will be nothing more than a footnote, like dirigibles: an idea that didn't work."

"Then he's wrong," Bellmon said.

"I don't think so," Cronin said. "I think you're wrong."

"There's no telling what Johnson is going to do," Bellmon insisted. "Felter is doing the same thing for Johnson he did for Kennedy, and you know how McNamara hates him."

That announcement clearly surprised General Cronin.

"I hadn't heard that," he confessed, then added, "You're telling me you have a mouth at Johnson's ear, is that it?"

"I devoutly hope so," Bellmon said, "but what I'm telling you is that I think we've already gone too far to stop, no matter who thinks what about Army Aviation. And you know as well as I do that we're going to get deeper and deeper in Vietnam. I don't think Johnson is going to pull the rug out from under us—not now. For one thing, we're right. More importantly, McNamara thinks so. I don't think Johnson gives a damn one way or another who has the aircraft. And I don't think he would risk humiliating McNamara by reversing him that way. What did McNamara make at Ford? A million a year? He wouldn't stand for being humiliated."

Cronin digested that, his face moving as he did, but he didn't reply.

"The 11th Air Assault is going to Vietnam," Bellmon went on. "I think that's really a given. And it needs the Chinook, that's a given. And we need, *now*, the necessary training in its use. Equally important, we need the logistic data the Board tests are developing. Christ, we don't even have avionic radiation patterns for it yet! We have to fly the Chinook, Dick, and right now. We don't have the time to wait for an accident report, passed through channels, by Air Force types who know the Chief of Staff hopes they drag their feet."

"It isn't the Chinook alone," General Cronin said. "I really don't think we would object to that. But the Caribou is a transport airplane, and the Army isn't supposed to have transport airplanes. And the Mohawk!"

"The Mohawk is a reconnaissance airplane," Bellmon said.

"Come on, Bob, damn it!" General Cronin said furiously. "A reconnaissance airplane you've armed in Vietnam with fifty-caliber machine guns. I know all about your simple reconnaissance airplane: I even saw movies a week or so ago of your simple reconnaissance Mohawk shooting up a tank at the Yuma Test Station with thirty-millimeter cannon. That makes it, if not a fighter, then an armed ground-support airplane. And you know the Army's not supposed to have them."

"We're talking about the Chinook," Bellmon said. (*And just a little lamely,* Oliver thought.) "We've got to get that grounding lifted. If we don't, people are going to get killed. It is morally wrong to let that happen because we're fighting about roles and missions."

"Yeah, it is," General Cronin said after a long moment. "Goddamn you, Bob. But OK. With the clear understanding that this is it. This is the last time. Period. The end. Agreed?"

"Thank you," Bellmon said.

Helen Cronin appeared at the door at the moment. She had her hands on her hips and her lips were tight.

But what she saw was her husband and her brother shaking hands.

"Breakfast is on the table," she announced.

[ONE]
Main Post Chapel
Fort Rucker, Alabama
1450 Hours 14 January 1964

The parking lot between the Main Post Chapel and the Officers' Open mess was full; the overflow stretched blocks in all directions.

Was Jack Dant that popular, Oliver wondered as he walked quickly from the back door of Post Headquarters to the chapel, *or is some of this morbid curiosity*? The thought shamed him, and he came up with another reason for all the mourners: *It is a mark of respect to the widow. There, but for the grace of God, in other words. . . .*

He shouldered his way through the crowd standing outside. There were ushers at the door, but the panache of a general officer rubs off to some degree on his aide, and no one tried to stop him from entering the chapel. He quickly located the

Bellmons (just the General and Mrs. B; Marjorie was not in sight), walked up the aisle to them, bent over General Bellmon, and whispered, "This just came in, Sir."

Bellmon took it and read it.

PRIORITY

HQ DEPT OF THE ARMY WASH DC 1720Z 14JAN64

TO: COMMANDING GENERAL
US ARMY AVIATION CENTER FT RUCKER, ALA
COMMANDING GENERAL
11TH AIR ASSAULT DIVISION [TEST] FT BENNING GA
PRESIDENT USARMY AVIATION BOARD FT RUCKER ALA
INFORMATION: COMMANDING GENERAL,
CONTINENTAL ARMY COMMAND
COMMANDER-IN-CHIEF, US ARMY PACIFIC
COMMANDER-IN-CHIEF, US ARMY EUROPE
COMMANDING GENERAL, US ARMY ALASKA
COMMANDING GENERAL, US ARMY SOUTHERN COMMAND

1. REF TWK HQ DA 1600Z 11JAN64 SUBJECT: GROUNDING OF CH47-SERIES CHINOOK AIRCRAFT.

2. EFFECTIVE IMMEDIATELY CH47-SERIES CHINOOK AIRCRAFT ASSIGNED TO 11TH AIR ASSAULT DIVISION [TEST]; USARMY AVIATION CENTER; AND USARMY AVIATION BOARD, ONLY REPEAT ONLY, WHICH ARE CONSIDERED ESSENTIAL REPEAT ESSENTIAL TO CONDUCT OF PRIORITY TRAINING AND TESTING MAY BE FLOWN ON A RESTRICTED BASIS.

3. ALL REPEAT ALL OTHER CH47-SERIES CHINOOK AIRCRAFT REMAIN GROUNDED PENDING RESULTS OF JOINT USARMY/USAIRFORCE ACCIDENT INVESTIGATION BOARD.

4. RECEIPT OF THIS MESSAGE WILL BE ACKNOWLEDGED BY PRIORITY TWX. NO REPEAT NO REQUESTS FOR EXCEPTIONS ARE DESIRED.

FOR THE CHIEF OF STAFF:
WINDSOR, LT GEN, DCSOPS

General Bellmon read it, nodded his head, smiled at Oliver, and handed it back.

Oliver started back down the center aisle of the chapel. As he approached the rear, he saw Marjorie Bellmon and smiled. She stood up, stepped into the aisle, and gestured for him to sit down. When he looked hesitant, she made a gesture of insistence. He went into the pew and sat down and found himself sitting next to Liza Wood, who gave him a surprised look, and then an impersonal, perhaps uncomfortable, smile.

He dozed off during the chaplain's eulogy and woke suddenly to an elbow in his ribs.

''You were snoring,'' Liza Wood whispered intently. He could smell her breath, something like peppermint, and could feel its warmth.

Being awake did not turn his attention to what the chaplain was saying. He was conscious only of Liza Wood's perfume, of the black lace he could see inside her dress at the swell of her breasts and at the hem, and of the soft warmth of her thigh pressing, however unintentionally, against his.

He was somewhat startled when the pallbearers, Charley Stevens among them, second on the right, carried Jack Dant's flag-covered casket back down the aisle.

The chapel then emptied from the front. First the widow and her family, and then the close friends and the brass. The people in the rear, Oliver and Marjorie and Liza among them, were the last to leave.

By the time they were outside, the hearse had already driven off, and General and Mrs. Bellmon were waiting for them.

''Do you know my mother and father?'' Marjorie asked Liza, and made the introductions. There was no indication on either side that anyone remembered Liza slamming the door of Jack Dant's house in the Bellmons', and Johnny Oliver's, faces.

''Are you going to the house, dear?'' Mrs. Bellmon asked.

Marjorie nodded. ''Liza and I are going to help serving,'' she said.

"Johnny, why don't you go with Marjorie?" Bellmon said. "See if there is anything at all we can do."

"Yes, Sir," Johnny Oliver said.

"And then get yourself some sleep," General Bellmon went on. "I'll see you in the morning."

When they had gone, Liza Wood looked at him.

"Rough night last night, Johnny?"

"Unfair, Liza," Marjorie said. "Daddy had Johnny up in the middle of the night to fly them to Washington. And I heard him tell Mother that he wasn't tired, he'd slept both ways while Johnny flew."

"Sorry," Liza said with what Johnny decided was monumental insincerity. Then she asked, "What was going on in Washington that wouldn't wait?"

"We were trying to get the Chinook grounding lifted," Johnny replied.

"And did you succeed?"

"Yes, we did," he said evenly.

"Good for you. Now you soldiers can kill some other nice young man," Liza said, and turned and walked away.

"What was that all about?" Marjorie asked, shocked.

"I guess the service opened a scar," Johnny said.

"That didn't give her the right to jump all over you."

"Let it go, Marjorie, but thank you," Oliver said.

"I was about to offer you a ride," Marjorie said. "You look really beat. But I guess you're not going to stay a minute longer than necessary, are you?"

"No. I'm all right. But thank you anyway."

"Well, *I* like you, anyway," Marjorie said, and rose on her toes to kiss him on the cheek.

The guy that gets her, he thought, *gets the brass ring.*

[TWO]

The remains of First Lieutenant John M. Dant would be returned to his home for interment in the family plot. That would happen the next day. Oliver had seen the G-1's plans for that. An Otter had been laid on to fly the pallbearers to Ohio and to bring them and the escort officers back after the interment. The escort officers, a light colonel and a captain from the Aviation Board, would accompany the widow, and the remains, to Ohio, on Commercial Air.

Friends and neighbors of the widow had set up a buffet in the Dant home, to which other friends and neighbors went after the memorial service.

When Johnny Oliver reached the house, the street was full of cars. When he drove past Liza Wood's driveway, he thought for a moment of parking there.

Fuck it! She told me, however politely, to fuck off. If she sees that car there, she'll decide I don't know how to take no for an answer.

He drove around the block, finally found a place to park, and walked to the Dant house.

The widow, looking dazed and pale, was in an armchair in her living room. The callers passed by the chair, said something, and then went into the dining room where the buffet had been laid.

Johnny took his place in line. As he moved closer to the widow, he wondered what he should say.

Mrs. Dant, I really didn't know your husband, but when I was in the deep shit, in 'Nam, he put his balls on the chopping block for me, and I'm sorry as hell that goddamned rotor assembly came apart.

He bent over her, took her gloved hand, and said, "Mrs. Dant, I'm Captain John Oliver, General Bellmon's aide-de-camp. The General asked me to find out if there's anything, anything at all, that you need."

"Thank you very much," Mrs. Dant said.

She didn't hear a word I said.

He walked into the dining room and leaned against the wall.

I should be starved; the last thing I had to eat was breakfast in Silver Spring. But I'm not hungry.

Marjorie Bellmon appeared with a cup of coffee and extended it to him.

He shook his head, no.

"It's scotch," she said. "We decided we weren't going to have an open bar, but you look like you need it."

He took a sip and she smiled at him. And then someone

nudged him in the ribs and he saw First Lieutenant Charles J. Stevens standing beside him.

"Marjorie," Johnny said. "This is Charley Stevens. He's a classmate of mine, and he and Jack Dant flew together in 'Nam. I think I should warn you that he's been an admirer of yours, from afar, for some time."

"Hello," Marjorie said. "Why from afar?"

"Because my pal here has refused to introduce me," Charley said.

"Well, now that you've met me, what can I do for you?"

"I would really like to have some of the herb tea, or whatever it is, you just gave Johnny," Stevens said. "In exchange for which I will drag all the skeletons out of his closet for your inspection."

"All right," she said, smiling. "I'd love to know about Johnny's skeletons. Come with me."

She likes him, Oliver decided. *Well, why not? He's a good-looking guy, and amusing. The female of the species is as driven by nature as the male to find a mate.*

He watched as Charley opened the kitchen door for Marjorie, and then he turned, swiveling his head around. He would find the light-bird escort officer and tell him the General had sent him to see how he could help. And then he would get the hell out of here and follow his last order to get some sleep.

As he walked down the street to his car, he glanced toward Liza's house.

This is a goddamned fool thing to do, he thought as he turned toward Liza's house. *All you're going to do is get kicked in the teeth. Or make her uncomfortable. Or make an ass of yourself. Or all of the above. So why are you doing it?*

He walked up her driveway and to the kitchen door. She was inside, slicing the crust off delicate little sandwiches. He thought she did that with exquisite feminine grace.

I can still go. She hasn't seen me.

That option was removed when a middle-aged woman carrying a small blond boy in her arms walked into the kitchen, saw him, smiled, and said something to Liza.

The kid is almost certainly Liza's; that probably makes the woman her mother-in-law, Allan's mother.

Liza's surprise at seeing him showed on her face, but she said something to her mother-in-law, who came and opened the door.

"Hello," she said.

"Hello," Oliver said, and then looked over her to Liza. "Marjorie sent me to see if you need anything," he said.

"Come in, Johnny," Liza said.

She knows goddamn well Marjorie didn't send me here.

"How do you do, Captain?" Mother Wood said.

"And this is Allan," Liza said, picking up the child. "The kid."

She is pissed.

The boy hid his face in Liza's shoulder. Johnny saw Liza again as the madonna she had been when she was pregnant.

"Did you happen to know my son, Captain—Oliver is it?—Lieutenant Allan Wood?" Mother Wood asked.

"Yes, Ma'am, I did," Oliver said.

"He and Allan were buddies," Liza said. "They went through flight school together."

"Oh, I see."

She was smiling, but Oliver saw in her eyes the unfriendly question, *Why are you here, then, and my son dead?*

Liza handed the child to Oliver. The child didn't like that, and tried to get free.

"Here, let me have him," Mother Wood said, putting her hands out. "You're a stranger to him; he's always finicky with strangers."

Oliver started to hand the child over, whereupon he clung to him desperately and said, firmly, "No!"

"I'll hold him awhile," Oliver said.

The child stuck his tongue out at his grandmother.

"Can I offer you something to drink, Johnny?" Liza asked. "It'll be awhile until I'm finished."

"Please," he said.

"There's a bottle of scotch in the cabinet," she said, indicating the cabinet with a tilt of her head.

"Will you have one?" he asked.

"Please," she said. "A light one."

"Mrs. Wood?" Johnny asked.

"Mother Wood is a Baptist, Johnny," Liza said. "They don't use alcohol."

"But I never try to force my views on others," Mother Wood said.

"The hell you don't!" Liza said, laughing.

". . . so you just go right ahead," Mother Wood concluded, ignoring her.

In the next twenty minutes Mother Wood learned from John Oliver that he was a bachelor *("Good for you. Bide your time until the right girl comes along, I always say")*, that he was Bellmon's aide *("Then you must be something special; I'm sure they wouldn't let just anybody do that")*, that he was Regular Army and Norwich *("Until just now I had always been led to believe that Texas A & M was the oldest military school in the country; I can't imagine why I never heard of this Norwich University before")*, and that both of his parents were dead *("That's really a shame, I feel sorry for you")*.

And Oliver learned from her that Allan had been heavily insured *("Praise God that he understood his responsibilities; I know for a fact that a lot of girls in Elizabeth's position aren't one-tenth as well taken care of")*, that Liza had turned out to be a near-instant success as a real estate lady *("And I don't think I'm saying anything I shouldn't, surprising just about everybody, including Allan's daddy and me. She even now has her own business, with people working for her and everything")*, and that Liza was not without suitors *("Mind, if there's anyone special, Elizabeth hasn't seen fit to confide in me. Which, if you think about it, is not at all surprising, and is the way things should be. You can't mourn the dead forever. We Christians believe that our dead have gone to be with Jesus")*.

And then the three of them, the women carrying large plates of crustless sandwiches, Oliver carrying Allan, marched back to the Dant house.

Liza and Mother Wood promptly disappeared into the house, where tables of food had been set up, leaving Oliver in the kitchen, still holding the child. He tried to put the boy down, which produced an immediate, indignant, "No!"

What the hell do I do now?

Liza reappeared.

"There's more at my house," she said. "Will you help me?"

Without waiting for an answer, she took the child from him, ignoring another indignant "No!" and told him to go find Mother Wood.

He followed her back to her house, this time through the intervening backyards.

As they went into her kitchen, she said, "I saw you driving by, looking for a place to park. Why didn't you park in my driveway?"

"I didn't think I should."

"Then why did you come over here?"

"I don't know."

"I'm glad you did."

She smiled when she saw the look of surprise on his face.

"Really," she said. "That's why I asked you to come back over here. I wanted to tell you that, and I couldn't do it with Mother Wood around."

"Then I'm glad I came," he said.

She smiled at him. "Now I'll have to find something for you to carry back to the Dants' so that no one will wonder why we came back empty-handed."

He chuckled.

She turned to the kitchen cabinets, opened a cabinet door, and squatted down to look inside.

"Oh, I know," she said, closing the door, then standing up and going to another cabinet and opening its door. "A stockpot. We can fill it with ice from my freezer. That's credible. There's never enough ice."

She reached up to take a large stockpot from the shelf. Oliver stepped behind her and put his arms around her. She trembled. He kissed the side of her face, and moved his hand to her breast, and felt as well as heard her deep intake of breath.

"Oh, God, I wanted you to do that," she said softly.

Then she turned around and went into his arms and kissed him.

Twenty minutes later, when he carried the stockpot into the Dant kitchen, Marjorie Bellmon was there.

Liza said, ''Just put it anywhere, Johnny,'' and walked past Marjorie without speaking.

''What's that supposed to be for?'' Marjorie asked.

''Haven't the foggiest,'' Oliver said. ''I'm just making myself useful.''

''Uh huh,'' Marjorie said. ''It's a good thing I know you're a nice guy, Johnny.''

''And what is that supposed to mean?''

Goddammit, she knows. Does it show, or what?

''I wondered what that business at the chapel was all about,'' Marjorie said. ''She's a friend of mine, and she's a nice girl.''

''I know she's a nice girl.''

''That's why I'm glad I know you're a nice guy,'' Marjorie said, and then Liza walked into the kitchen with a nearly empty plate of cold cuts.

''Still here?'' Liza asked. ''I thought you were going.''

''Right now,'' Johnny said.

He saw that Marjorie Bellmon's eyes were smiling—or was it laughing?—at him.

[THREE]
Office of the Commanding General
The Army Aviation Center & Fort Rucker, Alabama
0840 Hours 17 January 1964

''Office of the commanding general, Captain Oliver, aide-de-camp speaking, Sir,'' Johnny Oliver answered the telephone in the prescribed manner.

''Captain, my name is Mary Margaret Dunne,'' a very pleasant, clear, soft voice announced. ''I'm Colonel Sanford T. Felter's secretary. May I speak to General Bellmon, please?''

The Commanding General of the Army Aviation Center and Fort Rucker, Alabama, was sitting at that moment on that throne on which all men are equal.

Felter! I wonder what General Cronin meant with that remark about Felter being a mouth at President Johnson's ear?

''I'm sorry, Miss Dunne,'' Oliver said. ''General Bellmon isn't available at the moment. May I help you some way?''

"But he's there? I mean, you can get a message to him right away?"

"Would you care to call back in a few minutes, Miss Dunne? I'm sure he'll be available then."

"Well, if you can get a message to him in a few minutes, perhaps that won't be necessary."

"I'll be happy to, Ma'am."

"Colonel Felter's on his way down there. He has to see General Bellmon today. At the moment he's on Delta Flight 204 to Atlanta, connecting with Southern Airways Flight 104, arriving at Dothan at three forty-five Dothan Time."

Oliver, who had learned to have a pencil and note pad at hand whenever he answered the phone, scribbled that information down.

"Yes, Ma'am," he said. "Delta 204 to Atlanta; Southern 104 to Dothan, arriving here at three forty-five local time. I've got it."

"If there is any change in that schedule, Colonel Felter will let you know."

"Yes, Ma'am."

"Thank *you*," Miss Dunne said. "God bless you, young man."

Two minutes later General Bellmon was back at his desk, and Oliver walked into his office.

"Sir, Colonel Felter's coming down here," he said. "ETA at Dothan 1545. His secretary called."

"Well, then, we can expect him at 1545," Bellmon said. "Sister Matthew is never wrong."

"Sir?"

"Oh, that's right, you don't know, do you?" Bellmon said, smiling. "Felter has a staff of two. He's got an office in the old State, War, and Navy Building. You know where I mean?"

"No, Sir."

"It's that ugly building next to the White House. They call it the Executive Annex now, but at one time it held all the Army, Navy, and State Department bureaucrats. My dad used to say it was the ugliest building in Washington. Anyway, Felter has two people working for him. One of them is an old Regular Army warrant officer, used to be a cryptographer.

He's a bishop in the Mormons. The other one is the lady you talked to. She's a Catholic nun—temporarily relieved, released, whatever they say—from her vows so that she can take care of her father, who's dying. Every once in a while she forgets herself and answers the phone, 'Sister Matthew.' I asked Felter what that was all about and he told me. President Kennedy had heard about her, that she needed a job, and asked Felter if he could use her.''

''That explains the 'God bless you, young man,' '' Oliver said. ''I wondered about that.''

Bellmon chuckled. ''Colonel Lowell heard about the bishop and the nun, and started calling Felter His Holiness, Moses the First, the first Jewish Pope,'' he said.

''Sir, Colonel Lowell told me Colonel Felter is a 'Counselor to the President,' '' Oliver said, but it was a question rather than a statement.

He thought he saw a flicker of ice in Bellmon's eyes, but after a moment, Bellmon apparently decided he should answer the question. ''That's true. That's his title. But no one but the President seems to know exactly what he does. I've often wondered who writes his OER''—Officer's Efficiency Report. ''Lowell says they probably classify it Top Secret—President's Eyes Only and leave the blanks empty.''

Oliver sensed that he was supposed to chuckle, and did so.

''Well, arrange to have Felter picked up, Johnny,'' Bellmon said. ''If he stays over, he'll stay with us. I'll tell my wife. I wonder what he wants.''

''She said he has to see you today, Sir.''

''Well, whatever it is, it will be interesting.''

Three hours later, just before lunch, the Cairns AOD called and reported that a U-9 had just called in, about to land. The Army had purchased ''off-the-shelf'' half a dozen Aero Commanders—six-place, high-wing, rather plush, light twin-engine aircraft—and designated them U-9. There was a Code Six aboard, and he wanted ground transportation, but no honors. The name of the Code Six was Fullbright.

''I wonder what that sonofabitch wants?'' Bellmon asked rhetorically when Oliver told him.

Oliver waited and Bellmon produced an explanation. ''That's Colonel Dick Fullbright, Johnny. Ostensibly, he's the

Army representative to the FAA. Actually, he's CIA. Among other things—which is the reason I suspect the sonofabitch is here—he's the recruiting officer for Air America."

"Sir?"

"The CIA owns Air America. Remind me to explain the whole operation to you some time—I don't have the time now—but they like to hire experienced people, aviators, preferably people with their twenty years in. They retire at twenty and go to work for Air America at a lot more money than they made in uniform, or we could afford to pay them if we hired them as civilians. In other words, Fullbright scoops the cream off the milk, hiring away from us the very people we really need. And there's not a damned thing I can do to stop him."

"I see."

"I think it highly unlikely that Colonel Fullbright will stop by to pay his respects," Bellmon said dryly. "But if he does, Johnny, you let the bastard cool his heels out there for at least fifteen minutes."

"Yes, Sir."

Twenty minutes later, Colonel Sanford T. Felter climbed up the narrow staircase to General Bellmon's second-floor office. He was in civilian clothing, a baggy gray suit.

He looks, Oliver thought, *like anything but a West Point full bull colonel of infantry with a second award star on his Combat Infantry Badge.*

Oliver was a little surprised how warmly, however suppressed, Bellmon greeted Felter. Bellmon was not a demonstrative man, and for him to wrap an arm around someone's shoulders was highly unusual.

"I got a ride down here with Dick Fullbright, Bob," Felter said.

"I figured maybe that was it," Bellmon said. "What's that sonofabitch up to?"

Felter chuckled. "He asked that I pass on his respects."

"While he's stealing my pilots, right?"

"I don't know what he's doing," Felter said.

Bellmon snorted.

"I can never understand how you can stand that sonofabitch, Sandy," Bellmon said.

"How can I answer that? How about a square peg in a square hole?"

"I'd like to pound Dick Fullbright into a square hole," Bellmon said. "With a sledgehammer."

Felter laughed and then got right down to business. "This is Top Secret, Bob," he said.

"With your permission, Sir?" Oliver said, expecting to be dismissed with a wave of Bellmon's hand. To his surprise, Felter insisted that he stay.

"You've got a Top Secret clearance, Captain," he said. "You might as well hear this."

Bellmon gestured for Oliver to take a chair. Oliver wondered how Felter knew he had a Top Secret clearance, and decided that it probably was a given for every aide—an aide couldn't do his job if he had to leave the room every time a Top Secret document was uncovered.

"This is in connection with OPERATION EAGLE," Felter said. "It deals with the Belgian—the ex-Belgian—Congo. But aside from that, and the name, that's all you have to know about it right now. Plus what we talk about here, of course."

"I understand," Bellmon said.

"I'm about to augment the staff of the military attaché in our embassy in Leopoldville with a U-8 and two pilots to fly it," Felter said.

"Where are you going to get the U-8?" Bellmon asked. "They're in short supply, Sandy. I've even heard talk they're going to buy some more U-9s off the shelf."

"One's on its way from the Beech Aircraft plant right now," Felter said. "Charley Augustus's people are going to fit it out with the avionics it needs and see that auxiliary fuel tanks are installed. It will be ferried over."

"What can I do to help?" Bellmon asked.

Oliver saw that the way Bellmon treated Felter was not at all like the way he had come to expect a major general to treat a colonel. The normal junior-senior roles seemed to be reversed, with Bellmon seeming to take as a given that Felter's authority was greater than his own.

"I need some people," Felter said.

"I was afraid you were going to say that," Bellmon said. "If I lose many more experienced pilots, Oliver and I will be out there in the back seat of an O-1, teaching Basic Flight.''

''This is important,'' Felter said.

Bellmon waved his hand in a gesture that said, ''I know.''

''What people?''

Felter took a folded sheet of typewriter paper from his bulging interior jacket pocket.

''DCSPERS came up with these three names,'' Felter said. DCSPERS is Deputy Chief of Staff, Personnel, pronounced, ''dee see ess purse.'' ''They're U-8-qualified, speak French, and have done a tour in 'Nam. I want to talk to them, to pick two of them.''

Oliver's mouth ran away with him. ''Is my name on there?''

Bellmon looked at him in surprise, almost shocked. Aides do not enter conversations like this until asked to do so.

Felter chuckled. ''You don't *speak* French, Captain. You *took French* for three years at Norwich. There's a difference.''

Jesus Christ, how did he come by that information?

''Sorry, Sir.''

''Would you like to use my office to interview these people, Sandy?'' Bellmon asked.

''Let's keep it informal. What about over a beer, at the club, after lunch?''

Bellmon nodded and handed Oliver the list.

''Johnny, get in touch with these people. Go through their department heads and inform them it is the General's desire that they attend him at the bar of the club at 1330. If you're asked for details, as I suspect you will be, tell them there is some Washington big shot here who wants to talk to them. OK, Sandy?''

''Make that State Department big shot,'' Felter said, smiling.

[FOUR]
Office of the Commanding General
The Army Aviation Center & Fort Rucker, Alabama
1535 Hours 17 January 1964

Captain John Oliver stood in General Bellmon's doorway and waited until Bellmon looked up from the paperwork on his desk.

"Colonel Felter got off OK, Sir," he said. "Very classily, as a matter of fact. There was an Air Force Special Missions Lear waiting for him out there."

Bellmon gestured for him to come in the office.

"You made a very good impression on Colonel Felter, Johnny," Bellmon said, "which may turn out to be a mixed blessing. Anyway, he telephoned me just now—"

"Just now, Sir? You mean he had to land again?"

"No. Apparently there's a telephone—a radio telephone, whatever it's called—on those airplanes. The sort of thing I'd like to have in my aircraft—"

"I haven't forgotten, Sir."

That's a bold-faced lie. Jesus Christ, why do I write things down in a notebook and then never look in the notebook?

"Anyway, he called just now and said that if I didn't think it would interfere with your other duties, and since you know, more or less, what's going on, he'd like you to keep an eye on that U-8 he's sending to SCATSA, and on the two officers who're going to the Congo for him. So, 'in addition to your other duties, Captain Oliver . . .' "

"I understand, Sir."

"You'd better let Colonel Augustus at SCATSA and Colonel McNair at the Board know about it," Bellmon said. "Exercise tact, just let them know that if they have any problems, they should tell you, and you'll tell me, and we'll do whatever we can to help."

"Yes, Sir."

"Put that pretty high on the priority list, Johnny," Bellmon said. "We have to presume that whatever Felter is up to is important."

"Yes, Sir. Sir, I'm pretty well caught up here right now. Would you like me to go see Colonel Augustus and Colonel McNair now?"

"Go ahead, Johnny. And don't bother to come back. I'm going to play a few holes of golf as soon as I'm finished here. I'll see you in the morning."

"Yes, Sir."

Colonel John W. McNair, President of the Army Aviation Board, wasn't in his office. His secretary—a statuesque blonde named Anne Caskie, whose good looks, Oliver had already learned, masked an extraordinary degree of hard-nosed competence—told him she had no idea where her boss was. Oliver was convinced she was not telling the truth; she just wasn't about to disturb him for anything unimportant.

"I'll try him again later, or in the morning," Oliver said.

"He'll be *so* sorry he missed you," Anne Caskie said, flashing him a dazzling smile.

When he went to Colonel Augustus's office in the SCATSA hangar, and asked Augustus's operations sergeant if he could see him, the sergeant said, "Go right in, Captain, they're expecting you."

Colonels Augustus and McNair were sitting around a coffee table with a third officer, an old major. He was wearing a flight suit and was introduced as "Pappy" Hodges.

"Colonel Felter called me," McNair said, "and said that you would run interference, where necessary, with the bureaucrats. We were wondering when you would show up."

"Sorry I'm late, Sir."

"Well, right now we don't see any problems," McNair said. "That doesn't mean we won't have any in five minutes. The airplane will arrive either tomorrow or the day after, from Beech. I'll run it through our contract maintenance people on a priority basis for installation of the auxiliary fuel tanks, and then Charley will install the avionics. Pappy feels, and of course, he's right, that they should train on the airplane they're going to use, so getting it ready is the first priority. While that's happening, why don't you get the pilots through the paperwork? Passports, shots, household goods, you know what they'll have to do."

"Yes, Sir. Sir, are the avionics here?"

"The stuff from ARC is on the way from Boonton," Colonel Augustus said, referring to the Aircraft Radio Corporation. "Collins will ship their stuff air freight from Cedar

Rapids no later than five o'clock tomorrow afternoon. The Sperry stuff is in stock here. Most of it belongs to Dick Fullbright, but we'll use it and then replace it when Felter's stuff arrives from Phoenix. No problems there, as I see it."

They've obviously done this sort of thing before. How much of this sort of thing is going on?

"In other words, Oliver, you walked in as the meeting ended," McNair said. "I wish I could learn to time it like that."

"Unless you've got something?" Augustus asked. "Pappy?"

Major Pappy Hodges shook his head, no.

"Oliver?"

"I'd be grateful for a moment of your time, Colonel," Oliver said. "Nothing to do with this."

Colonel McNair and Major Hodges left.

Colonel Augustus heard Oliver out about the equipment that would permit General Bellmon to talk on the telephone while airborne.

"If it was anybody but Bellmon, Oliver," Augustus said, "I'd tell you to send the aircraft over. I've got a couple of them in stock. But they belong to Fullbright—"

That's the second time he's said that. What the hell does it mean?

"—and Bellmon, as we all know, doesn't want to be indebted to Fullbright. They cost $9,100. Have you got $9,100 in funds you can lay your hands on to buy one?"

"No, Sir, I don't think so."

"Well, don't get your hopes up, but I'll look around and see what I can do," Augustus said. "Bellmon is one of the good guys. But don't hold your breath."

"Thank you, Sir."

Oliver used the sergeant's telephone to try to report to Bellmon, but the sergeant major told him that "The General is out swatting a small white spheroid with a weighted stick."

Because he had the rest of the afternoon off, Oliver took advantage of it by spending an hour in Daleville dropping off and reclaiming his laundry and dry cleaning and then having the oil in the Pontiac convertible changed.

When he got to the BOQ, he saw Jose Newell's MG of

Many Colors and Charley Stevens's Mercury in the parking lot and guessed, correctly, that they would be in Annex #1.

They were, sitting at the bar in flight suits, flying with their hands.

"There I was," Oliver said as he slid onto a barstool beside them, "at ten thousand feet with nothing between me and the earth but a thin blonde."

"Fuck you, dog-robber," Charley Stevens said.

"Hey, I'm the guy who introduced you to Marjorie Bellmon."

"You got me," Stevens said. "Sergeant, give the dog-robber whatever he thinks he's man enough to drink." Then he turned to Oliver. "Hey, I saw you leaving my new colonel's office this afternoon."

"I didn't see you," Oliver said truthfully.

"You had the glassy eyes of someone thinking profound thoughts," Stevens said. "What were you doing?"

"Trying to figure out how to tell the General he can't have an airborne telephone."

"Why can't he? I thought generals got pretty much what they damned well wanted."

"Because they're nonstandard, and they cost $9,100, and I don't think he wants to buy one with his own money."

"What's an airborne telephone?" Jose Newell asked.

"An *airborne telephone*," Oliver said. "You talk on the telephone while airborne."

"You said something about $9,100."

"That's what they cost. Colonel Augustus told me."

"Oh, hell. All they are is a switch," Jose Newell said. "You can get the parts in Radio Shack for no more than a hundred bucks."

"Why do I have this strange feeling, Jose, that you know what you're talking about?" Oliver asked.

"Because I do. I've made a couple of them myself." He then delivered a ninety-second lecture on the functioning of such a device. Oliver didn't understand a thing he said.

"Tell me, Lieutenant Newell, how would you like to do your commanding general—more important, your roommate—a large favor?"

"You mean, build one—"

"Two," Oliver said.

"Where would I do it?" Newell asked.

"Three," Stevens said. "You will build *three* of these things, and in the SCATSA workshop. My new colonel will be impressed with my genius when I show him what I have done."

"I will have a word with your IP, Lieutenant Newell. I will get you out of class For the Good of the Service," Oliver said. "How long will it take?"

"A couple of hours," Newell said. "I could do it in an afternoon."

"I'll drink to that," Stevens said, "since it's the dog-robber's turn to buy. Sergeant, three of the same, if you please?"

"Just two," Oliver said. "I have a date."

"I heard you melted the Ice Princess," Stevens said.

"Who told you that?"

"Miss Marjorie," Stevens said triumphantly.

"We're going to have dinner, that's all."

"Yes, Sir, if you say so, Sir," Stevens said.

"Screw you, Charley," Oliver said.

Bellmon gets his airborne telephone, Oliver thought, *and I seem to have indeed melted the Ice Princess. Right now, God is in his heaven and all is right with the world.*

"On second thought, Sergeant," Oliver said to the bartender, "I think another little nip might be in order after all."

XII

[ONE]
Quarters #1
Fort Rucker, Alabama
1610 Hours 19 January 1964

"Hi," Barbara Bellmon said to her husband and Captain John S. Oliver as she and Marjorie walked into the kitchen. "Nice flight?"

The women were dressed up, including hats. They looked good, Oliver thought—wholesome and pretty. He remembered vaguely that they had been to some kind of religious function, something about churchwomen. He hadn't paid a lot of attention to it. The General wasn't going to be involved, and it was happening on a Sunday, normally his day off.

General Bellmon and Oliver, in flight suits, looking a little worn, were slumped in chairs at the kitchen table, drinking beer from the bottle neck. There was a stick of pepperoni and a knife on a chopping block.

"Johnny's a very good IP," Bellmon said. "It was . . . *educational.*"

"Don't sound so surprised," Barbara said as she bent and kissed her husband.

If she's concerned that he's been flying the Chinook, Oliver thought, *it doesn't show. Which means that she's concealing her concern; she is certainly aware that a lot of people call the Chinook "the flying coffin."*

Oliver had been surprised when Bellmon had told him he thought he should get himself checked out in the Chinook. The General had, of course, been given seven hours of "familiarization" time in the helicopter, which meant that Colonel McNair at the Board had taken him for several rides and had let him steer.

Getting "checked out" was a more complicated process. Officially called "transition," it required a lot of preparation—ground school, so to speak—to prepare for the written examination, as well as in-flight instruction. Bellmon had cracked the books like any other candidate for Chinook qualification, employed Oliver as a tutor, taken and passed the written examination, and was, Oliver thought, about three flight hours away from the point where he would feel comfortable signing him off and turning him over to one of the school's flight examiners for the flight check.

Oliver was ambivalent about the whole idea. For one thing, it was highly unlikely that Bellmon, as a major general, would ever be called upon to fly a Chinook as pilot-in-command. For another, getting transitioned into the Chinook was costing Bellmon a lot of time, and he didn't have much—any—time that could be easily spared. And finally there was the question of risk. If another tail rotor assembly came off, for example, when a lieutenant or captain was driving, there would always be another lieutenant or captain to take his place. Major General Bellmon would not be easy to replace. He was, Oliver often thought, one of the very few general officers around Army Aviation who hadn't learned to fly last month, and whose expertise Army Aviation would really miss.

Would it be worth, Oliver wondered, *the loss of a general officer of Bellmon's value to Army Aviation just so that he could adhere to the philosophy that an officer should never order a subordinate to do something he was unable or willing to do himself?*

Oliver did not doubt that that was the only reason why Bellmon wanted to transition into the Chinook. There was no ego involved.

"Where did you go?" Barbara Bellmon asked.

"Birmingham," Bellmon said. "I rubbed salt into the wound of making Johnny work on Sunday by feeding him in the airport restaurant. They make the worst hot turkey sandwich I've ever had."

"Well, we'll make it up to him," Barbara Bellmon said, "I've got steaks."

"No, Ma'am," Oliver said. "I've got a date, thank you just the same."

"Speaking of *that*," Marjorie said, turning from a kitchen cabinet with two beer glasses in her hand and setting them on the table. "I relieve you, Johnny, of your obligation to take me to the Norwich Dinner."

"I was looking forward to it," Oliver said.

Marjorie laughed. "No, you weren't," she said. "You were wondering how to get out of taking me. Now you can. Charley will take me, and you can bring Liz."

He looked at her and smiled. "OK," he said. "If you'd really rather go with that Arkansas clodkicker than me, what can I say?"

"And speaking of the Norwich Dinner, Johnny," Mrs. Bellmon said. "What's the uniform?"

The Fort Rucker Chapter of The Association of Graduates of Norwich University had as a matter of courtesy sent a pro forma invitation to the Commanding General of the Army Aviation School and Fort Rucker and his lady.

"You're going?" Oliver asked, surprised.

"I like to keep an eye on the *untermenschen* at play," General Bellmon said, "whenever I can."

"Bob!" Barbara Bellmon said warningly. "It wasn't on the invitation," she added.

"I'm not at all surprised," Bellmon said, undaunted. "Norwich types think that full dress means tying their shoelaces."

"Daddy!" Marjorie protested loyally, but she had to giggle.

"Mrs. Bellmon," Oliver said, "if dress was not specified on the invitation it's because we believed that most addressees, being Norwich men, would understand without having it written down for them, that the proper attire for a dinner at that hour would be dress blues, or mess dress."

Dress blues is the Army Blue uniform, worn for formal occasions, with a white shirt and a black bow tie. Mess dress is far more elaborate. The short jacket, worn over a "white-tie-and-tails" shirt and cummerbund, is heavily decorated with gold. Rank insignia is worn on the lower sleeve, in the center of gold loops (the higher the rank, the more loops). The lapels are faced with the color of the branch of service. The uniform includes a cape, similarly lined.

"Good for you, Johnny! Let him have it," Barbara Bellmon said. "What are you going to wear?"

"I've been thinking about going whole hog," Oliver said. "Mess dress."

"Has Charley got mess dress?" Marjorie asked.

"Uh huh," Oliver said. "We got it together, as a matter of fact. We took our R and R in Hong Kong. We bought ours from a tailor in Kowloon."

Barbara Bellmon started to giggle.

"What's funny, Mother?" Marjorie asked.

"I was thinking about Craig Lowell and his mess dress," she said.

"Jesus!" General Bellmon said, and snorted a chuckle.

"What happened was . . . this was at Fort Knox, in what, Bob? Forty-six?"

"Forty-seven."

"Bob was a lieutenant colonel," Barbara Bellmon went on, "and Craig—this was before we really knew him—was a second lieutenant. No one, *no one,* except a very few senior officers, colonels and generals, had dress uniforms. But they were trying to get back to pre-war standards so the brass started putting *formal dress encouraged* on invitations. And the General and a few other people started getting dressed up, to set an example. Well, for the post commander's annual reception, they did this. Well, when Lowell got his invitation, he did what any second lieutenant with X many million dollars would do: he got on the telephone and called Brooks Brothers and told them to send him whatever it was he was being encouraged to wear.''

''And he'd just been given the golden saucer,'' Bellmon said. ''You know about that, Johnny?''

''No, Sir.''

''He'd been with the Military Advisory Group to Greece, and performed really well, and the King of Greece gave him the Order of St. George and St. Andrew, the highest award given to non-Greeks. It's a gold thing, about the size of a saucer, worn hung from a purple sash around the neck. It's spectacular.''

''So there is the reception line, at the main club,'' Barbara picked up the story, ''with the General, maybe the Deputy Commandant, and three, four colonels, standing in it, all dressed up in dress *blues,* and everybody else in pinks and greens. And in walks this *second lieutenant* in dress *mess*, complete to cape, looking like Errol Flynn playing George Armstrong Custer in a movie . . .''

''With this enormous gold medal,'' Bellmon said, laughing and demonstrating, ''which no one had ever seen before, hanging down over his chest from a purple sash.''

''Poor Uncle Craig,'' Marjorie said.

''The General promptly decided he was being mocked,'' Barbara said.

''And I still think maybe he was,'' Bellmon said.

''He was not,'' Barbara said. ''Craig was innocent!''

''Whatever Craig Lowell is, he has never been innocent.''

''Now I'm not so sure dress mess is such a hot idea,'' Oliver said.

''Don't be silly,'' Barbara Bellmon said. ''You wear it. Bob will wear his.''

Oliver glanced at his watch and stood up. ''I've got to be going.''

''You're pretty close to Lieutenant Stevens, aren't you, Johnny?'' General Bellmon asked. ''He's a classmate, you said?''

''Yes, Sir, and we were together in 'Nam.''

''What's his background?'' Bellmon asked.

"Daddy! My God!" Marjorie protested.

"It's a perfectly reasonable question."

"If you're filling out a stud book, it might be," Marjorie snapped. "All I'm going to do with Charley Stevens is go to the Norwich Dinner with him."

"Why don't you leave, Johnny?" Barbara Bellmon said. "Before Marjorie belts him with a frying pan? Or I do?"

"His father has a Buick dealership, Sir," Oliver said. "They're very nice people."

"That's right, stick together," Marjorie said, and stuck her tongue out at him.

[TWO]
123 Brookwood Lane
Ozark, Alabama
1705 Hours 19 January 1964

Liza's car was in the driveway, and there were lights on in the house, but there was no response to his knock at the kitchen door. He shrugged and tried the door.

"Anybody home?"

"I'm giving Allan a bath," Liza called. "Be out in a minute. Fix yourself a drink or something."

He went inside and walked to her bathroom.

"Johnny, Mama! Johnny, Mama!" Allan announced happily if quite unnecessarily.

Allan was having a fine time with his bath, Oliver saw. He had discovered the joys of splashing water. Liza was soaked to the waist.

"You don't seem to be very good at that," Johnny said.

"Go to hell!" Liza said.

"Gotohell, Gotohell, Gotohell," Allan said.

"Shame on you, teaching that innocent child language like that," Johnny said, and ducked back out of the bathroom just in time to miss the bathwater Liza tossed at him from a plastic cup.

He went back to the carport, put the roof down on the convertible, removed a large box from the rear seat, and then put the roof up again.

By the time Allan came running into the living room, the

contents of the box, a red pedal car, with real headlights and horn, was sitting in the middle of the carpet.

Allan stopped in midstride and looked at the car, his eyes wide.

"Don't run over any old ladies, sport," Johnny said.

He walked to the boy, picked him up, and set him inside the car. He took his hand and put it on the horn button, which Allan then proceeded to sound enthusiastically. It made a piercing, blatting noise, and Johnny winced even before Liza's voice came from her bedroom:

"What the hell?"

She had apparently been in the process of changing out of her wet clothing, for she came into the room wearing only her underpants, her arms crossed modestly over her breasts.

"Oh, my God!" she said. "Johnny, you're crazy! He's much too little for that!"

"He'll grow into it."

"Can you shut that horn off?"

"Probably."

"Then do it!"

She walked back into her bedroom. Johnny watched appreciatively until she was out of sight, then went to the pedal car and disconnected the horn wire.

"Broke, Johnny!" Allan said, hammering on the horn button.

"Looks that way, pal."

He got down on his knees and pushed the car, trying without much success at all to teach the boy how to steer. There was no way the boy could reach the pedals.

Liza came out shortly afterward, in a sweater and slacks.

"Who'd you buy that for, you or him?" she asked.

"The both of us."

He stood up and looked at her.

"You're crazy," she said.

"I know," he said. "It's more fun that way."

Allan got out of the car, went behind it, and pushed. It ran into the coffee table.

"I don't suppose it occurred to you that would happen?" she said.

"Every young man should have a convertible," Oliver said.

He put his hand out and touched her shoulder. He wanted very much to kiss her, but had learned she didn't like to be kissed, or, for that matter touched, when Allan was in the room.

"Well, it was sweet of you," Liza said. "Thank you."

She touched his hand and then moved away from him.

"Hey, we're fixed for the Norwich Dinner," he said.

"What does that mean?"

"Charley Stevens is going to take Marjorie."

"I'm sorry, Johnny, if you're suggesting that now I can go with you."

"Why not?"

"I just don't want to go, that's all. Leave it at that."

"I don't want to leave it at that."

"Is that so?"

"I had this really wild idea," he said. "You want to hear it?"

"I think I'm going to whether I want to or not," Liza said, and walked into the kitchen.

He followed her, and saw that she was taking things out so that she could feed Allan his supper. Afterward, a kid down the block was going to come in and baby-sit, and they were going out for supper and a movie.

He walked behind her, put his hands on her arms, and kissed her neck.

"Ummmm," she said, pressing back against him for a minute. "Nice."

"My wild idea is that before the dinner, we get you a ring."

"What kind of a ring?" she asked flatly, as she freed herself of his touch.

He chuckled. " 'Whatever you would like, he says, praying his beloved hates ostentation.' "

"I was afraid this was going to happen. I didn't think so quickly."

"*Afraid* it would happen?" Oliver asked, surprised.

She spun around and looked at him.

"I never proposed before," he said. "I guess I don't know how to do it."

"Johnny," she said. "You're a nice guy. . . . Oh, Christ,

you're more than that. But I'm not going to marry you. Not as long as you're wearing a uniform."

"Why?"

"You have to ask? I went down that path once. I'm not going to go down it again."

"That's it? Period? Nothing would change your mind?"

"You told me your wild idea. You want to hear mine?"

"Yes, I do."

"Get out of the Army. Come to work for me."

"Work for you?" he asked incredulously.

"With me . . . or find something else to do. But get out of the Army."

"This is what I do."

"Then the subject would seem to be closed, wouldn't it?"

"It does sound that way, doesn't it? I mean, why should we even think about something absolutely extraneous, like I love you?"

"Stop it."

"Goddammit, don't tell me you don't feel something for me!"

"I didn't say that," she said. "My God!"

"Then I don't understand."

"I've already lost one husband. I don't want to lose another. Is that so hard to understand?"

"When your number is up, it's up. When it's not, it's not."

"Except that the numbers of people in the Army seem to come up pretty often. Such as Allan's . . . and Jack Dant's. . . . Johnny, don't fight with me. I'm not being coy. I've thought this over pretty carefully. I can't take it. And, a couple of years from now, or next week, for that matter, I don't want to have to tell Allan that Johnny's not coming home anymore, he's dead."

There was the sound of breaking glass in the living room. She rushed in. Allan had pushed the red pedal car into an end table and knocked a lamp and a vase to the floor.

"Get that damned car out of here!" Liza flared.

She scooped Allan up and he started to howl.

"Where should I put it?"

"I don't give a damn. In with the washing machine. Just get it out of here."

He picked up the car and carried it to the utility room.

When he started to go back in the kitchen, she stood in the door, blocking his way. He could hear Allan crying, in fury, inside.

"He's pitching a fit, thanks to you," she said.

"Sorry."

"That was a bitchy thing to say," she said. "I'm sorry."

"It's OK."

"Johnny, go home. I don't want to be with you right now."

He met her eyes for a moment, then turned and walked out the door.

"Johnny," she called as he got behind the wheel of his car. He looked at her.

"You asked if I didn't feel anything for you . . ."

"Yes, I did."

"You really had to ask? Think about what I said."

He looked at her a moment, started the engine, and backed down the driveway.

[THREE]
Building T-124
Fort Rucker, Alabama
2035 Hours 19 January 1964

When the telephone listed in the book for *Oliver, J S Capt* rang, Oliver was absolutely sure it would be Liza. He had been on the verge of calling her, although he didn't know what he would say if he did. But she would call and say she was sorry, and he would go back over there, and at least they could talk about it.

"Captain Oliver," he said to the telephone.

"Capitaine John Ol-iv-aire?" a male voice in a thick French accent demanded.

"This is Captain John Oliver."

"You 'ave a pink Pontiac auto-mobile? A con-vair-tible?"

"I have a Pontiac convertible. Who is this, please?"

"My name is Antoine," his caller said. "Henri-Philippe Antoine."

"How may I help you, Mr. Antoine?"

"How may you 'elp me? You *ask* how you may 'elp me?"

"Yes, Sir."

"I will tell you, M'sieu le Capitaine Ol-iv-aire, how you can 'elp me. You can stop the . . . how you say? *foo-king* of my wife zee second I take my eyes off the bitch."

There was no French accent on the last part of the sentence.

"Who the hell is this?" Oliver demanded angrily. He was not in the mood for sophomore humor.

"Whaddasay, Slats? How they hanging?"

"Father, you sonofabitch!" Oliver said, all anger gone. "What the hell was that all about?"

"I was practicing my French accent. Not bad, huh? Had you going, didn't I?"

"Things a little dull at Fort Bragg, are they? All you can find to amuse yourself on a Saturday night is to make sophomoric telephone calls? Why don't you call the drugstore and ask them if they have Prince Albert in the can?"

"Actually I'm in Dothan," Captain George Washington Lunsford said. "At the airport."

"What are you doing in Dothan?"

"At the moment, I'm in a phone booth," Father said.

"Oh, Jesus!"

"Are you going to come pick me up?"

"I'll be there in twenty-five minutes," Oliver said and hung up.

Father Lunsford was standing outside the Dothan Airport terminal when Oliver drove up. He was wearing a dark-blue suit under a double-breasted camel's hair overcoat. He pulled the door open, threw a suitcase in the back seat, and got in.

"I knew it had to be you," he said. "There's not too many people outside the pimp profession with pink automobiles."

"Screw you, Father," Oliver said, chuckling.

"I am famished," Father said. "Is there someplace we can eat?"

"Best place, I suppose, is the club."

"Then head for the club."

"What brings you here?"

"A couple of things," Father said. "What the hell, get it out of the way. I want to leave a letter with you for my father."

"What kind of a letter?"

"You know the kind, Johnny," Lunsford said. "To be delivered only in case of my death, heroic or otherwise."

"Meaning what?"

"Meaning I'm being sent on a job; and, the eternal Boy Scout, I want to be prepared."

"You mean overseas?"

"In a manner of speaking, yes. Across an ocean. But not to a theater of operations."

"What the hell does that mean?"

"You don't have the need to know," Lunsford said seriously.

"So what are you doing here? And don't tell me I don't have the need to know."

"I have to see some people. People I will see later."

"They have names?"

"They're assigned to the Aviation Board," Lunsford said. "I'm scheduled to see them Monday morning. So I figured I'd come early and let you buy me dinner."

Oliver glanced over at him.

At the Aviation Board? What connection does a Green Beret who's about to do something lunatic have with people at the Aviation Board?

And then he understood.

"The name Felter mean anything to you, Father?" Johnny asked, glancing at Lunsford as he spoke. The surprise he expected to see was there.

"No," Lunsford said. "Can't say that it does."

"And how do you feel about going back to the land of your ancestors?" Oliver asked. "Got your spear and tiger skin G-string all ready?"

"You're guessing, and that's dangerous."

"Not for those of us with an EAGLE clearance, it isn't. Nobody thinks *we're* Russian spies."

"How the hell did you get involved in this?" Lunsford asked. "Where the hell did you meet Colonel Felter?"

"I'm good ol' Sandy Felter's right-hand man at Rucker," Oliver said. "In addition to my dog-robbing duties, of course. I can't imagine why he didn't tell me you were coming."

"He doesn't know. My coming here was General Hanrahan's idea. You know anything about a U-8?"

"I even know where they're going, and when. What I don't understand is where you fit in."

"I'm taking an A-Team over there. The U-8 is to support us."

"Support you while you do what?"

"If Felter hasn't told you, I'm not going to," Lunsford said.

"Christ, why you? You just came home from 'Nam!"

"I speak the language."

"But you volunteered, right? They didn't order you."

"So what?"

"So why?"

"This is what I do for a living," Lunsford said. "You rob dogs, and I take long walks in the woods. I was already getting a little bored with Bragg."

"When are you going?"

"If Felter didn't tell you, I can't, Johnny. You want to get off this conversation before we both get in trouble?"

"I told you I know about it."

"You know a U-8 and people to fly it is going to the Congo. You only *think* you know why. And you now know, my fault, that I'm going over there. You know too much, in other words. So as I was saying, how's your sex life?"

"Hey, Father!"

"I'm serious, goddammit," Lunsford said. "Change the goddamn subject!"

After a long moment Oliver said, "Well, since you have this prurient interest in my personal life, I will tell you. A couple of hours ago I proposed marriage."

"Who is she?" Father Lunsford asked, surprised and interested.

"She was married to a guy I went to flight school with. He got blown away in 'Nam. She's got a kid, a really nice little boy."

"And you're going to marry her? That was quick, wasn't it? You sure you know what you're doing?"

"I'm sure," Oliver said, "but that's a moot point. She turned me down."

"Why?"

"She said she doesn't want to marry another soldier."

Father grunted.

"She says once, losing a husband, is enough."

"Maybe she's onto something," Father Lunsford said. "Women are intuitive. People make jokes about it, but it's true, they are. I gather this was more than a splendid roll in the hay?"

"For me it is."

"And for her?"

"For her too, I think."

"OK," Father said. "Taking you at your word. Why else would a woman turn somebody like you down? You have all the Brownie points. Nice-looking guy, steady job. You obviously like her kid, and kids need daddies. So why not? Unless she's got you pegged, intuitively, for what you are, in which case turning you down makes a lot of sense."

"Pegged me for what I am? What am I?"

"You're a warrior. Not just a soldier, a warrior. Warriors should not get married. Smart women don't marry warriors. Warriors tend to be gone, temporarily or permanently, when women need them."

Oliver thought that over a moment. Lunsford was obviously serious.

"Taking your philosophy to its natural end, Aristotle," he said finally, "if that's true, then how is the race going to be perpetuated? If women didn't marry warriors, in a couple of generations all that'll be left is feather merchants."

"Warriors get to rape the enemy's women," Lunsford said. "Even if that's temporarily out of fashion. That's one way. The other, of course, is that most women are too dumb to know what they're getting into when they latch on to a warrior."

"You really believe all this bullshit you're spouting?"

"Sure," Lunsford said. "Am I going to get to meet the lady?"

"No. She sort of threw me out after I proposed. Or, really, after I turned down her counterproposal."

"Which was?"

"That I get out of the Army and go to work for her. She's in the real estate business. Does pretty well at it."

"You didn't mention that," Lunsford said. "Sort of proves my point, doesn't it? Since she doesn't need a meal ticket, she can look a little closer. And looking closer, she has decided she doesn't have to run the risk of having another husband disappear permanently after he gets her in the family way. Intuition. I told you. My advice is to let it drop."

"Thanks a lot."

"Anytime."

[FOUR]
Building T-124
Fort Rucker, Alabama
1605 Hours 28 January 1964

Jose Newell came into Johnny Oliver's room via their shared bathroom. He was in a flight suit. Oliver, fresh from a shower, was in his underwear.

"And what did you learn in school today?" Oliver greeted him. "Do you have a gold star for being a good little boy that you want to show Daddy?"

"At 1300 they gave us a slide show on the Chinook," Jose said. " 'This is the front and this is the back, and these are the rotors,' they told us . . . can I have a drink?"

"Help yourself. Make me one while you're at it."

"Anyway, when the slide show was over, they told us that if they were lucky, they would be able to arrange a static display of a Chinook for us before we finish flight school. No ride, of course, that would be out of the question—"

"Hell, Jose," Oliver interrupted, "the Army's bleeding for Chinooks. There's not enough to give to the 11th Air Assault, and we have half as many as we need here to train pilots and mechanics. They don't have any to spare to give fledgling birdmen a ride for the hell of it."

"Let me finish, Johnny," Newell went on. "And when that was over, I went out to Cairns and got in the right seat of one of the thousand-hour-test Chinooks and flew it back and forth to Mobile."

The Army Aviation Board developed spare-parts levels,

time-before-maintenance, and related data for new aircraft by flying a number of aircraft, usually at least three, for 1,000 hours each. The "time was put on" as quickly as possible by relays of pilots, flying round the clock, seven days a week.

Oliver, who had been pinning his double row of miniature medals to the lapel of his mess dress jacket, stopped, stood erect, and turned to look at Newell.

"With Charley Stevens?" he asked levelly.

Jose Newell nodded as he handed Oliver an inch of whiskey in a waterglass.

"That's what's known as goddamn dumb, Jose. If that gets back to Augustus, you'll both be in the deep shit. Christ! What the *hell* was Charley thinking about?"

"It was *Augustus's* idea," Newell said, sitting on Oliver's bed and sliding upward to rest his back against the headboard. "That's what I wanted to talk to you about. You got a minute? What the hell are you doing, anyway?"

"I'm getting dressed."

"Now? I thought that dinner started at eight."

"It does. What do you mean, it was Augustus's idea?"

"I mean it was Augustus's idea. I was talking to Charley, waiting for them to put gas in it, and Augustus walked up and said they were short a pilot, and why didn't I ride along with Charley and work the radios and get a little bootleg instruction?"

"That's hard to believe," Oliver said. "McNair will have a fit if—when—he finds out."

"McNair was there with Augustus," Newell said. "All he said was, 'Try not to bend our bird, Lieutenant.' "

"I don't think you're putting me on," Oliver said. "So what's going on?"

"That's what I wanted to talk to you about. McNair endorsed, 'in the strongest possible terms,' a letter Augustus wrote to DCSPERS, asking that Second Lieutenant Newell, US Army Reserve, be ordered to extended active duty and assigned to SCATSA as a critically needed expert."

"Go over that slowly," Oliver said. "I thought you were in the National Guard, not the Reserve."

"You're in both when you're in the Guard."

"I didn't know that," Oliver said. "How'd you get to meet Augustus?"

"He came in the SCATSA shop when I was making those voice-actuated switches for General Bellmon. And he started asking me questions, where was I from, where did I learn about avionics, that sort of thing. And then he apparently checked me out, and the next thing I know he called me in and said he can get me called to extended active duty with a shot at a Regular Army commission."

"What about the no college degree?"

"He said that if you know how to do it, there's a waiver for everything in the Army."

"So you told him yes?"

"Yeah," Newell said. "And now I'm not so sure that was such a smart idea. That's what I wanted to talk to you about. Can I trust him?"

"If he says he can get you called to extended active duty, I'm sure he can. He's got a lot of clout in the Signal Corps, and if McNair endorsed it—"

"Augustus wants to put me in charge of the shop," Newell said. "They've got a captain in charge who's not really sure of the difference between an ohm and a volt. Good technicians, though. I could do the job."

"Augustus has a reputation for being ruthless."

"Meaning I can't trust him? I shouldn't have?"

"Meaning he's ruthless. He doesn't let things get in the way of his mission."

"What are you saying?" Newell asked.

"And he's on orders to 'Nam. So what I'm saying is that he won't be around to make good his promises to you. What he gets from you is somebody to run his avionics shops, at least for as long as he's here. After that the shop is somebody else's problem. And Jose Newell's career plans are Jose Newell's problem."

Newell grunted and drained his drink, then looked at the empty glass. He shrugged and raised his eyes to Oliver.

"Opportunity knocks but once," he said. "You ever hear that?"

"No, but now that I have, I'll write it down so I won't forget it."

"You—and for that matter, Charley Stevens—are different about flying than I am," Newell said. "Why did you become an aviator? The flight pay?"

"That, sure, and because it struck me as a desirable alternative to standing around in a blizzard on the East German or North Korean border changing the tracks on a cold and dirty tank."

Newell chuckled, pushed himself off the bed, and asking permission with his eyebrows, went back to the bottle of scotch. He made himself another drink, then turned around and leaned against the chest of drawers.

"I *like* to fly," he said.

"So do I."

"I *love* it," Newell said. "I mean, I really *love* it. I was as happy as a pig in mud flying that Chinook this afternoon. And I'm good at it. I guess what I'm trying to say is that I'm one of those guys who were meant to fly. I'll bet that if the check-ride IP didn't know I have three hours, more or less, total time in a Chinook, I could go out right now and pass the flight test."

"There are old pilots, and there are bold pilots, but there are no old, bold pilots!" Oliver said sonorously. "You ever hear *that,* Jose?"

"Hey, I'm as cautious as you are. Probably more cautious."

"Just better, huh?"

"Yeah, I think so," Newell said softly. "But what I'm saying, Johnny, is that I *have* to fly. I have two options. I go back home and fly CH-34s for the Guard, and pick up what time I can in light business-aircraft, and maybe somewhere down the line I can get a job as a corporate pilot. Big damned deal; you're an airborne chauffeur—'Please pass the canapes, Captain.' Or I can trust Augustus and get to fly these new aircraft, all of them. And even if I can't wrangle a Regular Army commission, I think I could probably hang on in the Reserve, on active duty, until I get my twenty in. Then I could retire and see what happens. I would have a pension, which is something to think about. I've got a family to consider. If a corporate pilot busts a flight physical, the next step is standing in a welfare line."

''And you could come on active duty and six months later find yourself in 'Nam with a Russian ground-to-air missile up your ass,'' Oliver said.

''I have to take that chance.''

''Well, I'm proud that you have sought my advice and are taking it so much to heart.''

Newell laughed and met his eyes: ''You're my buddy,'' he said. ''I had to tell you.''

[FIVE]
123 Brookwood Lane
Ozark, Alabama
1740 Hours 28 January 1964

Captain John S. Oliver, in his mess dress uniform, sat in his Pontiac convertible just around the corner from Liza Wood's house in a position he hoped would permit him to see Liza come home without spotting him.

He had no idea how she would react when he showed up at her house, uninvited. He wondered if he was just making an ass of himself.

He looked at his watch. It was 1740, thirty minutes after her usual time to drive down Brookwood Lane and into her driveway. He decided that she had spotted him and turned off, so that an awkward confrontation could be avoided.

What I should do is leave.

He looked at the watch and pushed the button that started the elapsed-time function. The sweep-second hand began to move. Two smaller dials on the watch's face would now indicate elapsed time up to twelve hours.

I won't need that much time. If she doesn't get here in five minutes, I'll leave.

Five minutes passed, and he swore, and started the engine. Then he shut it off. He pushed the buttons starting the elapsed-time function again.

''Once more. Another five minutes. That's it,'' he said, and put his right hand on the steering wheel so he could watch the sweep-second hand marching in half-second jerks around the dial.

The watch, like his mess dress uniform, had come from

Hong Kong. He'd gone there with two months' pay and the proceeds of a mostly drunken poker game. And he'd returned to 'Nam with the watch. They had shipped the uniform home.

The watch was an Omega aviator's chronograph, over an inch in diameter, with a circular slide rule bezel, three elapsed-time dials, and a little window which showed the date. It had a waterproof stainless steel case and a matching band.

When he was back in 'Nam, he heard all the remarks about the way you could tell an Army Aviator in the shower was because he would be wearing an enormous watch and a miniature masculine appendage. His company commander, two days before he went in, told him that if he really wanted a watch like that, he should have ordered it through the PX, because the watches on sale in Hong Kong for such marvelous prices were actually forgeries, made in Japan, or right in Hong Kong, and he had probably been screwed.

That had seemed to be a real possibility at the time. He and Charley had been at the grape when they went shopping; and not only was the watch probably made of Budweiser cans, but the beaming, toothy tailor who offered such great prices on uniforms was probably beaming because he had no intention of ever making them, much less shipping them to the States, like he promised, at no extra charge.

For two weeks he had carefully removed the ''Waterproof to 100 Meters'' stainless steel Omega Chronograph when he showered so that it wouldn't rust off his wrist before he could somehow get rid of it. Then the Old Man had gone in, and they'd given him the company, and he hadn't had time to worry about his watch, or to pay particular attention to a letter he received from his sister. It said that a huge package had arrived from Hong Kong, and that she had to pay the duty at the Post Office, and would he please send her a check for $32.05, since it was his personal stuff.

The watch had survived 'Nam, but he cracked the crystal shortly after coming back to Rucker when a wrench slipped. So he'd gone to the PX and bought a regular watch, which he wore for two weeks—until he missed the phony Omega. So he took the phony Omega to a jeweler in Dothan and told him it probably wouldn't be worth it, but how much would a new crystal for this old junker cost?

"About nineteen dollars," the jeweler told him. "You wear a really top-of-the-line watch like this, and abuse it, you have to expect to pay a little more when you break it. I'll have to send it off to Omega in New York. I don't have the equipment to seal it, to make it waterproof again. You just don't see many watches like this in Dothan."

The sweep-second hand had just begun its fourth trip around the face when Liza's car appeared. He watched it intently. She did not even glance in his direction.

He waited, timing it, three minutes more. And then he started the engine and drove down the street and into her driveway. He got out and walked to the kitchen door and knocked.

Liza came from inside the house and opened the kitchen door, but she did not unlatch the screen door. She just looked at him.

"I just happened to be in the neighborhood," Johnny Oliver said with a brightness he didn't feel, "and thought, what the hell, I would just pop in."

She looked at him without any expression he could read. And she didn't reply for a long moment, long enough for him to decide that coming here like this was a bad idea, and that he was about to be turned away.

"I just got home," she said finally, resignedly. She unfastened the screen door latch, then turned and walked back into the kitchen. She went to the sink and leaned against it, watching him as he came in.

"I know," he said.

"What were you doing? Lurking in the woods? With a pair of binoculars?"

"Around the corner," he confessed. "No binoculars."

"Whatever will the neighbors think?" she said.

"I hope they were dazzled. I paid a fortune for this costume."

"What do you want, Johnny?" Liza asked coldly.

"Well, there I was, as I said, in the neighborhood, when all of a sudden there was a brilliant flash of lightning and a deep voice—I'm not saying it was God, but it could have been, I don't know anybody else who talks like that—said, *Remember, my son, that women reserve the right to change their minds!*''

Liza smiled faintly and shook her head.

''Remember, my son,'' she said, ''that when this woman saith no, this woman meaneth no.''

''Ah, what the hell. Come on,'' he said. ''There's plenty of time. Not only are Marjorie and Charley going to be there, but you can wear that black dress that's open to your navel and make all the girls jealous.''

''I was a camp follower once, Johnny. Never again. Get that straight. I mean that.''

Am I wasting my breath? My time? Was Father right? Has she somehow sensed that Captain John S. Oliver, Jr., Warrior Third Class, is really bad news? For her? And for Allan?

They locked eyes for a moment and finally he shrugged.

''I need a shower,'' she said. ''Fix yourself a drink if you like.''

She walked out of the kitchen. After a moment he started into the living room in search of the whiskey.

''But, good try, Johnny. I will admit I was tempted,'' she called to him from her bedroom. ''You are spectacular in that outfit.''

What she will do now, I hope, I hope, is change her mind. And when she comes out of the bedroom, she will be wearing a formal dress. And I will be one more rung up the ladder. Screw you, Father, and your damned female intuition!

He wondered where Allan was. He couldn't ask her. He could hear the sound of her shower and knew that meant she couldn't hear him if he asked. He took his drink and went and looked in the boy's room. He wasn't there. So Mother Wood must have him.

Did she park him with Mother Wood, hoping I would call and ask her to change her mind, or even come the way I did?

He went back in the living room, turned the television on, and sat down in what had been Lieutenant Allan Wood's chair, and which was now, he thought, by default, at least sometimes considered to be his.

Liza came out her bedroom, wearing a bathrobe, with her head wrapped in a towel.

She has washed her hair; women about to go to a formal dinner party do not wash their hair.

"I guess I can take that as a final no, huh? The washed hair?"

"Your powers of deduction are fantastic," she said, and walked across the room to where the whiskey sat on a table. "I probably shouldn't tell you this, but you have an ally in Mother Wood."

"All contributions gratefully accepted."

"She thinks you would make a good daddy for Allan."

"So do I."

"Anyway, when I told her I wasn't going with you to the Norwich thing, she said the same thing you did, that women are allowed to change their minds. So he's spending the night with Grandma."

"I'll send her a dozen roses," Oliver said. "So go with the wet hair. You're a fashion setter. You show up with wet hair, and there will be twenty women at the next party in wet hair."

She smiled at him over the rim of her glass.

"You're an imaginative fellow," Liza said. "Tell me, does the fact that we're alone here, behind locked doors, give you any ideas?"

"I have those ideas whether or not the doors are locked."

"I know."

She reached up and unwound the towel turban on her head. Then she met his eyes. Then she pulled the belt of her bathrobe loose, let the robe fall open, and shrugged out of it. Then she walked, stark naked, back into her bedroom.

Johnny Oliver opened his eyes and saw Liza Wood curled up next to him. He could make out the individual vertebrae in her back.

I must have dozed off, he thought. *The last I remember, she had sort of crawled onto me.*

He raised his left wrist and looked at his watch.

It was time to go.

Very carefully, so as not to disturb Liza, he sat up and swung his legs out of her bed.

Her hand touched his back, and he looked over his shoulder at her.

Goddamn, she's beautiful! Whoever said that having a kid ruins a woman's body was full of shit.

"If I asked you—begged you—not to go out there," Liza Wood asked, "would you stay?"

"I have to go."

"Why?"

"The Bellmons are going to be there. And Charley and Marjorie. I'm expected."

"And you want to go," she said, a challenge rather than a question.

"I *want* to go with you," he said. "Failing that, I *have* to go. Come with me."

"Do what you think you have to do," Liza said, and rolled over on the bed, facing away from him.

"I could come back," he said. "I'll eat, and make my excuses. I am a very talented liar. I'll think of something wholly credible to tell them: I have to get my alligator back from the vet. I have been named man of the year by the Ozark Horticultural Society and they're going to name a rose after me."

"If you go out there now, don't come back, period."

"Hey, that sounds like a threat," he said softly, after a moment.

"More like a statement of fact. We can't go on like this. I don't want to get to the point where you are so much a part of my life—of Allan's too—that I can't cut you out of it."

"You and Allan are the most important part of my life."

"We're next in line, right after the goddamned Army," Liza said. "So that's not true."

"Liza, I'm a soldier. I wouldn't be any good doing anything else."

"You're beginning to convince me of that. I thought maybe You Samson, Me Delilah would work. Obviously it didn't."

"What?" he asked, not understanding her.

"You don't think she really cut off his hair, do you?" she asked bitterly.

"As I remember that story, she also blinded him. And then

he died, when he pulled the walls in on him,'' Oliver said. ''Honey, I told you, I have to go.''

She shrugged her shoulders but didn't say anything.

He shrugged, stood up, and started to get dressed.

After a minute or so she rose from the bed and walked into the bathroom. He heard the toilet flush and then the sound of the shower. The sound of the shower ended before he was dressed, but she did not come out of the bathroom.

He tied his bow tie and checked his appearance in her hall mirror.

''Have a good time,'' she called.

''Oh, Jesus,'' he muttered. Then he walked out to the driveway and got in his Pontiac.

She came to the kitchen door in her bathrobe. He rolled down the window.

''I meant that,'' she said. ''Have a good time.''

''Can I come back?''

She shook her head, no. ''Not tonight,'' she said. ''Not for a while. Let's see what happens.''

She gave him a little wave and went back in the house.

He sat there with the engine idling for more than a minute, wondering what would happen if he didn't go out to the post, if he went back in the house instead.

That wouldn't solve a goddamn thing, he decided finally. *If I go back in there, she'll think I'm giving in. And when she found out that's not true, that would just make things worse.*

He put the Pontiac in gear and backed down the driveway.

[SIX]
The Officers' Open Mess
Fort Rucker, Alabama
2320 Hours 28 January 1964

''I'm sorry your girl couldn't come,'' Mrs. Robert F. Bellmon said to Captain John S. Oliver as they danced. ''It's been a great party. Even the Great Stone Face seems to be enjoying himself.''

She nodded, and he looked in that direction and saw Major General Robert F. Bellmon doing the Charleston with Marjorie.

He laughed, and then blurted, ''The problem is that she lost one husband and doesn't want to go through that again. She just told me I have to make up my mind between the Army and her.''

''Oh, I'm sorry, Johnny,'' Barbara Bellmon said. ''For the both of you. But mostly for her. A woman is kidding herself if she thinks she can make a man do something he really doesn't want to do.''

''I've been trying to tell myself that girls are like streetcars. If you miss one, another will be along in a while.''

''I guess that's true.''

''They don't have streetcars anymore.''

''Not like Mrs. Wood, anyway, huh?'' she said sympathetically.

''I didn't mean to bore you with this.''

''Don't be silly,'' she said. She started to say something else, changed her mind and stopped, and then changed it again. ''This is none of my business, *but* . . .''

''Go ahead.''

''You're going places in the Army, Johnny. Statement of fact. I have been around the Army all of my life. You get so you can tell.''

''I will order a larger hat tomorrow.''

''A wife who doesn't like the Army, or who spends all of her time waiting for the chaplain to knock at the door, is a burden you don't need.''

''Oddly enough, the same thought has been running through my mind.''

''Maybe I shouldn't have said that.''

''I need a shoulder to weep on,'' Johnny said. ''My problem is that I may not need the Army as much as I need that lady.''

She pulled back from him and looked into his eyes.

''You had better think that over very carefully, Johnny,'' she said.

''I am. I have been all night.''

''And for God's sake, don't tell Bob. Or anybody else, for that matter.''

''There's nobody else I could tell. I don't know why I told you.''

"I think I do, and I'm flattered," Barbara Bellmon said. "It means you like me nearly as much as I like you."

He could think of nothing to say.

"Damn," she said. "I wish you and Marjorie had hit it off."

He nodded across the dance floor, toward Marjorie and Charley Stevens.

"Marjorie seems to be otherwise occupied."

"That's not him," Barbara Bellmon said. "I don't know who it will be, but that young man is not him." A moment later she added, "I've had three drinks. Whenever I have three drinks, I tend to talk too much."

There were forty-two officers and their ladies present at the Annual Dinner of Graduates of Norwich University. There were cocktails and hors d'oeuvres, and a shrimp cocktail and a roast-beef dinner, and remarks by Colonel J. Franklin Dampell ('45) (the senior graduate); Second Lieutenant Karl Massbach ('63) (the junior); and Major General Robert F. Bellmon, the post commander. Dinner was followed by dancing, with music provided by the New Orleans Fox Trot Orchestra, imported from New Orleans for the occasion.

A good time was had by all . . . except Captain John S. Oliver, Jr. ('59).

XIII

[ONE]
Office of the Commanding General
The Army Aviation School & Fort Rucker, Alabama
1805 Hours 9 March 1964

Captain Johnny Oliver had seen lights glowing in the second-floor corner windows of General Bellmon's office when he drove up to the headquarters building. But neither the staff car nor Bellmon's Oldsmobile was parked in the space reserved for him near the front door, so he decided that it wasn't the General; the carpets were being vacuumed, or the furniture polished, or something.

That was annoying, too. He had work to do, and it was a pain in the ass to try to concentrate with some surly maintenance man shoving his vacuum cleaner hose under your nose, while he sang along with "And here's a real toe-tapper from Bobby-Joe Jones and His Arkansas Stump-Stompers" on the transistor radio in his shirt pocket.

Oliver nodded politely at the FOD sitting at his desk in an anteroom off the main lobby. Then he went up the narrow staircase, two steps at a time, pulling his tie down and unfastening his blouse as he did so.

Major General Robert F. Bellmon, Jr., was not only in the office, he was sitting at Johnny Oliver's desk in the outer office.

''Obviously you are an affront to uniform regulations,'' Bellmon greeted him. ''You did not expect to find your general in here.''

''Sorry, Sir,'' Oliver said, starting to pull up his tie.

''Hey, I'm pulling your leg,'' Bellmon said. ''Relax.''

''Did you need me, Sir?'' Oliver said, continuing to adjust his tie.

''Not really. There was a call from Colonel Felter for you, so I thought I'd better see what he wanted. Then there were a couple of loose ends—''

''Colonel Felter called me, Sir?'' Oliver asked as he finished buttoning his blouse.

''He wanted to know if there were any problems with those two officers, and their airplane, for Africa. He said he didn't want to bother me. I said, if there were any problems . . .'' He stopped and looked inquisitively at Oliver until Oliver shook his head, no. ''. . . you would have said something. So he said to tell you thank you and give you his regards.''

''I was with General Rand, Sir. He invited—it was more in the form of a command—me to have a drink with him.''

Bridgadier General George F. Rand had come to Fort Rucker that morning to begin his flight training.

''I knew where you were,'' Bellmon said. ''Everything go all right?''

''Yes, Sir,'' Oliver said. ''He's set up in the Magnolia House. I drew his books, and the rest of the student crap, and got him flight suits and a helmet. And, not without trouble, I got the signal officer to promise to put in a private telephone line for him tomorrow. I introduced him to the kid who'll be driving him, and checked with the club to make sure they'll send somebody first thing every morning to make the bed, et cetera. He's all set up.''

Bellmon grunted and nodded his head.

''We're having him for dinner,'' Bellmon said. ''I told Mrs. Bellmon I knew you had other plans. But you're welcome, of course. . . .''

''Thank you, Sir. For telling Mrs. B. I had other plans, I mean.''

''Do I infer you're not especially fond of General Rand's company?''

''No, Sir. I think he's a fine officer—''

''But he asks one hell of a lot of questions, right?'' Bellmon interrupted. ''It's like being interrogated by the NKVD?''

''Well, maybe the IRS.''

''You're not alone,'' Bellmon said. ''I told my wife that she is to get him started down Memory Lane and keep him there.''

Oliver chuckled.

''But that desire to know everything that it's possible to know,'' Bellmon said, ''is one of the reasons George Rand is one of the best planning types in the Army. He was pumping you about Vietnam, right? Not his going through flight school?''

''No, Sir, today he wanted to know about flight school. He pumped me about 'Nam the time I flew him to Benning,'' Oliver said.

''Flight school generally, or vis à vis Vietnam?''

''Both, Sir. But mostly, come to think of it, about how well we're training people to fly in 'Nam.''

''He's probably going to have trouble here because of that. I'm going to bend his ear about it at dinner.''

''Sir?'' Oliver asked, not understanding.

''He will go through the training here, unless I can talk him out of it, trying to relate that training to what will be required when the division goes operational in Vietnam . . . instead of putting that aside and just learning how to fly.''

''Oh,'' Oliver said. ''Yes, Sir, I see what you mean.''

''Part of the trouble with sending senior people like George Rand through flight school is their perception of aviators, generally.''

''I don't think I follow you, Sir.''

''Kids going into the program think of John Wayne,'' Bellmon said. ''Flying is something only supermen can do.

They're not at all sure they're supermen, so they pay attention. A senior officer, particularly a general officer, has had experience with some really stupid people sporting wings. *'If that moron can fly, anybody can. I'm going to breeze through this.'* See?''

''I never thought of that, Sir.''

''It's a problem,'' Bellmon said, then changed the subject. ''One of the loose ends I've been tying up is the leave program. You remember that, Johnny?''

''Yes, Sir.''

''As a matter of fact, I think you wrote it for me, didn't you?''

''Yes, Sir, I drafted it for you.''

''Then you will remember that it is the policy of this headquarters that the accumulation of leave beyond forty-five days is discouraged, and that it is the desire of the commanding general that no one will accrue leave to the point where it will be lost?'' Leave is earned at the rate of 2.5 days per month, or 30 days a year, except that no individual may accrue more than 60 days.

''Yes, Sir.''

Oh, shit! I know what's coming.

''And you will recall that I directed the G-1 to inform the immediate superior of individuals who have accrued in excess of fifty days' leave, so that he may counsel such individuals vis à vis the leave policy of this headquarters and strongly encourage them to comply with the commanding general's desires in this area?''

''Yes, Sir.''

''The G-1 has followed his orders,'' Bellmon said, and handed Oliver a mimeographed form. ''So tell me, Captain Oliver, now that I've counseled you, where are you going on your leave, and when?''

''Sir, I can't take off.''

''You've been in the Army not quite five years, and you've already lost about three weeks' leave, and you are losing leave at the rate of 2.5 days a month. You have *sixty* days' accrued leave, Johnny.''

''Sir, I don't mind losing the leave,'' Oliver said.

''Sometimes you're a little dense, Johnny,'' Bellmon said.

"For one thing, and I am not being facetious, all work and no play does indeed make Johnny a dull boy. And for another—and this is certainly not a criticism—disabuse yourself of the notion that you are indispensable around here. I've already talked to General Wendall, and he will send Jerry Thomas back here on TDY to fill in for you, whenever and for however long you're on leave."

"Yes, Sir."

"The other thing, Johnny, is that whether you like it, or I like it, or not, we're role models. If I force you on leave, then a hundred other captains—for that matter, fifty lieutenant colonels—will take the leave they're supposed to. If I don't, I am setting the wrong example. *Verstehst Du?*"

The intimate Du rather than the formal Sie. I'm touched.

"Jawohl, Herr General!"

Bellmon chuckled.

"Well, now that I've eaten your ass out," Bellmon said, "can I get you to give me a ride home?"

"Yes, Sir, of course."

"One final thing."

"Yes, Sir?"

"I had a look at the FOD's log a couple of minutes ago. You've been in the office after hours just about every day, including weekends. Are you really that inefficient, or could some of the stuff you do after hours, like what you're planning to do here now, really wait until tomorrow morning?"

"I like to stay on top of things, Sir."

"When you fall behind, I will let you know. I realize you'll think this is the pot calling the kettle black. But beyond a certain point—I'm talking of hours, or fatigue—your efficiency—anyone's efficiency, my own certainly included—drops to the point that when you think you're working, you're really spinning your wheels."

"I take your point, sir."

"Remember what I'm telling you, Johnny."

"Yes, Sir."

"When *you're* a general officer, and you catch your aide putting in eighty-hour weeks," Bellmon added.

Oliver's surprise showed on his face.

"Yeah," Bellmon said. "I added up the times in the FOD's after-hours log. Now, if you will be so kind, drive me home."

As Oliver reached for the switch to turn out the lights, the telephone rang. He went to the telephone and picked it up. "Office of the Commanding General, Captain Oliver speaking, Sir."

"You weren't in your room, and you weren't in either the club or Annex One, so I figured you'd be working," Liza Wood said.

"I could have been out chasing women."

He had not seen her in two weeks. Whenever he had called her, she had been "busy." Despite many solemn talks with himself—pointing out the growing evidence that so far as she was concerned, the whole thing was over, and the logical thing for him to do was face facts—he went to sleep at night thinking about her. And she was the first thing he thought of when he woke in the morning. Or, for that matter, in the middle of the night.

"I'm glad you weren't," she said softly.

"God, I've missed you," he blurted.

"The most interesting thing has happened."

"Can I call you back in ten minutes? You home?"

"I'm in no hurry, Johnny," General Bellmon said. "Go ahead."

"You can't talk now?" Liza asked.

"Tell me about the most interesting thing that's happened."

"How would you feel about five all-expenses-paid days, including air fare, in exciting New York City?"

"I don't know what the hell you're talking about," he said.

"I was nationwide Kingsford Salesman—Sales*person*—of the month."

What is she talking about? Some kind of prize? Is she actually asking me to go with her?

"I don't know what that means, either," he said.

"It means I sold more Kingsford Houses—they're the ones that come on a truck, and all they do is assemble them on the lot—than anybody else. The prize is the New York City trip for you and your wife, or husband."

He didn't reply immediately.

"Or friend," she said.

"Oh."

"You don't sound very thrilled."

"I'm thrilled that you just called me," he said. "But—"

"But you can't get leave, right? The goddamned Army would collapse without you, right?"

"When are we going? And are we taking Allan with us or not?"

"Take him, or leave him with Mother Wood, whichever you'd like."

"Let's take him. I missed him, too."

There was no reply.

"Maybe I could come by later and we could settle the details," Johnny said.

"I'll be home all night," Liza said. "Have you had supper?"

"No."

"Well, then, I'll make us something. Or fetch fried chicken."

"I'll be there in thirty minutes."

"OK," she said very softly, and then the phone went dead.

Oliver put the handset in its cradle.

The feeling of euphoria was almost instantly replaced by anger.

Goddammit, now she's making a fool of me. She puts me down, and then she maybe *changes her mind, and I obligingly raise my ass in the air so she can kick it again!*

Why the hell did I do that?

Because I'm in love with her, goddammit!

When do I get enough?

Jesus! The General heard the whole damned conversation.

When he turned to face Bellmon, he found Bellmon's eyes on him, thoughtful. But all the General said was, "Let me know when, and for how long, you'll be on leave, Johnny."

[TWO]
The Gramercy Park Hotel
New York City
17 March 1964

When Liza Wood came out of the bathroom in her bathrobe, she found Johnny Oliver in the living room of the two-room suite. He was sitting with Allan on the made-up convertabed. Allan was asleep, sitting up, in his lap. The television was on. The picture was flickering. Liza wondered about that; she would have thought that a TV image in New York City would be perfect.

"Isn't that uncomfortable?" she asked.

"Allan doesn't think so."

"Sssh, you'll wake him up."

"No, I won't," Oliver said. "But if you whisper, that'll have him hanging from the chandelier."

She said what she was thinking: "He really has been hanging on to you, hasn't he?"

"If I were his age, and in this place, I would be hanging on to the nearest friendly large body myself."

"Well, you wanted to bring him."

"And I'm glad we did."

"But you're not having a good time, right?" Liza asked.

"There are *moments*," Oliver said, "from time to time, when I am in hog heaven, but on balance—"

"Well, get on the phone, call the desk, and arrange for a babysitter."

"You have someplace you want to go?" he asked, seeming surprised. "I don't want to leave him alone. Jesus!"

"I said that to please you," Liza said. "Now you're making me feel lousy."

"I didn't mean to. How did we get on this subject, anyhow?"

"Because I walked in here and saw the look on your face," she said. "We should have left him with Mother Wood."

"Allan's not the problem."

"What is, then?"

"New York City," he said. "I am appalled at the prospect of another four fun-filled days in this place."

"Three."

"Ah, you've been counting, too."

"What would you really like to do?"

"You're dressed for that."

She flushed slightly and shook her head in resignation.

"Aside from that?"

"Go skiing."

"Skiing?"

"You put these boards on your feet," he said, "and go sliding through the snow."

"You're serious, aren't you?"

"And afterward, you sit—full of hot buttered rum or other booze of your choice—in front of a fireplace and fool around."

"You mean go to Colorado?"

"I mean go to Vermont."

"You mean go see your family."

There was a moment's hesitation before he replied.

"I guess we could. But I was thinking of Northfield."

"What's in Northfield? I never heard of it."

"There's a small motel, for one thing, and a real cheap ski lift, and my alma mater."

"We don't have skis, or the right clothes, not to mention that I have never been on skis in my life. And how would we get there?"

"Fly into Boston, rent a car, and drive. It's about a hundred and fifty miles from Boston. Then we drive back to Boston, get rid of the car, and fly back to Alabama. So far as skis and ski clothes go, no problem. And I think you would be adorable with both legs in a cast."

"You're crazy," she said. "The whole idea is crazy. But I like it."

"Good."

"What did you mean, no problem about skis and clothes?"

"I meant, no problem. I called a guy I know there, a math professor, and I said if I happened to come up, what would I do about skis and ski clothes. And he said, no problem."

"You mentioned Allan and me?"

"He said to get two rooms at the motel. General Harmon does not approve of officers sharing quarters with ladies to whom they are not lawfully joined in holy matrimony."

"Who is General Harmon?"

"President of Norwich."

"You get to be a general as a college president?"

"You get to be a major general by commanding the 2nd Armored Division and then you get to be president of Norwich."

"How far is this place from your sister's?"

"About sixty miles."

"Why don't we stay there . . . or near there?"

"Can I take that as a 'Yes, whoopee, I'd love to go skiing!'?" Oliver said, and then added seriously: "I'm not sure I want to see her, Liza."

"If we go up there, you'll have to see her," Liza said practically. "My God, what happened between you, anyway?"

"Nothing, really. I'm just not in the mood for her."

Liza looked at him, concern and curiosity on her face, but she didn't pursue the issue.

He noticed.

Another manifestation of our unspoken agreement not to talk about things that might be awkward and uncomfortable, he thought. *I didn't ask her if she had changed her mind about me, and I didn't ask her how come she wanted to go away with me for a week.*

He had a theory—a theory that was in a way flattering, even if it didn't offer much hope of a solution: She didn't want to give him up, which was flattering. But neither had she changed her mind about not marrying a soldier. She was giving him a chance to see all the benefits that would accrue to him, providing he put on two-tone shoes and started selling real estate. She was trying to get him to back down.

He had given backing down a good deal of thought and concluded it just wouldn't work. Not only would he probably be a lousy real-estate salesman, but he just didn't want to get out of the Army.

"Well, I suppose you better get on the phone and see about plane reservations," she said, "while I am temporarily bereft of my senses."

"Eastern 203, departing LaGuardia at eight-fifteen, arriving Logan eight fifty-five, where the friendly folks at Avis promise to have a Cadillac or equivalent luxury automobile waiting for us."

"A *Cadillac?*"

"They don't rent Rolls-Royces—I asked."

"You want to tell me what that's all about?"

"Two reasons," he said. "I couldn't make my triumphal return to Norwich driving a Ford, for God's sake."

"And the second?"

"I don't think you want to hear that."

"Oh, yes, I do."

"I always wanted to rent a Cadillac, and see how the rich people live."

"That's not true. You're lying."

"Yes, I am."

She met his eyes for a moment and then shrugged.

"If the plane leaves at eight-fifteen, we'll have to get up early. You want to come to bed or would you rather watch television?"

"I'll go to bed with you now," he said. "To be a nice fellow. And then I will get up afterward and watch Johnny Carson."

"You would, too, you bastard!"

"Only if modesty overwhelms you again, and you insist on putting a nightgown on," he said. "I have this rule: never leave a naked woman's bed."

Liza gave him the finger and walked into the bedroom.

Oliver very carefully removed Allan from his lap and slid the child under the covers. He looked down at him a moment, then leaned down and quickly kissed him.

Then he went in the bedroom and quietly closed the door.

[THREE]
Burlington, Vermont
1730 Hours 19 March 1964

"There it is," Johnny Oliver said to Liza Wood, gesturing with his hand.

Allan, in a car seat, and Liza looked in the direction where he pointed.

"What am I looking at?" Liza asked. All she could see was a truck stop, a sprawling, concrete block building, garishly lighted, topped by an enormous sign: JACK'S. It was surrounded by fuel pumps and fifty or sixty enormous tractor trailers.

"My truck stop," Oliver said.

"It says 'Jack's,' " Liza said, chuckling.

"Jack was my father."

"You're not kidding, are you?" Liza asked, leaning forward on the seat of the Cadillac to look at his face.

"No, Ma'am. Allan and I never kid pretty ladies, do we, pal?"

"Uh uh," Allan said.

"See?" Johnny said.

"You have stock in it, or what?" Liza asked.

"Yeah. It's a corporation. The Bank of Burlington owns ten percent of the stock, and my sister and I own the rest."

"So that's what this Cadillac is all about," Liza said. "Your oh so cleverly subtle way of letting me know you have money."

"No," he said immediately and automatically.

"No, what?"

"It's kind of complicated, honey."

"Meaning it's none of my business?"

"Oh, Jesus, Christ!" he said. "No, that's *not* what I meant. I have no secrets from you. Or I don't want to have."

"OK, so tell me why we're riding around in a rented Cadillac when I know how much you make as a captain on flight pay."

"I don't think you want the answer to that."

"Try me."

"Fantasy," he said. "We are on our honeymoon. You don't worry about how much things cost on your honeymoon. You just want it to be perfect. So you go in a Cadillac."

"Taking an eighteen-month-old baby with you, of course," Liza said.

"Tell her you're not a baby, Allan," Oliver said. "Tell her you go on all my honeymoons with me, to fill in the dull periods."

"OK, OK," Allan said.

"Goddamn you, Johnny," Liza said. She sounded close to tears.

"Mommy said a bad word," Johnny said. "Mommy is a naughty girl."

"This could *be* our honeymoon," Liza said, "if you'd get out of the goddamned Army."

"Can I take that as a 'yes, I love you'?"

"Go to hell."

[FOUR]
242 Maple Avenue
Burlington, Vermont
1915 Hours 19 March 1964

Tom and Shirley fed Johnny, Allan, and Liza a pot roast. Tom and Shirley's kids wolfed down their meals, and then Shirley drove them to what she called "their activities," the Boy Scouts and something for the girl at the church.

When the oldest Chaney child, Jerry, who was almost as old as Johnny Oliver, made a brief, awkward appearance, Shirley told Johnny that Jerry had had a little trouble in college and had left school. He was now working at the truck stop. He was spending a lot of time now with the Dowell girl, Shirley said. "You remember Steve and Dottie Dowell, Johnny, their girl?" And she was afraid it was getting serious.

As Shirley was leaving, she asked Liza to ride along with her, and there was no way Liza could decline. The purpose of that, Johnny knew, was to give Shirley a chance to put Liza through an interrogation, because she was having a hard time concealing an enormous curiosity about her. It was also pretty clear that Shirley didn't think a married woman, even a widow, should be running around the country with a single man.

Allan did not want to go with his mother. He had been building a wall with small, colored plastic cups; and when he had grown hyperactive with that, and Liza had taken them away from him, he had started to throw a fit. When Liza slapped his hand, he glowered at her and sought the comfort of Johnny's lap. And so when she asked him if he wanted to go for a ride, he replied with a firm no and wrapped his arms tightly around Johnny. A minute after she and Shirley left, he was asleep.

There had been an invitation to spend the night. Liza and the baby could sleep in Johnny's room (which was no longer Johnny's room; the girl was in there now), the girl could sleep on the couch, and Johnny could sleep in the other bed in Jerry's room.

But the invitation was declined. Johnny thought it was pro forma and was surprised at his sister's disappointment and insistence.

"Shirley, they expect us in Northfield," Johnny finally said, firmly. "What I told you on the telephone was that we could come for supper if that wouldn't interfere with anything."

"But we never see you," Shirley protested.

That was when Johnny realized there was a reason for her insistent hospitality: she wanted something. Aside from satisfying her curiosity, or perhaps delivering a moralistic message on his relationship with Liza, he couldn't imagine what.

His openness to Shirley's request would have been more profound if he and Liza had come here because he had insisted. But it was *Liza* who was the one who wanted to meet his sister, to see where he had grown up.

Well, now she's truly finding out. She's off with Shirley, enjoying the full force of her friendliness and concern. . . . I'd rather walk through land mines than spend an hour alone with my sister.

"So how long have you had the Cadillac?" Tom Chaney asked as he came back in the dining room carrying a bottle of Canadian whiskey.

He was a small, muscular man in his forties, bald, with a neatly trimmed pencil-line mustache.

"I rented that in Boston," Johnny said. "You don't have any scotch, do you, Tom?"

"No, but I can run out and get a bottle."

"Canadian's fine."

"They're great cars," Tom Chaney said. "I just got a new Coupe de Ville."

"Did you?"

"That's right, the garage doors were closed when you came, weren't they? No way you could have seen it."

''The one I rented is very nice,'' Johnny said. ''It does everything but bark.''

''Excuse me?'' Tom said, pouring two inches of the whiskey in a small glass and setting it in front of Johnny. ''You want Coke with that, or ginger ale?''

''A little water. I've got some right here.''

''There's 7-Up, too, if you'd like.''

''Water's fine, Tom, thank you.''

''What did you say before—the Caddie you rented barks?''

''I said it does everything but bark,'' Johnny said. ''Even automatically low-beams the headlights.''

''You have to adjust that very carefully,'' Tom said. ''Otherwise it puts them on low everytime you get near a street lamp. Or else it doesn't put them on low at all.''

''The dimmer on the car I rented seems to work fine,'' Johnny said.

He took a sip of the whiskey. It burned his mouth and throat, and he quickly chased it with a large sip of water.

''I guess you pretty well have decided to stay with the Army, huh, Johnny?''

''Pretty well.''

''What exactly have they got you doing? I mean, I know you're a pilot, but what *exactly* do you do?''

Why do I suspect, Tom, that you really don't give a damn what exactly *I do?*

''I'm an aide-de-camp, Tom,'' Johnny said. ''What they call a dog-robber.''

''Interesting work?''

There's the proof, Johnny thought. *He didn't even ask what a dog-robber is.*

''Fascinating.''

''What exactly does that get into?''

''I work for a general, a man named Bellmon. He's the commanding officer of Fort Rucker,'' Johnny said. ''And what I do, or try to do, is keep him from wasting his time on details.''

''How does that tie in with you being a pilot?''

''Sometimes when he has to go someplace, I drive.''

''I asked about being a pilot.''

"I meant to say 'fly,' " Johnny said. "I fly him around, Tom."

"Pretty good work, then?"

"I think so."

There was the glow of headlights against the dining room drapes, and the sound of wheels crunching the snow.

"Well," Tom said, "I guess the girls are back."

"It would seem so."

Shirley Oliver Chaney came into the dining room a moment later, still wearing her coat—a light blue, nylon, quilted affair that reached halfway down her thighs. She was a tall woman, a little plump. Her hair was cut short and her only makeup was a slash of bright red lipstick. She wore glasses, "stylish," with the earpieces mounted to the lower part of the glass frames.

"Well, if you've started that," she said, indicating the whiskey, "then you're going to have to stay. I won't have it on my conscience that you skidded off a road half drunk on whiskey I gave you."

"Hey, this is my first drink," Johnny protested. "And while we're at it, I'm a big boy, now, Shirley. I know when I've had too much to drink."

"We really have to start thinking about getting back," Liza said.

The ride around town must have been something less than unbridled joy, Johnny thought. *You asked for this, lady.*

He beamed at her.

"Nice ride?" he asked. "Get to see ye olde hometown?"

"Look," Shirley said, "the baby's already sound asleep. Sitting up. Johnny, why didn't you put him to bed?"

"He's a weird kid," Johnny said. "He likes to sleep like this."

"That's a terrible thing to say," Shirley said. "He's not weird. He's precious."

"You want me to take him, Johnny?" Liza asked.

"He's fine, leave him alone," Johnny said. "But Liza's right, Shirley. We should be getting back. Do you suppose I could have some more coffee, and then we'll go?"

"I wish you weren't being so obstinate about not spending the night," Shirley said.

"I wish you weren't being so obstinate about us staying," Johnny said. "Or is there something on your mind, Shirley?"

"As matter of a fact, there is. I thought maybe Tom would have mentioned it while we were gone."

"No. All we talked about was Tom's new Cadillac," Johnny said.

"The accountant said to do that," Shirley said quickly. "He said that the government's really paying for most of it."

"Yeah, it's not in my name," Tom said. "It's registered to the truck stop."

This beating around the bush is beginning to piss me off. Cool it. Get out of here without a scene.

"What did you think Tom might have mentioned to me while you were gone, Shirley?" Johnny asked, smiling at her.

"Well, I really hate to get into family business," Shirley said, "but since you insist on leaving, there's no help for it."

"Would you like me to wait in the kitchen?" Liza asked.

"No," Shirley said quickly. "The thing is, Liza, I don't know how much if anything Johnny has told you about this. . . ."

"Why don't I just go into the kitchen?" Liza replied. "Will this take long?"

"Sit there," Johnny said, more forcefully than he intended. Liza looked at him in surprise, but she didn't get up.

"The thing is, Liza," Shirley went on, "our parents were killed. Did Johnny tell you about that?"

"Yes, he did."

"Well, when that happened, and there was no place for Johnny to go, Tom and I, who were just married, of course took him in. We were glad to do it, of course."

"John told me about that," Liza said.

"Well, Dad had a business—a truck stop—" Shirley said.

"I showed it to her," Johnny interrupted.

"Which was left to the both of us," Shirley went on. "The children, I mean. And Tom went out there and worked himself nearly to death and made something out of it. I mean, our living, and he built it up. You know what I mean?"

"Yes, I think so," Liza said.

"Well, all these years, we never did anything about it *legally*, if you know what I mean."

"No, I don't," Liza said.

"Well, let me put it this way. *Legally*, the property is still owned by Dad's estate. I mean, it was never turned over to us the way the will said, when Johnny turned twenty-five. But now he's twenty-five and it's time we took care of that."

"I don't know what that means," Johnny said.

"It means—" Tom Chaney began. His wife interrupted him.

"What we have done, Johnny, is start the paperwork. I mean, we've come up with what we think is a fair price for your share of the business. I mean, you don't want to work there, with you being in the Regular Army and all, and Tom has worked out there all these years. You know how hard he's worked—"

"I've washed a trailer or two out there myself," Johnny said.

"But you had none of the *responsibility*," Shirley said. "You know that, Johnny." He didn't reply. "Now we want to be fair, just as fair as we can," she went on. "And see that you get what's rightfully yours. There's a lot of money, Johnny. More than I think you understand. Your share would come to almost three hundred thousand dollars."

"Jesus Christ!" Johnny said.

"I would appreciate it if you didn't take Jesus's name in vain," Shirley said.

"Sorry," he said. "But that's a lot of money."

"It's an awful lot of money," Shirley agreed. "But Tom and I want to be fair." She looked at him a moment and smiled. "Tom, go get those papers from the lawyer."

Tom got up from the table and went into the living room, where there was a rolltop desk. He opened it.

"Now I don't want to put my nose in where it doesn't belong," Shirley said, "but if anybody just happened to be thinking of marriage, that much money would be a real nice nest egg to get started."

Liza smiled wanly but said nothing.

Tom returned with a very large manila envelope.

"Now, Johnny," Shirley said, "just to make sure in your mind that everything's on the up and up, I'm going to suggest that you don't sign anything right now. Get yourself a lawyer, or somebody you trust, and have him read all that over before you sign it. If you have any questions, just call, and we'll explain what you don't understand—''

What she means with all that reasonableness, Johnny thought, *is that I will be an ungrateful sonofabitch if I don't sign that right now, without even reading it.*

''Johnny,'' Liza said, ''we have to go.''

''OK,'' Johnny said. ''I'll check it over and I'll be in touch.''

''Take all the time you think you need,'' Shirley said.

As soon as they got on the highway back to Northfield, it began to snow. The flakes were large and wet and stuck to the car, so that the windshield, except for the wiped area, was covered.

Liza rode slumped down in the seat, her arms folded on her chest. Johnny took his eyes from the road several times to look at her, but she didn't look back.

''If I didn't know that you have the temperament of a saint,'' Johnny said, ''I would harbor just the faintest suspicion you're pissed about something.''

''You bet your ass I am,'' Liza snapped.

''Hey, you wanted to come over here, I didn't.''

''If I hadn't gotten you out of there when I did, you would have signed whatever she put in front of you.''

''You underestimate me, baby,'' Johnny said calmly. ''Whenever my sister is sweet and kind, I grow very suspicious.''

''Huh!''

''I figure if she offered me three hundred thousand,'' Johnny said, ''it's worth four. And she never got into an accounting of how much it cost her to raise me, vis à vis how much she got from the estate to pay my bills. Nor a profit-and-loss statement for the business, all these years.''

Liza didn't reply for a moment.

''That place is worth at least a million five, maybe two million,'' she said finally. ''Half of a million five is seven hundred and fifty thousand.''

''Ah, come on.''

''It's on an interstate highway. It's the only one I saw. It's bigger than the truck stop I sold in Troy, and that wasn't even on an interstate. That went for one point six million."

"Jesus H. Christ!"

" 'I would appreciate it if you didn't take Jesus's name in vain,' " Liza quoted Shirley bitterly.

"Hey, she's not all black," Johnny said. "There are considerable areas of gray. She did raise me. And Tom has always run the place. And we don't know it's worth as much money as you say."

"You're a goddamned fool."

"Hey, why are you really so mad?"

"You told me your fantasy," Liza said slowly, softly, after a moment. "So I'll tell you mine. When we get back from this trip, you realize that Allan and I are more important to you than the Army. Your obligation is over in December. I explain how much money there is to be made in real estate if you know what you're doing. And I tell you I have enough for both of us to go into business together, get a couple of hundred acres I have my eye on—"

"And me sell real estate?" he asked, gently sarcastic.

"It's not really like walking the streets," she said softly but sharply. "But, no. What I meant was supervising the contractors, handling the business end. I'll handle the sales. We could do it. And with seven, eight hundred thousand dollars in capital . . . Johnny, we could be really rich!"

"I'm a soldier, honey. I can't turn in my suit right now."

"The Army needs you, right?" she asked sarcastically.

"Yeah, right now it does."

"That's what I meant. You're a goddamned fool," Liza said bitterly.

"I like you, too."

"Oh, *screw you*!"

But a minute or two later she slid across the seat and cuddled up under his arm, and they drove that way back to Northfield.

XIV

[ONE]
Office of the Commanding General
The Army Aviation Center & Fort Rucker, Alabama
3 April 1964

"Captain Oliver," Sergeant Major Harrison James called very courteously across the room. "Telephone for you, Sir."

There was a by-now familiar tone in Sergeant Major James's voice that told Johnny Oliver the incoming call was at least unusual . . . and more likely a problem the sergeant major did not choose the deal with himself. Ordinarily James would just snap his fingers to catch Oliver's attention. When he had it, he'd point at the telephone.

Even warned, Oliver was not prepared for what he got.

"Captain Oliver, Sir," he said to the telephone.

"This is the White House, Captain, please hold for Colonel Felter."

Oliver looked across the room at Sergeant Major James, who was beaming.

Oliver heard, faintly but clearly: ''Air Force One, we're ready for Colonel Felter.'' Then there was a pinging sound, and Felter's voice.

''Felter.''

''We have Captain Oliver for you, Sir,'' the White House operator said.

''Oliver?''

''Yes, Sir.''

''Sanford Felter, Johnny. I need a favor.''

''I'm at your service, Sir.''

''I just tried to get Mac McNair at the Board,'' Felter said. ''He's out flying. And Annie Caskie, who's the only other one out there who knows what's going on, is out of the office. So you're elected.''

''Yes, Sir?''

''A very clever sergeant named Gonzales in DCSPERS has come up with a very interesting PFC. Before he got drafted, he flew for a bush-aviation airline in the ex-Belgian Congo. Just the guy we need, I think. Anyway, I've arranged his transfer to the Board. He's at Benning, where he just graduated from jump school. As soon as you can, get to McNair and ask him to give this guy to Pappy Hodges. I mean, I don't want him mislaid. There's a chance Benning will send him back to Fort Knox before the DCSPERS TWX catches up with him. You still with me?''

''Yes, Sir, I think so.''

''His name is Portet, Peter Oboe Roger Tare Easy Tare, Jacques Emile. PFC. I don't have his serial number, damn it, but I don't think there's too many guys in jump school with a name like that. Got it?''

''Yes, Sir.''

''So if PFC Portet doesn't show up there by tomorrow, call Benning and see what they did with him. If they sent him back to Knox, I think you'd better go get him. We're pressed for time, and this guy is apparently an encyclopedia of remote Congolese airfields. Can you handle this yourself or would you rather I spoke with General Bellmon?''

"I'm sure I can handle it, Sir," Oliver said. "I'll get back to you, Sir."

"Not necessary, unless there's a problem. If there is, call Warrant Officer Finton in my office in Washington. He can move mountains of paper if necessary. You've got his number?"

"Yes, Sir. I'll call Mr. Finton either way, Sir."

"OK, then. I appreciate this, Johnny. And it's important."

There was a hissing noise, and then a voice said, "White House operator?" and Oliver realized that Felter had hung up without wasting his time on something unimportant like saying goodbye.

Oliver put the phone down, then looked across the room at Sergeant Major James, who was staring at him quizzically.

"Sergeant Major James," Oliver called, "do you think you could spare me a moment of your very valuable time?"

"My time is your time, Sir," James said, coming across the room to him.

"Would it be a reasonable assumption on my part to think that a distinguished long-term soldier such as yourself would know someone at Fort Benning of whom you could make a discreet inquiry?" Oliver said.

"I think that would be a reasonable assumption for the captain to make. Yes, Sir."

"The operative word is 'discreet,' " Oliver said. He wrote *PFC Jacques Emile Portet* on a slip of paper and slid it across his desk to James. "See if you can find out where this guy is. A TWX was sent to Benning ordering him to the Board, but it may not have got there in time to keep Benning from sending him back to Knox. Can you find out?"

"I will give it my best effort, Sir," Sergeant Major James said. "May I infer this is a matter of some importance?"

"Yes, you may."

"It isn't every day that we have the privilege of chatting with someone in the White House, is it, Sir?" James said, and then walked to his desk.

Oliver called the Board. Annie Caskie was back in the office, and she told him that Colonel McNair was due at any moment.

"I'll either call back, Anne, or come out there," Oliver said. "Please don't let him get away."

When he hung up, he saw that Sergeant Major James was on his telephone, and he could hear what he was saying: "Hello, you bald-headed old bastard, how the hell are you? Jack, I need a favor. . . ."

Five minutes later the telephone rang, Sergeant Major James listened briefly, said, "Thanks, Jack, I owe you one," hung up, and turned to Oliver. "The TWX got there; new orders were cut; PFC Portet is en route here. No details about that, but he says he can probably find out if it's important."

"No, I don't think that's necessary. There would have been a problem if he was on his way back to Knox. Thanks, Harrison. You're remarkable."

"Good-looking, too," Sergeant Major Harrison James said.

Oliver got up and stood in General Bellmon's office door until Bellmon noticed him.

"Sir, Colonel Felter called. He needed an errand run. Do you want to hear about it?"

"Is it done?"

"Yes, Sir, just about. I have to go see Colonel McNair."

"Then I don't want to hear about it," Bellmon said, and then, "Oh, hell, I guess I'd better." He made a "come on" gesture with his hand.

Bellmon heard him out, nodded, and said, "Well, you better go bring McNair in on it. And when all the round pegs are in the round holes, be sure you call Mr. Finton. Otherwise Felter will call. And if he can't get you, he'll call me, at half past three in the morning."

[TWO]
123 Brookwood Lane
Ozark, Alabama
4 April 1964

Allan Wood, crying, "Johnny, Johnny, Mama, Johnny!" ran across the kitchen floor to Captain John S. Oliver, who scooped him up, made a growling noise, and then nuzzled his neck.

Then he grimaced, set the boy on the floor, and called out, "We have a child here who requires a mother's attention."

"What?" Liza called from inside the house.

"If you're going to run around with me, pal, you're going to have to stop crapping in your pants," Johnny said to Allan.

Allan stuck his lower lip out and began to pout. When that did not produce the sympathy he wanted, he started to howl.

When Liza appeared, she was in the act of attaching an earring.

"What happened?" she said, looking at the howling child.

"Ol' craps-in-his-pants did it again."

"What did you say to him?" Liza challenged as she bent to pick Allan up.

"I said, 'Hooray for you, kid!' "

"He's only a little boy!"

Allan stuck his tongue out at Johnny, who returned the gesture.

"Great, set an example," Liza said.

"He started it," Johnny said.

Liza snorted. Then, carrying Allan, she disappeared into the back of the house. Johnny went to the refrigerator and searched for a beer.

When Allan came back in the kitchen a minute or two later, Johnny pretended not to see him. Allan finally made his way to the kitchen table where Johnny sat and held out his arms to be picked up.

"You're the guy who stuck his tongue out at me? And you want to get picked up? No way!"

Allan started to pout and Johnny scooped him up. Allan kissed him.

"You want a little nip, pal?" Johnny said, and extended the beer can. Allan took it and had it at his mouth when Liza came in the kitchen.

"I've asked you not to do that," she said.

"He stole it," Johnny said, unrepentant, but he reclaimed his beer.

"Allan going?" Allan asked.

"I don't know, pal," Johnny said. "Liza, is Allan going?"

"We're going to the Craigs'," she said. "If that's all right with you."

''Fine with me,'' he said. ''A little neighborhood get-together. Just like married people. That has a certain appeal, I will admit.''

''Stop, or I'm not going anywhere with you.''

''Color me stopped,'' Johnny said. He looked down at Allan. ''You're going, pal.''

''Allan going,'' Allan said with satisfaction.

''Tupperware party, or what?'' Johnny asked.

Liza laughed. ''Ursula called and said Geoff had some steaks flown in from Chicago. And did I think you would like to come?''

''He did what?''

''He had steaks flown in from Chicago,'' Liza said. ''You've seen those ads: 'The World's Best Steaks. Air Freight Free to Your Door. Only Five Dollars an Ounce.' ''

''It must be nice to be rich,'' Johnny said.

''It must. Speaking of which, I don't suppose you've had time in your busy schedule to talk to a lawyer about you know what?''

''I thought I told you my strategy was to wait them out and let them come to me with a better offer.''

''I remember,'' she said. ''And I remember telling you, oh, bullshit!''

''Are we going to fight tonight?'' Johnny asked. ''Is that why we're going to the Craigs'? So we'll have an audience?''

''Fight, fight,'' Allan said.

''Shut up, pal, we're already in trouble,'' Johnny said.

Liza walked out of the kitchen, returning in a minute shrugging into her overcoat.

''I guess we'd better take a car,'' she said. ''It rained all afternoon and the backyards are a swamp.''

They drove Johnny's Pontiac around the block. When they reached the Craig driveway they were a bit surprised at what they saw. In addition to the Craigs' Oldsmobile and Volkswagen, there was a strange car parked there. It was a glistening, fire-engine-red Jaguar.

''I didn't know the natives had cars like that,'' Johnny said.

''Natives meaning what?'' Liza said.

''There's no post sticker on it; ergo a native car.''

"I wonder whose it is?" Liza asked as they got out of the Pontiac.

There was another surprise inside, in the person of Miss Marjorie Bellmon.

"Johnny," Marjorie said, "say hello to Jack."

"Hello, Jack," Johnny said. "John Oliver."

He offered his hand to a tall young man with closely cropped hair. That identified him as a soldier. The Jaguar more than likely meant he was an officer, and on flight pay. His age (early twenties, Oliver judged), and the fact that he was with Marjorie, identified him further as probably the scion of some Bellmon-like military family. There was no post sticker on the car, which meant that he had just reported onto the post. And unless you had some sort of social in—that is, unless your father-the-general was an old pal of Bellmon's—you didn't get to take the General's daughter out within a day or two of your arrival.

Charley Stevens ain't going to like this competition at all.

"Hello, Johnny," Jack said.

"I like your wheels," Johnny said.

"I like your little boy," Jack said.

"Thank you. Takes after me, wouldn't you say?"

"Oh, damn you, Johnny," Liza said.

Geoff Craig came over.

"You see the Jag?" he asked.

"I saw, and am green with jealousy," Johnny said.

"You want a beer, Johnny, or something stronger?"

"Give him something stronger," Liza said. "If you give him a beer he'll feed it to Allan."

"Beer, beer, beer," Allan said.

"He's a regular chip off the old block, you see," Johnny informed them.

"It's not good for him," Liza said.

"My mother would argue with you, Mrs. Oliver," Jack said. "She says it's good for kids. I don't mean a lot of it, of course, but a sip now and again."

"It's not Mrs. Oliver," Liza said.

"But it does have a nice ring to it, wouldn't you say?" Johnny said.

"Sorry," Jack said.

"Me, too," Johnny said. "I can't begin to tell you how sorry I am."

Liza stormed deeper into the house.

"I guess I put my foot in my mouth, huh?" Jack said.

"It wasn't your fault," Marjorie said. "It was Johnny's."

"If you're waiting for an apology, don't hold your breath, Marjorie," Johnny said.

"I didn't mean it that way and you know it," Marjorie flared. "I'm on your side in that one, Johnny. But you did put Jack on a spot claiming Allan as yours."

"Well, in that case, I am sorry, Jack," Johnny said. "That wasn't my intention."

Geoff Craig returned with a scotch and soda and handed it to Johnny.

"Who pissed Liza off?" he asked. "She marched through the kitchen wearing a marvelous look of self-righteous indignation."

"I guess I did," Jack said. "I called her Mrs. Oliver."

"Ouch," Geoff said. "Well, if she had any sense, that's what she would be."

"She's a widow, Jack," Marjorie explained. "Her husband was killed in 'Nam."

"Oh, I'm sorry," Jack said.

" 'Quickly getting off a painful subject,' " Johnny said. "So you just reported in, did you, Jack?"

Jack nodded. "Yesterday."

"Where?"

"The Aviation Board," Marjorie answered for him.

"I think you'll like it out there," Johnny said. "What are they going to have you doing?"

"First they'll have to teach him the Aviation Board swagger," Geoff Craig said, "and that smugly superior tilt of the nose."

Marjorie giggled and Johnny smiled.

"I don't know," Jack said.

He's lying. How do I know that?

"You fixed, rotary, or both?" Johnny asked.

"That depends on who you ask," Jack said. He looked into Oliver's face. "I'm a PFC. I'm a pilot, but not so far as the Army is concerned."

"And your last name is Portet," Johnny said. "And you came here yesterday from Benning, and you will be working for Major Pappy Hodges."

"I hate to sound like a character in a Grade-B spy movie," Jack Portet said, "but Major Hodges made it pretty clear that I wasn't supposed to talk about what I'm doing here."

"What do you know that I don't know, Johnny?" Marjorie asked.

"He's your old man's dog-robber," Geoff said. "He probably knows a lot you don't know."

"You don't have a need to know," Johnny said, "and I don't want Colonel Felter on my case."

"Now I *really* want to know what's going on," Marjorie said. "Sandy Felter is involved in this?"

"You know?" Jack Portet asked. "The both of you know? Colonel Felter?"

"I thought everybody knows Colonel Sanford Felter," Geoff said. "Sometimes known as Uncle Sandy."

" 'Quickly getting off another painful, not to mention classified, subject,' " Johnny said, "so you and Marjorie are old pals, are you?"

Jack Portet looked uncomfortable. "Not really."

"Johnny," Marjorie said, "I met Jack today. He came into the bank, to cash a check, and he asked me to have dinner. And . . . well, here I am."

"Just before you arrived," Geoff said, "I offered the opinion that Marj looked like she was in the Garden of Eden and Jack was that famous apple."

Marjorie flushed. "Damn you, Geoff!" she said and went into the kitchen.

"I'll tell you what," Geoff said. "I'll call Ursula in here, piss her off, and then we can all be in the same boat."

Johnny and Jack laughed.

Johnny Oliver looked at Jack Portet and remembered what Barbara Bellmon had said to him at the Norwich Dinner; that she didn't think Charley Stevens was the one for Marjorie. He didn't think she would say that about Jack Portet, not if she saw the way Marjorie looked at him.

[THREE]
Norman, Oklahoma
1020 Hours 18 April 1964

"Norman, this is Army Four Seven One."

"Go ahead, Four Seven One."

"Norman, Army Four Seven One is a U-8 aircraft, at ten thousand, about fifty miles west of your station."

"Say again your aircraft type?"

"Norman, Four Seven One. U-8. Beech Twin Bonanza. I just had to shut down my port engine. I am not, repeat, not, declaring an emergency at this time. But I want to make a precautionary landing, and it might be a good idea to have a crash truck standing by. I guess we'll be there in about twenty minutes."

"Four Seven One, Norman. Norman will have emergency equipment standing by. Suggest the use of runway one four. Suggest you begin your descent at this time. The winds are negligible, ceiling and visibility unlimited. The altimeter is two niner niner seven. Suggest reporting passing through five thousand and ten minutes out."

"Norman, Four Seven One understands runway one four. Four Seven One leaving ten thousand."

"Norman, Four Seven One passing through five thousand. ETA ten minutes."

"Four Seven One, are you IFR?"

"Norman, Four Seven One, negative. We're VFR."

"Four Seven One, you are cleared for a straight in approach to runway one four. Report over the outer marker."

"Norman, Four Seven One understands straight in, runway one four."

"Four Seven One, emergency equipment in place. The winds remain negligible, ceiling and visibility unlimited."

"Norman, Four Seven One, I have the airfield in sight."

"Four Seven One, roger. Attention all aircraft in the vicinity of Norman Airfield. We have a possible emergency on runway one four. All aircraft approaching Norman will immediately begin a sixty-second turn and maintain position until further notice. Repeating, Norman has a possible emergency on runway one four. All aircraft approaching Norman will begin to execute a sixty-second turn immediately and hold altitude and position until further notice."

"Norman, Army Four Seven One over the outer marker."

"Norman clears Army Four Seven One for a straight-in landing on runway one four. The winds are negligible, the altimeter is two niner niner seven."

"Oh, shit, there goes the other engine."

"Four Seven One, say again?"

"Norman, we're not going to make it. Goddammit!"

"Four Seven One, emergency equipment is in place."

"Oh, goddammit—he went in!"

[FOUR]
Cairns Army Airfield
Fort Rucker, Alabama
1015 Hours 22 April 1964

Major General Robert F. Bellmon, trailed by Captain John S. Oliver, walked out of the Base Operations building across the concrete parking ramp to a glistening Learjet in Air Force markings. The fuselage door opened and a young black woman wearing the chevrons of an Air Force staff sergeant climbed down the in-door steps.

She saw Bellmon and saluted. Crisply, but not in awe. Learjets of the Air Force's Special Missions Squadron got to see a lot of brass. The day before, Air Force 311 had carried two four-stars, an admiral and the Commander in Chief of the Strategic Air Command.

"I don't believe Colonel Felter is quite ready to deplane, Sir," the staff sergeant said to Bellmon.

"May I go aboard?" Bellmon asked.

"Of course, Sir."

Bellmon entered the airplane and Oliver followed him.

Colonel Sanford T. Felter was pulling on uniform trousers. He hooked suspenders over his shoulders, then reached for his blouse.

"I'm suitably awed, Sandy," Bellmon said.

Jesus Christ, so am I, Oliver thought.

He had never seen Felter in a uniform before. There was an awesome display of fruit salad on Felter's blouse. Under a Combat Infantry Badge (with a star signifying the second award) were parachutists' wings with two stars for combat jumps. There was a Distinguished Service Cross, the nation's second-highest award for valor, a Distinguished Service Medal, two Silver Stars, two Bronze Stars, and a Purple Heart with three oak leaf clusters. Below these were two rows, three ribbons to a row, signifying foreign decorations, only a few of which, including the French Legion of Honor, in the grade of Chevalier, Oliver recognized. Below these were two rows of ''I Was There'' ribbons going back to World War II.

On the other side were insignia representing service on the General Staff of the U.S. Army, United States and Korean Distinguished Unit citations, and another set of wings that Oliver recognized after a moment as those awarded to members of the French *Troisième Régiment Parachutiste*. The *Troisième* had died at Dien Bien Phu.

''Hello, Oliver,'' Felter said as he buttoned his blouse.

''You're awed with me or the airplane, Bob?''

''Both,'' Bellmon said.

''I asked my boss if I could come down here for a couple of days,'' Felter said, putting his brimmed hat on his head and adjusting it. ''And he asked why, and I told him, and he said, 'Take a jet and be back tomorrow.' ''

''Very nice,'' Bellmon said.

''I admit I could learn to like traveling like this,'' Felter said. ''Every time the level in my coffee cup dropped below three quarters, that sergeant filled it up. I'm about to burst.''

''I presume the uniform is for the memorial service?'' Bellmon asked.

''Yeah. I thought it appropriate. In a sense, I was their commanding officer.''

''Damned shame,'' Bellmon said.

''Anything new on how it happened?'' Felter asked, looking at Oliver.

''Best guess now is contaminated fuel, Sir,'' Oliver said. ''As nearly as we can construct their flight, they took on fuel, the last three times, at some dinky little airports.''

''Damn,'' Felter said.

''The memorial service is at eleven,'' Bellmon said. ''Would you like me to introduce you to the families?''

''That's why I'm here,'' Felter said. ''To try to make the point they bought the farm doing something important. That's not much, but they're entitled to that, for what it's worth.''

''I think the gesture is entirely appropriate, Sandy,'' Bellmon said. ''I think they will appreciate your coming.''

''That's not the only reason I'm here, of course,'' Felter said. ''One of Dick Fullbright's people will deliver another airplane later today.''

''Today surprises me,'' Bellmon said. ''How did you arrange that?''

Felter shrugged. ''This is important, Bob.''

''But in another way I think we're probably ahead of you,'' Bellmon said. ''I alerted that other officer, the one you didn't pick before. I told him he might be asked to volunteer as a replacement. And Johnny came up with another list of people who've done a Vietnam tour, speak French, and are U-8 qualified. His name is on the list, Sandy. If it's as important as you say, you can have him.''

Felter looked at Oliver and smiled. ''Didn't anyone ever tell you not to volunteer for anything, Oliver?''

''It looks like a pretty interesting assignment, Sir.''

''Well, I think you're more useful right where you are,'' Felter said. ''And so far as that other guy goes, I don't want him, volunteer or not. I didn't like his attitude. I'll look at your list, Johnny, and I'm grateful you made it up, but what it looks like right now is Pappy Hodges and Geoff Craig.''

''Young Craig's still in flight school,'' Bellmon protested. ''*Rotary*-wing school.''

''And he has just passed the FAA check for multiengine land instrument whether you know that officially or not.''

''I didn't know he passed the FAA check ride,'' Bellmon said. ''And if I knew, officially, that he'd even been taking instruction, I'd have had to do something about it. Off-post instruction is absolutely forbidden.''

''Well, he has, and I need him,'' Felter said. ''You're going to have to run him past a Civilian Experience Board and get him certified.''

That was an order, not a suggestion, Johnny realized. *I wonder how the General's going to take that?*

Bellmon's lips tightened and he looked at Felter coldly.

"Which will make me look like a damned fool, you realize?" he said finally.

I'll be damned, he took it.

"That can't be helped, Bob. Geoff Craig was a Green Beret and he speaks French fluently. Pappy Hodges's experience in flying in the bush makes them a pretty good pair."

And that was the senior explaining to the junior why he has to do something he doesn't want to. Their roles are reversed.

"What about that PFC from the Congo you sent to the Board?"

General Bellmon asked, "Portet? Since you apparently have DCSPERS in your pocket, why don't you get him a commission, or at least a warrant, and send him?"

"You've met him?"

"Johnny has," Bellmon said.

"What do you think of PFC Portet, Johnny?" Felter asked.

"I like him," Oliver said. "Levelheaded. I have heard rumors that he's the one who got Geoff Craig through the FAA examination. If a suggestion wouldn't be out of place, Sir, Portet may be the man to send."

"Your suggestions are always welcome, Johnny," Felter said. "Even when they don't fit into what has to happen. Portet, like you, is more valuable on 'hold until needed' than he would be in the Congo. Anyway, he wouldn't go."

"What do you mean by that?" Bellmon said. There was a shade of bitterness in his voice. Or resignation.

" 'Hold until needed'?" Felter parroted. "Just what it sounds like."

"I meant what you said about Portet not being willing to go."

Damn, I wish he had answered the first question, Oliver thought. *What the hell is he talking about?*

Felter's eyes smiled naughtily.

"The story I get, Bob," he said, "is that a team of horses couldn't drag him from Marjorie's side."

"My God, how did you hear about that?"

"Portet has been reciting Marjorie's many virtues to Pappy

Hodges, apparently by the hour,'' Felter replied with a smile. ''Pappy told me.''

Bellmon grunted. ''That doesn't answer the basic question: what do you mean, he won't go? He's a soldier. Soldiers go where they're told to go.''

''His family is in the Congo. He told Mr. Finton that he would go to Vietnam tomorrow, but he would desert before he put his family in danger by going to the Congo.''

''Nonsense,'' Bellmon snorted.

''Finton believes him. So do I. Anyway, that's moot. I have other plans for him here. I'm afraid it comes down to Pappy Hodges and Geoff Craig, Bob. I've already talked to Pappy. He's willing to go, of course. After the memorial service, I want to see Geoff Craig.''

[FIVE]
Cairns Army Airfield
Fort Rucker, Alabama
0815 Hours 2 May 1964

The AOD was the same pompous sonofabitch who had given Johnny Oliver trouble about using the telephone for personal reasons back in January.

He was now practically beside himself with curiosity. First, he had been directed by the FOD on the post to permit the landing of a civilian Cessna airplane. The FOD hadn't known anything about it, except that the word had come down from Sergeant Major Harrison James.

And now the General's dog-robber had shown up, just as the civilian Cessna was due to land. And in civilian clothing.

Sensing the bastard's curiosity, Oliver resolved not to tell him a damn thing. With a little bit of luck, Lieutenant Colonel Craig W. Lowell would show up in civvies, too. And in civvies, Lowell looked more like a movie actor than a serving officer.

''May I be of any help, Captain?''

''No, thank you, Sir. I'm just waiting for someone.''

''There's a civilian Cessna about to land,'' the Major said. ''Special permission came down from the FOD.''

''Really?''

The Cessna taxied up to the transient parking ramp. The door opened, and Lieutenant Colonel Craig W. Lowell came out. He was wearing a tweed sports coat, an open-collared shirt, and a foulard.

"That must be him," the AOD said. "I wonder who he is?"

Oliver walked out of Base Operations without replying. He decided to forgo saluting a senior officer.

"Good morning, Sir," he said.

"Hey, Johnny," Lowell called as he jumped off the wing root. "I appreciate this. Sorry to take your Saturday morning."

"No problem, Sir," Oliver said as Lowell offered his hand. "My car's right behind Base Ops." And then he gave into the temptation. "Colonel, you speak French, don't you?"

"Uh huh. Why?"

"When we walk through Base Ops would you mind talking in French?"

Lowell looked at him appraisingly. "Putting somebody on?"

"The AOD, Sir."

"D'accord, mon ami," Lowell said. "Any special reason, or is he just an all-around pain in the ass?"

"No special reason, Sir."

And even that went better than Johnny could have hoped. The AOD came up to them and identified himself, and asked if he could be of any help. Lowell gave him a look of righteous indignation, and let loose a torrent of French, ending with a gesture which had his hand raised, index finger pointing skyward. Then he marched out the back door of Base Ops and got into Oliver's Pontiac.

"You think that fixed the bastard?" Lowell asked as they left Cairns Field.

"I think we've ruined his day," Oliver said.

"I know the type. The Army is full of them. I suppose naturally."

"Sir?"

"The Army, by its very nature, attracts people who prefer to be ordered around rather than make their own decisions. If it's not specifically authorized, it's forbidden, in other words. That type is necessary, even important, but it does them good to be shaken up every once in a while.''

''Yes, Sir, I suppose that's true.''

Lowell changed the subject.

''I was sorry I couldn't get here before Geoff left. Or even Ursula. But they did get off all right, I take it?''

''Yes, Sir. Ursula and Mrs. Hodges left yesterday. Mrs. Bellmon and Marjorie took them to the airport.''

''My cousin, Geoff's father, has arranged to take care of them in Frankfurt,'' Lowell said. ''Getting them from here to New York was the problem.''

''Yes, Sir.''

''My cousin's wife is having a fit about some of the furniture in the house in Ozark,'' Lowell said. ''Apparently some of it is from her family, and rather valuable. That's what I'm going to do here, stick labels on some of the antiques so the movers can come and send the good stuff back to New York. And then I want to see about renting the house.''

''General Bellmon told me, Sir,'' Oliver said. ''Colonel, my girl is in the real estate business. Maybe she could help you about renting the house.''

''The thought that came to me on my way up here, Johnny, is that maybe you'd like to move in. The rent would be whatever your housing allowance is. That way, with somebody we know, Geoff wouldn't have to pay for storage for the rest of his furniture.''

For a moment the idea was exciting, but then reality shot the balloon down.

''Colonel, I appreciate the offer, but General Bellmon keeps me on a pretty tight leash. I don't think he'd like it, when he blows his whistle, to have to wait for me to drive all the way from Ozark.''

Lowell chuckled.

''That's the same reason Bellmon gave when I said you and Bobby could share the house,'' Lowell said.

''Sir?''

''Bobby's coming here right after graduation,'' Lowell said. ''You didn't know that?''

''No, Sir.''

''Interesting,'' Lowell said thoughtfully. ''The school's

running a test. Four classes, two fixed and two rotary wing. Two—one of each—will be warrant officer candidates, but they won't be sergeants with three years of service. They'll be kids right out of basic training. And one of each will be brand-new second lieutenants, right out of college ROTC—without even going through their branch basic-officer course first. Except for four kids from the Point, one of whom, by what I am sure is the purest of chance, is Bobby."

"I'd heard about the test courses," Oliver said, "but not about Bobby."

"I can't imagine why he didn't tell you," Lowell said dryly. "Unless, maybe, he didn't want to shatter your illusions about being the sort of sterling character who would never use his connections, including the West Point Protective Association, to get his kid a favor."

"Sending someone to flight school isn't always a favor," Johnny said.

" 'Said the aide loyally,' " Lowell mocked him gently.

"Well, what the hell, why not?"

" 'Said the aide loyally,' " Lowell repeated, laughing. "No wonder Bellmon likes you so much."

"I don't know about that, but I admire him," Johnny said.

"Yeah, me, too. Beneath that stuffed shirt there's a pretty decent human being. Sometimes you have to dig pretty deep to get at him, though."

They rode on in silence until they were on the far side of Fort Rucker, on the Ozark Highway.

"So you don't know anyone else we could move into that house, Oliver?" Lowell asked.

"No, Sir," Oliver said after a brief hesitation.

"You hesitated," Lowell accused.

"Far-out suggestion, Colonel?"

"Shoot."

"I have a friend," Oliver said. "A second lieutenant."

"Beneath your dignity, Captain. Although I suppose you'll have one whether or not you want one when Bobby joins the Long Gray Line and comes here."

"This is sort of a special guy," Oliver said. "He was in the Texas National Guard. And then Colonel Augustus at the Board—"

"Pancho Villa," Lowell interrupted.

"Sir?"

"Little Tex-Mex guy? Knows avionics?"

"Yes, Sir."

"Dick Fullbright met him, told me about him. Fullbright's very impressed with him. He calls him Pancho Villa. What about him?"

"Well, Sir, for a long time, quarters on the post were no problem. But the minute Jose—"

"Is that his name? Jose?"

"Yes, Sir. Anyway, the minute he got his orders to active duty, and sent for his wife, the quarters all filled up. He and his wife and kids, two of them, are in a dump in Daleville."

"Two kids?" Lowell asked doubtfully.

"Yes, Sir. Little ones."

"You vouch for this guy, Oliver?"

Oh, shit! Me and my big mouth. His kids will probably set the carpet on fire and kick holes in the wall.

"Yes, Sir."

"OK. Same deal. His housing allowance, and he pays for unusual wear and tear. I'll have my lawyer send the standard contract. If that doesn't work, we'll try something else."

"Sir, if you don't mind my asking, why don't you just sell the place? Houses are in demand, and my girl, I'm sure, could get you a good price for it."

"Your girl being the widow who won't marry you because she already lost one husband?"

"Yes, Sir."

Now who the hell told him about that?

"Hang tough," Lowell said. "I understand her problem, but husbands get killed falling out of bed. For what it's worth, Barbara Bellmon likes her. I trust her judgment."

"So do I," Johnny said.

"The answer to your question, why don't I sell it," Lowell went on, "is that I am a very rich man because my ancestors had a real estate philosophy: Buy! Cheap if you can, but *buy.* And *never* sell. My own philosophy in this area is of course far more intellectual: If it ain't broke, don't fix it."

Oliver laughed.

"Don't laugh. That's a damned good philosophy. What you

should do as a young officer is buy a house every place you get stationed. Phrased simply, you use your equity in the first to make the down payment on the second, and you use the rent money to pay off the mortgage. Never take a mortgage longer than twenty years, and fifteen if you can afford it. By the time you're a general, you won't have to worry about living on the chicken feed the Army pays."

"I've got a piece of real estate now, or half of one, I don't know what the hell to do with," Johnny said.

"What kind of real estate?"

"A truck stop. But I don't want to bother you with this."

"I'm fascinated."

"Why do you say that, Colonel?" Oliver challenged. "What's fascinating for someone like you about a truck stop?"

"We've got some of them. Ordinarily, they're a license to steal. Real money machines. What's wrong with yours?"

"Sir, I didn't mean to get into this—"

"If it's none of my business, fine. But if you're worried about taking advantage of my good nature, you're not that smart."

"My sister and brother-in-law want to buy me out," Oliver said. "Liza, my girl, doesn't think they're offering me enough money."

"Real estate people never think the numbers are right," Lowell said. "But I think I'd go with your girlfriend."

"Why do you say that?"

"You won't like the answer."

"I'd like to hear it, anyway."

"Let me put it this way," Lowell said. "I went through the Wharton School not because I was fascinated with high finance, but because my cousin, Geoff's father, was running my half of my inherited business and I wanted to be in a position to know that his definition of fair coincided, at least roughly, with mine."

"Jesus!" Johnny blurted.

"Touched a nerve, did I? Tell ya what I'm going to do for you, young fella. We have a management office in Atlanta. The lawyer I spoke about works out of there. Instead of having him send you the lease, I'll send him down here with it. While he's here, explain it all to him."

"Colonel, I don't know what to say."

"Say thank you."

"Colonel . . ."

"Hey, Barbara Bellmon likes you. Bellmon himself likes you. Geoff likes you. Even the Jewish Pope likes you. You're part of the family. It may not be much of a family, but we take care of each other. Do what you're told, Captain. I rank the hell out of you."

XV

[ONE]
Office of the Commanding General
The Army Aviation Center & Fort Rucker, Alabama
1015 Hours 13 May 1964

Major General Robert F. Bellmon stood up from behind his desk and walked to the door of his outer office.

"Johnny, can you come in here a minute?" he asked. "You, too, please, Sergeant James."

When they had followed him into the office, he told Sergeant Major James to close the door and then waved them into the chairs in front of his desk.

"Second Lieutenant Robert F. Bellmon, Junior," he said dryly, "having graduated from the Academy, is on the standard thirty-day delay en route leave to his first duty station. His first duty station is Fort Rucker, Alabama. Lieutenant Bellmon has been selected as one of the four just-out-of-the-

Point young officers we are going to run through flight school in that test program."

"Well," Sergeant Major James said, smiling, pleased with the news.

Bellmon flashed him an impatient look. "I had nothing to do with his selection," he said. "But I am not so much of a fool to believe that it is unrelated to the fact that I am his father. As his father, I'm pleased. As Commandant of the Army Aviation School, I'm not so sure about that."

"Bobby's a bright kid, General," Sergeant Major James said. "He'll get through the program no sweat."

"That's not what I'm worried about, Harrison."

"Oh," Sergeant Major James said. "Yes, Sir, I see what you mean."

"I've known about this assignment for a month," Bellmon said. "I seriously considered having his orders changed. In the end I decided that would be unfair to Bobby. He wants to become an aviator, he's qualified to come here, and I didn't think it would be fair to penalize him because his father happens to be the commandant of the school. I'm not sure, even now, if that is the commandant speaking, or Daddy. In any event, he's coming here."

"I think you did the right thing, Sir," Sergeant Major James said.

"Well, thank you. Specifically, Bobby is out in Carmel, with his grandmother Waterford. She told me it is her intention to buy him an automobile. Knowing Mrs. Waterford, the odds are that that automobile will be the kind that befits a bushy-tailed Armored second lieutenant. That is to say, it will probably go two hundred miles an hour, cost him half his pay for insurance, and attract the military police like a magnet."

Sergeant Major James and Captain Oliver chuckled.

"I will also lay odds that he will not be in California anything like a month," Bellmon said. "In other words, we can expect him here in, say, a week or ten days. I want to set the SOP for his presence on Fort Rucker. He is to be treated exactly like any other second lieutenant. That is the first and great commandment."

"Yes, Sir!" Oliver and James said in unison, chuckling.

"For example," Bellmon said, "he is no more welcome

in this office at any time than any other second lieutenant, which means I do not expect to see him in here, period. I will explain this to him, of course, but I will need some help. If he ever shows up outside, throw his ass out."

"I get the picture, Sir," Sergeant Major James said.

"He will be living in the BOQ," Bellmon said. "The student BOQ, Johnny, not in yours."

"Yes, Sir."

"You will not offer your aviation expertise, Captain Oliver, in any way, shape or form, to Lieutenant Bellmon. And you will please spread the word among your peers that the best way you know for them to incur my rage is for me to find out that anyone else is giving him a special helping hand. Got that?"

"Yes, Sir," Oliver said.

"And I would be grateful to you, Harrison, if you would spread the word around afternoon tea at the NCO Club how I feel about this."

"Yes, Sir, of course," the sergeant major said. "Sir, I don't think this is going to be any problem—"

"Oh, bullshit, Harrison. You know better than that. And so do I. I was a captain at Knox when my father-in-law was post commander. It was a pain in the ass for both of us."

"Yes, Sir," Sergeant Major James said.

"But thank you for saying that, anyway," Bellmon said with a smile. "That will be all, thank you both."

[TWO]
Dothan Municipal Airport
Dothan, Alabama
0955 Hours 23 May 1964

There was a Caribou with 11th Air Assault Division markings on it on the parking ramp when the Southern Airways DC-3 landed and taxied up to the small, nearly forlorn, frame terminal building.

When he saw the crew of the Caribou in the small, bedraggled coffee shop, Johnny Oliver decided that they'd set down here for no better reason than they could land and get a cup of coffee without the bureaucratic hassle that landing at Cairns, twenty miles away, would entail.

He eyed the crew and they eyed him. The pilot and copilot, both first lieutenants, looked like they could be the sons of the crew chief, a gray-haired sergeant first class in his forties.

Johnny laid a dollar on the counter to pay for his coffee and doughnuts and walked to the terminal door as the DC-3 taxied up and shut down its engines.

The first two people down the DC-3's stair door were the pilot and copilot. They probably needed a cup of coffee, too, Johnny decided as they walked toward the terminal. Then curiosity got the better of them and they walked over to the Caribou to take a good, professional look at it.

The two airplanes had much in common in that they were twin piston-engine transports and roughly the same size. But more than a generation of technology separated them. The Caribou was, all around, a far superior airplane to the DC-3. It could carry larger and heavier loads, and get into and out of really short airfields. And it had weather-avoidance radar in the nose that the DC-3 didn't have. There was no telling how old the DC-3 was; the first of them had entered airline service before World War II. This one, he decided, was very likely nearly as old as the pilots of the Caribou.

He had the somewhat unkind thought that when these two silver-haired airline pilots with their eyes of blue walked into the coffee shop and saw who was flying the 'Bou, they would be just a smidgen less pleased with themselves and their role in the scheme of things than airlines pilots usually seemed to be.

He then turned his attention to the deplaning passengers. He had no trouble spotting Foxworth T. Mattingly, Esq., Attorney-at-Law. Mattingly, a short, pale-faced, slight, anemic-looking man, was wearing a dark-gray suit and a rep-striped necktie, and he was carrying an attaché case. He looked like a lawyer, and no one else getting off Southern Flight 413 looked even remotely like a lawyer. Still, he was surprised to see how young Mattingly was. From listening to his voice on the telephone, Johnny had decided Mattingly was at least in his forties. He didn't look much older than Oliver did.

"Mr. Mattingly?" Oliver asked as he intercepted him. When Mattingly nodded, he added, "I'm John Oliver. How was the flight?"

"Actually it was dreadful," Mattingly said. His grip was

limp when Oliver shook his hand. "Very good of you to meet me."

"Oh, my pleasure," Oliver said.

"Just give me a sec to reconfirm my departure," Mattingly said, "and then we can be about our business."

As he waited for Mattingly to conduct his business at the Southern Airways counter, Oliver glanced into the coffee shop and saw that he had misjudged the reaction of the DC-3 pilots to the 'Bou pilots. They were all at the same table, engaged in what appeared to be a pleasant conversation.

"I'm out of here at four-ten," Mattingly said. "Will that give us enough time?"

"Well, I don't see why not," Oliver said. "What would you like to do first?"

"Well, examine the property, and then have Lieutenant Newell sign the lease," Mattingly said.

"I don't think anyone is home," Oliver said. "So that we could get inside, I mean."

"Excuse me?"

"Lieutenant Newell is flying," Oliver said. "And Mrs. Newell told me she was taking the kids shopping."

"Are you saying they are already in occupancy?" Mattingly asked.

"Yeah, they've been in there for two weeks."

"I wasn't aware of that. It's more than a little unusual. Who authorized that?"

"I suppose Colonel Lowell did," Oliver said. He was already annoyed with Mr. Mattingly. "Jose Newell asked him when he could move in, and Colonel Lowell said the sooner the better. So they moved in."

He gestured for Mattingly to head for the parking lot.

"The thing is," Mattingly said as he pulled the Pontiac's door closed and looked askance at the top, which was down, "what we like to do is conduct a survey of the property together with the lessee so there is no question later as to the condition of the property when the lessee assumed responsibility for it."

"Lieutenant Newell will stipulate the property is in perfect condition, Mr. Mattingly," Oliver said.

"Well, there's nothing to be done, I suppose," Mattingly

said. "But there would be no problem in my having a walk-around, would there?"

"You mean walk around the house? Sure, why not?"

When they reached Ozark and pulled in the driveway, Mattingly took from his pocket a leatherbound notebook and what looked like a sterling silver mechanical pencil, and almost immediately started taking notes.

"Well, I see you were wrong," he said. "The Newells are at home."

"No," Oliver said, confused, "they're not."

"Then how many automobiles do they have?"

Oliver chuckled. "The Olds and the Volkswagen belong to the Craigs," he said. "I'm trying to sell them for them."

"The Craigs?"

"The previous occupants."

"Do you happen to know, Captain Oliver, anything about the previous occupants?"

"Yeah. They're friends of mine. What do you want to know?"

"I don't suppose you'd happen to know—what I'm driving at, Captain, is that the chairman of the board of Craig, Powell, Kenyon and Dawes, of which Sutton Holdings is a subsidiary—his name is Porter *Craig.* I wondered if there was any connection."

"Pretty close one," Johnny said. "Porter Craig is Geoff Craig's father."

"I wonder why I wasn't informed?" Mattingly said.

Probably because you're such a stuffed shirt, and whoever sent you down here wanted to pull your chain.

"I can't imagine," Oliver said. "Probably he's a little embarrassed—Mr. Porter Craig, I mean—about having a son in the Army. You know: 'Soldiers and Dogs, Keep Off the Grass'?"

Mattingly looked at Johnny with very sad eyes.

"I suppose I do come across as rather a horse's ass, don't I? I have immediately offended you, and I'm sorry."

"Hey, I didn't say that!"

"No, but you were thinking it."

"OK, the thought did run through my mind that you are

just a little stuffy,'' Oliver said. ''But not that you were a horse's ass.''

''Well, thank you,'' Mattingly said. ''I suppose I've had my comeuppance.''

''I beg your pardon?''

''They apparently have that opinion of me—I know they do, and now there's proof—in the office. They told me that word had come down from New York to send me, specifically, down here. Well, I don't mean to blow my own horn, but I generally deal with industrial and commercial properties, not something like this. . . . ''

The poor little bastard is crushed.

''Did they mention anything about me?'' Oliver asked.

''As a matter of fact they did. They told me you were one of Colonel Lowell's subordinates, and that you had a real estate problem, and that I was to do whatever was necessary to straighten it out for you. To take whatever problems there are off your hands, as it were.''

''I do,'' Johnny said.

''Let me guess,'' Mattingly said. ''A house not quite as large as this? Or perhaps a mobile home?''

''Actually, it's a truck stop,'' Johnny said. ''My part of a truck stop.''

''Oh, really?'' Mattingly said with visible relief. ''I have some expertise in that area. Is there somewhere we could go to talk?''

''My BOQ,'' Johnny said.

''Your what?''

''My room,'' Johnny said.

''Oh, I'd like that,'' Mattingly said. ''I've never been in a barracks.''

Foxworth T. Mattingly, Esq., could not quite conceal his fascination with Johnny Oliver's spartan BOQ, but Oliver decided it was just that, fascination, not snobbery. He was surprised to realize that he felt a good deal of sympathy for Mattingly. He was obviously the sort of guy who had been, since he was a little kid, the one the gang picked on. And he had never learned how to deal with it.

Johnny gave him the large envelope his sister had given him, and Mattingly sat down at Johnny's desk, perched a pair of half glasses on his nose, and started to read, very slowly, through it. From time to time he frowned, and several times he made grunting noises.

"Can I offer you a drink? It's a little early—"

"No alcohol, thank you," Mattingly said. "It makes me ill."

"Coffee?"

"Coffee would be nice."

"I'll go next door to the annex and get us some."

"Thank you," Mattingly said and returned his attention to the legal documents.

You have your orders, Oliver. March!

"Cream and sugar?" he asked.

"If it's real cream, please. No sugar."

"I'll see what I can do."

He really doesn't understand why he pisses people off!

When he returned from the annex with two mugs of coffee and a can of condensed milk, Mattingly was scribbling furiously on a lined pad.

"All I could get was the canned cow," Oliver said.

"The what? Oh, the condensed milk. No, thank you. It reminds me of boys' camp. I'll just have it black."

He took a sip, burned his lips on the hot mug, and spilled coffee on his lined pad.

So you're a slob, too. What do you do for an encore?

Johnny got a paper towel and mopped up the mess.

"I tend to be a bit messy," Foxworth T. Mattingly, Esq., said.

"Really?"

"Now you're mocking me," Mattingly said resignedly.

"Sorry."

"What you have given me, Captain Oliver, raises more questions than it answers. For example, there is a release from all trust obligations, but I haven't the trust documents, so there is no way I could tell what you would be signing away."

"Oh."

"And 'all' could mean one trust or a dozen," Mattingly said. "How many trusts are involved?"

"I haven't the foggiest."

"Oh, dear. Well, that would be a *starting* point."

"What I'd like to know is whether I'm being offered a reasonable price," Johnny said.

"Well, we're a good way down the pike yet from that."

The unlisted telephone rang.

"Yes, Sir?"

"Another Chinook just went in, Johnny," General Bellmon said.

"Oh, shit. How bad?"

"No fatalities. They lost it on landing. I'd like you to go out there with me."

"Yes, Sir. You want me to pick you up?"

"I'll pick you up," Bellmon said, and the line went dead.

Oliver looked at Foxworth T. Mattingly.

What the fuck am I going to do with him?

"Something's come up, Mr. Mattingly. I'm going to have to break this off."

Oh, shit! Jose and Charley are flying a thousand-hour Chinook.

He furiously dialed the telephone.

The phone rang a long time before somebody picked it up.

"Board Pilots' Lounge."

"Who was flying the Chinook that went in?"

"I'm sorry, I can't—"

"This is Captain Oliver, General Bellmon's aide. Don't give me that 'I'm sorry I can't' bullshit."

"Charley Stevens and Jose Newell," the voice said.

"Are they dead?" Oliver asked softly.

"No. They've got them on stretchers—the ambulance isn't here yet."

Oliver hung up without saying another word. He found Mattingly's eyes on him. They were very sympathetic.

"If I can make a suggestion—" Mattingly said.

"I don't have time to fuck with this right now," Oliver said, and quickly started to slip out of his civilian clothing.

"Is there anything I can do?" Mattingly asked.

Oliver pulled his shirt over his head, hearing cloth rip as he did so.

"Can you drive?"

"Why, yes, of course. Is there somewhere I can drive you?"

Oliver found his car keys and tossed them to Mattingly.

"Ask somebody how to find the Dothan Road," he said. "Leave the keys at the Southern ticket counter."

"Why, I'll just call a cab," Mattingly said. "I certainly don't want to inconvenience you at a time when—"

"There are no cabs, asshole. And it's too far to walk."

"Oh, I see. Well, in that case—"

"Take the damned car," Johnny said.

"You're very kind."

Oliver quickly put on a shirt and trousers and tied a necktie. He was vaguely aware that Mattingly was scribbling furiously on his lined pad again.

Oliver took the first blouse that came to hand and shoved his arms into the sleeves. When he had buttoned it, Mattingly was standing by the desk, extending a pen to Johnny.

"What's this?" Oliver asked as he looked around the room for his hat.

"It's a simple authorization appointing me as attorney-in-fact to represent you in this matter."

"I just told you, I don't have the time to fuck around with this now."

"I doubt if they'll give me access to the documents we need without it," Mattingly persisted. "As a matter of fact, I'm sure they won't."

"Then it will just . . ." Oliver said, and then: "Oh, to hell with it." He leaned over the table and quickly glanced at what Mattingly had written, in a tiny but very legible hand.

Fort Rucker, Alabama
May 23, 1964

The undersigned herewith appoints Foxworth T. Mattingly as his counsel of record, with all appropriate powers provided in the law, to represent him in the matter of the property commonly know as "Jack's Truck Stop" of Burlington, Vermont, this authority to last until properly revoked.

Johnny scrawled his name.

"Close the door when you leave," he said, and left the room.

Foxworth T. Mattingly, Esq., caught up with him in the parking lot of the BOQ as General Bellmon's Oldsmobile drove up.

"Now what?" Oliver snapped.

"It has to be notarized," Foxworth T. Mattingly, Esq., said. "Witnessing your signature."

"Where the hell am I going to get a notary? Give it to me and I'll mail it to you with Newell's lease."

"I just remembered that a commissioned officer of the regular military establishment has the de jure authority to act as a notary public for another member of the military service," Foxworth T. Mattingly, Esq., said as Bellmon skidded to a stop.

Oliver ran to the car and got in beside Bellmon.

Foxworth T. Mattingly rapped imperiously on the door glass by General Bellmon's head. Bellmon rolled the window down.

"Pardon me, are you a commissioned officer of the regular military establishment?"

"I suppose you could say that, yes," Bellmon said, torn between gross annoyance, impatience, and incredulity.

"Oh, *good*!" Mattingly said. "Then perhaps you would be willing to affix your signature to this, attesting that you know the signer, and that this is his signature?"

Bellmon looked at Oliver.

"I'm sorry, Sir," Oliver said.

"You want me to witness your signature?" Bellmon snapped.

"Sir, please—"

Bellmon snatched the paper from Mattingly's hand and scrawled his signature.

"And under it, please print your name, rank, serial number, and the date," Mattingly said. Bellmon sighed audibly and did as he was told.

"Is that all?" he asked, sarcastically polite.

"I think so, thank you very much," Mattingly said. "Goodbye, Captain Oliver. It was very nice to have met you."

Bellmon rolled the window up as he backed out the parking spot, sending gravel spinning under his wheels.

''Curiosity overwhelms me, Oliver,'' he said. ''Who was that obnoxious little turd?''

''A lawyer Colonel Lowell sent me to help with a personal problem, Sir.''

''Well, if Lowell sent him, he's probably going to charge you two hundred dollars an hour. And be worth every dime of it. Anything I can do to help with the problem?''

''No, Sir,'' Oliver said. ''Thank you. But it's not important.''

''Don't be bashful, if I can help, say so.''

''Yes, Sir, I will. Sir, I called Cairns. There have been no fatalities.''

''Who was it? You find out?''

''Yes, Sir. Newell and Stevens.''

''God, and his wife and kids just got here!''

''Yes, Sir.''

''You hear how it happened?''

''No, Sir,'' Oliver replied. ''I just asked who.''

''It comes at a particularly rotten time,'' Bellmon said as they drove past Post Headquarters at what Johnny saw was precisely twice the twenty-five-mile-per-hour speed limit. ''Just when I was beginning to think we might be out of the woods.''

''Sir?''

''We lost one of the thousand-hour Chinooks,'' Bellmon said. ''That leaves two. One of the remaining two just passed the thousand-hour mark. The other has almost nine hundred hours, Mac McNair told me this morning. If that's the one that went in, we're finished. The Air Force will say we can't base any logistics data on one aircraft. And since we have wrecked two of the three, the Army is obviously not qualified to conduct the tests, period. They will volunteer to take the tests over, McNamara probably will go along and let them, and we will hear from Wright-Patterson in two years or so, if ever.''

''Damn,'' Oliver said.

''So what I'm hoping is that the one that went in is the one that they've already put a thousand hours on.''

''You think they'll ground all of them again, Sir?''

"Absolutely, and they won't even bother with a TWX. The Chief of Staff will tell me so personally on the telephone."

"Are you going to call the Chief of Staff, Sir?" Oliver asked, curious.

"Yes, I am. I have been ordered to do so. He called me right after we came home from Washington the last time. I have to call him whenever there is a Chinook accident worth more than a thousand dollars or involving personnel injury of any kind."

"Well, we have that. They told me that they have Charley Stevens and Jose on stretchers."

"I don't know why the hell I'm speeding," Bellmon said. "The damage is done, there's really no reason to rush out there."

But he did not slow down.

[THREE]

The Chinook had gone down on the grass between runway one six and the concrete parking ramp which ran next to Hangars 102, 103, and 104. Two of the brand-new crash trucks were in place beside it, their foam cannon pointing at the helicopter. But there were no signs that there had been a fire.

When they came closer, they could see that the Chinook had come down on top of a Cessna O-1, collapsing its gear and flattening the two-seater's fuselage. The O-1's wings were crushed.

It looks, Oliver thought, *like a big bug eating a little bug.*

He saw ambulances, one GI and olive drab, the other a civilian-type ambulance on a Cadillac chassis. And there were people in medic's whites standing around, but no sign at first of either Charley Stevens or Jose Newell.

Then he saw them, on their feet, standing with Colonel Mac McNair, the Aviation Board president, a very young looking sergeant in a flight suit, obviously the crew chief, and a gray-haired medic who was visibly upset.

General Bellmon apparently saw what Oliver saw.

"Thank God they're not badly hurt," he said. He drove to where they were standing and got out of the car.

Colonel McNair saluted, a reflex action. Charley Stevens

and Jose Newell, a fraction of a second later, followed suit. And then the medic, who wore captain's bars, finally became aware of his obligations under the Code of Military Courtesy.

"You fellows all right?" General Bellmon asked.

"General, I'm sorry," Charley Stevens said.

"That wasn't the question, Lieutenant."

"Yes, Sir, we're all right."

"Sergeant?" Bellmon asked. "Are you hurt?"

"No, Sir," the crew chief said.

"Newell?" Bellmon challenged.

"I'm all right, Sir."

"You don't know that," the doctor said.

"Piss off," Stevens snapped.

"That will be enough of that, Lieutenant," Bellmon said. "What happened?"

"Sir, I just don't know," Stevens said.

"General, I'd like to get these men to the hospital," the doctor said.

"In a moment, Doctor," Bellmon said. He looked at Stevens. "You were saying what happened, Charley?"

"Sir, I don't know," Stevens said, torn between anger and humiliation. "I was coming in to park the sonofabitch, and all of a sudden it just stopped flying."

"I don't think I understand," Bellmon said.

"Yes, Sir, that's it, neither do I," Stevens said. "It just . . . *stopped flying.*"

There was the sound of another Chinook, and they turned over their shoulders in the direction of it, toward the Board Building. The Chinook came in quickly and stopped over the parking ramp at the south end of Hangar 102. When the helicopter turned, Oliver saw Colonel Charles Augustus in the pilot's seat. Augustus put it on the ground and was out of the machine and running toward them before his copilot could apply the rotor brakes and shut it down.

"You guys all right?" he asked, putting his hands on the crew chief's arm and looking intently into his face. He had not, Oliver noticed, saluted Bellmon. When he was satisfied the sergeant was not injured, or at least in need of immediate attention, he went to both Stevens and Newell and took a close look at them.

"OK, so what happened?" he demanded. "Who was flying?"

"I was, Sir," Stevens said. "Colonel, I don't know what happened. I guess I was thirty, forty feet in the air, coming in to touch down here for fuel, and it just stopped flying. We came down tailfirst on top of the O-1."

"Helicopters just don't stop flying," Augustus said.

"This one did, Colonel," Stevens said. "I'm sorry to say."

"Augustus," Bellmon said, "which one is it?"

Augustus looked at him a moment, not understanding the question, and then comprehension came.

"The one Stevens dumped is the one that just finished the thousand hours," he said. "SCATSA took it over to run radiation patterns."

"Thank God for small blessings," Bellmon said.

"Is that going to do us any good?" McNair asked.

"Probably not," Bellmon said. "I know goddamned well the moment the Chief of Staff hears about this, he'll ground them."

"Don't tell him, then," Colonel Augustus said.

"I have been ordered to tell him," Bellmon said flatly.

"We only need eighty-six hours on the other one," McNair said, pointing toward the Chinook Augustus had just landed.

"You're not suggesting I put off reporting this to the Chief of Staff until we can put the rest of the hours on the other one, are you, Mac?"

McNair didn't reply.

"I can't do that," Bellmon said.

"Pilot error," Augustus said significantly.

"I don't think so," McNair said. "Not from what Stevens says."

"Think again, Mac," Augustus said. "What else have we got?"

Oliver suddenly felt chilled as he understood what Augustus was proposing.

"A tired pilot," Augustus went on. "And an inexperienced copilot. How many hours have you got in Chinooks, Newell?"

"About sixty, Sir," Jose said.

Whatever caused this accident is not pilot error. Charley

Stevens is not only a natural pilot, but he's got a lot of hours in helicopters a lot harder to fly than the Chinook, Oliver thought. He saw in his mind's eye an H-37. The Sikorsky H-37, the second-largest helicopter in the world, was so large that a jeep and trailer could be driven into the fuselage through a clamshell door in the nose. Charley was flying, setting a 105mm howitzer in a sling load down on a tiny pad on a mountainside in the Au Shau valley in 'Nam. He was way over maximum gross weight, the density altitude conditions were horrendous, and the winds had been gusting to thirty knots. It had been a spectacular demonstration of skill.

"There you have it," Augustus said.

If it's pilot error, ergo it's not the fault of the Chinook. That would provide a chance, a slight one, but a chance, that the Chief of Staff could be talked into not grounding the remaining thousand-hour Chinook until it had completed the thousand hours. But a charge of pilot error of this magnitude on Stevens's and Newell's record would probably see the both of them lose their wings. Charley can forget making captain and Jose can kiss any dreams of a regular commission goodbye.

"It could have been my fault," Charley Stevens said. "Pilot error, I mean. I don't have any other explanation."

You fucking fool! You know what's being proposed as well as I do!

Oliver looked at Newell. He had just understood what was happening. He looked sick.

"No," Bellmon said flatly. "There will be the usual investigation of this incident. The Accident Investigation Board will determine the probable cause of the accident. It may turn out that Stevens is at fault. I doubt it. But in any case, I have no intention of trying to offer him or Newell up as a human sacrifice."

"General—" Augustus started to argue.

"No, Augustus, I said no and I mean no. Let it drop right there."

Oliver had a disturbing thought: *I expected that response from Bellmon. But I expected it much more quickly than it came. He was thinking about it. Did he decide against it on moral, ethical grounds, or because he didn't think they could get away with it?*

"What now, General?" McNair asked.

"Well, these three will be taken to a telephone so they can call their families and tell them they're all right, and then they will go to the hospital and have themselves checked over. And I will call the Chief of Staff and tell him we have had a little accident here."

"And that politician in a soldier's uniform will ground the Chinooks, and there goes the fucking ball game," Augustus said bitterly.

"I don't like your vocabulary, Colonel," Bellmon said sharply. "And you're wrong. It ain't over until the fat lady sings. Come on, Oliver, let's get out of here."

He started back toward his car, and then turned to look at the sergeant, Stevens and Newell.

"I want the three of you to know that you have my highest admiration for your behavior here, today."

[FOUR]

As they passed under the sign at the main gate, Bellmon said, "I have suddenly developed an awesome thirst, which is the real reason I'm going to see if George Rand is in the Magnolia House. The official reason is that I will brief him on this incident and ask him to relay the information to General Wendall at the 11th."

"Yes, Sir," Oliver said.

"Augustus is a ruthless bastard, isn't he?" Bellmon said. "He probably would have made a fine Armor officer."

"Sir?" Oliver asked, wholly confused.

"I didn't expect you to understand, Johnny," Bellmon said. "I'm just running off at the mouth."

Susan Rand answered their knock at the Magnolia House.

"Hello, Susan," Bellmon said. "A pleasant surprise! I didn't know you were here."

"I didn't intend that you should," she said. "You and Barbara would have put yourselves out."

"Don't be silly," Bellmon said.

"Hello, Captain Oliver," she said. "How are you?"

''Ma'am,'' Oliver said.

''He's in the kitchen,'' she said. ''We were studying. Is there anything either of you would like to know about the formation of stratocumulus clouds?''

General Rand heard the voices and came out from the kitchen, wearing a battered sweater and corduroy pants.

''Welcome to the Honeymoon Motel,'' he said. ''Can I offer you a drink?''

''That's exactly what I had in mind,'' Bellmon said. ''To give me a little liquid courage before I call the Chief of Staff.''

''Come on in the kitchen,'' Rand said. ''Johnny Oliver laid in more booze for me than there is in the club.''

''I know how to pick aides, George,'' Bellmon said, and then thought of something. ''Johnny, get on the horn to Colonel McNair. Tell him I would be grateful if he would check with the hospital about those three, and call me and let me know what he finds out, good or bad.''

''Yes, Sir.''

''Something happen, Bob?'' Susan Rand asked.

''Yeah,'' Bellmon said. ''We just dumped another thousand-hour Chinook.''

''Jesus! Anybody hurt?''

''I don't think so,'' Bellmon said. ''But they fell straight down from forty, fifty feet. Right on top of an O-1. They look all right, but they're going to the hospital, of course, to make sure. That's why I had Johnny call McNair.''

''What's this going to do to us, Bob?'' Rand asked. ''Won't they ground all the Chinooks again?''

''I think the Chinooks will be grounded in a couple of minutes,'' Bellmon said. ''Just as soon as I interrupt the Chief of Staff's Saturday afternoon with this pleasant new information.''

''Damn,'' Rand said resignedly.

''General,'' Oliver called.

''What?''

''Sir, Colonel McNair wants to speak with you.''

''Now what?'' Bellmon said as he went to a wall-mounted telephone and picked it up. ''What is it, Mac?''

His face was creased with thought when he hung the telephone up, and he shook his head no as if he didn't believe what he had just heard.

"That was very interesting," he said, "topping off what else has happened today." He looked at Oliver. "According to Colonel McNair, as soon as we left, Colonel Augustus loaded Stevens and Newell and the crew chief in the other Chinook and took off."

"You mean he flew them to the hospital?" George Rand said. "Well, it may not be authorized, but what the hell, Bob."

"Before he took off, the assigned copilot and crew chief left the aircraft," Bellmon said. "The copilot told Colonel McNair that Colonel Augustus had said, and I quote, 'Get your ass off and don't ask any questions.' End quote.

"When it dropped off the Cairns radar, the Chinook was approximately thirty miles west of New Brockton, Alabama," Bellmon said dryly. "The last communication with the aircraft was a message for me from Colonel Augustus: Would I please call the wives and tell them they would be away for a few days? When the tower tried to respond to that, Colonel Augustus reported that they were coming in garbled and he couldn't understand them; he probably had a radio problem of some sort."

"Jesus!" Rand said.

"Charley Augustus is going to see that that Chinook completes the thousand-hour test come hell or high water," Bellmon said. "Hell being the very good chance that the Chief of Staff will rack his ass when he hears about this. A court-martial is possible, even likely. And he certainly shouldn't have involved Stevens and Newell, and the sergeant, in this."

"What are you going to do?" Rand asked.

"Officially, I am outraged," Bellmon said. "But, not for dissemination beyond the walls of this kitchen, I confess a certain admiration for that ruthless little sonofabitch."

"What are you going to tell the Chief?"

"That I can immediately ground all Chinooks but one, and that as soon as I am able to get that one on the radio, I will order him to land at the nearest airfield."

"But you said he was having trouble with his radios," Susan Rand objected.

"I forgot you were here, Susan," Bellmon said. "Please forgive my language."

"I didn't mean to butt in," she said.

"Don't be silly," he said. "About the malfunctioning radios: Strange, isn't it? You'd think that the CO of SCATSA could keep the radios working in at least the aircraft he flies, wouldn't you?"

Bellmon took a sip of his drink.

"Johnny, would you see if you can get through to the Chief of Staff for me?"

"Yes, Sir."

"I just hope Stevens, Newell, and that sergeant are as healthy as they think they are," Bellmon said as Oliver looked in his notebook for the telephone number of the Chief of Staff of the United States Army.

[FIVE]

Captain John S. Oliver looked in his cooler and saw that he was right; he had forgotten to replenish the ice. What he saw was four cans of beer floating around in dirty water which, beyond any doubt, had the ambient temperature of the room.

"Shit!" he muttered, and started to button his blouse again. He didn't want to go to the annex because the word of the Chinook crash and probably of the "missing" Chinook was out by now and he would be asked questions he didn't want to answer. Could not answer.

There was a knock at the bathroom door.

Well, that fucking well ties it in a bow. I should have known that sooner or later they would put somebody in there to replace Jose Newell.

"Come," he called.

A second lieutenant of Armor marched into the room, came to attention, and saluted.

"Sir!" he barked. "Second Lieutenant Bellmon reporting for the booze hour, Sir."

"What were you doing in that room, Bobby?"

"I moved in there."

"You were not supposed to," Oliver said. "As a matter of

fact, I think your father had a chat personally with the housing officer on that specific subject.''

''Well, I told the sergeant in billeting that we were buddies and he gave it to me,'' Bobby said. ''You going to tell my father?''

''Eventually I'll have to,'' Oliver said. ''But not today. He has other things on his mind right now.''

''You don't want me in there?''

''What is important is that your father doesn't want you in there,'' Oliver said. ''We have all been given a lecture about how you are to be treated like any other second john.''

''I'm not asking for any special privileges,'' Bobby said, hurt.

''I understand Grandma bought you a car.''

''Yeah.''

''What?''

''A Pontiac convertible, like yours,'' Bobby said. ''This year's of course. And they didn't make them in pink this year. So mine's red.''

''Well, I will let you take me for a ride in it,'' Oliver said. ''My car's at the airport in Dothan. En route you will be lectured on the behavior to be expected of you.''

''Why's your car in Dothan?''

''It's a long story, one I don't feel like getting into right now.''

''OK. So what else is new? I hear Marjorie's got a new boyfriend. True?''

''You heard about that?''

''I even heard he's a classmate of yours,'' Bobby said.

''That was boyfriend number one. That's history. You're going to be thrilled about boyfriend number two.''

''Am I? Why?''

''He's a PFC,'' Oliver said.

''Oh, come on!''

''Boy Scout's honor, Bobby,'' Oliver said. ''Come on, let's go.''

''A PFC?'' Bobby asked incredulously. ''You're putting me on, right?''

XVI

[ONE]
The Magnolia House
The Army Aviation Center & Fort Rucker, Alabama
0715 Hours 29 May 1964

Magnolia House was Fort Rucker's VIP house. It had begun life in 1942—rather rapidly; only thirty-six hours had passed from the time the first concrete foundation-block had been set until the contract compliance inspection officer had passed it as complete. It had been built to plans provided by the Corps of Engineers for ''Bachelor Officers' Quarters [Brigade or Regimental Commander's], temporary, frame.'' The Corps of Engineers had projected the useful life of such structures to be no more than five years. All this one was originally required to do was provide a place where a regimental or brigade commander, a colonel or a brigadier general, could sleep and take a shower in privacy while training his regiment or brigade for service in War II.

As originally constructed, it had three rooms: a bedroom, a living room, and a bathroom. The two-by-fours in the walls had been left exposed. There was a toilet and a shower, but no other comforts, not even a door for the crapper. But from the day after it had gone up, there had been modifications, some prescribed by the Corps of Engineers and some not quite legal.

When its first occupant, a brigadier general of the Wisconsin National Guard, moved in, he told his aide to do something about getting a door for the bathroom. . . .

A door had been found and installed, and a concrete sidewalk poured. And the sergeant who did that was a man who took pride in his work, and so he uprooted a dozen small magnolia trees from someplace and installed them on what would have been a nice place for a lawn—if he could only lay his hands on some grass seed.

When the National Guard went off to war, Camp Rucker became a POW camp for Germans and Italians captured in North Africa. Among the prisoners were a number of skilled craftsmen, who decided, after some debate, that fixing up the shack where their head captor resided did not really constitute giving aid and comfort to the enemy.

There was heart pine on the Rucker reservation, with which the walls and floors were covered, and from which cabinets were made. A room and another bath were added to the right of the original structure; and two more rooms, a dining room and a kitchen, were added to the rear.

When the war was over and the POWs went home, the captain commanding the caretaker crew at deserted Camp Rucker lived in the little house near what had been the main gate. Then the Korean War came along, and midwestern National Guardsmen came to the deep south again, and their colonels and generals moved into the little house with the magnolias on the lawn.

And then that war was over too, and another small caretaker crew waited at Camp Rucker for the contracts to be let by the General Services Administration to tear the barracks and the theaters and everything else down so the place could finally be closed.

But in Ozark there was a lawyer named James Douglas

Brown, who was the mayor, and who had come to realize that a military payroll was a nice thing to have in a little town without much else to offer. And he had a long talk with the Honorable John S. Sparkman, of the United States Senate.

The Army was looking around the deserted air bases of the nation for a place where it could train pilots for the helicopter and light fixed-wing aircraft that had come into the Army after Korea. There were a number of surplus military air bases, mostly in the southwest, which had all the necessary facilities in terms of runways and hangars and fuel storage tanks. A list was made up. And Camp Rucker wasn't even on it.

But none of the others were represented in the United States Senate by John S. Sparkman. And in due course the Secretary of Defense announced, with as much of a straight face as he could muster, that a careful study of the problem indicated that Camp Rucker was the best place to station the Army Aviation Center. And it was so ordered.

Colonel Jay D. Vanderpool, a distinguished and flamboyant paratrooper, moved into the little house by the gate, which by now was known as the Magnolia House. Vanderpool commanded the Aviation Combat Developments Agency, a kind of Army think-tank devoted to investigating the best way aviation could serve the Army.

Vanderpool believed that an officer should never order his subordinates to do what he could not do himself. In his mind this was of greater importance than some still wet-behind-the-ears chancre mechanic's notion that he was too old and too beat-up to be allowed in an airplane, much less taught how to fly.

He learned how to fly, and he flew, and he and his boys put machine guns and rockets on helicopters, the first time either had been done. And if anyone noticed that there were no aviators' wings on his chest, no one said anything.

After Congress came through with a multimillion-dollar authorization to build family housing at what was now *Fort* Rucker (by this time a permanent military installation), Vanderpool moved into family quarters appropriate to his grade on Colonels' Row.

The Magnolia House was turned into transient VIP quarters.

Suitable furniture was acquired, some from government stocks, some purchased with Officers' Open Mess funds, and some donated as gifts. Central air conditioning and heating were installed.

There is a guest book there now, and the signatures in it are a who's who of important military brass (both American and foreign), the defense industry, and the upper echelons of the government. Many guests of the Magnolia House, especially foreign officers, have seen fit to express their appreciation for the hospitality shown them by sending a memento. This has often been an ornate plaque bearing the insignia of their army. A china cabinet is full of them. The overflow hangs on the walls.

And outside, the magnolia trees planted so long ago have matured. They now tower over the building and give it both privacy and shade.

Magnolia House was full today. In addition to General George F. Rand, who occupied the facility while attending flight school and who was set up in bedroom #3, there were some VIPs from Washington: a Deputy Assistant Secretary of Defense, an Air Force Major General, and an army Brigadier General. The latter two were forced to share bedroom #2.

One of the orderlies, a tall, thin, blond-headed corporal in a starched white cotton jacket, laid the telephone handset down and walked to bedroom #1. Once inside, he went to the open door of the bathroom, where a man was standing over the washbasin. He knocked on the doorjamb.

"Mr. Secretary," he said, "there's a Colonel Lowell outside, who said to ask you if you could spare him a moment of your time."

"Who?"

"Lieutenant Colonel Lowell, Sir," the orderly repeated.

John Xavier O'Herlihy paused in mid razor stroke. O'Herlihy was a stocky, redheaded man of thirty-nine, who was Deputy Assistant Secretary of Defense for Research and Development. The name Lowell was unfamiliar to him.

"Did he say what he wanted?"

"No, Sir."

"Oh, hell, ask him to wait, please."

"Yes, Sir."

Jack O'Herlihy was a product of Seton Hall High School, Fordham, and the Harvard Law School. After a year with the law firm of McRae, McRae, Henderson, Belker and Saybrook, 38 Wall Street, in New York City, he went back to school and took a degree at the Wharton School of Business Administration of the University of Pennsylvania.

He returned to McRae, McRae, Henderson, Belker and Saybrook and specialized in the practice of contract fulfillment, which he rather liked, because it gave him the opportunity to plead his clients' cases in court and sometimes even before a jury. Very few of the lawyers at McRae, McRae, Henderson, Belker and Saybrook ever went near a courtroom. Five years after he graduated from Wharton, he was named a partner, making him both the youngest partner (of thirteen) in the firm, and the man who had been appointed a partner in the shortest time since joining the firm..

He had married in his last year in law school; and he and Mary Margaret bought a house in South Orange, New Jersey, not very far from Seton Hall.

Sometimes a limo took him to the airport in Newark. Often on those occasions, he would be driven past the Seton Hall High School campus (shared with Seton Hall University). Whenever he passed by there, he allowed himself to remember how far he'd come from the kid who used to ride his bicycle to the campus from the Rosewood section of Newark. The O'Herlihy family had occupied the upper floor of a frame house there, across the street from the Rosewood fire station. He had stocked groceries in the Acme Supermarket to help pay the Seton Hall High tuition.

As a partner in McRae, McRae, Henderson, Belker and Saybrook, Jack O'Herlihy was making more money than he ever dreamed he would—though what he was getting as Deputy Assistant Secretary of Defense for Research and Development was peanuts. But he resisted the temptation to think that working for forty-odd thousand was a sacrifice. For one thing he really believed that serving his country was a privilege. (An otherwise nontroublesome heart murmur had kept him from serving it in uniform.) And for another, it was a learning experience which would be of great value to him in his future career. And finally, he had been led to believe that when his time with the Defense Department was up (he intended to serve two years, no more), McRae, McRae, Henderson, Belker and Saybrook would make up the lost income in the form of a bonus. The firm knew the importance of contacts within the government.

Jack O'Herlihy finished shaving, wiped his face clean with a towel, liberally splashed on his face St. John's Island Spice after-shave . . . and recalled the U.S. Virgin Islands, which is where he first discovered it. And that triggered a thought that had come with greater and greater frequency: when his time with Defense was over and his income was back to normal (or maybe with the promised bonus), he dreamed of buying a little place down there in the islands, just for him and Mary Margaret, a place where they could get away from the kids.

He tied his necktie, slipped into the jacket to his dark-blue, very faintly pencil-striped Brooks Brothers suit, and left bedroom #1.

The soldier who wanted to see him was standing by the door almost at attention. *Jesus, he didn't even dare to sit down!*

O'Herlihy glanced around the living and dining rooms, looking for the two officers who had accompanied him here from Washington to settle this Chinook-testing business once and for all. But neither Major General Richard F. Stone, the Vice Deputy Chief of Air Force Research and Development, nor Brigadier General Max Kramer, Vice Deputy Chief of Staff for Operations, U.S. Army, was in sight. So this poor colonel was paying him that kind of respect. Jack O'Herlihy was a little embarrassed, but told himself, *What the hell, I* am *an Assistant Secretary of Defense. . . .*

"Good morning, Colonel," O'Herlihy said, offering his hand. He had learned that lieutenant colonels like it when you call them colonel.

"Good morning, Mr. Secretary," Lieutenant Colonel Lowell said politely. "Thank you for seeing me, Sir."

Good-looking man, O'Herlihy decided. *Even handsome.*

And he's been around the block. He didn't know what all the ribbons and other insignia hanging on Lieutenant Colonel Lowell's uniform were, but he recognized the Distinguished Service Cross and a Purple Heart dotted with oak leaf clusters. This man was a pilot, and a parachutist, and he'd seen a lot of combat. *I wonder what the hell he wants?*

"How may I help you, Colonel?"

"Actually, Mr. Secretary, this is completely unofficial," Lieutenant Colonel Lowell said.

"Oh, I see." *What the hell does* that *mean?*

"Dinky Saybrook said that if I ever bumped into you around the Army, I should do what I could. Dinky's apparently rather fond of you."

Haynes D. Saybrook was the youngest of the three managing partners of McRae, McRae, Henderson, Belker and Saybrook. He had inherited the necessary stock in the firm from his father when old Mr. Saybrook had retired. So far as Jack O'Herlihy recalled, the only partner who dared refer to him as Dinky was old Mr. McRae. O'Herlihy had only recently stopped calling him sir.

"You're a friend of Mr. Saybrook?"

"Dinky and I go way back, Mr. Secretary," Lieutenant Colonel Lowell said. "We went to school together."

"Groton?"

"St. Mark's, Mr. Secretary," Lieutenant Colonel Lowell said. "And then we were in Cambridge for a while."

By Cambridge he means Harvard. What the hell is going on here?

"Mr. Secretary, I realize you have a very busy schedule, but I thought I'd hate to have to tell Dinky that we got this close and couldn't get together, so I hoped, Mr. Secretary, that maybe we could have breakfast."

"You see Mr. Saybrook regularly, do you?" O'Herlihy asked.

"I'm going to see him tomorrow, Mr. Secretary, as a matter of fact," Lieutenant Colonel Lowell said. "He asked me to fill in as his number two. They're playing the Argentines."

"Excuse me?"

"Fellow named Hopper took ill, and Dinky asked me, Mr.

Secretary, if I could come over to Palm Beach and fill in for him.''

Polo! Polo! That's what he's talking about. This guy plays polo at Palm Beach with Saybrook! What the hell is he doing in the Army?

''Well, that's very kind of you, Colonel,'' O'Herlihy said. ''But let me invite you to breakfast. They send a cook over here, and putting a couple of extra eggs in the pan wouldn't be any problem at all, I'm sure.''

''With respect, Mr. Secretary,'' Lieutenant Colonel Lowell said, ''I'm a lowly lieutenant colonel. I'm a little uncomfortable around general officers.''

''No need to feel that way. No need at all.''

''What I had in mind, Mr. Secretary—I thought perhaps you might find it interesting—was that we could have breakfast with the WOCs.''

''With the who?''

''The WOCs, Mr. Secretary. The Warrant Officer Candidates—the kids they're teaching to fly.''

''Could we do that?''

''You're an Assistant Secretary of Defense, Mr. Secretary. I don't think there would be any problem at all. And I could have you back here in under an hour.''

''Well, it sounds interesting,'' O'Herlihy said.

''And then I could tell Dinky that I at least fed you, Mr. Secretary.''

What the hell, why not? Even if curiosity does kill cats.

''On one condition, Colonel,'' O'Herlihy said. ''That you stop calling me Mr. Secretary. My name is Jack.''

''Thank you—Jack—that's very gracious of you.''

O'Herlihy raised his voice and spoke to the orderly.

''When General Stone comes out, would you tell him that I'll be back in an hour? I'm going to have breakfast with Colonel Lowell.''

''Yes, Sir,'' the orderly said. ''I'll give him the message.''

Lieutenant Colonel Lowell held open the door for Deputy Assistant Secretary O'Herlihy. Parked at the curb was an Oldsmobile 98 sedan. As O'Herlihy walked around the back, he noticed the post sticker.

He waited until Lowell had the car moving and then asked,

''If you're uncomfortable around general officers, Colonel, how is it you're driving a car with a number one on the sticker? From what I understand that sticker goes with the commanding general's car.''

''Well . . . Jack, there are general officers and then there are general officers,'' Lowell said. ''Bob Bellmon is one of the good ones.''

''The implication is that Generals Stone and Kramer are not.''

''Just between us boys, Max Kramer is a miserable shit,'' Lieutenant Colonel Lowell said. ''I don't know Stone.''

''Isn't it a little dangerous for a lieutenant colonel to say that to someone like me—about a general officer?''

''Well, there are lieutenant colonels and then there are lieutenant colonels.''

''I'd just love to know what's going on here, Colonel.''

''Well, Stone is here to convince you that the Air Force should take over the testing of the Chinook. . . . And down the road, he wants the Air Force to take over the Chinook itself, which would effectively kill the whole idea of an airmobile division. If the Army loses the Chinook to the Air Force, that's the end of Army Aviation, which I'm sure I don't have to tell you. And Max Kramer, that spineless shit, is down here to roll over and wave his arms and legs in the air.''

''Not that I should be discussing this with you—and not that that was the question I asked—but General Stone offers some very persuasive arguments.''

''Well, I thought I would offer some very persuasive counterarguments.''

''General Bellmon sent you?''

Lowell laughed.

''Hell, no. If he knew I was here, he'd have me thrown in the stockade. He doesn't even know I have his car. We may get arrested at breakfast.''

''I don't think you're kidding,'' O'Herlihy said.

''I'm not,'' Lowell said. ''Well, here we are.''

They were outside a brand-new concrete-block mess hall building. Young men in flight suits were standing in a line.

''This is what it's all about, Jack,'' Lowell said. ''These

are the kids who are going to fight in Vietnam. If you don't let the Air Force delay the Chinook into the next century, you'll save some of their lives."

"I don't need any lectures from you, Colonel," O'Herlihy said.

Lowell ignored him. "I'm a lieutenant colonel," he said. "While lieutenant colonels ain't much, we do get to go to the head of line. Come on, Jack, we'll chow down."

"I don't think so, Colonel," O'Herlihy said. "I think I would rather go back to the Magnolia House."

"I would hate to have to tell Dinky that you couldn't find time in your busy schedule to even have breakfast with me," Lowell said.

"May I speak frankly, Colonel?"

"Please do, Jack. I like to get right to the heart of things myself."

"You are implying that you have influence with Mr. Saybrook, which I find rather difficult to swallow, if it is based, as you say, on the fact that you went to prep school and Harvard together. . . ."

"I didn't last long at Harvard, Jack. I was expelled, and they drafted my ass."

"And to judge by your decorations, you have been in the Army for some time," O'Herlihy went on, growing more angry by the moment. "Frankly, Colonel, I am offended by the name dropping, and I disbelieve that you have any influence on Mr. Saybrook. I am even more offended at the suggestion that he would not only attempt to exert improper influence on me but also—in the unlikely happenstance that he would attempt to so do—that it would influence my official judgment in any way."

"Well, that's blunt enough. And well said. Dinky said you were a pretty good guy as well as a good lawyer. Now let *me* be blunt."

"Go ahead."

"I called Dinky yesterday. Haven't seen the stuffy bastard in years. And I said, 'Dinky, I understand this guy O'Herlihy works for you.' And Dinky allowed as to how that was so, and I said, 'Dinky, I need a favor,' and Dinky said, 'Name it,' and I told him what it was, and he said, 'If you have any trouble with him, have him call me.' And then he asked me to pop over to Palm Beach and play the Argentinians."

"I find this whole conversation incredible," O'Herlihy said. "I was about to simply forget it happened. But you have crossed the line, Colonel. I feel I must tell you that I intend to make an official report of this entire incident."

"Before you do that, Jack, why don't you call Dinky?"

"Why should I?"

"Because if you tell him what you intend to do, Dinky will tell you he hopes you will be happy with your new law firm—wherever you can find one to take you on."

"You shouldn't make threats you're not prepared to back up, Colonel," O'Herlihy said and started to open the car door.

Lowell reached over and grabbed his arm.

"Take your hands off me!"

"How much, expressed as a percentage, would you say the legal business of Craig, Powell, Kenyon, and Dawes represents of the legal practice of McRae, McRae, Henderson, Belker, and Saybrook?" Lowell asked.

"Just for your information, Colonel," O'Herlihy said, "I am personally acquainted with Mr. Porter Craig of Craig, Powell, Kenyon, and Dawes. And he would be as justifiably outraged by this as I am. Now let go of my arm!"

"Yes, Mr. Secretary," Lowell said. "Of course. Go write your report. But I think I should tell you that Porter Craig's son Geoff is an Army Aviator."

O'Herlihy looked at him.

"That's sort of scraping the bottom of your little barrel, isn't it, Colonel Lowell?" he asked icily.

"And so is the vice chairman of the board," Lowell said. "To tell you the truth, Jack, I never really liked Dinky. Nothing would give me greater pleasure than to call him up and say, 'Dinky, you hire dumb people. You're fired. And you look like a horse's ass on the polo field.' "

"You're telling me you're . . . you couldn't do that."

"I have enough stock to control five of the nine seats on the Board," Lowell said. "If you write your report, I'm through in the Army. McNamara doesn't like me anyhow. If that happens, the first thing I would do when I got to Wall

Street would be to get Dinky's word that he would fire you, and if he didn't I'd fire him. This is hardball, Jack."

"I don't know why I'm listening to this."

"Because you're smart enough to recognize the truth when you hear it. Which is all I'm asking of you, O'Herlihy, that you listen to what I have to say and recognize the truth when you see it."

O'Herlihy did not reply, but neither did he get out of the car.

"Sometime today," Lowell went on, "a Chinook will land here. When it does, it will have completed the one-thousand-hour test."

"That's the one the Signal Corps colonel . . . *stole*?"

"He didn't steal it; he had every intention of bringing it back. He's playing hardball, too. He and the two kids with him. If the Air Force is right, and the Chinook is unsafe, they have put their balls on the chopping block. The Air Force is wrong, of course. There's nothing wrong with the Chinook. But the three of them, at the very least, put their careers on the line. I suppose they could even be court-martialed. Or Colonel Augustus could. And they deserve more than to have an asshole like Max Kramer come down here and roll over for the Air Force just to increase his chances for a second star."

"I don't like to be threatened," O'Herlihy said.

"Nobody does," Lowell said. "Sometimes it comes with the territory."

They locked eyes for a moment.

"There's a pay telephone just inside the mess hall entrance," Lowell said. "Why don't we get on it and call Dinky and tell him how we're getting along? And afterward, O'Herlihy, if you'd like, we could have some breakfast."

[TWO]
Officer of the Commanding General
The Army Aviation Center & Fort Rucker, Alabama
1605 Hours 29 May 1964

Captain John S. Oliver was waiting in the downstairs lobby of the Post Headquarters Building when the staff car pulled up before the door. The driver ran around the car and opened the curbside door, and Deputy Assistant Secretary of Defense for Research and Development John X. O'Herlihy and Major General Richard F. Jones, USAF, stepped out of the back seat of the Chevrolet. Brigadier General Max Kramer, USA, who had been riding in front with the driver, opened his own door.

Oliver met them just inside the door of Post Headquarters.

"Good afternoon, Mr. Secretary," he said. "General Jones, General Kramer. General Bellmon expects you, gentlemen. If you'll just follow me, please?"

He led them up the narrow stairs to the second floor. Sergeant Major Harrison James came to attention as they walked in.

Oliver walked quickly to Bellmon's open door.

"General, Secretary O'Herlihy and his party are here," he said.

"Ask them to come in, please, Johnny," Bellmon said, rising to his feet and walking around his desk. He offered his hand to O'Herlihy.

"Good afternoon, Mr. Secretary," he said. He nodded at the two general officers.

"Good afternoon, General," O'Herlihy said.

"May I offer you some coffee?" Bellmon said.

"That would be very nice," O'Herlihy said.

"Johnny?" Bellmon said, and Oliver left to see about the coffee. "Please sit down, gentlemen," Bellmon added.

Sergeant Major James entered, carrying a silver coffee set, and set it on the coffee table.

"Without objection, Mr. Secretary, I'll ask my aide to stay," Bellmon said. "When there's an important meeting like this, a second set of ears to remember it is valuable."

"Certainly," O'Herlihy said.

"Well, have you been able to accomplish what you came for, Mr. Secretary?" Bellmon asked as he went to the coffee table and poured coffee.

"It's been a very interesting day," O'Herlihy said, "right from the start. I had breakfast in the WOC mess."

He saw what had to be a genuine look of surprise on Bellmon's face.

I'll be damned, O'Herlihy thought. *He didn't know.*

"Your Lieutenant Colonel Lowell came to the Magnolia House," Brigadier General Kramer said, "and practically kidnapped him."

There was another look of surprise, this one mingled with concern, on Bellmon's face.

"Oh, I wouldn't say kidnapped, General," O'Herlihy said. "Actually, I found it fascinating. They're a fine group of young men, General Bellmon."

"I think so," Bellmon said. "And just for the record, Max, Lieutenant Colonel Lowell is not assigned here. He's the Army Aviation Officer at STRIKE." The U.S. Army STRIKE Command, an in-place headquarters organization commanded by a four-star general, was based at McDill Air Force Base, Florida. When needed, tactical forces of all the armed services were placed under its command for operations around the world.

"So I understand, General," General Kramer said. "I wondered what he was doing here."

"He didn't tell me," Bellmon said. "He flew in yesterday. He's an old family friend, and he stayed with us. But he didn't tell me what he was doing here. And I didn't ask him."

"Very interesting man," O'Herlihy said. "We have some mutual friends."

"Is that so?" Bellmon said.

"Anyway," O'Herlihy said, "to move on with this . . . we want to return to Washington today—"

"Any problems with that, Mr. Secretary?" Bellmon asked.

"No. The aides are packing us up right now. And while I'm on that subject, I'd like to thank you for the splendid hospitality."

"Thank Captain Oliver," Bellmon said. "I left that in his very capable hands."

"Well, Captain, you did a fine job. Thank you," O'Herlihy said.

"My privilege, Sir. I'm glad you were comfortable."

"To get on with this," O'Herlihy said. "Colonel McNair offered some very convincing arguments that inasmuch as two one-thousand-hour tests have been completed, there is really no purpose in the Air Force starting them from scratch—''

''If I may interrupt, Mr. Secretary,'' Bellmon said, ''for the record, I wish to associate myself, that is, the Aviation Center with whatever Colonel McNair said.''

''I thought you might feel that way,'' O'Herlihy said. ''General Jones still feels—and I think I should add he feels rather strongly—that further testing is required and that it should be conducted by the Air Force for the very good reason that they have the experience and the facilities. And General Kramer has said that to avoid any suggestion of parochiality, he, speaking for the Army, will raise no objections to whatever I decide.''

Bellmon flashed General Kramer a look of pure contempt. But after a moment he forced a smile on his face and looked at O'Herlihy. ''And what is your decision, Mr. Secretary?'' he asked.

''I think General Jones is right, of course,'' O'Herlihy said. ''We're talking not only about a lot of money, but about the lives of those fine young men I saw at breakfast. On the other hand, however, I think we all know that sooner or later, probably sooner, the 11th Air Assault Division will be sent to Vietnam. When it goes, it has to have the capability the Chinook will provide. I think this is one of those cases where we have to accept the risk involved.''

''Permit me to say, Mr. Secretary,'' Bellmon said, ''that I really think that is the correct decision.''

''I will arrange to have the next two production Chinooks off the assembly line diverted from here to the Air Force at Wright-Patterson,'' O'Herlihy said. ''And I will ask that the Air Force give Chinook testing their highest priority.''

''Their input will will be most welcome, Mr. Secretary,'' Bellmon said. ''Thank you very much.''

''And that would seem to be it,'' O'Herlihy said. ''As I said, we're anxious to return to Washington.''

''May I address the question of Colonel Augustus for a moment?'' General Kramer said.

"Certainly," O'Herlihy said.

"I'm sure the Chief of Staff will want to know how you're going to handle that, General."

"I intend to discipline him of course," Bellmon said.

"A general court-martial?" General Kramer asked.

"A letter of reprimand," Bellmon said. "I've already prepared it."

"Colonel Augustus defied an order of the Chief of Staff. That is not the sort of the thing you punish with a mere letter of reprimand," General Kramer said.

"General, for one thing, Colonel Augustus was unaware when he took off that the Chinooks had been grounded. For another, so long as I command here, I will decide how to discipline my officers," Bellmon said.

"You say you've already prepared the reprimand?" O'Herlihy asked.

"Johnny, would you ask the sergeant major to bring it in?" Bellmon asked.

"Yes, Sir."

"I've done everything but sign it," Bellmon said.

That is not the truth, the whole truth, and nothing but the truth, Oliver thought.

What actually happened was that Colonel Lowell, just before he flew back to McDill, spent five minutes behind closed doors with Bellmon. Then he came out of the office, took over Sergeant Major James's chair and typewriter, and with what Oliver had thought was astonishing typing speed, wrote a draft. He carried it in to Bellmon for another three-minute session behind closed doors. And after he finally left, Bellmon handed James the letter and told him to have it typed up for his signature.

When Oliver walked into the outer office, Sergeant Major James had all five copies in his hand, waiting for him, which told Oliver that James had been listening to what was going on in Bellmon's office over the intercom.

Oliver took the sheath of paper into Bellmon's office.

"Give me the original, Johnny," Bellmon ordered, "and I'll sign it. Let these gentlemen see the carbons."

"Yes, Sir."

HEADQUARTERS

THE ARMY AVIATION CENTER & FORT RUCKER ALABAMA

201-Augustus, Charles M 375545

29 May 1964

SUBJECT: Letter of Reprimand

TO: Colonel Charles M. Augustus
USA Signal Aviation Test & Support Activity
Fort Rucker, Alabama

VIA: The Chief Signal Officer
Headquarters, Department of the Army
Washington, D.C.

1. The fact of the situation as understood by the undersigned are that you, during the period 20-29 May 1964,

a. Without appropriate authority, participated in an unknown number of flights [totaling 103.25 flight hours] in a Chinook helicopter assigned to the U.S. Army Aviation Board, Fort Rucker, Alabama, and temporarily assigned to the USA SCATSA, for which, as Commanding Officer of USA SCATSA, you were therefore responsible, and

b. That inasmuch as these flights, against standard operating policy, were not between military air bases, but between an undetermined number of civilian air terminals and other flight facilities, you denied yourself the opportunity of being informed as you would have, had you availed yourself of the use of any military air base, that all flights of Chinook aircraft had been suspended by the Deputy Chief of Staff for Operations, U.S. Army, and,

c. That you not only failed to inform your flight crew that these flights were unauthorized, but implied to two splendid young officers, 1st Lieutenant Charles Stevens, Signal Corps, and 2nd Lieutenant Joseph M. Newell, Signal Corps, that their participation in these flights, which involved long hours at the controls, far beyond that routinely expected of officers, was of great importance to the One-Thousand-Hour Service and Logistics Testing Program, thereby inspiring them to a level of performance that under other circumstances would more than likely have seen them commended for a demonstration of superior flying skill and extraordinary devotion to duty, and which instead will see them officially reprimanded for performing aerial flight without first ascertaining beyond reasonable doubt that the flight in question is specifically authorized.

2. If the facts are not as stated above, you may reply by endorsement hereto, citing your exceptions to them.

3. If the facts are as stated above, and you do not wish to challenge them, you are herewith officially reprimanded. Your behavior in this matter is not only reprehensible, but baffling when considering your previous long and distinguished record of service in positions of great responsibility.

4. A copy of this reprimand will be placed with your service record, and kept there for a period of twelve [12] months, unless sooner removed by competent authority, and will be considered when any personnel actions in your regard are undertaken.

ROBERT F. BELLMON
Major General, USA
Commanding

Brigadier General Max Kramer's face first grew white as he read through the carbon copy Oliver had handed him. And then his face grew red.

"Reprimand, my foot. Bellmon, this is more in the order of a commendation. The Chief isn't going to like this."

"Max," Bellmon said, "I don't recall giving you permission to address me by my last name."

"That is not a reprimand," Kramer insisted.

"Actually, General," Deputy Assistant Secretary of Defense for Research and Development John X. O'Herlihy said, "I think it covers the situation rather well. Colonel Augustus deserves to be reprimanded, and General Bellmon has termed his conduct reprehensible."

General Kramer looked at him.

"Yes, Sir," he said. "If you look at it like that."

O'Herlihy stood up and offered his hand to Bellmon.

"Thank you, Mr. Secretary," Bellmon said.

"Just doing my job, General," O'Herlihy said.

When Oliver returned from escorting the party to their car, Bellmon was sitting behind his desk, looking thoughtful. It was a moment before he sensed Oliver in the doorway, and then he waved him into the office.

"That was close, Johnny," he said. "It could have gone either way."

"Yes, Sir."

"Well, take that letter and write the same sort of thing for Stevens and Newell. That will cover them in case that bastard Kramer tries to get at me through them. And he's capable of it."

"Yes, Sir."

"And Colonel Lowell does write a great letter, doesn't he?"

"Yes, Sir," Oliver said. "I'd say that qualifies as masterful."

"I wonder that the hell was in Lowell's mind when he took O'Herlihy to the WOC mess for breakfast? He didn't say anything about that to me."

"Well, maybe he thought it would be a good idea for O'Herlihy to see the WOCs."

"With Lowell you never know," Bellmon said. "Well, get right on that, will you, Johnny?"

"Yes, Sir."

XVII

[ONE]
The Magnolia House
Fort Rucker, Alabama
0615 Hours 10 July 1964

Brigadier General George F. Rand opened his eyes suddenly, looked around the master bedroom of the Magnolia House, and groaned, ''Oh, shit!''

The lights were on. *TM-1—HU-1-Series, Operations Manual, Bell HU-1-Series Aircraft* was in his lap. When he went to sleep, he'd been reading it propped up against the headboard of one of the two double beds in the room. Apparently he had hardly moved since. His lower back ached from being propped against the pillows. His neck ached from the weight of his head hanging downward. His legs had been crossed; now the right one was asleep.

General Rand had been enrolled in the senior officers' flight program almost exactly four months. If things went well today, he would be authorized to wear the silver wings and shield of an Army Aviator. If they didn't go well, if he busted his check ride, he'd made up his mind to leave the division. There was absolutely no question in his mind that anyone wearing the hat of Assistant Division Commander-B, 11th Air Assault Division [Test] should be a qualified aviator. Preferably a long-time aviator, with thousands of hours in the air, fixed- and rotary-wing qualified, with all the bells, multiengine, land and sea, and a special instrument ticket. But an aviator.

If all went well today he would be designated an aviator. But of rotary-wing aircraft only (and only Bell H-13 and HU-1B helicopters, narrowing his qualifications even further), with no instrument ticket of any kind, and with a grand total of 210 hours at the controls.

That wasn't enough and he knew it. But at least the General would be a pilot. There was a hoary adage which General Rand devoutly believed: *An officer should be able to do himself anything he orders someone else to do.*

And there was more to it than that. An assistant division commander should be with his division. And he wasn't. More important, during the four months he had been at Rucker, the division had undergone significant changes: the Pentagon had ordered the testing program to be accelerated so that it would be completed by the end of the year.

By stripping aviation assets—aircraft, crews, maintenance personnel, and support equipment—from other units in the Army and ordering them to Benning, there were now four aviation battalions, more or less up to strength, in the 11th. These included the 226th Aerial Surveillance and Escort Battalion (Mohawks and Armed Hueys); two assault-helicopter battalions (the 227th and 229th), also equipped with Hueys; and, finally, an up-to-full-strength Chinook Battalion, the 228th.

The infantry brigade, the foot soldiers, was now not only up to strength, with three battalions (the 1st Battalions of the 187th, 188th, and 511th Parachute Infantry Regiments), but it had been augmented by three additional battalions from the 2nd Infantry Division.

And finally, five artillery battalions were now assigned to

the 11th: three 105mm Howitzer battalions, one aerial rocket battalion, and one Little John Missile Battalion. And the whole force had been augmented by supporting-troop units, Signal, Military Police, Ordnance, and so forth.

Trouble had come with the troop augmentation. For instance, relaxed flight-safety standards had caused some really unpleasant accidents. Specifically, an attempt to fly a battalion of Hueys from Camp Blanding, Florida, to Benning in bad weather had been an unmitigated disaster, with helicopters scattered in farmers' fields all over northern Florida and Georgia.

General Rand had tried to keep on top of what was happening, spending his weekends and his few holidays at Fort Benning. But keeping up with what was going on was not the same thing as making a contribution to it. That required an assistant division commander at Benning, not another guy spending his days at Rucker as an overprivileged basic flight student.

Rand had twice gone to General Wendall to point this out . . . and to suggest that Wendall replace him as assistant division commander and find someone to put in there who could do what assistant division commanders are supposed to do. Both times, Hok Wendall turned him down.

The first time Rand went to him, Wendall explained that he didn't need him so much now as later. He was looking down the road to the time when the 11th Air Assault would be deployed. That's when he would need Rand's talents.

The second time he went to Hok Wendall, Wendall bluntly told him the subject was no longer open for discussion. "You've been ordered to flight school," he said, "and you're expected to obey your orders."

Hok Wendall's premise—that the contribution he would make later justified his absence at this critical period—depended of course on his getting himself rated as an aviator. And Brigadier General Rand was not at all sure that was going to happen. He was not a boy any longer, with marvelous reflexes and an ability to retain all sorts of technical minutiae. There was a very good chance that he would bust his check ride.

If that happened, he'd decided not just to insist on being

relieved. That wouldn't be enough: he couldn't just do it the pro forma way and go to the division commander. That would put Major General Harrison O. K. Wendall on the spot. Rand had decided that he would go to Washington and wait until the Chief of Staff had time to see him. He would then explain the situation as he saw it and request relief and transfer someplace else where he could make a contribution. If that was denied, he was going to retire. He had twenty-three years' service. If necessary he could live on his pension.

Brigadier General George Rand's shoulder joint ached as he raised his right wrist to look at his watch, and again as he tossed the Huey tech manual onto the adjacent bed, and still again as he threw the covers off his lower body.

He grimaced and grunted as he swung his feet out of bed and then stood up. He was wearing a white T-shirt and Jockey shorts. The pajamas his wife had packed for him when he came down here would return to Fort Benning unworn. He forced himself to stand upright and then hobbled out of the bedroom through the dining room and into the kitchen. His aide had set out an electric percolator and a can of Maxwell House coffee on a counter in the kitchen.

He filled the percolator with water, and then the basket with coffee, closed it and plugged it in. He waited for it to grumble and spit and then hobbled back to the bedroom.

He opened a drawer in a chest of drawers and took from it a fresh set of underwear, a pair of heavy woolen socks, and a Nymex flight suit. The flight suit had a number of embroidered insignia sewn to it. There were the insignia of the Army Aviation Center, a name tag, and on either side of the collar, a single five-pointed silver (actually white) star of a brigadier general.

General Rand pulled off his T-shirt and boxer shorts and stuffed them into the bottom drawer of the chest of drawers, which he was using as a hamper. Then he walked into the bathroom, turned the water on in the shower, waited for it to warm up, and stepped under the steam.

Ninety seconds later he became aware that the telephone was ringing. He shut the water off and listened, hoping that his aide had shown up and would grab the phone.

When that didn't happen, he decided that it was the aide

who was calling. He had a new aide, a pleasant kid from the class of '60, who had gone through the Basic School, done two years as a platoon leader in the 18th Infantry with the 1st "Big Red One" Infantry Division, and then gone to flight school.

Once he had received his orders to flight school, General Rand had replaced his old aide, who couldn't fly either. He had tempered the relief with a fine efficiency report, and he'd pulled hard enough at the strings available to him to get his ex-aide into flight school. But it had been perfectly clear to General Rand that an aide to a general who flew should be able to fly himself.

Howard F. Mitchell had been on orders to the 11th Air Assault from Rucker when Rand picked him as his new aide. Rand had subsequently decided that choosing him had not been one of his brighter decisions. For one thing, Mitchell didn't know much more about flying than Rand did, and it would have made more sense to have an aide with a good deal more time driving airplanes than he did himself.

That of course was not Mitchell's fault. Neither was what Rand was coming to think of as Mitchell's affinity for malfunction. When Mitchell came near them, things seemed to break. Automobile batteries died. Telephones refused to function. Shoelaces broke. Since Mitchell had been the one who set out the percolator before leaving the previous night, Rand would not have been surprised if it had refused to function—or burst into flames.

Mitch was probably calling now to report that the staff car had thrown a rod, or that on the day of his check ride there was about to be a hurricane, or the check pilot had come down with a sudden attack of hoof and mouth disease.

Naked, dripping soapy water onto the carpet, General Rand walked to the bedside telephone and picked it up.

"Rand," he barked into it.

"I can see we're in a fine, cheerful mood, aren't we?" his wife said.

"Susan, I was in the goddamned shower."

"I just called to wish you luck."

"For the check ride, you mean?"

"Is there something else?"

"How'd you hear about it?" he asked.

"I'm psychic," Susan said. "I *know* about you. When you're going to have a check ride. When some pneumatic nineteen-year-old waitress decides you're pretty cute for an old man. Things like that."

"You heard about that, too, huh?"

"You can tell me about that when you come home," she said. "And when, by the way, is that going to be?"

"I'll have to call you. But, one way or the other, by supper tomorrow."

"I'll get steaks."

"You might get a brace of crow, just in case. It is not graven on stone tablets that I will pass the check ride."

"Don't be silly, of course you will," Susan said firmly. "I'll let you go."

"Thanks for calling," he said. "Keep your fingers crossed."

"Wash behind your ears," she said, then chuckled and hung up.

Brigadier General George F. Rand was extraordinarily fond of his wife, whom he had married in the chapel at West Point the day after he had graduated. He wondered how she would take it if he busted out of flight school and had to leave the division.

Well, he decided as he hung the phone up. *Just as she has taken every other disappointment, every other exigency of the service. Of which, viewed dispassionately, we have had more than our fair share.*

He was halfway across the room when the telephone rang again.

"Goddammit!" he said as he returned to the bedside. He picked the phone up and barked "Rand" into it again.

"Good morning, General. This is Captain Oliver. General Bellmon's compliments, Sir."

"What does he want, Oliver?" General Rand snapped, aware even as he spoke that jumping on Bellmon's aide was unfair.

"General, General Bellmon hopes that you will be able to have breakfast with him."

"This morning?"

"Yes, Sir."

"Please tell General Bellmon that I appreciate his invitation, Johnny, but that this morning is a little awkward for me. I've got a check ride at half past seven."

"Yes, Sir," Oliver said. "General Bellmon is aware of the check ride."

Now what the hell is this all about?

"Captain, please tell General Bellmon that I am about to soft-boil a couple of eggs, and that I would be pleased to have him join me, and you too, Johnny, if that is convenient."

"Soft-boiled eggs would be just fine, General, thank you very much," Oliver said. "We'll be there shortly. Goodbye, Sir."

Rank hung the telephone up again and finished his shower. Lieutenant Howard Mitchell came in as he was shaving.

"Good morning, General," Mitchell said.

"What's broken, Howie?" Rank asked.

"As far as I know, nothing, Sir," Mitchell said a little uncomfortably.

"Then our breakfast guest, *guests,* are the bad news," Rand said. "General Bellmon just invited himself and Johnny Oliver for breakfast. They're on the way. If they get here before I'm dressed, pour them a cup of coffee, will you, please?"

"Yes, Sir. He didn't say what he wanted?"

"If you want to make somebody nervous, Howie, you never tell them what you want. That puts their imagination to work."

"What about your check ride, General? That's scheduled for 0730."

"I'll ask General Bellmon to give me a note explaining why I'm tardy."

"Yes, Sir," Mitchell said and walked out the bedroom.

[TWO]
Quarters #1
Fort Rucker, Alabama
0630 Hours 10 July 1964

Captain John S. Oliver replaced the handset on the wall base on the kitchen wall and turned to General Bellmon.

"General Rand's compliments, Sir," he said, gently mockingly. "He will be pleased to share soft-boiled eggs with you, Sir. With both of us."

"I don't eat soft-boiled eggs," General Bellmon said. He turned to the refrigerator, removed a package of bacon from it, and handed it to Oliver. Then he took out a jar of English orange marmalade and a package of English muffins. "Breakfast is the most important meal of the day," he said. "I am unable to understand why most people refuse to acknowledge that."

He walked out of the kitchen toward the driveway, carrying the muffins and marmalade. Oliver turned to follow him. Marjorie Bellmon, in a bathrobe, sleepy-eyed, appeared at the door from the living room.

"I will not ask what that's all about," she said, smiling. "But I'm sure you'll have a *wonderful* time whatever it is."

Oliver smiled at her, chuckled, and followed Bellmon. The staff car driver had turned it around so that it was headed down the driveway, removed the covers from the red major general's plates, and, having installed the General in the back seat, was already behind the wheel starting the engine. Oliver slipped into the front seat.

"Magnolia House, Dick," General Bellmon ordered the driver.

"Yes, Sir."

Their route to the Magnolia House took them past the new, concrete-block, two-story barracks of the 31st Infantry. A platoon of troops was being inspected by a very short, very dapper second lieutenant. All of a sudden—someone had obviously spotted the two-starred plate—he did a quick about-face and saluted.

Bellmon had been reading the overnight TWXs, but somehow he sensed that he was being saluted and returned it.

Logically, Oliver thought, he could not be expected to have seen the saluting second john. But he had.

When they got to Magnolia House, they were saluted again, this time by the driver of the staff car assigned to General Rand. He had been leaning on the fender, and his eyes followed Bellmon's car as it pulled into the drive.

The door was opened by General Rand's aide, a tall, ascetic-looking young first lieutenant who wore both a West Point ring and aviators' wings. He was wearing stiffly starched fatigues. The embroidered wings were visibly much newer than the fatigues.

"Good morning, gentlemen," Lieutenant Mitchell said. "General Rand is expecting you."

After Bellmon walked past him, Mitchell looked questioningly at Oliver, curious about the reason for this early-morning visit. Oliver shrugged his shoulders, signifying he was just as puzzled.

" 'Morning, George," Bellmon said.

"Good morning, General," General Rand replied. He was sitting at the dining room table, dressed in a flight suit, drinking a cup of coffee.

They shook hands.

"I was not kidding about the soft-boiled eggs, General," Rand said. "Is that going to be enough for you?"

"No, it won't," Bellmon said. "And it's not enough for you, either, George. Breakfast is the most important meal of the day." He turned to look at Rand's aide. "Can you cook, Lieutenant? Bacon and eggs? And toast an English muffin?"

"I'll give it my best, Sir," Mitchell said.

"Give him that stuff, Johnny, and let him have a shot at it," Bellmon ordered.

"With pleasure, Sir," Oliver said, handing Mitchell the groceries. "They also serve, Lieutenant, who stand and fry."

"General," Rand said, "I didn't know what to do about my check ride."

"You can call me Bob, George," Bellmon said. "For the moment, at least, we're old friends . . . classmates. Your check ride has been rescheduled for fifteen hundred."

"What's going on, Bob?" General Rand asked.

There was a coffeepot on the table, a battered silver one,

on loan from the Officers' Open Mess. Bellmon went to it and poured half a cup before replying.

''Actually, George, it's a rather interesting problem in command responsibility,'' he said.

''Why do I feel I'm not going to like this?'' Rand asked.

''You probably won't,'' Bellmon said. ''But I've given it a lot of thought, and I hope you'll consider that before you start throwing things.''

''Now I *am* worried,'' Rand said seriously.

''As soon as we have our breakfast, you're going to go out to Hanchey with Johnny Oliver.'' Hanchey Army Air Field was then the main Fort Rucker heliport. ''You and Johnny are going to get into a Huey, and you will fly him around, wherever he wants to go. To Benning, if he wants. Anywhere he wants to go, just so long as that gives him a fair opportunity to judge your flying skills, and more important, your attitude and aptitude. If you pass that muster you can take your check ride at fifteen hundred.''

''I don't think I understand,'' General Rand said. It was obvious to Johnny Oliver that Rand was furious.

''Well, George, you're entitled to an explanation,'' Bellmon said. ''The thing is, I'm more than a little uncomfortable with the senior-officer flight program. People our age tend to forget we're not twenty-one any more. Or even forty-one.''

''I passed the same flight physical you did,'' Rand said. ''And they wouldn't have set me up for the check ride if they didn't think I was ready for it.''

''That's what's been bothering me,'' Bellmon said. ''I'm not sure what you just said is so.''

''How would you like your eggs, Sir?'' Lieutenant Mitchell called from the kitchen.

''See if you can find some cyanide out there,'' Rand called back.

Bellmon laughed. ''Up, please,'' he called.

''Mine, too,'' Captain Oliver called cheerfully, ''Thank you *ever so much*, Lieutenant.''

Bellmon gave him a hard look and then smiled.

''That's what you get, Bob, when you have an aide who doesn't want to be an aide,'' Bellmon said.

General Rand was not in the mood for pleasantries; he did not allow the conversation to move off the subject.

"I really don't think I've been given a free ride, Bob," he said. "The course has been, pardon the French, a ball-buster."

"I'm not saying that," Bellmon said. "What I'm saying, George, is that it's *possible* that whoever is scheduled to give you your check ride this afternoon—and I think it's very important to tell you I have no idea who that is, and don't want to know—would give you the benefit of the doubt—beyond what you should get."

"In other words you don't think I can fly," Rand said, and anger took over. "Well, then, why don't you give me the goddamned check ride?"

"I considered that," Bellmon said, oblivious to Rand's anger. "But that would set a precedent I'd rather not set. They sent me down here to run the school, not give check rides. I don't have the time—nor are there other senior officers who have been flying a while who have the time—to give every senior officer who comes through here a check ride."

"Then why don't you let the system work the way you set it up?" Rand asked.

"The senior-officer flight program hasn't been in effect long enough to really be called a system," Bellmon said. "This is one modification to it I think is necessary."

"What you're saying in effect is that you don't trust your own people."

"Don't push me, George," Bellmon said. "I told you I don't even know who's scheduled to give you your check ride. But whoever it is, I think there's a risk of an overly generous benefit of the doubt. For one thing, you're a general. I would hate to be a captain, for that matter, a lieutenant colonel, who was the guy who said, 'Sorry, General, you just don't cut the mustard.' And there's something else, in your case. You ever notice, George, that people feel sorry for ex-POWs, that they treat them with a little extra consideration—as if they're old women?"

General Rand's face reddened and his lips tightened. He had been captured when Corregidor fell. He'd spent nearly four years as a Japanese prisoner. All logic aside, he felt there was something shameful about losing a battle, burning the colors, becoming a prisoner. There were very few people in the service who dared talk to Rand about his having been a POW. General Bellmon was one of the few who could. Bellmon had been captured by the Germans in North Africa, and had spent three years as a prisoner in Germany.

Bellmon stared him down. " 'He's a nice guy. He can't fly too well, but what the hell, he's a general and he won't be flying by himself anyway. And the poor bastard was a POW. I'm not going to kick him, too.' Get the picture, George?"

Rand didn't reply.

"And I considered the other alternative, George," Bellmon went on. " 'Let the old bastard kill himself; what the hell, he's a big boy.' And I decided against that, too. For one thing I don't want Susan mad at me. And for another, the Army needs you. Preferably flying with the 11th, but if not that, somewhere else."

"OK, Bob," Rand said. "You've made your point."

Bellmon looked at Johnny Oliver. "Johnny, aside from 'I'd really rather not be doing this' have you got anything to say?"

"No, Sir," Johnny Oliver said.

[THREE]
Hanchey Army Airfield
Fort Rucker, Alabama
0805 Hours 10 July 1964

Brigadier General George F. Rand walked around HU-1D Tail Number 610977 and performed the pre-flight check. Captain John S. Oliver walked with him, watching him.

What is involved here, General Rand thought, *is my goddamned ego. I am a general officer of the United States Army. I have fought in two wars, and commanded a regiment in combat. Therefore I have every right to be annoyed at having a captain young enough to be my son watching my every damned move as if I'm a plebe whose mess kit he suspects is greasy. How dare he?*

The point is he has every right to. The system is out of whack. The junior officer knows what he is doing, and there is a strong possibility that the general officer doesn't.

He finished the pre-flight and turned to Oliver and raised his eyebrows in question. Oliver returned the facial expression.

"I think this machine, Captain, is safe to fly," General Rand said.

"If you say so, Sir," Oliver said.

"Where would you like me to sit?"

"Wherever you would like to, Sir."

Rand locked eyes with him a minute.

This is one tough little sonofabitch. He is not awed by Brigadier General Rand. What I need is someone like him for an aide.

Rand put on his helmet and then walked around the nose of the Huey and climbed in the right, the pilot's seat. The seat was too far forward.

Whoever flew this thing last must have been a goddamned midget.

He reached down and unfastened the seat lock and slid the seat as far back as it would travel. Then he put the lap and shoulder harnesses on and adjusted them. He looked at Oliver and saw that Oliver was strapped and plugged in, but obviously had no intention of being helpful; Rand understood he was not going to get any special courtesy because he was a general officer.

Oliver reached over and up and grabbed the plastic-coated white checklist, which was fastened to the sun visor with a length of key chain.

"Are you ready for this, Sir?" Oliver asked, his voice sounding metallic in the earphones.

"As ready as I'm likely to get," General Rand said.

"Cyclic, collective pitch, and pedals?" Oliver read.

Rand moved the cyclic control, between his legs, in a small circle, then to the outward perimeters of its movement and then centered it. He moved the collective control, on his left, up and then down, and pushed on the rudder pedals.

"Checked and centered," Rand replied.

"AC circuit breakers?"

"In."

"Radios?"

"Off and set."

"Governor switch?"

"Automatic."

"Main and starter fuel switches?"

"Off."

Rand was aware that Oliver was checking for himself after every question. Oliver was not, in other words, giving him the benefit of any doubt.

"Altimeter?"

"Set."

"Starter/generator switch?"

"Start."

"Main generator switch?"

"On."

"Inverter switch?"

"Off."

"DC circuit breakers?"

"In."

"Battery switch?"

"On."

"Inverter switch?"

"Spare."

"Fire-detection light?"

"Checked."

"RPM warning light?"

"On."

"Master caution panel warning light?"

"Tested and reset."

"Main fuel switch?"

"On."

"Starting fuel switch?"

"On."

"Governor RPM increase/decrease switch?"

Rand pushed on the switch for ten seconds and then reported, "Decreased."

"Throttle?"

"Set."

"Fireguard?" Oliver asked, and then, after looking out the window, answered that one himself: "He's there."

"Rotor blades?" Oliver asked. He looked up and behind him, and around, to see if, for sure, the blades were unrestrained, and Rand waited for him to again answer his own question. He didn't. He looked at General Rand.

''Clear,'' Rand said.

''Intercom and radios?''

''On.''

''Ignition system?''

''In.''

''Starter circuit breaker?''

''In.''

''Inverter switch?'' Oliver asked.

''Main,'' Rand replied.

''Starter generator?''

''Set.''

''Main generator?''

''On.''

''Fuel warning light?'' Oliver asked, and Rand reached forward and pushed the push-to-test light. It came on.

''Check,'' Rand replied.

''Fuel gauge?''

''Check.''

''Caution panel warning light?''

''Check.''

''Throttle?''

''Fully closed.''

Rand looked at Oliver, expecting him to say something. Oliver didn't.

''May I start it?'' General Rand asked.

''You're the pilot,'' Oliver said, not appending the usual ''Sir.''

General Rand caught the eye of the fireguard, who was standing beside an enormous fire extinguisher mounted on what looked like giant bicycle wheels. He took his hand off the cyclic, raised it to the level of his head, and, index finger extended, made a whirling motion. The fireguard nodded his understanding.

''Battery?'' Oliver read.

''On,'' Rand replied.

''Fuel main switch?''

''On.''

''Oil valve?''

"On."

"Fuel start switch?"

"On."

"Governor?"

"On."

"Throttle?"

"Ground idle."

"Rpm control?"

"Minimum."

"Starter ignition switch?" Oliver asked.

Rand did not reply. He pulled on the starter switch. There was a whine and a just barely perceptible vibration.

"Ergo sum," General Rand said, and was pleased with himself.

The engine rpm began to wind up. The rotor blades began, very slowly, to turn. Rand examined the control panel. No warning lights came on.

A new voice came over the intercom.

"Crew chief aboard, Sir."

"You go catch a cup of coffee or something, Sergeant," Oliver said.

"You don't want me along, Sir?" the crew chief asked.

"Not on this ride," Oliver said.

"Yes, Sir," the crew chief said. Even over the frequency-clipped intercom system, his disappointment, or annoyance, was evident.

Rand looked at him curiously, but Oliver offered no explanation.

What is this arrogant young sonofabitch doing? Is he trying to spare me the humiliation of having the sergeant hear him telling the General off? Or, with infinite courtesy and kindness, telling him, "Sorry, you don't cut the mustard?" What the hell else could it be?

Rand ran his eyes over the instrument panel. Just to the left of the center were six round dials, in two columns of three. The two indicators on top reported fuel pressure and fuel quantity. Pressure was all right, and the tanks were full. The needles of the two gauges below, engine-oil pressure and temperature, were in the green. So were the needles of two gauges on the bottom, which indicated transmission-oil pressure and temperature.

Directly in front of him were four instruments mounted horizontally: the tachometer, which had two needles, one reporting engine rpm and the other rotor rpm. Beside that was the airspeed indicator, then the attitude indicator, and finally the altimeter. Immediately below the altimeter was the vertical-speed indicator, which reported how fast the aircraft was gaining or losing altitude.

There were more indicators and gauges and switches, and the first time General Rand sat where he was sitting they had baffled and intimidated him. He'd thought then that it was a hell of a lot to ask of a man his age to learn not only what they were for, but their relationship to each other.

But he knew now. He could have sat down at a table and drawn the instrument panel (actually panels, plural) from memory.

Rand pressed the intercom switch, one of several on what he thought of as the "handle" of the cyclic control.

"Everything's in the green, Captain," he said. "Permission to take off?"

Oliver balled his fist, thumb extended, and made an upward movement.

Rand pressed the radio-transmit switch on the cyclic.

"Hanchey, Huey Niner Seven Seven."

"Go ahead, Niner Seven Seven," the tower replied.

Before Rand could continue, Oliver's voice came over the airwaves.

"Niner Seven Seven to the active for takeoff. Local IFR. We have a Code Seven aboard. This is Captain Oliver."

"Hanchey clears Niner Seven Seven to the threshold of the active. Army Four Six One, hold your position. You will be number one to take off after a VIP Huey about to move to the threshold."

"Four Six One, Roger."

"Why did you do that?" Rand demanded.

"Take us to the threshold of the active—two seven—please," Oliver replied.

"Niner Seven Seven, Hanchey."

"Go," Oliver said.

That was not correct radio procedure, either, General Rand decided.

''Niner Seven Seven, Four Six One is holding on the threshold. You are number one for takeoff on two seven. The time is one five past the hour, the winds are negligible, the altimeter is two niner niner eight.''

''Got you, thank you,'' Oliver's voice came metallically over the earphones.

He turned to General Rand and made a lifting gesture with his right hand, ''pick it up.''

Rand slowly pulled upward on the collective control, by his left side. The Huey trembled and then lifted an inch or so off the ground, and then six inches. Then he moved the cyclic just perceptibly, which caused the nose of the Huey to dip just perceptibly and just perceptibly start to move.

He moved the cyclic again, and touched the rudder pedals, and the nose slowly swung until it was pointing at the threshold of runway two seven.

''I've got it,'' Oliver's voice came over the earphones. Rand looked at him in surprise as he let go of the controls. With Oliver's hands on the controls, the Huey rose six feet off the ground, sharply dropped the nose, and moved, accelerating all the time, toward the threshold. He was still a hundred yards away when he pulled up on the collective, pulling the Huey upward sharply, and then into a steep climbing turn to the right.

''Hanchey, Niner Seven Seven gone at one seven past the hour,'' Oliver said, and then, immediately, ''OK, General, take it.''

Rand put his hands and feet back on the controls.

''Maintain this heading, and this rate of climb, and take us to thirty-five hundred,'' Oliver said.

Rand leveled the Huey and set up the rate of climb.

''May I ask, Captain, what that was all about?''

Oliver looked over at him.

''Any time you declare a Code Seven, the tower will more often than not, whether or not you want them to, put you at the head of the line. That means you are holding other people up. So you can either tell the tower you will take your place in the line or the landing stack or you can get out of the way as quick as possible.''

''That's never happened before,'' General Rand protested.

''This is the school, General. Things are different in the field,'' Oliver said. ''When you get to thirty-five hundred, take us to Troy.''

''I don't know that heading,'' General Rand said.

''Then you'd better fly over the post to Ozark and see if you can find it by flying up the highway,'' Oliver said, adding, ''you'd have a hell of a time getting the chart out of your Jeppesen case right now.''

Rand's face colored. That was error one, and a major one. His ''Chart, Aerial, Local, Low-Level, Fort Rucker, Ala, Vicinity'' was neatly folded and stacked with the other charts in the leather Jeppesen case in the back of the Huey.

Every time before, when there was an indication that he would be flying out of sight of the Rucker complex, he had found his chart, neatly refolded to show the route to the destination, sitting on the sunshade over the instrument panel. The instructor pilots had done that for him, as a courtesy to a brigadier general. Oliver had not felt obliged to be similarly courteous, and hadn't mentioned charts on the ground either.

General Rand looked over at Captain Oliver, who added to his discomfiture by smiling tolerantly at him.

For the first time in a very long while, Brigadier General George F. Rand considered how nice it would be to have the opportunity to take a brother officer out behind a supply room somewhere and punch the living shit out of him.

[FOUR]
Near Eufaula, Alabama
0905 Hours 10 July 1964

With the exception of a very few special-purpose aircraft that use the thrust of their engines to overcome gravitational force, and of course, rockets, all aircraft rise and remain in the air using the flow of air over their airfoils—more commonly known as wings—as a lifting force. If the upper surface of the wing is longer (larger) than the undersurface, the aircraft (under suitable propulsion) can rise into the air—fly.

In fixed-wing aircraft, the power of the engine is used to propel the craft through the air, thus causing air to flow over an airfoil. In aircraft equipped with a piston engine, that engine turns an airscrew (propeller) in a vertical plane that pulls (or pushes) the craft forward. Jet aircraft use the force of the jet to push the aircraft forward through the air, accomplishing the same thing.

When the engine of a fixed-wing aircraft fails, or is shut off, the aircraft cannot maintain altitude. But it can glide for varying distances—depending on a factor called wing load. That is to say, if the pilot is able to maintain an adequate airspeed, by lowering the nose and permitting the aircraft to enter a shallow dive, enough air will continue to pass over the wings to provide some lift and keep the machine from dropping like a stone. With a little luck there will be enough "glide" for the pilot to find some farmer's field to land in.

Things are a little different with helicopters, because it is the wings of rotary-wing aircraft that rotate. The engines of helicopters use their power to turn the rotary wings in a horizontal plane around a hub.

When a helicopter engine fails and power is no longer available to turn the rotary wings, it is possible for the pilot to use the same physical principles that the pilot of a fixed-wing aircraft can use in similar circumstances: he can exchange altitude for velocity and thus maintain some lift. In other words, the helicopter is permitted to lose altitude, which builds up airspeed, which builds up the speed at which the unladen rotary wings are turning. Then, just before the helicopter strikes the ground, the pilot uses up the stored energy in the turning rotor blades and changes the pitch of the rotor blades again, giving him enough lift to halt his descent and to lower the machine gently onto the ground.

A miscalculation of the moment when he chooses to haul up on the collective and stop the descent, of course, can lead to disaster. Too early, and the machine stops high above the ground, momentarily, and then with no lift remaining, falls the rest of the way like a stone. Too late, and the same thing happens—except that there's no momentary stop.

This had all been explained in some detail to Brigadier General George F. Rand in pre-flight training, and there had been both written and oral quizzes to ensure that he understood it.

The technique of rotary-wing-aircraft flight known as autorotation had also been explained to him.

Instruction and practice of the autorotation technique is ordinarily accomplished at some distance above the ground, so that if the neophyte hauls up on the collective at the wrong time, no real harm is done. The ground is still some distance below him, and he can correct from either a too early or a too late application of upward collective movement.

When, in the opinion of the IP, the student has mastered the basic technique, he permits the student to make a *real* autorotation from a position close to the ground, almost invariably giving him plenty of time to prepare himself for the maneuver.

Brigadier General George F. Rand fully expected that Captain John S. Oliver would test his ability to perform the autorotation maneuver. He was not at all surprised when, at thirty-five hundred feet, some eight or ten miles from Troy, Alabama, when he momentarily took his hand off his collective control, Captain Oliver put his hand on *his* collective and cranked the throttle back to ground idle.

"Flare out at three thousand," Captain Oliver ordered with what Rand thought was an unnecessarily smug self-satisfaction.

General Rand did his very best to comply with the order. And, he thought, after he had dropped five hundred feet, and flared it out, that it hadn't been half bad.

Oliver would now crank the throttle open again, and they would resume the flight, possibly, even probably, dropping to two hundred feet over some convenient field, where he would autorotate again and actually settle the helicopter, powerless, onto the ground.

But Oliver made no move to restore power to the engine.

"May I advance the throttle?" Rand asked as the controls grew mushy in his hands.

Sonofabitch! I'm going to have to autorotate again while the sonofabitch makes up his goddamned mind!

"No, I don't think so," Captain Oliver said as Rand

dropped the nose again to swap altitude for velocity. "Sit it down someplace, General, please."

"What?" Rand asked disbelievingly.

"Engines have a tendency to fail at higher altitudes," Oliver said, infuriatingly smug. "Find someplace to set it down, please, and set it down."

Rand was aware that his hands inside the thin pigskin flying gloves were now sweaty. He looked out the windows, searching for someplace to land the damn thing, even as he watched the dials and the rotor rpm.

The altimeter unwound alarmingly. And he had been taught that the altitude indicated by the instrument was not their altitude at the moment, but what the altitude had been seven seconds before. And he realized suddenly that he had no idea how far above sea level the ground beneath him was. Altimeters indicate height above sea level, not above the ground.

For all practical purposes that goddamned altimeter is useless to me; I'm going to have to judge how far off the ground I am by looking out the windows.

He dropped and flared and dropped and flared and dropped and flared, and finally dropped and flared one last time and HU-1D Tail Number 610977 ran completely out of the aerodynamic forces required for flight about four feet over the stubble of a cutover cornfield and returned to earth. There was a dull thump and the sounds of groaning metal.

Brigadier General George F. Rand looked over at Captain John S. Oliver.

Gross goddamned mistake number two.

"May I take off?" General Rand asked.

"I think I had better have a look and see if we broke something," Oliver said. "I don't think we did, but it will take only a minute to look. Just keep it running."

He's about my size and weight, General Rand thought, *and I have twenty years on him. But I still think I can punch his ass into next week.*

No damage to HU-1D Tail Number 610977 as a result of what would be entered in the flight-log as a "hard landing" was detected by Captain Oliver.

Oliver climbed back in the copilot's seat, and as Rand

watched, carefully noting the time on his aviator's chronometer, entered the time and circumstances, including who was at the controls, of the hard landing in the flight log.

"Well, Sir," he said, smiling smugly at General Rand, "if you're feeling up to it, why don't you see if you can get our little birdie in the air again?"

This sonofabitch is trying to make me mad. Well, to hell with him. I won't let him.

When General Rand did not reply, Captain Oliver went on, as if talking to a backward six-year-old. "Why don't we see if we can find Eufaula? Take us to twenty-five hundred feet, please."

When they were at two hundred feet, Captain Oliver retarded the throttle to ground idle again. General Rand was so taken by surprise that he performed another autorotation in the belief that this one was necessary, not a demonstration of his skill at performing the technique. Then he saw Captain Oliver's smile and understood what had happened.

"One never knows when there will be a loss of power," Captain Oliver intoned solemnly. "Therefore, it behooves one to always be prepared to execute an autorotation maneuver. That one was considerably smoother than the previous one."

With what he recognized to be a demonstration of considerable willpower, General Rand kept his mouth shut, except to ask for permission to take off.

Over the next hour and a half, above the farms and pine forests of what is known as the Alabama Wire Grass, Captain Oliver called upon General Rand to demonstrate his mastery of the various flight maneuvers he had learned while a student in the senior officers' flight program. Though General Rand was reasonably but not entirely sure that he had performed them above minimum standards, Captain Oliver offered no comment, congratulatory or otherwise.

Finally they flew back to Fort Rucker and Hanchey Army Airfield, entered the landing stack without announcing a Code Seven was aboard, and landed. By the time Captain Oliver had observed General Rand going through post-flight procedure, Lieutenant Howard Mitchell walked up to HU-1D Tail Number 610977 and announced that he had the car anytime the General was ready.

"Are you going to tell me how I did, Captain Oliver, or not?" General Rand asked.

"Sir, with respect, no," Oliver said. "General Bellmon specifically said I was not to offer an opinion."

"Well, thank you for your time, Captain," General Rand said.

"My pleasure, Sir."

General Rand, not without effort, managed a smile as he returned Captain Oliver's salute. And then he walked across the grass of the parking ramp and the concrete of the runway, and stepped into the staff car.

They had been at the Magnolia House ten minutes when the telephone rang. It was General Bellmon's secretary. She told Mitchell that General Rand's check ride, scheduled for 1500, was canceled and would he instead please come to General Bellmon's office at that time.

When he had relayed the message, Lieutenant Mitchell looked at General Rand with what could have been concern, curiosity, or pity.

"If I busted that check ride, Mitchell, which is what it looks like, I'm going to protest," General Rand said softly but firmly. "I may be a little rough, I may not have the finesse I suspect Captain Oliver expected me to have, but I can fly that thing. I'll demand another check ride."

"Yes, Sir," Lieutenant Mitchell said uncomfortably.

At 1455 hours, General Rand, accompanied by his aide-de-camp, presented himself at the office of the Commanding General of the Army Aviation Center & Fort Rucker, Alabama.

He was courteously informed that the General was tied up at the moment and then offered a cup of coffee, which he declined.

At 1500 hours the door to General Bellmon's office opened and Bellmon himself appeared.

"Come in, please, George," Bellmon said. "Lieutenant, you keep your seat."

Rand followed Bellmon into his office, turning to close the door after him.

"You want some coffee, George?" Bellmon asked, settling

himself in the high-backed chair behind his desk. ''Sergeant Major James just made a fresh pot.''

''No, thank you,'' General Rand said.

''OK,'' Bellmon said. ''I've heard one version of your ride with Johnny Oliver. Now let's hear yours.''

''All right,'' Rand said. ''I hoped you'd give me that opportunity. Bob, I'm forty-five years old. My reflexes are not what they were when I was twenty-five, and I have no illusions that I'm one of these people you hear about who are born to fly. I am not smooth, I have to work at it every damned second. And I readily confess that taking off without a chart was pretty damned dumb. Having said that—''

''You took off without a chart? I didn't hear about that,'' Bellmon interrupted, visibly incredulous. ''How did you manage to do that?''

''I left the Jepp case in the back. I didn't think. I said it was dumb.''

Bellmon shook his head from side to side. ''You did remember, George, to count the shoes on your feet?''

''But despite everything I did wrong today, and I'm not going to challenge whatever Oliver reported to you—''

''Well, I'm glad to hear that,'' Bellmon said, holding up his hand, cutting him off.

He pushed a lever on his intercom. ''Would you send those people in here, please?''

Rand looked at him in confusion.

''What Johnny Oliver said to me,'' Bellmon said, ''was that you flew a lot better than he thought you would.''

''He said that?''

''And he said you didn't get flustered, even when he did his damndest to shake you.''

''I'll be damned.''

In the split second that he smelled perfume and sensed a feminine presence, a hand touched his, and there was breath against his ear, and his wife said softly, ''I told you you were going to pass.''

He looked down at her and then around the office. Captain John S. Oliver had also come into the room, and Lieutenant Howard Mitchell, and a sergeant with a U.S. Army photographer brassard around his arm.

"Bring him over here, Susan," Bellmon said. "In front of this wall. I will shake his hand and smile benignly at him while you pin on his wings and Sergeant Sanderson records this momentous occasion for posterity."

General Rand found Captain Oliver.

"You sonofabitch," he said, but he was smiling.

"George!" Susan Rand said. "Captain, I know you know he didn't mean that, but he shouldn't have said it anyway."

"No problem, Ma'am," Johnny said.

"I want you to know that *I'm* very grateful—"

"Hell, Oliver," General Rand interrupted his wife, "so'm I."

"—because General Bellmon told me," Susan Rand went on, "that if you didn't think he could safely fly, you wouldn't have passed him."

"This was rougher on him than it was on George," Bellmon said. "Johnny, why don't you knock off for the day? And I mean knock off. Get off the post. Go see your girlfriend. No work, in other words."

XVIII

[ONE]
Ozark, Alabama
1545 Hours 10 July 1964

Marjorie Bellmon's MGB was in the gas station at the corner of Ozark Highway and Spring Street when Oliver made the turn to go to Liza's house.

He tooted the horn, and she waved, and then it occurred to him that despite Jose Newell's expert and continuing attention, that damned little car was broken again. He could think of no other reason she'd be in a civilian gas station. He turned around to go back, pulling up beside her as she was handing money to the attendant.

''Anything wrong?'' he asked, a little ashamed at his relief to find that she had really stopped for gas. He was in no mood to have to fool around with the car.

''No,'' she said, ''and yes.''

"Tell me. I was a Boy Scout and I remain sworn to be helpful to ladies in distress."

"Jack called the house, collect, and I wasn't there," she said. "I was working. So Mother called me and told me. No sooner did she get off the phone than Uncle— Colonel Lowell called me at the bank and told me he didn't know what was going on in detail, but Jack was in some kind of trouble and he thought I might want to know about it and maybe even go down there."

"To McDill? That's halfway to Miami."

What did PFC Jacques Emile Portet do, punch out some arrogant second lieutenant?

"No. He's at Hurlburt Field," Marjorie said.

Hurlburt Field, the home of the Air Force Air Commandos, is on the Gulf of Mexico, in the Florida Panhandle, not far from the Alabama border.

Oliver said what popped into his mind.

"That's where the Air Commandos hang their funny little hats."

"I know," she said. "What would Jack be doing there?"

"Haven't the foggiest."

"I'm going down there," she said.

"That's going to go over like a lead balloon with your old man."

"I know," she said. "But I've got to go if he's in trouble."

"Why don't you come with me to Liza's," Oliver said, "and I'll get on the phone and call down there and see what I can find out."

"I wouldn't know where to call," she said. "I've got to go."

"I've got the afternoon off. Want some company?"

She kissed his cheek.

"That's sweet, but I'm the one in love with him."

"I'm not granting the point, but what if he *is* in trouble? What do you think you can do about it?"

"I don't know," Marjorie said. "Be there. If I need some help I'll call you." When she saw the look of doubt on his face, she added: "I will, Johnny."

"OK."

"We're friends, right?" she pursued, and he smiled and nodded.

"Yeah."

"So, friend, how's it going with you and Liza?"

"We're flying in circles, waiting for the other one to run out of gas," Oliver said. "No change, in other words. Catch-22. She won't marry me unless I get out of the Army. And I can't get out of the Army."

"You've thought about that?"

"That wouldn't work," he said. "If I thought it would, I would resign."

"You're like Daddy. I can't imagine either one of you doing anything else but being in the Army."

"Like I said, Catch-22."

"Well, if I were Liza, *I'd* marry you," Marjorie said.

"Maybe we could give Jack to Liza. He's really a civilian. That would straighten our romantic problems."

She laughed and kissed him on the cheek.

"Be careful, Marjorie," Oliver said as she climbed in her car.

"You, too."

When he reached the house he was surprised to find Liza's car in the driveway. He'd expected her to be at work. It had been his intention to get out of his uniform, take a shower, pick Allan up at Mother Wood's, and fool around with him until Liza got home.

He really liked the little guy. And the reverse seemed to be true as well, which was understandable on Allan's part. A little boy likes a daddy. But he sometimes wondered if he wasn't, at least subconsciously, using Allan as a lever on Liza's emotions.

Before he'd met the kid, he'd thought that whoever had called small children house apes was right on the money. Whenever these uncomfortable thoughts occurred to him, he consoled himself with the profound, age-old wisdom that all's fair in love and war. And with the somewhat self-righteous notion that whatever the reason, he genuinely cared more for Allan Wood than Tom Chaney had ever cared for Johnny Oliver.

"You're home early," Liza said when he walked into the

kitchen. It was more of a challenge than a question or statement.

And she said home, which is an interesting Freudian slip.

Allan came running from inside the house and Oliver scooped him off the floor and growled in his neck.

"I spent the day giving General Rand a check ride," he said, hoisting Allan so that he sat with his legs around his neck. "Bellmon turned me loose early."

"What did you say to your sister about me?" Liza demanded.

"Horsey! Horsey!" Allan said, pulling on Oliver's ears.

"What?"

"I said, what did you say to your sister about me?" Liza repeated coldly.

"You were there, baby," Oliver said. "What did you hear?"

"*Horsey,* Johnny!" Allan demanded, and Oliver obligingly flexed his knees and bounced him around.

"I mean, since we were there," Liza snapped.

"I haven't talked to her since we were there. What the hell are you talking about?"

"She called me up."

"She called you up?" Oliver asked, genuinely surprised. "What did she want?"

"Among other things she called me a grasping bitch and said I would never get a dime of your father's money if she had to take it to the Supreme Court."

My God! She's telling me the truth.

"Honey, I don't know what brought that on," Oliver said.

"*Horsey,* Johnny!" Allan demanded, and Oliver bounced him around again.

"Hold on to him," Liza said sharply. "I tell you that and tell you that!"

"I'm not going to let him fall," Oliver said. "Jesus!"

"I think she was drunk," Liza said. "I know she was hysterical."

"I wonder what that's all about."

"Maybe if you called her on the telephone you could find out," Liza said sarcastically.

Oliver reached up and swung Allan off his shoulders.

"Go in the living room and break something," he said, smiling, as he set the child on his feet.

"That's nice," Liza said furiously.

"Hey, take it easy," Johnny said and glared at her a moment. "Until otherwise proven, I'm innocent."

He turned and took the handset from the wall telephone. When the operator finally came on the line, he put in a person-to-person call to Mrs. Thomas Chaney in Burlington, Vermont.

As the number was ringing, he motioned for Liza to stand by him so that she could listen in. She shook her head, no.

"Then go get on the extension," he said. "You know you're curious."

She glared at him, but then walked out of the kitchen. He heard the click of her picking up as Tom Chaney came on the line.

"Tom, this is Johnny," Oliver said. "Is Shirley there?"

"Shirley can't come to the phone right now, Johnny," Tom said. His voice was cold and unfriendly. *And wary.*

"She called my girl today, Tom," Oliver said. "Mrs. Wood. Do you have any idea what that was all about?"

Shirley Chaney came on the extension at that point. "You ungrateful sonofabitch!"

"I'm fine, Sis, and how are you?" *She's drunk, that's why Tom said she can't come to the phone.*

"Take it easy, honey," Tom Chaney said.

"Take it easy? After what he's done?"

"You want to tell me what I've done?" Johnny asked.

"You know goddamned well what you've done, you and that greedy slut of a girlfriend of yours. Mother and Daddy must be spinning in their graves."

"Watch what you say about Liza, Shirley!" Johnny flared. "She hasn't done a damned thing to you!"

"Huh!"

"You want to tell me what all this is about?"

"I'll tell you this," Shirley said. "I'll burn the fucking place to the ground before I'll see you, you ungrateful bastard, or your goddamned slut getting a goddamned dime—"

"John," Tom Chaney said, interrupting her, "maybe it would be best if you—"

''Now you won't get a goddamned dime!'' Shirley screamed. ''Put that in your pipe and smoke it, Johnny!''

He heard the telephone being slammed down.

''Tom, you still there?'' Oliver asked in a moment.

''I'm here,'' Chaney said.

''Tom, you want to tell me what the hell is going on?''

''I think we better let the lawyers handle this, John. You'll be hearing from our lawyers.''

There was a second click and the line went dead.

Oliver hung up, leaned against the wall, and waited for Liza to return to the kitchen. In a moment she was standing in the doorway.

''I think I would have to say that my beloved sister is annoyed about something,'' he said. ''Pity she wasn't sober enough to tell me what's bothering her.''

''You don't know?'' Liza asked incredulously.

''Haven't the foggiest. But, clever fellow that I am, I think it may have something to do with Foxworth T. Mattingly, Esquire.''

''Who?'' Liza asked, smiling at the name, and then remembering. ''Oh, that lawyer. What about him? You think he's done something?''

''I would hazard a guess that he has. Lawyers, I have noticed, do seem to tend to piss people off.''

''You're going to have to start watching your language,'' Liza said. ''Mother Wood told me what Allan said to her: 'Don't piss me off!' he told her.''

''Really?'' Oliver said, for some reason delighted.

''It's not funny, Johnny,'' Liza said, but she was unable to restrain a smile. ''Well, call him and find out what this is all about.''

''I don't know where to call him.''

''Come on!''

''I don't. All I know is that Colonel Lowell said he worked out of Atlanta.''

''What's the name of the firm? Wouldn't the Yellow Pages list lawyers?''

Atlanta information reported there was no listing for an attorney by that name.

''Are we to presume that Foxworth T. Mattingly, Esquire,

is practicing law without a degree?'' Johnny asked rhetorically.

''This is serious, Johnny, do something?''

''I'm thinking.''

''I hate to do this, but . . .'' he said, and dialed a number from memory.

''General Bellmon's quarters, Lieutenant Bellmon speaking, Sir.''

''Bobby, ask your mother if she can come to the phone,'' Oliver said.

''Mom! It's Johnny. Maybe he knows where she is!''

''Hello, Johnny,'' Barbara Bellmon said.

''Was he talking about Marjorie?'' Johnny asked.

''Yes, he was.''

''I know where she is,'' Johnny said. ''Is there anything I can do to help?''

''Maybe a little prayer,'' Barbara Bellmon said.

''You know where she went?''

''Yes,'' Barbara Bellmon said. ''Do you want to talk to my husband, Johnny? He's standing right here.''

''He doesn't know?''

''No.''

''Jesus Christ!''

''That isn't exactly the prayer I had in mind, Johnny,'' Barbara Bellmon said.

''Well, you have the other kind, too, I guess you know that.''

''I know, dear,'' she said. ''But thank you. Do you want to talk to my husband?''

''I'm now embarrassed,'' Oliver said. ''What I called for was a sort of desperate hope that you might happen to know the phone number of Colonel Lowell's lawyer in Atlanta.''

''Oh, dear. I was so concerned with what's been going on around here since Marjorie called and told us she was going away for a few days that I completely forgot about your sister calling. Did she manage to get in touch with you?''

''Oh, boy!''

''Yes, she called here, too. Is there anything I can do to help, Johnny?''

She called the Bellmons' quarters! And, if I'm reading Mrs. B right, she was drunk when she did. Oh, Jesus Christ!

"No. Ma'am, unless you happen to know that number, or even the name of the firm."

"It's in the den," Barbara Bellmon said matter-of-factly. "Hang on, I'll get it for you."

General Bellmon came on the line.

"Johnny, are you privy to Marjorie's idiocy?"

"Mrs. Bellmon just told me she called and said she was going away for a few days," Oliver replied carefully.

"That wasn't the question, Johnny."

"Sir, please don't ask me to answer that question."

"You just did, Johnny."

"Johnny?" Barbara Bellmon picked up on the extension in the den. "It's 555–4586 in Atlanta."

He wrote the number down. "Thank you, Ma'am," he said.

Very faintly, but clearly, he heard Bellmon's voice in the background. "I will be damned, my aide has just decided his greater loyalty is to my wife and daughter!"

"Bob!" Barbara Bellmon said, "that's an *utterly despicable* thing to say!"

And then the phone went dead.

"What was that all about?" Liza asked.

He looked at her and motioned for her to come to him. She hesitated a moment, and then went to him. He put his arms around her.

"Jack Portet is in some kind of trouble with the Air Commandos at Hurlburt," he began.

"I don't know what that means," Liza said against his chest.

"It doesn't matter. Marjorie heard about it and went down there. I saw her on my way here. And I just refused to answer Bellmon when he asked if I know where she is."

She raised her face to his.

"Good. I hope he fires you. I hope he's mad enough to throw you out of the Army."

"He won't do that," Oliver said. "He may fire me. Why not? I have just proven myself to be pretty fucking disloyal."

"Fucking dissel," Allan said very clearly.

"Oh, shit," Oliver said.

"Oh, shit," Allan said, very clearly.

"Allan! Naughty!" Liza said, giving Johnny a dirty look.

"Fucking dissel," Allan said, very pleased with himself.

Oliver told the operator to get him 555–4586 in Atlanta.

"Sutton Holdings," a pleasant female voice said.

Meanwhile, Allan, bent over the kitchen counter with his pants lowered, had his bottom whacked and began to howl.

"Mr. Foxworth Mattingly, please," Johnny said.

"One moment, please, I'll connect you."

"Mr. Mattingly's office," a different but equally pleasant voice said.

"Mr. Mattingly, please. Liza, *please* take him in the other room. I can't hear."

"I'm sorry, Sir, Mr. Mattingly is out of the office. If you'd care to give me your name and number, I'll tell him you have called."

"My name is John Oliver," Johnny said. "Captain John Oliver—"

"Oh, *yes,* Captain *Oliver.* You're Colonel Lowell's friend."

Well, hardly. But why argue?

"Yes, Ma'am. I really have to talk to Mr. Mattingly as soon as possible. Is there some other number where I could get him?"

"I doubt it," she said. "He just left St. Croix for Mexico City. Until he arrives in Mexico City and checks in, I won't have even a number for him. But if it's an emergency—"

"No, it's not an emergency," Johnny said. "But as soon as you do hear from him, would you ask him to please call me?"

"Has he your number?"

"I think he does, but here it is again," Oliver said, and gave her his office, BOQ, and Liza's numbers.

Liza came back in the kitchen as he took a Millers High Life from the refrigerator. He could hear Allan howling in his room, as if his heart were breaking.

"That's your fault—I feel like beating *you,*" she said.

"I'm sorry," he said, genuinely contrite.

"What happened in Atlanta?"

"Mr. Mattingly is out of town, between St. Croix and

Mexico City. When he comes down to earth, he will call me."

"So we have to wait?"

"Oh, no. The ever resourceful John Oliver never says die." Oliver opened the beer bottle, took a swallow from the neck, and went back to the telephone.

"Operator, person-to-person, Colonel Craig Lowell, at Headquarters STRIKE Command, McDill Air Force Base, Florida," he ordered.

He had to repeat the directions twice before the operator understood him, and there was a long delay when she finally got McDill on the line.

"Sir, they want to know who's calling," the operator said.

"Captain John Oliver, aide-de-camp to General Bellmon." *This is personal business; you had no right to say that. Fuck it!*

"Hello, Johnny, what's up?" Lowell came on the line thirty seconds later.

"Sir, there are two things."

"One having to do with the fair Marjorie, no doubt? Are you calling for an enraged Bob Bellmon?"

"No, Sir. General Bellmon doesn't know I'm calling. I saw her just before she drove to Hurlburt."

"I was playing cupid," Lowell said. "Apparently things got a little out of hand. Barbara Bellmon called me awhile back. Have you spoken to her?"

"Yes, Sir."

"Well, relax. Felter sent Portet up there to teach people how to fly in an area he is familiar with. You take my meaning?"

"Yes, Sir."

"Portet's not in trouble. But I'm touched with your concern."

"Sir, there's something else."

"Shoot."

"My sister called up in a rage and said some very rough things to my girl. And me. I suspect it has to do with Mr. Mattingly."

"I guess she is a little pissed," Lowell said. "When people carefully lay plans to screw other people, and then those plans go awry, they tend to become very annoyed."

"Sir?"

"Mattingly called me and told me he'd found out that the trust provided an optional buyout."

"Sir, I don't know what that means."

"It means that either party—that is, you or your sister—is authorized to make a buyout offer to the other party. The other party then has the option of accepting the offer or of sending a check in the same amount and buying it themselves. When I heard what the offer was, I told Mattingly to send the check."

"Sir?"

"They offered you—your sister offered you—a little over three hundred thousand in round figures," Lowell said. "Which meant she *thought*, to be kind, the property was worth six hundred thousand. Mattingly valued the property at a little over two million. He had it appraised by an outside firm, and they said two million three. So I told him to send the check. The exact figure, I think, was three hundred seventeen thousand and change."

Oliver could hardly believe what he was hearing. He was sure he didn't understand it all.

"What check? How could he send a check?"

"Well, he had your power of attorney. So he borrowed the money from the firm, using your share as collateral. That's what investment bankers do, Johnny, loan money on sure things."

"So what happens now?" Oliver asked.

"If she's smart, your sister will come to you on bended knee and ask you to reconsider. If you want to, you can give her say, ninety days, to come up with a fair price—half of the two million three, in other words. Otherwise, according to the trust codicils, you own it—for three hundred thousand and change—thirty days after she signed for the registered letter."

"What would I do with it?" Johnny asked very softly.

"Oh, you'd have no problem getting someone to take it off your hands. You could hire management. . . . We'll cross that bridge when we get there. My guess is that as soon as she talks to a lawyer, she will come crawling. People will crawl long distances on their knees for a million-odd dollars."

"Jesus H. Christ!"

"I told Mattingly to tell you what's going on. But he's in the Virgin Islands. Or Mexico. But trust his judgment, Johnny. He knows what he's doing."

"Sir, this is all beyond me."

"May I speak bluntly?"

"Please do."

"Your sister was trying to cheat you out of a million dollars. She got caught at it."

"That word upsets me," Oliver said. "It's unreal."

" 'Cheat'?" Lowell asked, chuckling. "Or 'a million dollars'?"

"Both."

"You will be surprised how quickly you get used to having a million dollars," Lowell said. "Don't spend it all in one place, Johnny. I have to go."

"Sir, thank you very much." Oliver hung up the phone and turned to face Liza.

"Well?" she said. "What's unreal?"

"A million dollars."

There was concern on her face.

In the movies, he thought, *it wouldn't be like this. People would shout and scream and jump around. I feel like somebody died.*

"What about a million dollars?" Liza asked.

"According to Lowell, that's what my sister was trying to cheat me out of," he said. "And the reason she was so pissed was that Mattingly caught her at it."

"Stop saying pissed," Liza said automatically. "Oh, Johnny, I'm so sorry for you."

"I guess I'm going to have to cry all the way to the bank."

[TWO]

The chimes of the Mrs. Elizabeth Wood residence played, slightly off-key, "There's no place like home."

"Who the hell can that be?" Oliver asked. He was sitting

with Liza on the couch in the living room, slumped down, a glass of scotch resting on his stomach. Allan was on the floor, trying to get a too-large red plastic block into a plastic glass.

"Watch your mouth," she said, and left the couch and answered the door.

"I hate to bother you," Bobby Bellmon's voice said, "but I have to speak to Captain Oliver."

"Come in," Liza said.

"Thank you, no. Could you ask him to come to the door, please?"

"Come in, Bobby, damn it!" Oliver called.

"I'd like to see you alone for a moment, please, Captain Oliver."

"Oh, Jes— Oh, *darn*," Oliver said, and got up and walked to the door. "What's the matter, Bobby?"

"Can I speak with you a moment privately?"

Johnny exchanged a glance with Liza, then went outside and closed the door. It was like stepping into a steam bath.

"OK. What?"

"I want to know where my sister is," Bobby said.

"I don't really know. But I don't think I'd tell you if I did."

"You're a disloyal sonofabitch, Oliver."

"Thank you for the vote of confidence."

"My sister is off no one knows where—fucking an enlisted man—and you probably think that's just fine."

"I don't know that, and neither do you. But if it were true, it's not any of your business, or mine."

"You tell me where she is or I will kick the living shit out of you."

"Your ass is showing, Bobby," Oliver said patiently, with a slight tone of disgust.

Second Lieutenant Robert F. Bellmon, Jr., thereupon struck Captain John S. Oliver upon the face with his fist, causing Captain Oliver's lip to split and throwing him backward against the front door of the Wood residence.

Mrs. Liza Wood, hearing the heavy thump against her door, opened the door.

She saw Captain Oliver stagger to his feet, muttering a foul obscenity. He then struck Lieutenant Bellmon's face and body several times with his fists, and this caused Lieutenant Bellmon, his nose bleeding, to fall upon his back on the lawn and then become nauseated.

"Johnny!" Liza called.

"You dumb little shit!" Oliver said furiously, apparently not hearing her. He bent over Lieutenant Bellmon.

"Johnny, don't!" Liza screamed.

He looked at her in confusion.

"Help me get him in the house," Oliver said, hauling Bobby to his feet. "God, I hope I didn't break his nose."

"What *happened*?" Liza said.

"Go get some ice in a towel."

"You sonofabitch," Bobby said, breathing heavily. "You miserable sonofabitch!"

Jesus, he's going to cry!

"You are in the Army, Lieutenant. I am a captain," Oliver said coldly. "You will shut your mouth and march into the house. That's an order."

[THREE]
123 Brookwood Lane
Ozark, Alabama
1505 Hours 12 July 1964

"Funny," Liza Wood said to Johnny Oliver, "you don't look like a man with a million dollars."

Captain John S. Oliver, aide-de-camp to the commanding general of Fort Rucker, Alabama, was sitting on the concrete floor of the utility room at the end of Liza Wood's carport. He was wearing a pair of athletic shorts and a torn T-shirt, both of which were heavily stained with thick black grease. As were his face and hands. His forehead was beaded with sweat, and there were large sweat damp areas on the T-shirt. In his lap were the parts of the mechanism which was supposed to drive Liza's washing machine. Sitting next to him, similarly attired, and just about as filthy, was Allan.

"That's probably because I don't have it yet," Johnny said as he took the glass of lemonade she held out to him. "Thank you."

"Allan drink."

"Allan says please, Allan gets," Johnny said. "Otherwise Allan can go suck a lemon."

"God, you look awful," Liza said. "It keeps getting bigger. I think you should go see a doctor."

"If and when I get this sonofa— *gun* back together, I'll put an ice pack on it."

"*Please*, Johnny," Allan said.

Allan extended the lemonade to Allan and held the glass as the child drank.

"Can you fix it?" Liza asked.

"Probably not," he said. "But hope springs eternal."

"Why don't you just give up and I'll call Sears tomorrow and have them fix it."

"When I start something, I like to finish it," he said. "Give me another thirty minutes."

He took the glass back from Allan.

"Enough?"

"Nuf."

Oliver handed the glass to Liza, said "Thank you" again, and then watched her legs as she walked back in the house.

"Allan fix," Allan said, handing him a grease-soaked gear.

"Well, you're way ahead of me, pal," Oliver said.

He heard the telephone ring, but paid no attention to it until he heard the screen door from the kitchen to the driveway open.

"It's for you," she said, and added, "General Bellmon."

He pursed his lips and blew against them; there was a faint, shrill whistle.

Allan tried to copy it but failed.

"You finish fixing it while I'm gone, pal," Oliver said, and hoisted himself to his feet with a grunt.

"You can't leave him here alone," Liza said.

"Well, then, you pick him up—he's filthy," Oliver said, and went into the kitchen and took the wall phone from its hook.

Well, what happens now? Has Bobby thought over that ridiculous, if painful, episode for forty-eight hours and decided to manfully confess all to Daddy? Christ, I told him to forget it! Jesus, I hope General Bellmon doesn't try to thank me for not making a case out of it.

"Captain Oliver, Sir," he said to the telephone.

"I hate to break into your off-duty time, Johnny."

"No problem, Sir."

"This is not a secure line, Johnny, so this may sound a little vague."

"Yes, Sir?"

"Sandy's having a little party down at the Gulf. I said I couldn't get away and he suggested that you fill in for me."

What the hell does that mean?

"Yes, Sir?"

"I told him that was fine with me, and then he asked if you could pick him and Red up. Sandy's with Red. And then take the both of them to the Gulf."

"Yes, Sir," Oliver said. "When, Sir?"

"I think it would probably be best if you went over there this afternoon. Would that be possible?"

"Yes, Sir."

"They'll be waiting for you, and they'll fill you in on the details. And then, when you get here, you can bring me up to date on what's happened."

"Yes, Sir. Sir, I'm about to have dinner."

"Well, don't let this interfere with that. Just so long as you get over there sometime today."

"Yes, Sir."

"I'm sorry to do this to you, Johnny, but these things come up."

"No problem, Sir."

When he turned from the telephone, Liza was standing there, watching him, holding Allan on her hip.

"You got your dress all dirty," Oliver said.

"Tell me about it," she said. "Well?"

"I've got to go to Fort Bragg."

"Today?"

"After I've had dinner."

"That's funny," Liza said. "I would have thought that a man with a million dollars could take Sunday afternoon off like a real human being instead of flying halfway across the country on ten minutes' notice at some general's whim."

He met her eyes.

"That's what happens if you're a soldier."

"Really?" she asked sarcastically. "And you're a super soldier, right, so that means you work fourteen hours a day, seven days a week?"

"So it starts again, huh? I wondered how long it would be before it did."

"When you look back on this in your later years," Liza said, "please remember that it started before your million dollars. Whether or not you are spending those sunset years with me."

"I don't suppose you would be interested in taking a shower with Allan and me? I'll let you play with my rubber duckie."

Liza handed Allan to him.

"You got him dirty, you get him clean," she said.

"Or anything else of mine you would like to play with."

"You're wrong, Johnny, if you think you're getting to me through Allan. That backfired on you. I told you once: I have no intention of telling him next week, or five years from now, that 'Sorry, Johnny won't be coming home anymore.' "

"Johnny go bye-bye?"

"Just as far as the shower, kid," Oliver said. "Hey, people get killed by falling out of bed."

"Not out of my bed, they don't," Liza said.

"You'd feel differently if you were old, fat, and flat-chested."

"No, I wouldn't," Liza said sadly. "Be careful when you wash your lip. You don't want to get it infected on top of everything else."

XIX

[ONE]
Pope Air Force Base, North Carolina
1945 Hours 12 July 1964

Johnny Oliver parked the U-8 on the transient ramp, shut it down, and dealt with the Air Force ramp crew. He was wearing a flight suit under a nylon zippered jacket.

A very tall, very thin, Green Grunt captain, a black guy, in fatigues and field jacket, was waiting for him.

"You *are* the airplane for General Hanrahan?" the Green Grunt asked after Oliver climbed down, having reclaimed a zipper bag containing a Class A uniform and some extra shirts from the back seat of the U-8.

"No, actually, I'm the *pilot*," Oliver said, smiling, and offering his hand. "The *airplane* is that thing with the propellers."

"Where's the dog-robber?" the Green Grunt captain asked,

ignoring the hand. "You were supposed to be here by 1700 with the dog-robber."

"Are you constipated, Captain, or are you always this cheerful and charming?"

"I asked you a question."

"I'm General Bellmon's aide-de-camp, if that's what you're asking. If you heard I was supposed to be here by five, you were misinformed."

"General Hanrahan doesn't like to be kept waiting."

"Few people do," Oliver said. "But sometimes that's the way the ball bounces."

"I've got a pickup truck outside Base Operations."

"Where are we going?"

"Camp Mackall," the Captain said.

"What's going on out there?"

"You'll find out when you get there," the Captain said. "You get in the habit around here of not asking too many questions."

"I'll show you my Top Secret clearance if you show me yours," Oliver said.

"Top Secret won't cut it around here."

The pickup truck, painted in camouflage colors and equipped with GI headlights, had an unusual number of radios installed. As soon as he started the engine, the Captain picked up a microphone.

"Piano, Piano Nine," he said.

"Go."

"The dog-robber just got here."

"Hold one," the reply came. There was a ninety-second delay while they backed away from the Base Operations building and started to leave Pope Air Force Base. Pope abuts the Fort Bragg military reservation. "He wants to know if the aircraft is all right."

The Captain looked at Oliver.

"Airplane's fine," Oliver said.

"Piano, he says the airplane's fine."

"Hold one," the reply came, and then a moment later, "He said to bring him out here."

"On the way," the Captain replied. He hung up the microphone.

They were moving by then down a two-lane macadam road. It was growing dark, but Oliver could see known-distance rifle and machine-gun ranges on his right. "Is Camp Mackall a secret or what?" Oliver asked.

"We just don't talk about it much," the Captain said.

"Let's try something safe. Captain, I don't suppose you happen to know a guy named Father Lunsford, do you? A black guy?"

"Is that why you asked, because I'm black?"

"That fact did run through my mind, yeah."

"Well, around here we don't talk about who we know or who we don't know."

"Is your date of rank a military secret, Captain?"

"I made captain a couple of months ago. What's it to you?"

"I am senior to you, Captain," Oliver said, coldly furious. "And with that in mind, why don't you go fuck yourself?"

A few minutes later Oliver saw a civilian store, which meant that they had left the reservation. He was curious about that, but he was determined not to say one more damned word to this icy, nasty, self-satisfied sonofabitch.

And five minutes after that the headlights of the pickup illuminated a fading sign: CAMP MACKALL. U.S. MILITARY RESERVATION. TRESPASSERS WILL BE PROSECUTED.

But there was no gate, and no fence, and no sign of life. They drove another five minutes, and the pickup slowed. The Captain turned off the headlights. The blackout headlights, a narrow slit of light, barely illuminated the road. But as his eyes grew adjusted to the faint light, the Captain picked up speed.

Five minutes later they came out of a stand of trees to the edge of a field. Oliver saw a half-dozen vehicles, jeeps, pickups, a six-by-six, and then a Hughes Loach. The Captain pulled the pickup up beside the other trucks and shut it off.

"This is it," he said.

"No fooling?" Oliver said.

He climbed out of the truck, and only then saw Colonel Sanford T. Felter, in fatigues, and wearing a green beret. As he walked toward him, he saw Brigadier General Paul T. Hanrahan, the head Green Beret in the Army.

He walked up to Hanrahan and saluted. ''Good evening, Sir,'' he said.

Hanrahan and Felter returned his salute.

''If you had gotten here earlier, Oliver,'' Hanrahan said, ''you could have ridden out here with us in the Loach.''

''Sir, General Bellmon said I could have dinner before I came over here,'' Oliver said.

''He's been asking about Father Lunsford, General,'' the Green Grunt Captain said. It was more of an accusation than a simple statement of fact.

''He and Father Lunsford are old pals, Timmons,'' General Hanrahan said. ''They used to take long walks together in the woods.''

''I haven't heard from him lately,'' Oliver said, looking at Colonel Sanford T. Felter.

''He's in the Congo,'' Hanrahan said matter-of-factly, ''walking around in the woods. I thought you knew.''

''He's all right, Johnny,'' Felter said. ''I heard from him yesterday.''

There was just enough light for Oliver to be able to see the Green Grunt Captain's eyes widen in surprise at the exchange.

Up yours, buddy! Don't lay any of your Green Grunt bullshit on me!

''I'm really sorry General Bellmon couldn't get away,'' Hanrahan went on. ''I would have liked for him to see this.''

''Sir, what am I looking at?''

Felter chuckled.

''Johnny,'' Felter said, ''Sperry came up with a new navigation system. 'Inertial.' You familiar with it?''

''I've read about it, Sir,'' Oliver said. What he had read was that a combination of gyros and computers established an artificial departure point and then produced a second-by-second readout of how far the aircraft had come from that point. If the destination point was known, all a pilot had to do was fly the needles to get there. No contact with on-the-ground navigation aids was required. ''I didn't know it was operational.''

''It's not,'' Felter said. ''It's supposed to be accurate within a hundred yards per hundred miles. We're about to find out.

There's a couple of C-130s up there somewhere that took off from Fort Riley. When they think they're over here, they're going to drop an A-Team from each airplane.''

''It'll be handy as hell if it works,'' Hanrahan said. ''This is the first time we've really tried it. I'm beginning to have my doubts.''

''Sir?''

''The ETA was ten minutes ago,'' Hanrahan said.

''I don't hear any engines,'' Oliver thought out loud.

''Oh, you won't,'' Hanrahan said tolerantly. ''That's part of the whole idea. They'll be dropped from thirty thousand feet—HALO.'' High Altitude, Low Opening. ''They'll pop their chutes at ten thousand. That will give them some movement across the ground to home in on here. There's a little transmitter going *beep beep* over there.'' He made a vague gesture in the direction of the woods.

Oliver looked up at the sky. There was almost no moon, and he could neither see nor hear anything at all.

Three minutes later, however, there was a noise from the blackness at the end of the field. It sounded for all the world as if someone were beating on a child's tin drum. Someone was. To the musical accompaniment of a $1.98 drum and a harmonica, playing ''When Johnny Comes Marching Home Again, Hurrah! Hurrah!'' two nine-man A-Teams marched out of the darkness.

''I'll be goddamned,'' Hanrahan said in delight.

A man dressed in leather high-altitude flight clothing detached himself from the marching group, walked up to Hanrahan, and saluted.

''Very impressive,'' Hanrahan said.

''It worked like a goddamned jewel, General,'' the man said.

''You could hear the radio all right?''

''Came in five-by-five, Sir, but we didn't need it. We homed in on cigarette coals. I could see them the minute I popped my chute.''

''But the radio worked?'' Hanrahan insisted.

''Yes, Sir!''

''Christ, that's impressive!'' Johnny Oliver blurted.

Hanrahan chuckled. ''We Green Berets are very impressive

people, Captain Oliver. I'm surprised you haven't learned that. Major Dopp, this is Captain John Oliver. He's the guy who got shot down trying to extract Father Lunsford and then had to walk out."

"Father's told me about you," the man in the leather high-altitude clothing said warmly, offering his hand. "He said you're one hard-nosed sonofabitch."

"That would seem to be the pot calling the kettle black," Oliver said.

But I am delighted you said that in the hearing of the asshole here. . . . Up yours, Captain, again.

"We've got room in the Loach, Dopp, if you want to ride back to the post with us," Hanrahan said.

"I appreciate it, Sir," Dopp said. "But I want to eat a little ass before I go back."

"Suit yourself," Hanrahan said. He walked over to the A-teams, which were still in a rough formation. "You guys done good," he said. "Now see if you can stay out of jail." Then he walked down the double line and shook every man's hand.

Sanford T. Felter touched Oliver's arm and nodded toward the Loach, which already had its rotor turning. Oliver started walking to it, realized he was still angry, and turned back to Captain Timmons.

"It's been an experience meeting you, Timmons," he said. "Ranking right up there with the time I had an abscess on my ass."

Then, feeling very pleased with himself, he trotted toward the Loach.

He reached it as General Hanrahan walked up to it. Hanrahan put his hand on Oliver's arm.

"Timmons gave you a hard time?" he asked.

"No problem, Sir."

"Well, you probably won't see him again, Johnny, but if you do: he got the word yesterday that his brother got blown away."

"Oh, shit!"

"No way you could have known," Hanrahan said. He held open the Loach door so Oliver could climb in the back with Felter. Twenty seconds later they were light on the skids.

[TWO]
Hurlburt Air Force Base, Florida
0845 Hours 13 July 1964

"Hurlburt, Army Six Zero Six over the outer marker."

"Army Six Zero Six, you are cleared as number two to land after the C-130 on final. Beware of jet turbulence. The time is one five past the hour. The altimeter is two niner niner niner. Ceiling and visibility unlimited. The winds are ten to fifteen from the north. Please advise your Code Seven that he will be met."

"Roger, Hurlburt," Oliver said to the microphone. "Understand Three Six. I have the One Thirty in sight. You want to close me out, please? I filed to Eglin."

"Roger, we'll close you out."

"Hurlburt, Air Force Four Two, on the deck at one five past the hour."

"Four Two, roger. Four Two, take the night taxiway, left."

"Next left, roger."

"Army Six Zero Six, you are clear to land. If conditions permit, take your first left taxiway. The One Thirty went in a little long."

"First left, roger," Oliver said. He brought the U-8 in low over the bright blue waters of the Gulf of Mexico, flashed over the wide beach, and then a highway, and put the wheels of the U-8 on the runway a hundred feet from the threshold.

"Well, I see that we have cheated death again," Brigadier General Paul T. Hanrahan said solemnly.

Oliver looked over at him and smiled. The Commandant of the U.S. Army Special Warfare School, the titular head Green Beret, smiled mischievously back.

"Hurlburt Ground," Johnny said to the microphone, "Six Zero Six on taxiway two right. Where do I go?"

"A Follow Me will meet you, Zero Six."

"OK. I have him in sight," Oliver said.

A Chevrolet pickup, painted in a yellow and black checkerboard pattern, came bouncing over the grass toward them. He pulled in front of them and led them down the taxiway to another taxiway, and then to a remote corner of the field. There a Sikorsky CH-19 with Air Force markings sat waiting.

A man who was obviously its pilot was sitting on the main gear wheel.

Oliver was not at all surprised that Brigadier General Hanrahan and Colonel Felter, now in his customary baggy gray suit, helped him, *insisted* on helping him, tie the U-8 down. He had learned long ago that only majors and lieutenant colonels, especially newly promoted ones, considered that sort of thing beneath their dignity.

By the time they were finished, the Air Force had wound up the CH-19. And as soon as they sat down on the pipe-and-nylon seats it went light on its wheels.

''For an historical note,'' Felter shouted in Oliver's ear, ''Dick Fullbright found out the field we're using is the one Jimmy Doolittle used to practice taking B-25s off an aircraft carrier.''

Oliver nodded his understanding, but it was a moment before he really did understand, remembering that in the early days of War II, Jimmy Doolittle led a flight of B-25s to bomb Japan: they took off from an aircraft carrier. It turned out that they didn't really do much damage, but it was an incredible act of heroism, for which, Oliver recalled now, Doolittle had been given the Medal of Honor, that gave the Japanese a kick in the teeth—and American morale a sorely needed boost.

When they arrived, all they found was a small strip in the middle of the enormous Eglin Air Force Base reservation—and several rather bedraggled buildings. As they approached, a glistening B-26 appeared to their right, dropped its gear, lined up with the runway, and landed.

Oliver looked at it with a pilot's fascination for a new aircraft. He was watching an airframe that was nearly as old as he was. The first B-26 had been built for the Army Air Corps in 1940. But Felter had told him the night before, over a roast lamb dinner in Hanrahan's quarters, that the B-26Ks they were going to have a look at at Hurlburt were for all intents and purposes new airplanes. A civilian concern called On Mark Engineering had taken about seventy of the old twin-engine attack bombers from the Air Force aircraft graveyard at Davis–Monthan Air Force Base and rebuilt them from the wheels up. The original 2000hp engines had been replaced with 2500hp ones. Larger internal and new wingtip fuel tanks had been installed. Three .50 caliber machine guns had been installed in each wing, and on the ones at Hurlburt, the bombardier's plastic nose had been replaced with an eight-gun .50 caliber machine-gun battery. There were hard points under the wings for bombs and other external loads, and there was provision to fix six 1,000-pound-thrust JATO bottles to the fuselage. JATO stood for Jet Assisted Take Off, which allowed a heavily laden aircraft to take off from a short runway. The avionics were state of the art.

Felter told him that the aircraft were intended for use in Vietnam, and that the Air Force was "mightily pissed" that the first six off the On Mark production line had been taken away from them, no reason given, and ordered delivered to Supportaire Services at Hurlburt Field, Florida.

Oliver, looking at the airplane start its landing roll, sensed there was something wrong with what he was seeing. After a moment he realized what it was: there were no markings of any kind on the wings, or the fuselage, or anywhere else.

The CH-19 went into a ground hover and turned around. Through the open door Oliver could see five more B-26Ks, and none of them had any markings of any kind either.

Colonel Richard M. Fullbright walked up the CH-19. He was attired in a powder-blue coverall, on which SUPPORTAIRE, INC. was gaudily embroidered.

"We're a little short on brass bands, Red," he said to General Hanrahan. "But if you'd like I'll try to whistle a couple of ruffles and flourishes."

"I love your rompers," Hanrahan said as he climbed out of the helicopter.

"And I see you've brought your dentist with you," Fullbright went on. "And how are you, Doctor Felter, Sir?"

"Oh, for Christ's sake," Felter said impatiently.

"And Captain Oliver," Fullbright said. "The perfect dog-robber. How are you, Johnny?"

"Good morning, Sir."

"They're all here?" Felter asked impatiently.

"And most of the motley crew of drunks and misfits who will fly them," Fullbright said. "The *airplanes* are in fine shape."

"Did Portet get here?" Felter asked.

"That was him in the one that just landed," Fullbright said. "He's getting checked out."

"That's not what I sent him here for," Felter said sharply.

"Hey, Sandy. Don't tell me how to do what you tell me to do," Fullbright said. "If you want these planes in the Congo yesterday, I need him as an IP."

"Is he that good?" Felter asked.

"No. But he's way ahead of everybody else except the guy checking him out. Some of these guys haven't flown an airplane, much less a B-26, since the Korean War. I just told my guy to hire another ten pilots—which will require some funding, incidentally—because I don't think half of the ones I have been able to hire so far are going to be able to cut the mustard."

"Do what you have to do," Felter said after a moment. "Call Finton about the money."

"That's what I've been doing."

"But no military personnel, and that expressly means Portet, are to take these airplanes off the Eglin Reservation, much less to Africa. You understand that?"

"This isn't the first time I've done something like this, Sandy," Fullbright said. "I know the rules."

Jack Portet and a swarthy-skinned man walked across the taxiway to them.

After a moment's visible hesitation, Jack Portet saluted.

"Don't do that," Fullbright said. 'You're a goddamned civilian. Remember that."

"Right now you're in limbo," Felter said. "Red, this is PFC Jack Portet. Before they drafted him, he flew in the Congo. Jack, this is General Hanrahan."

"How do you do, Sir?" Portet said politely.

"How did it go, Jack?" Hanrahan asked. "The flight?"

"Sir, it's one hell of an airplane. With another ten hours I would feel reasonably comfortable to be a copilot," Portet said.

"If it went that well, congratulations," Fullbright said. "You are now an IP, Mr. Portet."

"Is this going to work, Dick?" Felter asked doubtfully.

"I'm wide open to suggestion, Sandy," Fullbright said.

"Particularly in the area of where I could find some qualified pilots."

"Then we'll have to go with what we have," Felter said. "The priority is to nip this Congo thing in the bud."

[THREE]
Aboard U.S. Army U-8D Tail Number 59-77606
Over Eufaula, Alabama
1745 Hours 13 July 1964

Major General Robert F. Bellmon, Sr., sitting in the co-pilot's seat, studied the lined pad in his lap for a moment, shrugged, and looked over at Captain John S. Oliver, who was flying.

He started to speak, then stopped when he saw Oliver reaching for the microphone.

"Lawson, Army Six Zero Six," Oliver said.

"Six Zero Six, Lawson."

"Six Zero Six is U-8 with a Code Eight aboard. I am at one zero thousand, forty miles south of your station. ETA about twelve minutes. Approach and landing, please. And my Code Eight will require ground transport."

As Bellmon listened to the conversation between Johnny Oliver and the Lawson tower, he thought that Oliver sounded tired.

Hell, of course he's tired. Not only has he been flying all over the country, but Felter, Hanrahan, Fullbright, and Company have been throwing a hell of a lot of information at him. And then, when he finally got back to Rucker, there I was waiting for him at Base Ops, to make him fly me up here. I have been pushing him too hard.

Bellmon waited until Oliver had begun his descent.

"I hate to do this to you now, Johnny," Bellmon said, "but it has to be done and I don't want anybody at Benning listening."

"Do what to me, Sir?" Oliver asked innocently.

Bellmon chuckled.

"I took notes during the first part of the lecture," he said. "Let me give it back to you, Johnny," he said, "to make sure I've got it right."

''Yes, Sir.''

''Felter believes the current situation in the Congo, known as the Simba uprising, is going to get a lot worse. Specifically, his scenario says that the rebels will manage to take Stanleyville, and probably within a matter of days. In the worst-case scenario it will be necessary to rescue the staff of the U.S. Consulate, and he presently has two Special Forces A-Teams training to do so. But in any event, there are presently a half dozen B-26Ks at Hurlburt, under Colonel Fullbright. Getting them to the Congo is at the head of the list.''

''Yes, Sir.''

''Rucker's role in this, starting with the B-26s, is to provide whatever assistance, including and especially avionics support, which is to come from SCATSA. The aircraft are in good mechanical shape, and the only thing that may need some help is the avionics.''

''Yes, Sir.''

''Plus ground-handling equipment, et cetera et cetera, as Colonel Fullbright may call for.''

''Yes, Sir.''

''And again in the worst-case scenario, we may need another U-8 with a crew in case something happens to the one Felter sent over there.''

''The one Pappy and Geoff took over there, yes, Sir.''

''Felter is having one sent here from the First Division at Fort Riley, with a crew. It will have extra tanks installed, and the crew will be trained like the other one was except that they won't know why they're being trained.''

''Yes, Sir.''

''And the whole operation is Top Secret,'' Bellmon said. ''How does he think he's going to be able to fly unmarked B-26s in and out of Rucker and not have people ask questions?''

''Sir, Colonel Felter told me to suggest—actually he said, 'politely suggest'—that the best way to handle it is to act as if it's entirely routine, that SCATSA is simply doing the Air Force a favor because they have experience with the avionics that Eglin doesn't. . . . In other words, if anybody asks, they're Air Force aircraft being outfitted at Eglin by Supportaire, Inc., for service in Vietnam.''

"Right now who's privy to all this? At Rucker, I mean? And what about STRIKE?"

"Yourself, Sir; Colonel Augustus; Colonel McNair; and me. At STRIKE Command, Sir, only the C-in-C"—Commander in Chief—"the Chief of Staff, and Colonel Lowell, Sir."

"I'd like to keep it that way," Bellmon said. "Can you stay on top of this by yourself or do you think it would be better if I brought the Chief of Staff, or the G-3, or both of them, in on this?"

That was dumb, Bellmon thought. *You know he's overworked. And you know what he will reply.*

"Sir, Colonel Augustus came down to Hurlburt. He anticipates no problems doing what has to be done. All Colonel McNair has to do is incorporate the standby U-8 and its crew in his flight operations. I don't see where we need the Chief of Staff or the G-3."

That's exactly what I thought you would say, General Bellmon thought.

And Captain Oliver realized what he had just said.

Jesus Christ! You arrogant sonofabitch! Railroad tracks on your shoulders, and you're telling a two-star general that "we" don't need two full colonels.

Bellmon looked at him thoughtfully.

"OK, Johnny, so be it," Bellmon said finally. "Tell Augustus I want any B-26s landing at Cairns to be taken immediately inside the SCATSA hangar."

"Yes, Sir."

"And tell the Cairns operations officer that I want to be notified immediately whenever a B-26 does come to Rucker and when it leaves. And if he can't get me, have him notify you or Sergeant Major James."

"Yes, Sir."

"Anything else?"

"I can't think of anything, Sir."

"The general rule of thumb, Johnny, in situations like this, is that you don't ask questions. If they want you to know something, they'll tell you. Having said that, the Portet boy is involved somehow, isn't he?"

"Yes, Sir. He's checking out the CI—the Supportaire—pilots in the B-26Ks."

"Fullbright has him flying?" Bellmon asked, surprised.

"Yes, Sir. Colonel Felter doesn't like it much, but Colonel Fullbright explained there was no other way."

"I'll be damned," Bellmon said. "You like him, don't you, Johnny?"

"Yes, Sir, I do."

"Well, I suppose that's something," Bellmon said resignedly. "That leaves me and Bobby against all-around popular opinion."

Oliver didn't reply. Instead, he reached for the microphone and told Lawson that he was passing through five thousand and estimated Lawson in five minutes.

What I should do, Bellmon thought, *is just get out of the airplane and tell him to go home and get some rest. But then how would I get home? Well, the least I can do is drive this thing home. And try to remember tomorrow to make him take some time off.*

[FOUR]
Room Seven, Building T-124
Fort Rucker, Alabama
2005 Hours 25 July 1964

Johnny Oliver walked into his room, took off his blouse, took a bottle of beer from the cooler, and looked again at the just-arrived copy of *Playboy.*

The centerspread was missing. A half hour before, while checking Liza's house to make sure everything was all right, he had thumbtacked it inside Allan's bedroom closet. At the time that had seemed to be a splendid idea: when Liza opened the door after she came back from visiting her parents, it would give her cause for thought. That no longer seemed like such a splendid idea.

It's done. To hell with it.

He propped a pillow against the headboard of his bed, stretched out on the bed, took a swig of beer, and started flipping through the magazine.

There was a knock at the bathroom door.

"Come!" Oliver called, and Second Lieutenant Robert F. Bellmon came into the room.

"I thought we were having dinner with Mommy and Daddy," Oliver said.

"Do you always have to be such a wiseass?"

"Why do I suspect that all is not right with your world, Lieutenant Bellmon?"

"How much do you know about what Jack Portet's doing?"

"That falls under a security classification to which you are not authorized access, Lieutenant," Oliver said. "Not to mention that what I know about Jack is none of your fucking business."

"I *know.*"

"I rather doubt that, Bobby," Oliver said. "Knock it off, will you?"

"But you *do know*?"

"Yeah, I know. OK? And it's none of your business, personally or otherwise, so drop the subject, huh?"

"He just took off for Africa," Bobby said. "Did you know that?"

"What are you talking about?"

"He just took off from Cairns in a B-26, and he's going to Africa."

"How do you know that?"

"He came by the house while we were having supper, in his Jaguar. And he asked Marjorie to take care of it for him, and then Cairns called and said that a 'Florida airplane' had just landed, and . . . it all came out. My father was furious."

"Jesus Christ!" Oliver said, and jumped off the bed and went to the three telephones.

"Who are you calling?"

"Your father."

"Johnny, if you do that, he'll know I told you!"

"You should have thought of that when you told me," Oliver said, and dialed the number. But when Bellmon came on the line, he did not speak the truth, the whole truth and nothing but the truth.

"Sir, I just heard there was one of the Florida aircraft in here, and I wondered if you had heard."

"I'd heard, Johnny," Bellmon said. "It was that friend of yours. He just left on a rather long trip."

"Sir, Colonel Felter told Colonel Fullbright in my hearing that—my friend—was restricted to the post."

"Yes, I know," Bellmon said. "I just put in a call to Colonel Felter, Johnny, to tell him. And to tell him that some of the more interesting parts of OPERATION EAGLE are known to my wife, my daughter, and Bobby."

"I was afraid that might be the case, Sir."

"I just read Bobby the riot act," Bellmon said. "When you see him, Johnny, it might be a good idea if you did the same. I get the feeling sometimes that he pays more attention to you than he does to me."

"When I see him, Sir, if you think I should, I'll speak to him."

"Do that, please," Bellmon said. "There's the other line, that's probably Felter."

The phone went dead.

Oliver turned to Bobby.

"Thank you," Bobby said, "for not telling him I told you."

"I should have," Oliver said. "You've got to learn to keep your fucking mouth shut. Goddammit, Bobby, this isn't West Point, this is for real."

Bobby looked crushed. Oliver took pity on him.

"As I suppose dear old Dad has already pointed out to you?"

Bobby nodded, and then managed a weak smile.

"Yeah, and that's not all he told me," he said.

"Really?"

"He said that Marjorie is going to marry Jack, and I had better get used to it."

"Well, then, that leaves you alone against the world, doesn't it?"

"My head is bloody but unbowed," Bobby said. "I just don't like that sonofabitch."

Oliver smiled at him.

"Let's go over to the annex," he said, "where I will tell you all about the birds and the bees."

[FIVE]
Room Seven, Building T-124
Fort Rucker, Alabama
1645 Hours 4 August 1964

Captain John S. Oliver, fresh from the shower, had just pulled on a pair of Levi's when there was a knock at the door. Bare-chested, barefoot, still buttoning his fly, he walked to it and pulled it open.

"Hi, there," Marjorie Bellmon said. "I'm the Ding-Dong lady and we're running a special. Can I come in?"

"Yeah, sure," he said. "Come on."

"This won't take long. I'm just glad I caught you. Daddy said he'd ordered you to take a seventy-two-hour pass. What was that all about?"

"Leave the door open!" he said sharply.

"Worried about your reputation or mine?" Marjorie asked.

"Come on. You're an Army brat. You know what kind of dame hangs around BOQs."

"My reputation is already compromised," Marjorie said. "I am the General's daughter who's fooling around with the PFC. You mean you haven't heard?"

"Come on, Marjorie," Oliver said uncomfortably.

"What's with the seventy-two-hour pass?" she asked.

"I fell asleep in the airplane on the way home," he said, a touch of embarrassment in his voice.

"You were flying?" she asked, horrified.

"He was," Oliver said. "But he now is convinced he's been overworking me."

"And he has," Marjorie said. "Mother even said so."

"He works more hours than I do."

"He told Mother he added it up, and you had flown twenty-six hours in four days," she said. " 'In addition to your other duties.' "

"Your father likes to move around a lot," he said. "I'm the guy who drives the airplane."

"And what if you had been flying when you fell asleep?" Marjorie challenged.

"Your father was too much of a gentleman to mention that. He just told me not to show my face for seventy-two hours."

"I don't know what was going on up there," she said. "Why did you have to fly so much? Where did you go?"

"From one farmer's field to another. It was Exercise HAWK BLADE, which was the dress rehearsal for AIR ASSAULT II."

"What did Daddy have to do with that?"

"Officially, nothing. But General Wendall knows he needs all the help he can get, so he put your father to work as another pair of eyes. We went around looking for things that had gone wrong, or were about to. It was important. If the 11th Air Assault blows AIR ASSAULT II, which is a real possibility, your father and I can go back to driving tanks. There won't be an airmobile division."

"Isn't that a little strong?" she asked.

"No, I don't think so. The story as I get it is that the Army has to produce. The 11th is now big enough and has enough equipment to conduct a real test. AIR ASSAULT II will either make or break the whole idea. The Army can field an airmobile division or it can't."

"But we know it can," she said loyally.

"The Air Force says not. And they're going to try to prove that they can do it better. When AIR ASSAULT II is running, the Air Force is going to run GOLDFIRE I, moving the 1st Infantry Division around in Air Force airplanes. If they can do that more efficiently, so long 11th Air Assault Division [Test]."

"Daddy didn't say anything about that," Marjorie asked.

"Then maybe I shouldn't have," Oliver said. "What's up, Marjorie?"

"Jack."

"What about Jack?"

"Jack is at Fort Bragg."

"He is?" Oliver said, genuinely surprised. "You sure?"

"He called me," she said. "I'm sure."

The last word Oliver had had on Portet was that after he had flown the B-26K to the Kamina Air Base in the Congo, Colonel Felter had had him sent to Berlin. Felter had been furious with Fullbright for ordering Portet to fly the B-26K against what he thought had been clear orders.

Unpleasant reality had overwhelmed even Felter's worst-case scenario. The rebellion had been more than the Army of the Republic of the Congo could handle. Thousands of square miles, including Stanleyville, had fallen to the ''Simba Army of Liberation.'' Sixteen hundred ''Europeans,'' including the staff of the U.S. Consulate and sixty-odd other Americans, among them Jack Portet's mother and sister, and Ursula Craig and her baby, who had been caught there returning from Europe, were being held hostage by people who regularly announced their willingness to execute them all if they didn't get their way.

Political opinion was sharply divided between those who felt American intervention was necessary and those who thought the problem could be resolved by diplomatic negotiation. Felter had explained to Oliver that if it became known to any of several people in what was known as ''the Congo Working Group'' that one of the B-26Ks had been flown to the Congo by someone in the military, it would be leaked to the press. Jack Portet was a soldier—even if he had flown the airplane over there in civvies and was ostensibly a civilian employee of Supportaire, Inc.

And that in turn could very well have meant the end of all efforts to rescue the hostage Americans. It could even possibly have resulted in America's having to give in to African Nationalist pressure to cease both overt and covert aid to the Congolese government. Felter's solution to the problem of PFC Portet and the B-26K was to have Portet assigned to the U.S. Army garrison in Berlin, as a German language interpreter.

''What's he doing at Bragg?'' Oliver asked.

''That's what I want you to tell me,'' Marjorie said.

''I don't know.''

''You don't know or won't tell me?''

''I don't know, but I probably wouldn't tell you if I did. Why don't you ask him? Or did you ask him and he told you to butt out?''

''He called me from the Fayetteville Airport and said he didn't know what he was going to do; he was assigned to the 7th Special Forces Group.''

I know what's he doing. He's working with those HALO A-Teams I saw, because of his knowledge of Stanleyville.

"Well, then, you know. He's running around in the woods, eating snakes," Oliver said.

"When I called the 7th Group, they said they never heard of him."

"You call Post Locator?"

"Of course," she said. "I started there. I know he's there, and I want to know why, and why they won't tell me."

"Marjorie, honest to God, I don't know," Oliver said.

She met his eyes for a moment.

"OK," she said. "How long do you think it will take me, in a Jaguar, to drive from here to Bragg?"

That's right, she's got Portet's Jag.

"Why don't you just sit still and wait till he calls again?"

"Because I can't, that's why," Marjorie said.

"You listen to Johnny, Marjorie," Bobby Bellmon said behind Oliver.

Oliver spun around, furious.

"You little shit!" he exploded. "How dare you eavesdrop at my door?"

"I recognized her voice," Bobby said, unrepentant. "She's my *sister*, for God's sake."

"Oh, goddammit!" Oliver said.

"You listen to Johnny, Marjorie," Bobby repeated.

"I'm going to Bragg," Marjorie said. "If Bobby doesn't get right on the phone and squeal on me, Johnny, would you call my mother later and tell her where I am?"

"At least let me try to find out something at Bragg," Johnny said. "Before you run off."

"Go ahead."

Both the officer of the day at Headquarters, U.S. Army 7th Special Forces Group and the sergeant on duty at the Fort Bragg, North Carolina, Post Locator denied any knowledge of a PFC Jacques Emile Portet.

"Call General Hanrahan," Marjorie said. "He'd tell you."

"I can't do that, Marjorie," Oliver said.

"He can't do that, Marjorie," Bobby said righteously.

"Bobby, I don't need any help," Oliver said.

"Sorry I asked," Marjorie said.

"Hey!" Oliver said.

"Call my mother and tell her where I went," Marjorie said and walked out of the room.

Oliver turned to Bobby.

"If I ever catch you with your ear to my keyhole again, Bobby," he said furiously, "I'll kick your ass into next week. You read me?"

Bobby nodded and then shrugged.

"I'll be gone in a couple of days, anyway," he said.

"What the hell does that mean?" Oliver demanded, still furious.

"It means I'm getting an elimination check-ride tomorrow and I don't think I'm going to pass it," Bobby said.

"Why not?"

"Because I can't *fly,* that's why."

"Oh, bullshit. Flying is no more difficult than riding a bicycle. What's wrong?"

"I just told you," Bobby said. "Great week for the Old Man, huh? His daughter runs off to Fort Bragg after a goddamned PFC and his son busts out of flight school for 'inadaptability'—read, stupidity."

"What are you having trouble with?"

"Does it matter? Everything."

"You really can be a pain in the ass sometimes," Oliver said as he picked up one of the three telephones and started to dial. "You're a pimple on an abscess."

Bobby started to walk out of the room.

"Come back here," Oliver ordered sharply. "Where the fuck do you think you're going?"

Bobby stopped and turned and looked at him.

"Major, this is Captain Oliver, General Bellmon's aide. Sir, I need a little Huey time and I just fell into several free hours and wondered if you've got something out there I could borrow." There was a brief pause, and then Oliver said, "Thank you very much, Sir. I'll be right out."

"What's that all about?" Bobby asked.

"You're pretty smart, what did it sound like?" Oliver said. "Put a flight suit on and meet me at that strip on the Ozark Highway."

"We can't do that," Bobby said. "That's against regulations."

"I am going flying. I am taking you along for a ride. What's against regulations?"

"I'll know," Bobby said. "It's dishonest. It's unfair to the others."

"So it is. Welcome to the real world, Bobby. Generals' daughters fall in love with PFCs and make asses of themselves over their men just like ordinary human beings, and generals' sons get a little bootleg instruction from their fathers' aides."

"I couldn't look him in the face," Bobby said.

"What do you think his face is going to look like when you tell him you've busted out of flight school? Or your mother's, for that matter?"

"If he found out he'd fire you. He'd have to."

"You want the fucking wings or not?" Oliver asked. "What I'm going to do now is go wind up a Huey and sit it down on the Ozark Highway strip. If you're there, fine. If you're not, you will be a selfish little prick who considers his high ethical standards more important than breaking his father's heart."

Oliver went to his closet, grabbed a flight suit and his helmet, and walked out of the room.

When he put the skids of the Huey on the ground at the tactical strip next to the Ozark Highway, Bobby was waiting for him.

XX

[ONE]
Headquarters, 11th Air Assault Division [Test]
Harmony Church
Fort Benning, Georgia
0845 Hours 14 October 1964

Brigadier General George F. Rand escorted into the VIP map room one more of the many distinguished visitors who were on hand to watch the beginning of Exercise AIR ASSAULT II.

There were simply too many senior officers there to permit them, and their aides and assistants, to wander at will around the maps in the G-3 Division's office space. As a consequence of that, an adjacent room in the white, two-story, frame, World War II building had been emptied of the rows of filing cabinets used by the G-1 [Personnel] Division and turned into a VIP map room. Duplicates of the G-3 maps were put up on the walls; and chairs, both upholstered and folding, were set up. The Signal Section had installed telephones, and two coffee machines and stacks of china mugs were placed on a folding table.

"The post," that is to say, Headquarters, Fort Benning and the U.S. Army Infantry Center, had been asked for help. And they had provided cars and drivers for the visiting VIPs; and, in response to a request for some bright enlisted people to help with the maps, they had sent over eight crisply turned out young enlisted people, six of them female.

The VIP who Brigadier General George F. Rand ushered into the VIP map room was Lieutenant General Richard J. Cronin, Deputy Chief of Staff for Operations, United States Air Force.

General Cronin looked around the room, found an upholstered chair with his name Scotch-taped to it, and then surprised General Rand by walking to the front wall of the room. There, under the eyes of a young captain, one of the female soldiers was marking the latest position of Hurricane Isbell with a grease pencil on a six-by-twelve-foot map of the eastern coast of the United States from Florida through Virginia.

"I thought you'd be out flying," he said, and Captain John S. Oliver turned in surprise to look at him.

"Good morning, Sir," he said, and took General Cronin's offered hand.

"You know Johnny, do you, Sir?" General Rand said.

"Sure," Cronin said. "What have they got you doing, Oliver?"

"I'm trying to make myself useful, Sir," Oliver said. "I had in mind flying, but I suppose we also serve who make grease-pencil marks on weather maps."

The female Spec Five actually working on the map looked over her shoulder and smiled at him.

"What's the weather like?" Cronin asked.

"I would say that God is on the side of the Air Force, Sir," Oliver said, and pointed to the map. "Here's the center of Hurricane Isbell, which is moving north-northeast at about twenty knots. On the Georgia coast here, we have severe rain, winds gusting to fifty knots, and a pretty good indication that conditions will worsen. We have an assault-helicopter battalion here"—he pointed to the airfield at Fort Stewart, Georgia, near Savannah—"where the winds have already turned over two choppers on their pads. Here on the right, where Colonel Buchanan's battalion is, visibility is down to zilch, with heavy rains. And in the center, on Colonel Seneff's battalion's route, in the mountains, some visibility, under a ceiling of five to seven thousand feet, which means a lot of rock-filled clouds."

"Just before we landed," General Cronin said, "it came over the horn that flight operations—*our* flight operations—have been suspended from here"—he pointed to a point in Florida near the Georgia border and then to a point near the North Carolina-Virginia border—"to here, and two hundred miles inland."

Then he turned to General Rand. "What are you going to do, George, call it off, reschedule it?"

"Not yet," Rand said.

"We think we can fly through this, General," Oliver said. "We've sent reconnaissance ships out, looking for holes in the soup."

"Visually, you mean?" Cronin asked. "Holes radar can't find?"

"Yes, Sir."

"That doesn't seem to be a very good way to become an old aviator," General Cronin said.

"Yes, Sir, that's just what I told General Bellmon when he took off in a Mohawk."

"He's out there flying in this stuff?" Cronin asked, genuinely surprised.

"Yes, Sir," General Rand said.

"I will not say, in front of this junior officer and this young lady, that I thought he had more brains than that," General Cronin said, "but that thought does occur to me."

"Sir," Oliver said, "those of us who aren't fortunate enough to have aircraft which permit us to fly over weather have to learn to fly through it."

Cronin looked at him and laughed.

"Touché, Captain," he said. Then he grew serious. "Straight answer, Oliver. Is it going to go?"

"We're going to give it a hell of a shot, Sir."

"Isn't that a little foolish, George?" General Cronin asked.

"I guess I meant to say dangerous. Wouldn't it be better to reschedule?"

"Sir," Rand said, "at the risk of stepping over the line, if we called off AIR ASSAULT II for any reason, those who feel the concept of an airmobile division is wishful thinking would consider their opinion proven. On the other hand, if we *can* move a battalion—carried in one hundred and twenty Chinooks—through these weather conditions, I think we'll be able to say that we have proved it will work."

"And the risk to those involved?"

"General Wendall called each aviation battalion and made it clear that anyone who was uncomfortable flying was free to stay on the ground."

"And did that offer extend to the troops aboard the Chinooks?" General Cronin asked.

After a pause General Rand said, "No, Sir. The decision whether or not to fly was left to the pilots."

General Cronin did not reply.

"It's 0900, Sir," Oliver said. "AIR ASSAULT II just began."

"I find myself ambivalent about this," General Cronin said thoughtfully. "I find myself hoping that you will fall flat on your faces and end this Army Air Force nonsense once and for all. And on the other hand, maybe, as a pilot, I sort of hope you make it."

Neither Rand nor Oliver replied for a moment, and then Rand said, "Thank you, General."

"How many pilots elected not to go?" Cronin asked.

"No one opted out, Sir," Rand said.

"I would hate to be General Wendall right now," Cronin said.

[TWO]
Office of the Deputy Commanding General
11th Air Assault Division [Test]
Harmony Church
Fort Benning, Georgia
1015 Hours 14 October 1964

Brigadier General George Rand was sitting at his desk, looking out at the driving rain. His feet were on the windowsill, and a now-cold china mug of coffee rested untouched in his hands. He turned and looked over his shoulder when he heard the knock.

''Captain Oliver, General,'' Lieutenant Howard F. Mitchell, General Rand's aide-de-camp, said.

''Come in, Johnny,'' Rand called, and swung himself around from his window.

''Sir, we just heard from Colonel Seneff,'' Oliver said.

''He's on the ground and can't move,'' Rand said.

''He's through the mountains with his battalion, Sir. The other two battalions are following. They should be at the LZ in forty-five minutes.''

''An hour late,'' Rand said.

''They came through, Sir. Through a hurricane.''

''The *edges* of a hurricane.''

''Through weather which caused the Air Force to ground everything they have,'' Oliver insisted.

''Anybody down?''

''No, Sir. There were five aborts, but the backup ships took care of that.''

''Thank God,'' Rand said.

''The Army today proved that not even a hurricane can stop a battalion-strength airmobile assault on a target one hundred miles inside the enemy's lines.''

Rand smiled at him.

''You sound like a press agent, Johnny,'' he said, ''You ever think about becoming a PIO?'' Public Information Officer.

''No, Sir,'' Oliver chuckled.

''Well then, how about becoming an administrative assistant?'' Rand asked.

''Sir?''

"To the Deputy Commanding General of the 11th Air Assault Division?"

Oliver hesitated.

"Sir, are you pulling my leg?"

"No. Not at all. Last night General Bellmon was talking about you. He said that your year's tour as his aide is about up, and he's really going to miss you. That started me thinking."

"Sir, with respect, I don't want to go from one aide's job to another."

"I didn't say aide. I have an aide. We're still writing the TO and E around here. It seems to me I need somebody who knows his way around a headquarters, is a dual-qualified aviator, and, most important, knows his way around Vietnam. Maybe administrative assistant is the wrong title. We could work on that."

"What would I do, Sir?"

"What you did today, make yourself useful. Probably as important, sit on me when I become a too-confident aviator."

"Sir, what I would like to have is a company. I had one, for a little while, in 'Nam."

"Aviation companies are now commanded by majors," Rand said. "The only way you're going to get a company is to become a major. Let me throw this in the pot, Oliver. If we go to Vietnam—and there's no doubt in my mind, as of two minutes ago, that we are going—General Wendall will have some leeway in promoting outstanding officers. What I'm saying is that if you came to work for me, you'd probably get to put a gold leaf on your collar faster than any other way I can think of."

"I hadn't really given much thought, Sir, to what I'll do after my tour with General Bellmon is over."

"Well, think about it. Let me talk about it to him. And think about my wife."

"Sir?"

"My wife would be a lot more at ease if she thought you were driving me around. She hasn't said it out loud, but I know she thinks they shouldn't let old men like me fly around by themselves."

"Sir, I'm flattered by the offer—"

"So think about it," Rand repeated. "Have you mentioned Colonel Seneff getting through to General Cronin?"

"No, Sir. I sort of thought you would like to do that yourself."

"Indeed, I would," General Rand said, standing up.

[THREE]
Office of the Commanding General
The Army Aviation Center & Fort Rucker, Alabama
1600 Hours 1 December 1964

Captain John S. Oliver knocked at the open doorjamb of General Bellmon's office, who waved him inside.

"The *New York Times*," Oliver said, laying a stack of newspapers on Bellmon's desk, "the *Atlanta Constitution*, and the *Baltimore Sun*."

"You are a very resourceful young man, Oliver," Bellmon said as he spread the newspapers on his desk. "How did you manage this?"

"I called the departing-passenger lounge at the Atlanta airport and had them page the senior officer headed for Fort Rucker. I got two lieutenant colonels and a captain with delusions of grandeur."

Bellmon chuckled. "Did you really?"

"Yes, Sir, and I just expressed to the senior Lieutenant Colonel your deep appreciation for the favor of bringing the newspapers."

"I'm going to miss you around here, Johnny," Bellmon said.

The headlines on all three newspapers said essentially the same thing.

BELGIAN PARATROOPS JUMP ON STANLEYVILLE;
100S OF HOSTAGES REPORTED KILLED; MOST SAVED

USAF DROPS BELGIAN PARACHUTE BATTALION
ON STANLEYVILLE; MOST HOSTAGES FREED

MOST OF 1600 HUNDRED STANLEYVILLE HOSTAGES
FREED BY JOINT US–BELGIAN PARACHUTE RAID IN
CONGO

The photograph in all three newspapers was identical. It showed a helmeted Belgian paratrooper, in camouflage uniform, a bloody bandage across his nose and upper face, carrying a blonde girl of about ten in his arms.

Bellmon and Oliver read the lead story and all the sidebars.

"Nothing about anybody named Portet, Craig, or Lunsford that I can find," Oliver said.

"Lunsford?" Bellmon asked.

"He's a Green Grunt captain, Sir. A pal of mine. He's been running around in the woods over there with the Simbas."

"Well, if there was bad news, we would have heard," Bellmon said. "Portet I'm not worried about." When he saw the look on Oliver's face, he added, "What I meant to say is if Jack Portet got to Europe, which I doubt—I think he's sitting at Camp Mackall under a quarantine—he wasn't involved in the jump. And if he did get to Europe, he's probably in the bar of the King Leopold Hotel in Brussels. But I was hoping I would see something about the Craigs."

He stood up and put the newspapers back together.

"Not that they'll do them any good," Bellmon said. "But Marjorie and my wife will be interested in these. I'm going home."

"Yes, Sir. Is there anything else you need from me, Sir?"

"Just the one thing, Johnny. I alluded to it before and you ignored me."

"Sir?"

"When I said I was going to miss you around here," Bellmon said. "By ten tomorrow morning, I want the names of six company-grade officers from whom I can pick your replacement."

"Sir, it's just the first of December."

"You'll report to General Rand 1 January. Spend the time between now and then in transition, easing out of here, and easing in up there. So far as I know, you will be the Army's first executive assistant to an assistant division commander. You owe me for that, by the way. 'Administrative assistant' would have sounded as if you were in charge of the Red Cross fund drive."

"Yes, Sir," Oliver chuckled. "I appreciate that. Thank you."

An hour later, Bellmon called Oliver in Annex #1. "I just talked to Felter," he said. "The Craigs and Portet's mother and sister are safe in Kinshasa. Your friend . . . what was his name?"

"Lunsford, Sir?"

"Captain Lunsford came through it all right. They're flying him to Walter Reed."

"Well, thank God for that," Oliver said. "And Jack?"

"What's the matter, Captain, don't you read the newspapers?"

"Sir?"

"You should really pay more attention to newspaper photographs."

"Sir, I don't understand."

"That Belgian paratrooper with the bandaged face?"

"Yes, Sir?"

"That was Jack. The little girl was his sister. Marjorie spotted it thirty seconds after I assured her Jack was at Fort Bragg, waiting for the security quarantine to be lifted."

"I'll be damned," Oliver said.

[FOUR]
123 Brookwood Lane
Ozark, Alabama
1730 Hours 1 December 1964

"Well, I'm happy for Marjorie," Liza said. "You don't think Jack is badly hurt?"

"We would have heard, I think, if he was. I expect he's already on his way home. Here, I mean. I think they'll get him out of the Congo as quickly as they can, even if his home is really there."

Liza grunted her agreement.

"Speaking of which," Johnny said.

"What which?"

"Home. Homes. Residence. Real estate."

"What are you talking about?"

"Why don't we go up to Columbus tomorrow and find a house? General Bellmon told me I was to 'ease in' up there between now and the first of the month." Fort Benning abuts Columbus, Georgia.

She walked into the kitchen without a word. Oliver followed her.

"What did I say wrong?" he asked.

"It's what you didn't say," she said, her back to him. "What I was waiting to hear was, 'Well, I submitted my resignation today.' "

"Jesus, honey, you're being unfair!"

"I haven't changed," she said. "I told you how I felt from the beginning."

"Liza, for God's sake! I love you."

"If you loved me you'd get out of the Army and let us build a life together. You're a damned fool, that's what you are. Don't tell me you love me!"

"I can't get out of the Army. I'm a soldier. I couldn't go into the real estate business. Think that through, for Christ's sake! Can you see me selling houses?"

"As a matter of fact I can. But you don't have to sell houses. You've got a million dollars . . ."

"Not yet, I don't," he said lamely.

"You'll have it soon enough. You can do anything you want to do. My God, we could go to the Virgin Islands!"

"The *Virgin Islands*? What the hell would we do in the Virgin Islands?"

"There was a story in *Real Estate Monthly* . . ."

"Jesus!"

"Lie on the beach. Make babies. You'd find something that would interest you. We would be together. In six months you'd wonder why you stayed in the Army as long as you did."

"In six months I'd be a drunk. A rich drunk, maybe, but a drunk."

"Thanks a lot," Liza said. "I didn't realize you thought I was that much of a bore."

"Honey!"

"Get out, Johnny. Just go."

He looked at her back. He saw it start to heave. She was crying. He went to her and touched her and she spun around and there was fury in her face.

"Just get the hell out!" she shouted, and he felt her spittle on his face.

"Liza!"

"Just go. For Christ's sake, just go!"

He looked at her a moment, then nodded and walked out of the house.

[FIVE]
Walter Reed U.S. Army Medical Center
Washington, D.C.
0930 Hours 12 December 1964

Brigadier General James R. McClintock, Medical Corps, U.S. Army, a tall, silver-haired, hawk-faced man of forty-six, arrived in the ward unannounced. He was wearing a white smock over a uniform shirt and trousers. The smock bore an embroidered caduceus, the insignia of the U.S. Army Medical Corps; but it did not have pinned to it, as regulations required, the small oblong black piece of plastic he had been issued, and on which was engraved his rank and name and branch of service.

He did not have to look down at his chest to remind himself who he was, General McClintock often informed his aide-de-camp when the question of the missing name tag came up. And if there was a question as to his identity in the minds of the staff, the aide should tell them.

General McClintock was alone when he stepped off the elevator. Usually he was trailed by at least his aide, and most often by a small herd of medical personnel. And these people were usually smiling nervously. In addition to being an internist of international repute, General McClintock had a soldier's eye. When he visited a ward, in other words, he was just as likely to spot a military physician whose hair was too long, or whose shoes needed a shine, as he was a misdiagnosis or something wrong with a patient's chart.

He walked across the highly polished linoleum floor to the nurses' station. There were three nurses and two enlisted medical technicians inside. The nurses looked busy, so General McClintock addressed one of the medical technicians:

"Hand me Captain Lunsford's chart, will you, son?"

"Yes, Sir," the technician, a Specialist Six, responded. Specialist Six was an enlisted grade corresponding to Sergeant First Class. He knew who General McClintock was, and consequently his response was far more enthusiastic and militarily crisp than was usually the case. So much so that it caught the attention of the senior nurse, Major Alice J. Martin, ANC, who had been standing with her back to the counter, talking on the telephone. She glanced over her shoulder, hung the phone up in midsentence, and walked quickly to the counter.

"May I be of help, General?" she asked.

"I thought I'd have a last look at Captain Lunsford before he's discharged," McClintock said.

He took the chart from the medical technician. The chart was actually an aluminum folding clipboard. With all the forms clipped in various places inside, it was nearly three inches thick. Then he nodded and smiled and said, "Thank you."

Major Martin headed for the opening in the nurses' station.

"That won't be necessary, Major," he said. "I won't need you. Thank you."

"Sir, he has visitors," Major Martin said, more than a little annoyed and disappointed not to be able to exercise her prerogative of accompanying the chief of internal medical services while he saw a patient on her ward.

"Well," General McClintock said, "he's about to have at least one more."

"He's in 421, General," Major Martin said.

"Yes, I know," General McClintock said. "Thank you."

He walked down the corridor, his rubber-soled shoes making faint squeaking noises on the waxed linoleum.

When he pushed open the door to 421, there were three men inside. Among these was the patient himself, who was sitting on the bed, dressed in civilian clothing, smoking a very large light-green cigar. The patient started to move off the bed when he saw General McClintock, but McClintock, smiling, quickly put up his hand to stop him.

"Stay where you are, Captain," McClintock said.

General McClintock saw that the room was decorated for the holiday season. The decorations, however, might seem somewhat eccentric unless one saw them through the eyes of an officer like this one. The patient had obviously visited the Post Exchange Branch, where he had purchased not only a plastic model of the HU-1B Huey, but four adorable little dolls. One of them was Santa Claus; two were dressed as nurses and one as a doctor.

The Huey was hanging from the central light fixture. The adorable nurse and doctor dolls were hanging, their necks realistically broken, from pipecleaner nooses attached to the Huey's skids. Santa Claus straddled the tail boom of the helicopter, cradling a machine gun in his arms.

The patient was a captain, a Negro male, twenty-six years old, five feet eleven and one half inches tall. At the moment he weighed 144 pounds, which made him twenty-one pounds lighter than he had weighed at his last annual physical examination.

Dr. McClintock noted quickly, professionally, that the whites of the patient's eyes were clear. When they had brought him in, he looked likely to bleed to death through the eyeballs. And he had been ten pounds lighter then than he was now.

His visitors were two Negro males. McClintock confidently identified them as father and brother, although they didn't really look very much alike. The younger of them, the brother, was a tall, light-skinned, thin-faced man who was elegantly dressed in a superbly tailored glen plaid suit and a white-collared, faintly striped blue shirt. The father was short, squat, flat-faced, very dark, and what Dr. McClintock thought of as "comfortably crumpled." He wore a tweed jacket, rumpled flannels, rubber-soled "health" shoes, and a button-down-collar tattersall shirt without a necktie.

"How do you feel, Captain?" Dr. McClintock asked.

"Frankly, Sir," the patient, whose full name was Captain George Washington Lunsford, Infantry, USA, said, "not quite as happy as I was an hour ago when I thought I was being turned loose."

Dr. McClintock raised his eyes from Lunsford's chart and smiled. "All things come to he who waits, Captain," he said. "We're still going to turn you loose. But not just now. Soon."

"Today?"

"Today," McClintock said. "Shortly."

"May I see the chart, Doctor?" Lunsford's father asked. When McClintock looked at him in surprise he added, "I'm a physician."

"Excuse my manners, General," George Washington Lunsford said. "Doctor, may I present my father, Doctor Lunsford? And my brother, Doctor Lunsford?"

"How do you do, Doctor?" McClintock said, handing the elder Lunsford the chart.

"Dad is a surgeon, Doctor. My brother is a shrink," Lunsford said. Then, when McClintock smiled, he added, "Before Charley became a shrink, Dad used to say that shrinks were failed surgeons."

"George, for Christ's sake!" the younger Dr. Lunsford snapped.

"I've heard that," Dr. McClintock said, smiling, "but rarely when one of them was in the same room."

"My God!" the elder Dr. Lunsford said. "I have never seen a case of that before." He extended the chart to McClintock, pointing at a line with his finger.

"It's pretty rare," McClintock said. "Your son has been regarded as a gift from heaven by our parasitologists. I understand he has his own refrigerator in their lab."

"I'll bet he does," the elder Dr. Lunsford said, and showed the chart to his other son, who shook his head in disbelief.

"And they are going to give him his own glass cabinet in the Armed Forces Museum of Pathology," Dr. McClintock said, smiling. "Several of our intense young researchers suggested more or less seriously that we just keep him here as a living specimen-bank."

"Do you *realize* how sick you were?" Dr. Lunsford demanded of his son. "For that matter, still are?"

"I didn't really feel *chipper*, now that you mention it, Dad," Captain Lunsford said, "but there is a silver lining in the cloud. I have been given so many different antibiotics that it is not only absolutely impossible for me to have any known social disease, but I may spread pollen, so to speak, for the next six months or so without any worry about catching anything."

Dr. McClintock and the elder Dr. Lunsford chuckled. The younger Dr. Lunsford shook his head in disgust.

"We think, Doctor," McClintock said, "that everything is under control. We were a little worried, frankly, about the liver, but that seems to have responded remarkably—"

He stopped in midsentence as the door to the room opened suddenly and two men in gray suits walked briskly in. One of them quickly scrutinized the people in the room, then walked quickly to the bathroom, pulled the door open, and looked around inside. Then he stepped inside and pushed the white shower curtain aside.

The other went to the window and closed the vertical blinds, then turned to Dr. McClintock.

"Who are these people, General?" he demanded.

"Who the hell are *you*?" Captain Lunsford demanded icily.

The wide, glossily varnished wooden door to the corridor opened again.

The President of the United States walked in. On his heels was a small, slight, balding man in a rumpled and ill-fitting suit.

"You can leave, thank you," the President said.

"Mr. President—" one of the Secret Service men began to protest.

"Goddammit, you heard me!"

The two Secret Service men, visibly annoyed, left the room.

"How do you feel, son?" the President asked Captain Lunsford with what sounded like genuine concern.

"I'm all right, Sir, thank you," Lunsford replied, a tone of surprise in his voice.

"This your dad?" the President asked.

"Yes, Sir, and my brother."

"Well, you can be proud of this boy, Mr. Lunsford. He's something special."

"It's 'Doctor' Lunsford, Mr. President," Captain Lunsford said.

"No offense, Doctor," the President said. "I didn't know. Usually Colonel Felter tells me things I should know, like that."

"None taken, Mr. President," Dr. Lunsford said.

The President turned to Captain Lunsford.

"I'm sorry I couldn't send the Peace Corps when you asked for them," he said.

"On the whole, Mr. President, I'll take parachutists over the Peace Corps anytime," Lunsford said.

The President ignored that. There was a suggestion that he was annoyed at being interrupted. He went on: "So I thought maybe this might make up for it."

He held out his right arm, behind him. The small man in the rumpled suit put an oblong blue box in it. The President opened the lid and took out a medal.

"That's the Silver Star, Captain," he said. "I understand it will be your third. I can't believe the others are more well deserved than this one."

He stepped to Lunsford and pinned the medal to the lapel of his coat. He did not do so properly; it promptly fell off. Lunsford, in a reflex action, grabbed for it and the open pin buried itself in the heel of his hand.

"Shit!" he said, and then, immediately, "Excuse me, Sir."

"I understand," the President said, chuckling, "that it's the thought that counts." And then there was concern in his voice, as Lunsford pulled the pin free from his hand. "You all right, son?"

"Yes, Sir."

"I told the Chief of Staff to find out if there is some reason your name can't be on the next promotion list to major. I have the feeling he's not going to find any."

Lunsford looked at him but didn't say anything.

"You're one hell of a man, Captain," the President said. "I'm grateful to you. Your country is grateful."

He shook Lunsford's hand, then punched him affectionately on the shoulder, nodded at McClintock, murmured, "General," and walked out of the room.

The small man in the rumpled suit handed Lunsford an 8-by-10 manila envelope.

"Citation's in there, Father," he said. "It's masterful. I wrote it myself."

"Thank you, Colonel," Captain Lunsford said.

"See you soon," the small man said, and left the room.

"Now you understand why we asked you to stick around awhile," General McClintock said.

"I certainly hope that someone will explain to me what just happened," the elder Dr. Lunsford said.

"Who was that little man?" the younger doctor demanded. "What did he call you? *'Father'?* What's *that* about?"

Captain Lunsford ignored him. He opened the manila envelope and took from it the citation that went with the award of the Silver Star. He chuckled. "It's masterful, all right," he said.

"May I see that, George?" the elder Dr. Lunsford asked. Captain Lunsford handed him the citation.

> *By Direction of the President of the United States, The Silver Star Medal is awarded to Captain George Washington Lunsford, Infantry, United States Army.*
>
> *CITATION:*
>
> *During the period 9 February 1964–25 November 1964, while engaged in a mission of great importance, MAJOR [Designate] [Then Captain] LUNSFORD performed extremely demanding duty in an outstanding manner, demonstrating extraordinary professional skill and knowledge, and inspiring his subordinates by the example of his impeccable character and devotion to duty, all in a manner which reflected great credit upon himself and the United States Army.*
>
> *Entered the Military Service from Pennsylvania.*

Dr. Charles Lunsford had stepped behind his father and read the citation over his shoulder.

"What the hell is this, George?" he asked. "It doesn't say a damned thing. It doesn't even say where you were."

"I like the part," George Washington Lunsford said, "where it says *Major* Lunsford. You've got to admit, Charley, that has a *nice* ring to it."

"Put your brain in gear, Charley," the elder Dr. Lunsford said. He looked at his younger son. "I liked the part, George, where the President of the United States looked me in the eye and said, 'You can be proud of this boy. He's something special.' I just wish your mother had driven down with us."

''Yeah,'' Major [Designate] Lunsford said. ''Me, too.''

''Are we free to go now, Doctor?'' the elder Dr. Lunsford asked.

''Absolutely,'' Dr. McClintock said. He put out his hand. ''I prescribe a rich protein diet, some bed rest, and reasonable amounts of alcohol.''

''That's all?'' Dr. Lunsford asked. It was a medical question, between doctors.

''You saw what I prescribed, Doctor. If you don't think that'll handle it, I'd welcome your advice.''

''All I meant to imply . . . the speed of the recovery is amazing.''

''Well, he's young, and he's tough, and he responded well,'' McClintock said. ''And when he gets to Fort Bragg, they'll do a very thorough serology workup and some liver and kidney tests. But that's just a precaution. Our experience here is that the antibiotics and the antiparasitic toxins work very well; possibly, probably, because they've had no chance to build up an immunity.''

''Anemia?'' Dr. Lunsford pursued. ''I didn't like that white cell count.''

''It was really bad when he came in. We decided, finally, that it was a combination of everything, plus malnutrition and exhaustion.'' He smiled at both of them. ''Feed him a lot of steak and eggs.''

''I'm sure his mother will take care of that,'' Dr. Lunsford said. He offered his hand. ''Thank you very much, Doctor.''

''My pleasure,'' Dr. McClintock said, then added: ''If the answer to this is yes, I'm going to feel like a fool. Are you connected with the Medical College of Pennsylvania, Doctor?''

Dr. Lunsford nodded.

''I was right, I feel like a fool,'' General McClintock said. ''Doctor, I just didn't make the connection. Sorry.''

''No reason to feel that way at all,'' Dr. Lunsford said. ''Thank you for the care you gave my boy.''

''Now, that *was* my pleasure.''

[SIX]
226 Providence Drive
Swarthmore, Pennsylvania
1735 Hours 12 December 1964

"Charlene," Major Designate George Washington Lunsford said to Charlene Lunsford Miller, PhD, Allan Whiteman Professor of Sociology at Swarthmore College, "you don't know what the fuck you're talking about."

Major Lunsford offered this opinion of Professor Miller's assessment of the political situation in the Congo at an unfortunate time—two seconds after their mother had pushed open the door to his room, bearing a tray of camembert on crackers and bacon-wrapped oysters.

"George!" their mother said, truly shocked. She was a slight, trim, light-skinned, gray-haired woman wearing a simple black dress with a single strand of pearls.

"Sorry, Mother," Father Lunsford said, truly embarrassed.

"You apologize to your sister!"

"Sorry, Charlene," Father Lunsford said, not very sincerely.

"It's all right, Mother," Professor Miller said, pushing herself out of an upholstered armchair. "I know what he's been through."

Just in time, Father Lunsford stopped the reply that came to his lips: *Screw you, don't you dare humor me.*

"I thought you might want something to nibble on," Mrs. Lunsford said, setting the tray on Father Lunsford's desk. There was an old blanket covering part of the desk. On the blanket were the disassembled parts of a Colt Combat Commander .45 ACP automatic pistol. Lunsford had been cleaning the pistol when his sister came up to welcome him home.

"Not for me, Mother, thank you," Professor Miller said. "I'd better go keep my husband away from the gin."

She walked out of the room.

Lunsford popped a bacon-wrapped oyster in his mouth and chewed appreciatively, mumbling his approval.

Mrs. Lunsford waited until she heard Charlene's heels on the wide wooden steps leading from the second floor to the foyer, then asked, "What was that all about?"

Lunsford shrugged. "It's not important, Mother. My mouth ran away with me. I'm sorry."

"What was it about, George?" Mrs. Lunsford insisted.

"The professor delivered a lecture," Lunsford said. "Apparently the collective wisdom of the faculty of Joseph Stalin U equates what we did in the Congo with some of the more imaginative excesses of Adolf Hitler."

His mother looked at him with troubled eyes and then smiled.

"As a special favor to me, George, could you refrain from referring to Swarthmore as Joseph Stalin University tonight?"

He stepped quickly to her, put his arms around her, and lifted her off her feet.

"You're my girl," he said. "Your wish is my command."

She kissed his cheek as he set her down.

"If you mean that. No politics tonight, agreed?"

"I don't start it," he said. "They start it. They get so excited to have a real live fascist in their midst that they slobber all over themselves waiting for their chance to tell me off."

"I don't think you're a fascist," she said. "Neither does your father. And I don't think the President would have personally given you that medal if he thought you were."

"On that subject," Lunsford said, taking a camembert cracker, "I don't think we should bring up that medal tonight. Not with half the faculty of *Swarthmore College* at table."

She laughed, not entirely happily.

"Too late," she said. "Your father's put it on the phone table in the foyer. He's greeting people, 'Good evening, and, incidentally, let me show you what President Johnson gave George today.' "

Lunsford laughed. "I wondered where the hell it was."

Her eyebrows rose.

"I wondered where, delete expletive, it was," he said.

"Better," she said. "George, these people just don't understand."

"That's what's known as a massive understatement."

"I'm not sure I do," his mother said. "All I know is that I'm proud of you and I thank God you're home."

"Then nothing else matters, Mom. And I give you my word as a field grade, designate, officer and gentleman that I will behave myself tonight."

"Then finish whatever you're doing with that gun, get yourself dressed, and come down. Just about everybody's here and they're all anxious to see you."

"For one reason or another," Lunsford said dryly. Then: "Sorry. Yes, Ma'am. I will be right down. Thank you for the oysters."

She raised her hand and gently touched his cheek. Then she walked out of the room.

Lunsford sat down at his desk again. He opened a drawer, took from it a bottle of Johnnie Walker Black Label and took a pull at its neck.

Then he started putting the Colt Commander back together.

He had been downstairs thirty minutes when he was called to the telephone.

"Captain Lunsford."

"I understand they cured the clap OK, but that they're having trouble with the scabies, crabs, and blue balls," his caller announced.

Captain Lunsford didn't reply for a moment. He was surprised at the emotion he felt.

Then he said, "How you doing, Slats? Robbed any good dogs lately?"

He expected something wiseass from Oliver in return; at the very least a suggestion that he attempt a physiologically impossible coital feat.

"Father," Oliver said seriously, "I know you just got home, but I'd like to buy you a drink."

"I accept. You have some sort of date and place in mind?"

"Now," Oliver said.

"Now? Oliver, you asshole, where are you?"

"In Philly."

"In Philly? How soon can you get here?"

"I'd rather not come out there."

"Why the hell not?" Lunsford asked, confused.

There was a pause and then Oliver said, ''I need to talk to somebody. You're elected.''

''Slats, you sound real down. The widow broke off that famous shaft of yours?''

''Ah, shit, I've got no right to dump this all on you.''

''In a pig's ass, you don't. That broad is giving you a bad time, right?''

''That's part of it. The other part is that I'm supposed to report to Benning as of 1 January to work for General Rand and I don't want to go.''

''They trying to make you a career dog-robber or what?''

''Something like that.''

''Listen to me, Slats. Where are you?''

''Out by some athletic stadium. I just got off I-95.''

''South Philly,'' Lunsford said. ''Is there a great big stainless steel diner—the Philadelphian, something like that?—anywhere around where you are?''

''I'm in it.''

''It'll take me thirty minutes to get there,'' Lunsford said.

''Can you drive? You just got out of the hospital.''

''Don't argue with me, I'm a goddamned major designate. All I want to hear from you is yes, Sir.''

''Yes, Sir.''

''I will come there, and we will find a saloon, and you can pour your heart out to me.''

''Thanks, Father,'' Oliver said emotionally.

''Be at peace, my son,'' Lunsford said sonorously. ''For someone like myself, who has just singlehandedly saved the Congo from the forces of international communism, your minor problems in interpersonal relationships are a mere bagatelle.''

Oliver chuckled. Lunsford was pleased.

''Keep your hands off the waitresses until I get there,'' Father said and hung up.

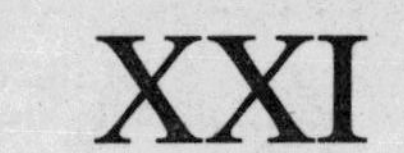

XXI

[ONE]
Office of the Commanding General
The Army Aviation Center & Fort Rucker, Alabama
18 December 1964

Major General Robert F. Bellmon had before him the draft of "The Commanding General's Christmas Message." It had been written for him by his aide-de-camp, Captain Richard J. Hornsby. Captain Hornsby was new on the job, but it had already become apparent to Bellmon that literary skill and finesse were not among his assets. Even worse, he apparently didn't know it. If he had, he would have looked in the file and stolen something from the year before—or the decade before.

Johnny Oliver's statement last year, he thought, might not have been original, but it was head and shoulders above this:

"It is the Commanding General's desire to express joyous wishes of the Yuletide Season to the officers, enlisted personnel, civilian employees and dependents of the Army Aviation Center.''

It went on from there, far, far longer than was necessary, and it grew more stilted and artificial with each sentence.

''Hello, down there, from Mount Olympus! This is your stuffy Commanding General speaking!'' Bellmon thought, and then concluded; *I really hate to jump on his ass so soon, but this just won't cut it.*

At that moment Captain Hornsby, an athletic young man in a well-fitting uniform, appeared at his door.

''Come on in, Dick,'' Bellmon said. ''I was just about to send for you.''

''Yes, Sir?''

''Have another go at this thing. It's a little too long, and see if you can't make it sound a little less like an operations order. See if you can work Mrs. Bellmon and my family into it, too, will you?''

''Yes, Sir,'' Captain Hornsby said. His face mirrored his disappointment and chagrin.

''Have you got something for me, Dick?''

''Yes, Sir. This TWX just came in and I thought you would like to see it.''

Bellmon took it and glanced at it very quickly. It was a Routine message, signed by some colonel for the Adjutant General. It was probably yet one more admonition to him to limit drinking by the troops over the holidays, or, failing that, to keep them from killing themselves on the highway, full of holiday cheer. Whatever it was, it wasn't all that important and could wait for a couple of minutes.

''Dick, there's no way you could have known what I wanted,'' Bellmon said kindly. ''Why don't you look in the file and see what Johnny Oliver wrote for me last year. For that matter, go back several years. General Cairns always wrote his own. He was possessed of greater literary skills than you and me.''

''Yes, Sir,'' Captain Hornsby said. ''Thank you, Sir. I'll do better the second time around.''

''I'm sure you will,'' Bellmon said. He smiled at Hornsby until the young officer had left.

I think I handled that rather well, he decided.

He picked up the TWX, which was printed on a roll of yellowish teletype paper, and read it. The smile vanished. His lips tightened. He clenched his teeth and was aware that his temples were throbbing.

"Sonofabitch!" he muttered and reached for his telephone.

Then he reminded himself of his solemn vow to count to twenty slowly twice before picking up a telephone when he was angry. He slumped back in his chair, and read the TWX again.

ROUTINE

HQ DEPT OF THE ARMY WASH DC 1005 18DEC64

COMMANDING GENERAL

FORT RUCKER AND THE ARMY AVIATION CENTER ALA

ATTN; AVNC-AG

INFO: PERSONAL ATTN MAJ GEN BELLMON

1. SO MUCH OF PARAGRAPH 23, GENERAL ORDER 297, HQ DEPARTMENT OF THE ARMY 29 NOVEMBER 1964 PERTAINING TO CAPT JOHN S. OLIVER ARMOR AS READS "IS RELIEVED OF PRESENT ASSIGNMENT AND TRANSFERRED TO HEADQUARTERS COMPANY 11TH AIR ASSAULT DIVISION FORT BENNING GA EFFECTIVE 1 JAN 1965" IS AMENDED TO READ "IS RELIEVED OF PRESENT ASSIGNMENT AND TRANSFERRED TO HEADQUARTERS JOHN F. KENNEDY CENTER FOR SPECIAL WARFARE FORT BRAGG NC EFFECTIVE 1 JAN 1965."

2. IT IS SUGGESTED THAT SUBJECT OFFICER BE NOTIFIED OF THIS CHANGE AS SOON AS POSSIBLE.

FOR THE ADJUTANT GENERAL
J.C. LESTER LTCOL AGC
ACTING ASSISTANT ADJUTANT GENERAL

Johnny Oliver had been a good aide, a very good aide, a *goddamned* good aide. And not only that, he'd gone above and beyond the call of duty and stuck his neck out as a friend for the Bellmons.

Bellmon wasn't supposed to know, and Barbara and Bobby certainly didn't know he knew, but he had his sources. And he had found out that Bobby was given an elimination check-ride that he had been almost certain to flunk. And then all of a sudden, Bobby had miraculously polished his skills—literally overnight. He'd passed the check ride and gone on and gotten rated.

Bellmon didn't believe in miracles. So he checked that out, first with the instructor pilot, who told him he wouldn't pass Jesus Christ himself if he didn't think he was safe to fly and up to snuff. Bellmon believed him and he looked elsewhere for the answer.

And it turned out that Johnny Oliver was responsible. Fully aware that if he was caught at it he would be permanently taken off flight status himself (not to mention the lousy efficiency report Bellmon would have been obliged to give him), Johnny had taken Bobby out in a helicopter and taught him enough to get him past the check ride.

And Johnny had not waved his General's Aide insignia in anybody's face, either, hiding behind the throne. He had taken the risk knowing that if Bellmon caught him he could kiss his career goodbye. He had done it because he liked Bobby and because he knew Bobby's father would be heartbroken if Bobby busted out.

Not without a certain uneasiness, Bellmon had decided in the end that more harm than good would come from his becoming officially aware of what had taken place. The Army would lose two pilots, and in Johnny Oliver's case, anyway, a bright young officer with great potential.

And that potential was going to be enhanced by work for George Rand in the 11th Air Assault. He would come out of that assignment knowing how a division functioned in combat—not any division, but the Army's first airmobile division. And he'd probably come out with a gold leaf on his collar point, too; and he'd have it justifiably. For he'd have unusual knowledge and experience for an officer of his age and length of service. It was a damned good assignment for him, and for the Army.

And now the orders were changed. Johnny was assigned to The John F. Kennedy Center for Special Warfare.

Those sonsofbitches in Green Berets again!

He was not going to stand still and have those bastards take a perfectly decent, upstanding, *out*standing young officer and ruin him!

He lit a cigarette, and when he saw that his hand was hardly shaking at all, he punched his intercom button and, proud of the control he was now exercising over his voice, he very calmly and politely asked his secretary to see if she could get Brigadier General Hanrahan at the JFK Center at Bragg for him.

"If he's not in his office, Mrs. Delally, try his quarters, please."

General Hanrahan was not in his headquarters. He was not in his quarters either. So General Bellmon had to settle for Mrs. Hanrahan. After he wished her a Merry Christmas, she told him Red was off somewhere with Craig Lowell and that she didn't really expect him back until Christmas Eve.

If he was off with Lieutenant Colonel Craig Lowell, God only knew where they would be. And God, if he had any sense, would probably not want to know.

When Mrs. Delally called the Office of the Adjutant General in the Pentagon, the only officer he could get on the phone, a light colonel, obviously didn't have the brains to blow his nose without illustrated instructions.

"No problem, thank you, Colonel, I'll call again in the morning."

He had less trouble getting Brigadier General George F. Rand on the telephone.

"I have a TWX here, George," he said. "Assigning Johnny Oliver to Red Hanrahan and the snake eaters. You know anything about it?"

"You don't?" Rand asked.

"First I'd heard of it. What do you know?"

"He called me a couple of days ago and very politely said that he'd been offered another job—"

"By Red Hanrahan?" Bellmon interrupted.

"He said 'at the Special Warfare Center,' but I'm sure he

meant Red, because—after I told him I wouldn't stand in his way—Red called me and asked if I minded. He said he had a job for him, with a little less pressure than he's been under. But that if I really needed him—et cetera et cetera."

"Hanrahan wanted him when he first became my aide," Bellmon said.

"But you didn't know about this, huh?"

"Oliver is on leave. It must have come up all of a sudden. George, if I can talk some sense to you, will you still take him?"

"Sure. Love to have him."

"I'm going to look into this. I'll probably get back to you. Thank you, George."

General Bellmon hung up. And then he broke, one by one, six #2 lead, rubber-tipped pencils into inch-long pieces. Then he walked out of his office, smiled at Mrs. Delally and said that he would be going to his quarters, now, to dress for the party.

[TWO]
Annex #1, Officers' Open Mess
Fort Rucker, Alabama
1645 Hours 18 December 1964

Second Lieutenant Robert F. Bellmon, Jr., sat at the bar of Annex #1 drinking Millers High Life from a can and feeling more than a little sorry for himself. He was about to lose the companionship of the officers sitting on either side of him at the bar, Captain John S. Oliver and (newly promoted) First Lieutenant Joseph M. Newell, Jr. Both of them were going to leave Fort Rucker for Fort Benning in the next couple of days; their transfers were official as of 1 January 1965. Jose Newell had been assigned to the Test and Support Directorate because Brigadier General William R. Roberts had convinced the Chief Signal Officer that he would be of more use there than he was at SCATSA, and Johnny was going to Fort Bragg. . . .

Bobby was staying on at Rucker so that he could be transitioned into fixed wing. After that he didn't know what was going to happen to him. But an era, clearly, was over. He was being separated from the best friends he had ever made in his life, and nothing would ever be the same again. Bobby didn't think much of his father's new aide. Goddamned stuffed shirt.

It was difficult for a second lieutenant to be stationed on a post where the commanding general had the same name. His peers were generally divided into two categories: those who thought getting close to the General's son was dangerous, and those who thought they might somehow be able to turn it to their advantage. Bobby was naive, but not a fool, and he knew that Johnny and Jose belonged to neither category. They were friends.

There were two tests of a friend, Bobby believed: Someone could do something for you that cost him. Or else he could do something for you when nothing was in it for him. Or both. The proof that Johnny Oliver was a friend had occurred several times, when he had done things for Bobby *even though* he was General Bellmon's aide *and not* because of it—things (one in particular) that would have enraged the Old Man if he had ever found out. And although there was nothing that General Bellmon could do for Jose Newell, Jose had—as a friend—spent long and dull hours tutoring him on the intricacies of Instrument Flight Regulations and Procedures. If it hadn't been for Johnny and Jose, Bobby knew, he wouldn't be wearing wings, period.

Bobby realized that what he really admired in both of them—in Johnny more than Joe, but in both of them—was their self-confidence. They decided what was right and then they did it. Bobby privately thought that he was still thinking like a plebe: *If a thing is not specifically permitted, it is prohibited.* Johnny and Joe reversed that: *If something isn't specifically proscribed, screw it, let's do it!*

Captain Johnny Oliver had signaled the bartender for another round of beers, and the bartender had just stooped over the cooler to get them, when the phone rang. Bobby picked it up.

"Annex #1, Lieutenant Bellmon, Sir," he said in the prescribed manner.

"Is Captain Oliver in there?" a male voice asked. "This is Major Ting. I'm the AOD."

"Hold one, please, Sir," Bobby said, and covered the phone with his hand. "It's for you. Major Ting. The AOD."

When Bobby handed him the telephone—and he knew goddamned well that he was again being summoned to duty, if probably for the last time—Captain John S. Oliver had actually been thinking that his year as General Bellmon's aide had gone very quickly, and that he was really far unhappier now that it was just about over than he ever thought he would be. Nearly, but not quite, he thought, as unhappy as he was over his ex-relationship with Liza.

The word for that, though, was not unhappy. It was *miserable.*

His replacement was already on the job. And so, when the Bellmons had a few (160) friends for dinner at 1845 tonight, Johnny would be there as a diner and not as the social secretary. He'd even received a formal invitation:

Major General and Mrs. Robert F. Bellmon
Request the Pleasure of the Company
of
Captain John S. Oliver
at dinner Friday, December 18, 1964,
at six forty-five o'clock
The Officers' Open Mess
R.S.V.P.

Actually he was going to be more than one more plate at the table. He was, more or less, the guest of honor. That was supposed to be a secret, but he had set up the same ceremony last year for Jerry Thomas, when Jerry's tour as an aide had been up. Just as it had been last year—and for God knew how many years before—there would be drinks and dinner, and when dinner was over, Bellmon would tap his wineglass with his knife and stand up, and when the conversation had died down, he would summon Oliver to the head table, and make his speech, and give Oliver a farewell present.

I will even miss this goddamn dump, Oliver thought, looking around Annex #1. *I am either losing my mind or drunk. Or both.*

He waited until the bartender had punctured the lid of the Millers High Life can and slid it to him before he took the phone from Bobby.

"Captain Oliver, Sir," Johnny Oliver said to the battered telephone at the end of the green linoleum bar.

"Major Ting, Oliver. I'm the AOD."

"Yes, Sir?" Oliver said.

"The tower just got a call from a civilian Cessna 310-H," Major Ting said. "They're thirty minutes out. They have a Code Seven aboard. No honors, but they request ground transportation."

A Code Seven, based on the pay grade, was a brigadier general. "No honors" meant the General didn't want a band playing or an officer of suitable—that is, equal or superior—rank to officially welcome him to Fort Rucker. All this Code Seven wanted was a staff car to take him to Ozark.

Oliver had no doubt about who it was. It was Brigadier General "Red" Hanrahan, Commandant of the U.S. Army John F. Kennedy School for Special Warfare at Fort Bragg. Oliver was sure that it was Red Hanrahan for a couple of reasons: When he had seen Hanrahan at Bragg the week before (having gone there with Father Lunsford), Hanrahan informed him he'd be visiting Rucker on Monday to deliver a briefing on Army participation in OPERATION DRAGON ROUGE (the Stanleyville jump) to Rucker officers.

More importantly, he was arriving in a 310-H. That almost certainly meant Lieutenant Colonel Craig W. Lowell's 310-H.

But it never hurt to check.

"Sir, have you got a name for the Oh Seven?"

"General Hanrahan," Major Ting said.

"Thank you very much for calling me, Sir," Oliver said. "I appreciate it."

It was not the time to mention that he was no longer aide-de-camp to General Bellmon, and that calls like this should be directed to his replacement.

"My pleasure," Major Ting said and hung up.

Captain Johnny Oliver, with visible reluctance, pushed his beer can away from him and then made several calls, dialing each number from memory.

He called the General's driver and told him to get a one-star plate, and the staff car, and to pick him up at Annex #1.

He called the billeting office and told them to make sure the Magnolia House was set up and prepared to receive Brigadier General Hanrahan and a party of God Only Knew.

Then he called the main club and told them to be prepared

to reset the head table for General Bellmon's dinner party on short notice; there would probably be Brigadier General Hanrahan and who else Only God Knew.

Finally he called Quarters #1. Mrs. Bellmon answered.

"Johnny, Mrs. B," Oliver said. "General Hanrahan will land at Cairns in about twenty minutes in a Cessna 310-H."

"That probably means Colonel Lowell."

"Yes, Ma'am, I think so. I've called the club and Magnolia House and laid on the General's car. They requested ground transportation to Ozark, but I figured I'd better cover all the bases."

"You're supposed to be retired, Johnny," Barbara Bellmon said.

"My last hurrah, I thought it would be better to spring General Hanrahan and Colonel Lowell on Captain Hornsby slowly. Or at least one at a time."

She laughed.

"Where are you?"

"At Annex One, with Bobby and Jose Newell," Oliver said, and then winced. Bobby, who did not like to be called "Bobby," was shamelessly eavesdropping on the conversation.

"We'll see you at the club, then," she said. "Thank you, Johnny. Again."

"One last time," he said then hung up and turned to Bobby. "Finish your beer, Roberto, duty calls. And you, Jose, better be at the club at the proper hour in the properly appointed uniform."

"Hey, I don't really belong in that company," Newell said. "Are you sure—"

"I'm not supposed to know this, but it's a surprise party for me and I want my friends there."

Newell shrugged. Oliver saw that he was pleased and was glad he had thought to get the Newells invited.

Until now Oliver hadn't paid much attention to today's weather—weather was important only when he was going to fly—but when they heard the horn of the Chevrolet staff car bleating and went outside, he grew concerned. It was drizzling and cold, which meant the real possibility of wing ice. And the visibility and ceiling were probably down to next to nothing.

It was a ten-minute ride before the General's driver pulled the nose of the Chevrolet into the parking space reserved for the commanding general at Base Operations.

"Come on, Bob," Oliver said. "The only way they're going to get into here is on a GCA. You ought to see that."

They entered the Base Operations building through the rear door, walked through the lobby past the oil portrait of Major General Bogardus S. Cairns, a former tank commander who crashed to his death in his white H-13 two weeks after he'd pinned on his second star, and climbed an interior stairway to the GCA room.

GCA—Ground Controlled Approach—which permits an aircraft to land through fog without any visual reference to the ground until moments before touchdown, requires three things, in about equal priority. A high-quality, precision radar so that the precise location of the aircraft is known second by second; a highly skilled GCA controller who interprets the position (speed, altitude, attitude, and rate of descent) of the landing aircraft with relation to the runway; and a pilot of high skill who can instantly respond to the controller's directions with precision.

The controller, a plump, thirty-five-year-old sergeant first class, looked over and glared at them when they entered his preserve. They had no business there, but the aide-to-the-general is a "more equal" pig.

"Is that General Hanrahan's aircraft?" Oliver asked.

"Yes, Sir," the sergeant said impatiently. "He's about five miles out."

Oliver then remained silent as Cessna 603 was talked down. It was not very exciting. The controller told the pilot what to do and the pilot did it. Johnny was a little disappointed. He was pleased, of course, that everything went smoothly, but it would have been more of an education for Bobby had there been terse, quick commands to change altitude or direction, or even an excited order to break it off.

But there were no such commands. The first Cessna 603 was heard from was when Lieutenant Colonel Craig Lowell's voice came over the speaker.

"We have the runway in sight, thank you very much, GCA."

"My pleasure, Sir," the sergeant said.

"We probably would have done much better if we were sober," Colonel Lowell's voice said.

The sergeant laughed and turned to them.

"You know the Colonel, Captain?"

"Yes, Sir."

"Quite a guy," the sergeant said. "Hell, that approach was textbook. Couldn't have been any better."

"We better go down and meet them," Oliver said. "Thank you, Sergeant."

They went down the stairwell and then through the plate glass doors leading to the transient ramp. As they pushed them open, the Cessna's engines could be heard, and then it could be seen, taxiing from the active runway.

The General's driver, a staff sergeant, followed them out. There was probably luggage, and brigadier generals are not expected to carry their own luggage.

"With a little bit of luck, Bobby," Oliver teased, "Sergeant Portet will have been given a ride over here by the General. Wouldn't that be a nice surprise?"

"Shit!" Bobby said.

General Robert F. Bellmon was finally reconciled to having his daughter marry a common enlisted man. Second Lieutenant Bobby Bellmon was not similarly adjusted, or even resigned, to having Jack Portet, the EM who had been fucking his sister outside the bonds of holy matrimony, accepted into the Bellmon platoon of the Long Gray Line.

The Cessna taxied past them. Both Captain Oliver and Second Lieutenant Bellmon saw that General Hanrahan had not given Sergeant Portet a ride over here. The reverse was true. Sergeant Jack Portet, smiling broadly, was waving at them from the pilot's seat.

"Well," Oliver said, chuckling, "that explains that textbook GCA, doesn't it, Bobby?"

"Goddammit, will you stop calling me Bobby?"

Lieutenant Colonel Craig W. Lowell came out of the sleek Cessna first. He was wearing civilian clothing: a Harris tweed jacket, gray flannel slacks, loafers, and an open-collared, yellow, button-down shirt. There was a paisley foulard around his neck.

He stood on the wing root and stretched his arms over his head. Then he looked down at Captain Oliver and Second Lieutenant Bellmon and smiled.

"Hello, Bobby," Colonel Lowell called down cordially. "How nice of you to come out here in the rain to meet us."

"Hello, Uncle Craig," Bobby said. He had known Lowell since he was a little boy; that, Oliver had noticed, gave Lowell the right to call him Bobby without his taking offense.

Lowell came down off the wing and offered his hand to Johnny Oliver.

"I thought you'd been retired," he said. "But thanks anyway, Johnny."

"My pleasure, Colonel," Johnny said. "How was the flight?"

"Humbling," Lowell said. "Safe, but humbling. You know we had to come in on a GCA?"

"Yes, Sir. We watched your approach. The GCA controller said it was textbook."

"What made it humbling was that he carried on a conversation with us while he was doing it," Lowell said. "When I make a GCA approach in weather like this, I resent the intrusions on my concentration of a watch ticking."

Brigadier General Paul T. Hanrahan emerged from the Cessna's cabin next. He was in uniform, wearing only his combat-jump-starred parachutists' wings and his Combat Infantry Badge with the star above the flintlock that indicated a second award.

"Oh, hell," he said. "I didn't expect you to come out to meet me. All we asked for was a ride."

"Our pleasure, General," Oliver said, saluting.

"And you, too, Bobby. Well, I appreciate it," Hanrahan said as he came off the wing root.

Lowell walked over to the baggage compartment and took out their luggage. He gave the first two pieces to the General's driver and then extended the rest to Bobby Bellmon.

Sergeant Jack Portet was the last to emerge. He stood on the wing root and pulled up his tie, rolled down and buttoned his shirt and cuffs, and then reached back into the airplane for his uniform blouse. He put that on and buttoned it, then reached inside a last time and came out with a green beret. He put that on, then stooped to adjust the "blouse" of his trousers around the top of his highly polished parachutist's jump boots.

He stepped off the wing root and saluted Johnny Oliver.

"Hello, Jack," Oliver said, returning the salute and then offering his hand. "That was a nice GCA."

"That wasn't quite what I hoped to hear," Portet said.

"So far as I know, she's at Quarters One."

"And doesn't know I'm coming?"

"She probably suspects by now," Oliver said.

Portet went to a compartment in the side of the airplane and took out wheel chocks and a cover for the Pitot tube. He then walked around the plane and put them in place. While he was doing that, Oliver took tiedown ropes from the compartment and tied the wings down. Then they walked together to Base Operations.

Just inside the double glass doors, an Asian-American major wearing an AOD brassard was talking to General Hanrahan. Oliver decided that had to be Major Ting, who had telephoned him in Annex #1.

Captain Oliver saluted as he walked up. Sergeant Portet did not, until he realized that Major Ting was looking at him at least curiously and probably disapprovingly.

It was more curiosity than disapproval. Ting had watched the passengers deplane, and knew the Cessna, and he knew that the pilot was the last man out. The Green Beret sergeant with the strange wings—two sets of them—over his right blouse pocket—in addition to U.S. Army parachutists' wings over the left pocket—had obviously been flying the Cessna.

Lieutenant Colonel Craig W. Lowell saw the Major's interest.

"This is Sergeant Portet, Major," he said. "He's been demonstrating Congolese Air National Guard GCA procedures to us."

Ting's eyes went up, and General Hanrahan looked at Lowell and just perceptibly shook his head resignedly.

"I've been looking at those wings," Major Ting said. "I don't think I've ever seen them before."

"Congolese pilots' wings, Belgian parachute wings," Lowell said. "Our Sergeant Portet is a remarkable young man. He also does very well with Fort Rucker belles."

"Are they authorized?" Bobby Bellmon asked.

"I'm surprised your father hasn't told you, Bobby," Lowell said. "We Green Berets are not bound by the petty regulations that affect lesser mortals."

"All right, Craig," Hanrahan said. "Sergeant Portet was involved, Major, in the Stanleyville operation. That's where he got the Belgian jump wings. I don't know where he got the Congolese pilots' wings."

"He was a member of the Congolese Air National Guard," Lowell explained solemnly. "Where *did* you get them, Jack?"

Portet was, just visibly, slightly embarrassed.

"General Mobutu came by the house to pay his respects to my mother," he said. "He asked me how I was doing in the Army—the U.S. Army—and I told him fine except they wouldn't let me fly. The next day, as I was getting on the airplane to come home, one of his aides showed up with the wings. And the appropriate certificate."

"I'm not sure they're authorized," General Hanrahan said. It was an observation, not a criticism.

"They are," Lowell said with finality. "You need Congressional approval to accept a medal, but wings are qualification badges. You can wear them. See Felter, Colonel Sanford, and Fullbright, Colonel Richard. Between them they must have a dozen sets—jump and pilots'."

"Yes, I guess that's right," Hanrahan said, chuckling. "Well, Marjorie will be dazzled."

"Yes, Sir," Portet confessed. "That was the idea."

"Now let's get this show on the road," General Hanrahan said. "The first priority, Johnny, when it can be arranged with his schedule, I'd like a few minutes with General Bellmon. The sooner the better."

"I don't think that will be a problem, Sir," Oliver said. "You're in the Magnolia House. Why don't you call him when you get there?"

"OK," Hanrahan said. "How did he react to the news that you're coming to work for me?"

"I haven't told him, Sir."

"You haven't?" Hanrahan asked sharply. "Why not?"

"I . . . Sir, I was about to say there hasn't been the opportunity. But the truth is I haven't made the opportunity. I plan to tell him tonight at his party."

"He already knows," Hanrahan said. "The orders were changed by DA TWX. I have a copy."

"Oh, God!"

"You should have told him, Oliver," Hanrahan said.

"Yes, Sir, I should have."

Hanrahan started to say something else but stopped when Marjorie Bellmon walked into the lobby.

"The USO has arrived," Lowell said sotto voce. He shifted into a thick but credible Southern accent. "Why, Miss Marjorie, *whateveh* brings you heah?"

"Oh, shut up, Uncle Craig," Marjorie Bellmon said. She went to General Hanrahan and kissed his cheek. "Thank you," she said.

"Thank me, it's my airplane," Lowell said. He extended his cheek.

"OK," she said and kissed him. "Thank you, too."

Then she went to Jack Portet and kissed him, lightly, on the cheek. And looked out of her intelligent gray eyes into his for a moment, and kissed him again.

"It's the wings," Lowell said. "I remember that from my youth. Wings'll get 'em every time."

"Uh uh," Marjorie disagreed, smiling. "It's the green beret. We girls go gaga over green berets. I'm surprised you haven't noticed."

She put her hand under Jack Portet's arm and leaned her head against his shoulder.

"May I presume," Lowell said, "from that awful display of affection, that I will not have to concern myself with Sergeant Portet's well-being while we're here?"

"I'll take care of him," Marjorie said. "You won't have to worry about him at all."

"In that case, let's get out of here," Hanrahan said.

XXII

[ONE]
The Magnolia House
Fort Rucker, Alabama
1820 Hours 18 December 1964

Major General Robert F. Bellmon, in mess dress uniform, pulled his Oldsmobile into the driveway of Magnolia House and walked quickly to the door. He knocked at the door but entered without waiting for a reply.

He found Lieutenant Colonel Craig W. Lowell in the living room. Except for the jacket, Lowell was also in his mess dress uniform. He was watching the news on the television, holding a drink in his hand.

"Hello, Craig," he said, signaling for him to remain seated. "Where's Red?"

"On the horn, checking in with his wife," Lowell said. "Would you like a little taste?"

"Please," Bellmon said. "What are you having?"

"Scotch," Lowell said. He stood up and walked to a sideboard on which sat a row of bottles and shining silver accoutrements. Before he reached them, the steward, a moonlighting GI in the employ of the Officers' Club, came into the room from the dining room.

"That's all right, Sergeant," Lowell said. "I'll pour the drinks. As a matter of fact, why don't you just pack it in?"

The steward, surprised, looked at General Bellmon for guidance.

"I've known these gentlemen long enough, Sergeant," Bellmon said, "to know they need absolutely no help in getting at the whiskey. Why don't you go over to the club and see if you can't help out with the bar for my party?"

"Yes, Sir," the steward said with a smile.

Lowell mixed a scotch and soda and handed it to Bellmon.

"Mud in your eye, Robert," he said.

"Nastrovya," Bellmon said, and took a sip. "That's good. What is it?"

"McNeil's," Lowell said.

"Never heard of it."

"I have it sent over," Lowell said.

"From Scotland, you mean?" Bellmon asked.

Lowell nodded.

Bellmon shook his head from side to side. "It must be nice to be rich."

"It is, as you well know," Lowell said, smiling. "Don't poor-mouth me, Bob. I know better."

"Not that I'm not delighted to see you, Craig," Bellmon said just a little sarcastically. "Especially since you brought your mess dress—I presume you brought the golden saucer, too?"

"I never leave home without it," Lowell said, gesturing toward one of the armchairs. On it, suspended from a purple sash, was the four-inches-across golden symbol of membership in the Greek Order of Saint Michael and Saint George.

"That always gives people something to talk about when the conversation pales," Bellmon said.

"A regular conversation piece," Lowell agreed.

"As I was saying, while I'm thrilled you're here, I can't help but wondering *why* you're here."

"Well, I was invited, for one thing," Lowell said.

"You know what I mean."

"OK. I suspected you were going to be annoyed with Red about now, and I came here to protect him from your righteous wrath."

"Then you know? Maybe you're involved?"

"Tangentially," Lowell said. "Peripherally."

"Well, Red better have a damned good explanation or I'm going to fight it, right up to the Chief of Staff if necessary. I like Johnny Oliver, and I'm not going to see him throw his career down the toilet—have it thrown down the toilet by you cowboys."

Brigadier General Paul T. Hanrahan appeared at the bedroom door. He was in his mess dress.

"Howdy, Tex," Lowell said. "Go for your gun. It's high noon. I told you he was going to be pissed."

Bellmon flashed Lowell a coldly furious look and then faced Hanrahan.

"Goddammit, Red, I wasn't even consulted!"

"I think I better have a drink," Hanrahan said.

"I think you better tell me what the hell you're trying to do to Johnny Oliver," Bellmon insisted.

"All right," Hanrahan said as he mixed himself a drink. "Captain Oliver came to me, asked if he thought there was someplace around the Center where he could be useful, and I said there was."

"He came to you?" Bellmon asked, genuinely surprised. "He had his assignment. George Rand, who is writing his own TO and E, came up with an executive-assistant slot for him. It's a damned good assignment."

"He came to me," Hanrahan repeated.

"I just don't understand that," Bellmon said.

"Well, he got together with his pal Lunsford—"

"He's mentioned him. Who is he?" Bellmon interrupted.

"They knew each other in 'Nam. He was the A-Team commander Johnny was trying to extract when he got shot down. Felter had him in the Congo, walking around in the woods with the Simbas. He got a Silver Star for it—from the President, incidentally—who put him on the Majors' List. Good officer."

"And this is his idea, then?" Bellmon asked.

"No, it was Oliver's idea. They showed up drunk."

"Drunk?"

"Drunk. That didn't surprise me about Lunsford, but I was surprised about Oliver. And then it occurred to me, Bob, that he was damned near as emotionally exhausted as Lunsford."

"You're suggesting I burned him out?" Bellmon asked coldly.

"I'm suggesting he broke his hump working for you," Hanrahan said. "He thinks the only reason you don't walk on water is that you don't like wet shoes. And then he had some personal problems."

"You mean the reluctant widow?" Bellmon asked.

"Yeah," Hanrahan said. "She told him fish or cut bait. Her and the kid or him and the Army. He chose the Army."

"And then there was the beloved sister," Lowell said.

"I don't know about that," Bellmon said.

"When he wouldn't let her cheat him out of a million point three, she told him what an ungrateful sonofabitch he was."

"I didn't hear about that," Bellmon said. "There was something about a sister, but—"

"From what I hear she is a real bitch," Lowell said. "But she did raise Johnny from a kid . . . I know why it bothers him."

"He told you all this?" Bellmon asked.

"No. He told Father Lunsford, and when I asked Father why Oliver wanted to join the Foreign Legion, he told me."

"Tell me?"

"Right now it's those two against the world," Hanrahan said. "Lunsford's on the outs with his family—or some of them, anyway. And Oliver has been kicked out by both family and the widow."

"And he thinks running around in the woods with you guys, eating snakes, is going to make things better?"

"They both need a rest," Hanrahan said. "After which I can find something for them to do. I don't intend to have them running around eating snakes. They've had all the on-the-job training they need in that area."

"If he goes to work for George Rand," Bellmon said firmly, "there is absolutely no question in my mind that he would make the Majors' five-percent list in a year. I just wrote him one hell of an efficiency report."

"What he does *not* need at this point in his career is another year or so of sixteen-hour days working for a general officer," Hanrahan said just as firmly. "Can't you see that? As soon as he gets home from 'Nam, you put him to work. He would work just as hard for George Rand. And his lady love, who threw him out, would be just a couple of hours down the road. That's a prescription for a breakdown if I ever heard one."

"I vote with the redhead," Lowell said.

Bellmon looked at him coldly, shrugged, then turned back to Hanrahan.

"So what would you do with him? Notice the tense. *If* you had him. I am still ten seconds away from calling the Chief of Staff."

"OPERATION EARNEST," Hanrahan said.

"What the hell is that?" Bellmon asked.

"I'm going to put both of them in it," Hanrahan asked, "so they can be together. Lunsford will be G-3 and Oliver will be the Aviation Officer. The TO and E slots are for majors, and I'll be writing their OERs. It's just starting, and I don't think anything is going to happen for six months at least."

"I asked what the hell it is," Bellmon said impatiently. "What is OPERATION EARNEST?"

Hanrahan looked at Lowell before replying. Lowell shrugged.

"Che Guevara has dropped out of sight in Cuba," Hanrahan said.

Guevara, Argentinian by birth, had helped Fidel Castro achieve his revolution in Cuba, first by fighting in his army and helping shape its strategy, then by holding several important posts in the new Cuban government, including that of minister of industry. Lately, however, he had taken more interest in spreading communism in Latin America by revolutionary warfare.

"His Christian name," Lowell said dryly, "is Ernesto."

"I'm not quite sure I understand," Bellmon said. He obviously did not like what he had heard. "You're going to try to locate him, is that what you're saying? Isn't that going a bit far afield from your mission? Isn't that the CIA's business?''

Hanrahan shrugged.

''What are you going to do if you find him?''

''Reason with him,'' Lowell said. ''Try to point out the error of his ways. He wasn't always a murderous sonofabitch who beats prisoners to death with baseball bats. And, as Father Whatsisname of Boys' Town said, there is no such thing as a bad boy.''

''You mean assassinate him,'' Bellmon said. When it became apparent that neither Hanrahan nor Lowell was going to respond to that, Bellmon asked, ''And Felter is going along with this?''

''You weren't listening,'' Lowell said. ''OPERATION EARNEST wasn't a Special Forces proposal. It came down, yea, from Mount Olympus, damned near graven on stone tablets. I suppose that someone convinced the powers that be that Red's people can handle this better than the CIA. I mean, what the hell, Bob, if the CIA did it, they'd get mud on their shiny loafers. Couldn't have that, could we?''

General Bellmon had absolutely no doubt that the ''someone'' was in fact Colonel Sanford T. Felter, and the ''the powers that be'' was in fact the President of the United States. No one else had the authority to assign to Red Hanrahan's Special Forces a mission that clearly belonged to the CIA. And after the Felter-run operation to rescue hostages from Stanleyville had gone off so well, he clearly enjoyed the admiration of the President, for the moment at least. The President admired results.

''I don't see why you would put Johnny Oliver in something like that,'' Bellmon said. ''He has neither the training nor the experience.''

''Something dirty and illegal, you mean?'' Lowell asked.

''Craig,'' General Hanrahan said, ''shut up.''

He turned to Bellmon. ''I have no intention—at least until somewhere way down the pike—of sending either Lunsford or Oliver operational on this. What we do need is some people at Bragg who know what it's like to be running around in the woods and can train people to stay alive. That's Lunsford.

And someone who knows what's going on and can take care of moving both bodies and paper. Someone who can control the air supply system, material, and aircraft. And someone, as Sandy put it, with not only a grasp of the situation, but who knows how to keep his mouth shut."

"What's Felter's involvement with this? I mean with Oliver. I can guess what it is with this assassination operation of yours."

"Who do you think had Oliver's orders cut?" Lowell asked.

"No one gets assigned to OPERATION EARNEST without Felter's approval," Hanrahan said. "And he said he thought Oliver was just the man for the job."

"I still think he'd be better off working for George Rand," Bellmon said.

"It's done, Bob," Hanrahan said. "If you raised a lot of hell about it, you might get it undone. But I'm not sure. Why don't you just let it be? If nothing else, for his sake, give him a little time to get over the woman. I'm probably betraying a confidence when I say this, but Major Lunsford told me he broke down and cried like a baby."

Bellmon looked at him. It was a moment before he spoke.

"Just within these walls, I am about out of patience with that goddamned widow." Then he shrugged. "OK. If the best thing for Johnny to do is go eat snakes, *bon appétit.*"

"There's one more thing, Bob," Lowell said. "He had planned to tell you about this tonight. Apparently he was afraid of your reaction. Red told him you already knew; that he'd gotten a copy of the TWX changing his orders."

"I'm not about to add to the poor guy's problems. A crazy widow and you two, plus Felter, is more than enough of a burden for a young captain to bear."

Lowell smiled and chuckled.

"Well, now that we're all old pals again," Lowell said, "would anybody like another drink before we go face the ladies?"

"Please," Generals Bellmon and Hanrahan said almost in unison.

[TWO]
The Officers' Open Mess
Fort Rucker, Alabama
2115 Hours 18 December 1964

When Major General Robert F. Bellmon had directed his then aide-de-camp, Captain John S. Oliver, to start setting up his official Christmas party, the direction had been in the form of a handwritten distribution form. On it he had written

Christmas Party
18 December. 1845. Dinner at 2000 sharp!
Mess Dress (preferred). Blues. Black Tie.
Dining Room A
General and Special Staff, including deputies
Class II activities, including deputies
31st Inf & 403rd Eng
Odd 0-6s
GS-13+
Mrs. B's orphans
Roast Beef
Cocktails and wine on me
Cash bar afterward
Decent Band in Club!!

Dining Room A of the Officers' Open Mess was usually the cafeteria. It was on the main floor of the club, separated from it by folding doors. When it was in use for a more formal purpose, such as the Commanding General's Christmas Dinner–Dance, the glass-covered steam trays of the cafeteria serving line were hidden behind folding screens, and the plastic-topped tables rearranged and covered with linen.

The tables tonight had been arranged in a long-sided "U," with a shorter line of tables in the middle of the U. Seating was determined by protocol, modified slightly by the unanticipated presence of Brigadier General Paul Hanrahan.

The Commanding General and his lady sat, naturally, at the head of the table, in the center of the U. To their left sat the Chief of Staff and his lady, and to the right, Brigadier General Hanrahan. No one sat across from the general officers and their ladies.

People were seated on both sides of the legs of the U, their proximity to the head of the table determined for the most part by their rank and sometimes by their seniority within that rank.

Protocol was always made more difficult at an affair like this because officers from all the units on Fort Rucker were involved. Several of these officers were not subordinate to the Army Aviation Center & Fort Rucker.

General Bellmon, in his DF, had directed that the General and Special Staffs of the Army Aviation Center & Fort Rucker be invited to the party with their ladies. The invitation was de facto a command, although—except for the initial cocktails and the table wine—those attending would be expected to pay for the dinner and whatever else they chose to drink.

There were four General Staff Officers. All of these except the G-2, who was a lieutenant colonel, were full bird colonels. The Special Staff were the officers who provided special services. The provost marshal, for example, was for all intents and purposes the Fort Rucker chief of police. The signal officer ran the telephones and other communication. The engineer maintained everything from dependent housing to airfield runways. There was a flock of others, including the post chaplain, the veterinarian, and the chemical officer. These ranged in rank from full colonel down to captain. Most of them had wives, and most of them had deputies, and most of the deputies had wives.

General Bellmon also wanted Oliver to send invitations to the commanding officers (and their wives) of the two troop units and of the Class II activities. The two troop units were the 2nd Battle Group, 31st Infantry—"The Polar Bears," a reference to their service in Siberia 1917-1919—and the 403rd Engineer Construction Battalion. The commanders of the Class II activities included three full colonels and a lieutenant colonel, and their deputies included two full colonels, a lieutenant colonel, and a major.

Both troop unit commanders were lieutenant colonels. And both were subordinate to the Continental Army Command [CONARC]. There were four Class II Activities at Fort Rucker that were not subordinate to the commanding general of Fort Rucker. The hospital was subordinate, for example, to the Office of the Surgeon General. The Combat Developments Agency belonged to the Deputy Chief of Staff for Operations, U.S. Army. The Army Aviation Board belonged to CONARC. The U.S. Army Signal Aviation Test and Support Activity belonged to the chief signal officer.

The "odd 0-6s" on General Bellmon's DF made reference to 0-6s (full colonels) whose presence was desired although they were not General or Special Staff officers, or Deputies, or whatever. "GS-13" refered to Department of the Army civilian employees. For protocol purposes, "senior civilians" in pay grades GS-13 and above were considered to be entitled to the courtesy normally accorded a field-grade officer (major through colonel). There were perhaps a dozen such who would attend the party, either because they wanted to or because they didn't think it politically expedient to send regrets.

And "Mrs. B's Orphans" meant those officers who fitted none of the other categories, but who Mrs. Barbara Bellmon felt should be invited. They included people she knew (relatives or other officers visiting invitees, for example) or people who she had been told were on the post. And those like Captain John S. Oliver, who was no longer officially the General's aide-de-camp, and his friend the Texas National Guard Lieutenant.

All of these officers had to be seated according to their rank. A cork board the size of a sheet of plywood mounted on the wall of the small office of General Bellmon's aide-de-camp had been used. Every invitee was represented by a small piece of cardboard on which had been typed his name, grade, and date of rank. These were thumbtacked to the cork board into a representation of the arrangement of the tables in Dining Room A and rearranged as necessary.

One of the things that Johnny Oliver had learned during his tour as aide-de-camp was that General Robert F. Bellmon looked forward to official parties (there were half a dozen a year) with slightly less enthusiasm than he would look forward to a session with the post dental surgeon where the agenda was the removal, without anesthesia, of all of his teeth.

This was not evident to the guests or to their wives. Bellmon had long ago decided that the parties, which were more or less an Army tradition, were part of his duties, and his duty was very important to him. He and Mrs. Bellmon, and the Chief of Staff and his wife (and both aides-de-camp, who took turns discreetly whispering the invitees' last names, read from invitations), stood in the foyer for forty-five minutes, shaking hands with, and smiling at, and more often than not coming up with a personal word of greeting for, everybody who showed up.

Once, sometime during the year, General Bellmon had come to his office late at night and found Johnny Oliver standing before the cork board, rearranging the guests for an official affair.

''It began, these official damned dinners, with the Brits,'' Bellmon had told him. ''Regimental 'dining in' once a month. Good idea. Once a month they got together, shop talk was forbidden, and they got a little tight. And that worked here too, before the war, when there was rarely more than a regiment on a post. Thirty, forty, officers on a post, including all the second lieutenants. This is out of hand, of course. But how the hell can you stop it? If it wasn't for these damned things, a field-grade officer could do a three-year tour on the post and never get to see the commanding general except maybe at an inspection or a briefing. And the wife never would.

''The most important element in command, Johnny, is making the subordinate believe he's doing something important. If he doesn't feel he *knows* the commanding officer . . .''

Johnny Oliver had also learned that sometimes getting to *personally* know the commanding general could get out of hand. Officers' wives were the worst offenders, but not by much. One of the aides' functions at official dinners was to rescue the General from people who had backed him into a corner, either to dazzle him with their charm and wit or to make a pitch for some pet project of theirs, ranging from getting use of the post theater for amateur theatrics to revamping the entire pilot-training program.

''General, excuse me, Sir,'' Captain Oliver had often said, to separate General Bellmon from pressing admirers, ''General Facility is calling.''

General Facility was a white-china plumbing apparatus hung on the tiled wall of the gentlemen's rest room.

Nobody in the men's room would bend his ear while the General was taking a leak. But from what Oliver had seen of the women—especially with a couple of drinks in them—the General would not be equally safe in the ladies' room.

When Johnny Oliver entered the club, Captain Richard Hornsby, the new aide-de-camp, was standing where Oliver had stood so often, behind General Bellmon. Hornsby was wearing his dress mess uniform for the first time, and he had a clipboard and a stack of invitations in his hand. He smiled and said softly, "Captain Oliver and Lieutenants Bellmon and Newell."

General Bellmon put out his hand.

"Good evening, Sir," Johnny Oliver said.

"Good evening, Captain," Bellmon said. "An officer is judged by the company he keeps. Try to remember that."

Then he withdrew his hand and offered it to his son.

"Good evening, Sir," Bobby said.

"Good evening, Lieutenant," Bellmon said. "I'm glad you could make it."

Barbara Bellmon violated protocol. After she took Captain Oliver's hand, she pulled him to her and kissed his cheek.

"We're going to miss you, Johnny," she said.

"Me, too," John Oliver said.

"So will I, Oliver," the Chief of Staff said.

"Thank you, General," Oliver said, touched by the comment.

"Well," Mrs. Chief of Staff said, "you're only going to Benning. We'll see you."

Next in the reception line was Brigadier General Paul T. Hanrahan. Oliver knew that he was in the line only because Bellmon had insisted on it. If it was true that it was a good thing for officers remote from the command post to shake the hand, and look into the eye, of the commanding general, it therefore followed that it was a good thing for officers to do the same thing with visiting—and in Hanrahan's case, near legendary—general officers.

"Hello, Johnny," Hanrahan said.

"Good evening, General."

"Do me a favor?"

"Yes, Sir. My privilege."

"Keep an eye on Colonel Lowell. Amuse him, see if you can keep him out of trouble."

"I'll do what I can, Sir," Oliver chuckled, and then surprised himself: "General, I'd like you to meet my good friends Lieutenant and Mrs. Jose Newell."

Hanrahan looked down the line, put his one hand on Bobby Bellmon's shoulder, and extended the other to Joe Newell.

"I'm General Hanrahan, Mrs. Newell," he said. "If Captain Oliver speaks well of your husband, he must be something special."

Beneath his darker-than-usual skin it was plain that Newell's face was flushed.

"Thank you, Sir," he said, and then blurted, "I never thought I'd get a chance to meet you."

Hanrahan laughed.

"Now that you have, and if you have a dollar, they'll sell you a drink," he said.

In Dining Room A, Captain Oliver spotted Lieutenant Colonel Craig W. Lowell at almost the instant Lowell spotted him. Lowell was standing near the bar, holding a drink in his hand. He looked, Oliver thought, *splendiferous* in his uniform. He was in the center of a group of people, predominantly female. Oliver remembered what Mrs. Bellmon had said about Lowell attracting the ladies as a candle draws moths.

Lowell beckoned to Oliver with his index finger. The three of them walked over.

"Good evening, Sir," Oliver said.

"Lieutenant Bellmon," Lowell said by way of greeting, "now that you're here, go around and locate our place cards—mine, Oliver's, Lieutenant Newell's, and yours—and relocate them to one of the tables at the rear of the room."

"Sir?" Bobby said.

"See if you can explain what I thought was a simple command to him, will you, Captain?"

Oliver chuckled. "Do it, Bobby."

Lowell turned to the others he was standing with.

"I have a standing rule at official dinners," he explained,

"to sit as close to the back of the room, and the exit, as possible."

There was laughter, some genuine, some a little nervous. Bobby, visibly uncomfortable, started to comply with his orders.

Major General Bellmon stood up and looked around the room. Some conversation stopped, but by no means all of it. Bellmon rapped on an empty wine bottle with the handle of a knife until the room fell silent.

"You all have met General Hanrahan," he said. "And I know that many of you are wondering what he's doing here."

He gave that a moment to sink in, and for a scattering of applause to die down.

"One rumor I heard going around is that they ran out of rattlesnakes for General Hanrahan's Green Berets to eat in North Carolina, and that he's here to talk me out of some of ours."

There came the expected laughter.

"That's not true, of course. And neither is another rumor about the Green Berets that most of us have heard: that Green Berets are all volunteers. I have two proofs of this. The first proof concerns an officer—he's here with us tonight whom General Hanrahan wished to become a Green Beret. Now this officer is not the type who would willingly eat snakes, sleep in the mud, wear an earring, or do many of the things expected of a Green Beret. So he said, 'Thank you very much, General Hanrahan, I am honored to be asked, but I don't happen to be a parachutist and therefore am not qualified.' "

There was more appreciative laughter.

"So General Hanrahan smiled that charming if mysterious smile of his and let this officer go. A few days later that same officer happened to be thirty-thousand feet over Fort Bragg, watching a Green Beret HALO—High Altitude, Low Opening—parachute jump. In the interests of safety, this officer was suited up like the Green Berets who were in fact about to jump from a C-130 at thirty thousand feet and land in the garbage can of their choice on the ground, although jumping himself was certainly not on his agenda."

''Uncle Craig,'' Bobby blurted, ''he's talking about you, isn't he?''

''It would seem that way,'' Lieutenant Colonel Lowell said. Oliver looked across the table at him. Lowell, shaking his head slowly, ostentatiously, was sitting with his arms folded on his chest and a large black cigar clenched between his perfect teeth.

''Have you got the picture?'' General Bellmon went on. ''There was this officer, standing at the open rear door of the C-130, dressed up in sheepskin flight jacket and trousers, an oxygen mask over his face, marveling at the brash—some might say foolhardy—courage of these muscular young men, and more than likely thinking how wise he was to refuse General Hanrahan's kind offer to join them.

''And then two of General Hanrahan's more muscular Green Berets went to this unsuspecting officer, pried his fingers loose from his handhold, and carried him between them to the end of the platform and jumped off with him.''

Only a few nervous giggles broke the pause.

''It's an absolutely true story,'' General Bellmon said. ''So when this officer finally got back on the ground, he understandably sought out General Hanrahan to report the outrage perpetrated against his body by two of Hanrahan's playful thugs.

'' 'Why, hello, there, Colonel,' General Hanrahan greeted him. 'Nice of you to drop by to see me. I presume that now that you're parachute qualified, you're here to volunteer to be a Green Beret?' ''

The laughter was now loud.

''There's a moral to this story, of course,'' General Bellmon went on. ''And that is, Never trust a Green Beret!

''I have had occasion recently to reflect on that great moral truth,'' Bellmon went on. ''Actually, it usually pops into my mind whenever I see General Hanrahan, but this was special. General Hanrahan is a frequent visitor to Fort Rucker. There's nothing I can do about it. The Chief of Staff told me that I have to keep in mind that even if he rarely acts like it, he *is* in the U.S. Army, and it would look bad in the press if it got out that I had issued shoot-on-sight orders to the guards at the gates.''

More laughter. But Oliver saw raised eyebrows on some of the senior brass that suggested that they too sensed there was something behind the funny story. Even in jest, a general officer rarely talked about having another general officer shot on sight. When Oliver looked at General Hanrahan, he didn't seem offended; the General was smiling broadly.

''During the past year, as you all know, Captain John S. Oliver has had the toughest job on the post—he's been my aide-de-camp. When General Hanrahan unfailingly mentioned Captain Oliver's all-around competence and high intelligence, I simply chalked that up as Captain Oliver's due. For he has indeed been a fine aide, and I like to think a friend, too. We will all miss him. The Command Group, my family, everybody on the post.''

There was a round of applause and heads turned, looking for Johnny.

''As those of you who have been around a couple of years know, there's sort of a new custom: At this Christmas Dinner, with everybody gathered together, I announce my departing aide's new assignment. There are many places in the Army where an officer of Captain Oliver's experience, devotion to duty, and extraordinary competence should be assigned. I made several recommendations along that line. Captain Oliver, will you please stand up?''

Oliver stood up.

''You remember what I just said about never trusting a Green Beret, Johnny?'' Bellmon asked.

''Yes, Sir.''

''Attention to orders,'' Bellmon said, and read from a sheet of paper: ''Headquarters, Department of the Army, 29 November 1964. General Order 297, Paragraph 23. Captain John S. Oliver, Armor, is relieved of present assignment and transferred to Headquarters, John F. Kennedy Center for Special Warfare, Fort Bragg, North Carolina, effective 1 January 1965.''

There was a scattering of applause and several audible snorts.

''General Hanrahan tells me that you will be assigned as the Aviation Officer on his Special Staff,'' Bellmon went on. ''And I'm sure you will serve him as well and faithfully as you have served me, and that he will in time become as fond of you as is the Bellmon family."

There was more applause.

"But if I were you, I wouldn't get near the open door of a C-130 in flight," Bellmon continued. "Now if you'll come up here, Johnny, we have a few little things to prepare you for your new assignment. There's a snakebite kit, and a Bowie knife, and an earring, and a book entitled *One Hundred and One Tasty Rattlesnake Recipes. . . .*"

Captain Johnny Oliver looked at Lieutenant Colonel Craig W. Lowell.

"He really is still pissed, isn't he?" Lowell said softly.

Oliver looked at him a moment and then started walking toward the head table.

General Hanrahan got to his feet as Oliver approached the head table. He smiled and handed Oliver a green beret.

"Put it on, Johnny," Mrs. Barbara Bellmon said. Oliver did so and turned to face the room.

There was applause, in which General Bellmon joined. But when Oliver looked at him, there was no laughter in his eyes.

[THREE]
Foster Garden Apartments
Fayetteville, North Carolina
1400 Hours 25 January 1965

"I am going downstairs to borrow a cup of sugar and whatever else I can get from that Puerto Rican nurse with the great hips," Major George Washington Lunsford announced. "You want to come? Or are you going to just sit there and get shitfaced again?"

"I may come down in a while," Captain John S. Oliver said.

"Hey, if you're not already too shitfaced, why don't you rent a plane and fly over and see the Merry Widow? Maybe absence *does* make the heart grow fonder."

"Why don't you mind your own fucking business, asshole?"

"Sticks and stones may break my bones," Father Lunsford

lisped credibly, placing one hand on a thrust-out hip, "but *names* will never hurt me."

Oliver laughed.

"Better," Lunsford said. "Come down, Johnny. A little piece—eye eee—and quiet will work wonders."

"For the absolutely last time, I will try to get her on the phone," Oliver said. "And then I'll come down to Chez Great Hips."

"If you don't come down, I will send the fat girl up after you," Lunsford said.

Oliver chuckled and reached for the phone.

The telephone rang for seven, eight . . . eleven rings. He put the receiver back into the cradle.

"Fuck it. I don't know what the hell I would say if you *did* answer the goddamned phone."

He went to the kitchen for ice.

The door buzzer rang.

That sonofabitch did *send the fat girl up here!*

He went to the door, opened it, and said after a moment, "What's this?"

"What does it look like?" Liza Wood said. "It's a god-damned camp follower and her fatherless child."

He didn't know what to do, so he scooped Allan up and growled in his neck.

"*Horsey*, Johnny," Allan said.

Johnny Oliver swung Allan so that he was on his shoulders, then put his arms around Liza and held her tight against him, and the three of them bounced up and down together.

I'd like to publicly thank the nearest thing I have to a little brother, Clifford Merritt Walker, Jr., for adding his expertise to the flying and combat portions of this book.

Colonel Walker, who began flying the Huey when it was still the YH-40, when he was a second lieutenant fresh out of flight school, won three Distinguished Flying Crosses in Vietnam. He was also awarded—as far as I know, the only time this happened—the Combat Infantry Badge by the Green Berets for exploits very much like those I had the fictional Captain Oliver doing in this book.

—W.E.B. GRIFFIN
Fairhope, Alabama
May 1988